DETECTIVE

DETECTIVE

ARTHUR HAILEY

a novel

CROWN PUBLISHERS, INC.

NEW YORK

Published by Crown Publishers, Inc., 201 East 50th Street, New York, New
York 10022. Member of the Crown Publishing Group.

Random House, Inc. New York, Toronto, London, Sydney, Auckland

CROWN and colophon are trademarks of Crown Publishers, Inc.

Printed in the United States of America

Design by Leonard Henderson

ISBN 0-517-70025-5

To the Memory of
Stephen L. (Steve) Vinson
Sometime Detective-Sergeant (Homicide)
Miami Police Department
Adviser and Good Friend
Who died, at age fifty-two, shortly before completion of this book

Life resembles the banquet of Damocles;
the sword is ever suspended.
—Voltaire

DETECTIVE

Part One

1

AT 10:35 P.M. ON JANUARY 27, Malcolm Ainslie was halfway to the outer door of Homicide when a phone rang behind him. Instinctively he paused to look back. Later, he wished he hadn't.

Detective Jorge Rodriguez moved swiftly to an empty desk, where he picked up a phone, listened briefly, then called to Ainslie. "For you, Sergeant."

Ainslie set down a book he had been carrying and returned to his own desk to take the call. His movements were ordered and easy. At forty-one, Detective-Sergeant Ainslie was solidly built, a half-inch short of six feet and not too different in appearance from his days as a high school fullback. Only a slight belly bespoke the junk food he often ate—a staple for many detectives, obliged to eat on the run.

Tonight, on the fifth floor of the main Miami Police Department building, the Homicide offices were quiet. In all, seven investigative teams worked here, each team consisting of a sergeant supervisor and three detectives. But the members of tonight's duty team were now all out, probing into a trio of separate murders reported in the past few hours. In Miami, Florida, the pace of human mayhem seldom slackened.

Officially, a Homicide duty shift lasted ten hours, but was often longer because of continuing investigations. Malcolm Ainslie and Jorge Rodriguez, whose own duty shift had ended several hours ago, had continued working until moments earlier.

Almost certainly the phone call was from his wife, Karen, Ainslie thought. Wondering when he was coming home, and eager to begin their long-planned vacation. Well, for once he'd be able to tell her he was on his way, the paperwork completed, loose ends tied, and the lights now green for Karen and Jason and himself to board tomorrow's early-bird Air Canada flight from Miami to Toronto.

Ainslie was ready for a break. While physically fit, he lacked the limitless energy he'd had when he joined the force a decade earlier. Yesterday as he was shaving, he'd noticed the ever-increasing gray in his brown, thinning hair. Some extra wrinkles, too; for sure, the stresses of Homicide caused those.

And his eyes—vigilant and probing—betrayed skepticism and disillusion-ment from witnessing, across the years, the human condition at its worst.

It was then that Karen had appeared behind him and, reading his thoughts as she so often did, run her fingers through his hair, pronouncing, "I still like what I see."

He'd pulled Karen toward him then and held her tightly. The top of Karen's head came only to his shoulders, and he savored the softness of her silky chestnut hair against his cheek, the closeness of their bodies exciting them both as it always had. Putting a finger beneath her chin, he tilted her face upward as they kissed.

"I come in a small package," Karen had said soon after they became engaged. "But there's lots of love in it—along with everything else you'll need." And so it had been.

Expecting to hear Karen's voice now, Ainslie smiled and took the phone from Jorge.

A deep, resonant voice announced, "This is Father Ray Uxbridge. I'm the chaplain at Florida State Prison."

"Yes, I know." Ainslie had met Uxbridge a couple of times and didn't like him. But he answered politely, "What can I do for you, Father?"

"There's a prisoner here who's going to be executed at seven o'clock tomorrow morning. His name is Elroy Doil. He says he knows you."

Ainslie said tersely, "Of course he knows me. I helped send Animal to Raiford."

The voice came back stiffly. "The person we're speaking of is a human being, Sergeant. I prefer not to use your description."

The response reminded Ainslie why he disliked Ray Uxbridge. The man was a pompous ass.

"Everybody calls him Animal," Ainslie answered. "He uses the name him-self. Besides, the way he killed makes him worse than an animal."

In fact, it had been a Dade County assistant medical examiner, Dr. Sandra Sanchez, who, on viewing the mutilated bodies of the first two victims in the twelve murders attributed to Elroy Doil, exclaimed, "Oh dear God! I've seen horrible things, but this is the work of a human animal!"

Her remark was repeated widely.

On the telephone Uxbridge's voice continued. "Mr. Doil has asked me to tell you that he wishes to see you before he dies." A pause, and Ainslie visual-ized the priest checking his watch. "That's slightly more than eight hours from now."

"Has Doil said why he wants to see me?"

"He is aware that you, more than anyone else, were the cause of his arrest and conviction."

Ainslie asked impatiently, "So what are you saying? He wants to spit in my eye before he dies?"

A momentary hesitation. "The prisoner and I have had a discussion. But I remind you that what passes between a priest and a condemned man is privileged and—"

Ainslie cut in. "I'm aware of that, Father, but I remind *you* that I'm in Miami, four hundred miles away, and I'm not driving all night because that wacko suddenly decides it would be fun to see me."

Ainslie waited. Then clearly the priest made a decision. "He says he wishes to confess."

The answer jolted Ainslie; it was the last thing he'd expected. He felt his pulse quicken. "Confess what? You mean to all the killings?"

The question was natural. Throughout Elroy Doil's trial for a ghastly double murder, of which he had been found guilty and sentenced to death, Doil had maintained his innocence despite strong evidence against him. He had been equally emphatic about his innocence of ten other murders—clearly serial killings—with which he was not charged, but which investigators were convinced he had committed.

The merciless savagery of all twelve murders had aroused a nationwide sensation and horror. After the trial a syndicated columnist had written, "Elroy Doil is the most compelling argument for capital punishment. Pity is, from electrocution he'll die too easily, not suffering as his victims did."

"I have no idea what he plans to confess. That is something you would have to find out for yourself."

"Oh shit!"

"I beg your pardon!"

"I said 'shit,' Father. Surely you've used the word a time or two."

"There is no need for rudeness."

Ainslie groaned aloud at the sudden dilemma he faced.

If, at this late stage, Animal was ready to concede that the charges at his trial were true and that he was guilty of other serial killings, it *had* to go on record. One reason: A few vocal persons, including an anti-capital-punishment group, even now supported Doil's claims of innocence, arguing he had been railroaded through the courts because an aroused public demanded the arrest of someone, anyone—and fast. A confession by Doil would crush those arguments.

What was in doubt, of course, was what Doil intended by the word "confession." Would it be a simple legal one, or something convoluted and religious? At Doil's trial he was described by a witness as a religious fanatic mouthing "crazy, garbled mumbo jumbo."

But whatever Doil had to say, there would be questions that Ainslie, with his intimate knowledge of events, was the most qualified to ask. Therefore he must, simply *must*, go to Raiford.

He leaned back wearily in his desk chair. This could not have come at a worse time. Karen, he knew, would be furious. Only last week she had met him at one o'clock in the morning just inside the front door of their home with a firm pronouncement. Ainslie had just returned from a grisly gang-related homicide for which he had had to miss their anniversary dinner. Karen, dressed in a pink nightshirt, blocked his entrance and said forcefully, "Malcolm, our life simply cannot go on like this. We hardly ever see you. We can't rely on you. And when you are here, you're so damn tired from sixteen-hour workdays, all you do is sleep. I'm telling you, things have got to change. You have to decide what you care about most." Karen looked away. Then she said quietly, "I mean it, Malcolm. This is not a bluff."

He understood exactly what Karen meant. And he sympathized. But nothing was ever as simple as it seemed.

"Sergeant, are you still there?" Uxbridge's voice was demanding.

"Unfortunately, yes."

"Well, are you coming or not?"

Ainslie hesitated. "Father, this confession by Doil—would it be a confession in a general sense?"

"I'm not sure what you mean."

"I'm looking for a compromise—not to have to come to Raiford. Would you agree to have Doil confess to you in the presence of a prison officer? That way it would be official, on the record."

A long shot, Ainslie knew, and the explosive reply didn't surprise him. "In God's name, no! The suggestion is outrageous! Our confession is sacred and private. You, especially, should know that."

"I suppose so. I apologize." At least he owed Uxbridge that. It had simply been a last-ditch attempt to avoid the journey. Now it seemed there was no alternative.

The fastest way to the State Prison was by air to Jacksonville or Gainesville, with the prison a short drive from either one. But the commercial flights all left during the day. Now the only way to reach Raiford before Doil's execution was to drive. Ainslie glanced at his watch. Eight hours. Allowing for time he'd need there, it was barely enough.

He beckoned to Rodriguez, who had been listening intently. Covering the receiver with his hand, Ainslie said quietly, "I need you to drive me to Raiford—now. Check out a marked car. Make sure it has a full tank, then wait for me at the motor pool. And get a cell phone."

"Right, Sergeant." Briskly, Jorge disappeared through the outer door.

The priest continued, his anger sharper now, "I'll make this clear, Ainslie. I find communicating with you distasteful. I am doing it, against my conscience, because I was asked by this pathetic man, who is about to die. The fact is, Doil knows you were once a priest. He will not confess to me; he has told me so. In his warped, misguided mind he wishes to confess to you. The thought is thoroughly repugnant to me, but I must respect the man's wishes."

Well, there it was, out in the open.

From the moment he heard Ray Uxbridge's voice on the phone, Ainslie had expected it. Experience had taught him two things. One, that his own past had a habit of surfacing unexpectedly, and clearly Uxbridge knew of it. Also, no one was more bitter or prejudiced toward an ex–Catholic priest than an incumbent priest. Most others were tolerant, even Catholic laity, and clergy of other denominations. But never priests. In his jaded moments, Ainslie attributed it to envy—the fourth deadly sin.

It had been ten years since Ainslie quit the priesthood. Now he said into the phone, "Look, Father, as a police officer the only kind of confession I'm interested in concerns the crime or crimes Animal committed. If he wants to tell me the truth about that before he dies, I'll listen, and of course I'll have some questions."

"An interrogation?" Uxbridge asked. "Why, at this stage, is that needed?"

Ainslie could not contain himself. "Don't you ever watch TV? Haven't you seen those little windowless rooms where we sit with suspects and ask a lot of questions?"

"Mr. Doil is not a suspect anymore."

"He was a suspect in some other crimes; anyway, it's in the public interest to find out all we can."

Uxbridge asked skeptically, "The public interest, or to satisfy your own personal ambition, Sergeant?"

"As far as Animal Doil is concerned, my ambition was satisfied when he was found guilty and sentenced. But I have an official duty to learn all the facts I can."

"And I am more concerned with this man's soul."

Ainslie smiled slightly. "Fair enough. Facts are my business, souls are yours. Why don't you work on Doil's soul while I'm on my way, and I'll take over when I get there?"

Uxbridge's voice deepened. "I insist on a commitment from you right now, Ainslie, that in any exchange you have with Doil, there will be no pretense that you possess any pastoral authority whatever. Furthermore—"

"Father, you have no authority over me."

"I have the authority of God!" Uxbridge boomed.

Ainslie ignored the theatrics. "Look, we're wasting time. Just tell Animal I'll be at the prison before he checks out. And I assure you there will be no pretenses about my role there."

"Do I have your word on that?"

"Oh, for heaven's sake, of course you have my word. If I wanted to parade as a priest, I wouldn't have left the priesthood, would I?"

Ainslie hung up.

•   •   •

Quickly picking up the phone again, he punched out the number of Lieutenant Leo Newbold, commander of Homicide, who was off duty and at home. A pleasant woman's voice, tinged with a Jamaican accent, answered, "Newbold residence."

"Hello, Devina. This is Malcolm. May I speak to the boss?"

"He's sleeping, Malcolm. Do you want me to wake him?"

" 'Fraid so, Devina. Sorry."

Ainslie waited impatiently, checking his watch, calculating the distance, the drive, and the time. If *nothing* got in their way they could make it. But with no time to spare.

He heard a click as an extension phone was lifted, then a sleepy voice. "Hi, Malcolm. What the hell is this? Aren't you supposed to be on vacation?" Leo Newbold had the same distinctive Jamaican accent as his wife.

"I thought so, too, sir. But something's come up."

"Doesn't it always? Tell me."

Ainslie summarized his conversation with Father Uxbridge, and the urgency to leave at once. "I called for your okay."

"You have it. Who's driving you?"

"I'm taking Rodriguez."

"That's good. But watch him, Malcolm. The guy drives like a mad Cuban."

Ainslie smiled. "Right now that's exactly what I need."

"Will this mess up your family vacation?"

"Probably. I haven't called Karen yet. I'll do it on the way."

"Oh shit! I'm really sorry."

Ainslie had told Newbold of their special plans for tomorrow, which would mark both the eighth birthday of their son, Jason, and the seventy-fifth birthday of Jason's maternal grandfather, Brigadier-General George Grundy, ex–Canadian Army. The Grundys lived in a suburb of Toronto. For the dual celebration an elaborate family reunion was planned.

Newbold queried, "What time does that Toronto flight leave here?"

"Five after nine."

"And what time are they burning Animal?"

"Seven."

"Which means you'll be away by eight. Too late to get back to Miami. Have you checked Toronto flights from Jacksonville or Gainesville?"

"Not yet."

"Let me work on that, Malcolm. Call me from the car in about an hour."

"Thanks. Will do."

On the way out of Homicide, Ainslie gathered up a tape recorder and the equipment to conceal it under his clothing. Whatever Doil's last statement, his words would live beyond him.

●   ●   ●

On the Police Building main floor, Jorge Rodriguez was waiting at the Patrol Office.

"Car's signed out. Slot thirty-six. And I got the cell phone." Jorge was the youngest Homicide detective, in many ways a protégé of Ainslie's, and his eagerness was an asset now.

"Let's move it."

They exited the building at a jog, feeling at once the oppressive humidity that had blanketed Miami for days. Ainslie glanced at the sky, which, apart from a few small cumulus clouds, was clear, with stars and a half moon.

Minutes later, with Jorge at the wheel, they left the Police Department parking lot, making a fast turn onto Northwest Third Avenue. Two blocks later they were on the Interstate 95 northbound ramp, from where they would continue north for ten miles, then switch to Florida's Turnpike, with three hundred miles ahead.

It was 11:10 P.M.

The marked car for which Ainslie had asked was a fully equipped, air-conditioned Miami Police blue-and-white Chevrolet Impala, unmistakably official.

"You want lights and siren?" Jorge asked.

"Not yet. Let's see how it goes, but put your foot down and keep it there."

Traffic was light and they were already doing seventy-five, knowing that a marked police car, even out of Miami jurisdiction, would not be stopped for speeding.

Malcolm settled into his seat and gazed out the window. Then he reached for the cellular phone and entered his home number.

2

"I CANNOT BELIEVE THIS, MALCOLM! I absolutely cannot believe it."

He told Karen unhappily, "I'm afraid it's true."

"You're *afraid!* Afraid of what?"

A moment earlier, on receiving Malcolm's call, Karen's first question had been, "Darling, when are you coming home?"

When he told her he wouldn't be home that night, the temper that she seldom showed exploded.

He tried to explain and justify what he was doing, but unsuccessfully.

Now she continued, "So you're afraid of offending that piece of human garbage who's about to be electrocuted, as he goddam well should be! Afraid of missing a juicy tidbit to one of your stupid cases? But *not afraid*, oh no!— not afraid at all—of disappointing your own son on his birthday. Your *son*, Malcolm, in case you've forgotten—your son who's been looking forward to tomorrow, counting the days, counting on you . . ."

Ainslie thought miserably: everything Karen was saying was true. And yet . . . How *could* he make Karen understand? Understand that a cop, especially a Homicide detective, was always on duty. That he was *obligated* to go. That there was no way he could *not* respond to the call he'd received, no matter what was happening in his personal life.

He said flatly, "I feel terrible about Jason. You must know that."

"*Must* I? Well, I damn well don't know. Because if you cared at all, you'd be here with us now instead of on the way to that *murderer*—the man you've put ahead of everything, especially your own family."

Ainslie's voice sharpened. "Karen, I *have* to go. I simply have no choice. None!"

When she didn't answer, he continued, "Look, I'll try to catch a flight out of Jacksonville and Gainesville, so I can join you in Toronto. You can take my suitcase."

"You're supposed to be traveling with *us*—the three of us together! You, Jason, me—your family! Or have you *totally* forgotten?"

"Karen, that's enough!"

"And of course there's the little matter of *my* father's birthday, the only seventy-fifth birthday he'll ever have, and who knows how many more there'll be. But clearly none of us count—not in comparison to that creature 'Animal.' That's what you call him, isn't it? An *animal*—who comes ahead of all of us."

He protested, "That isn't true!"

"Then prove it! Where are you now?"

Ainslie looked out at road signs on I-95. "Karen, I cannot turn around. I'm sorry you don't understand, but the decision's been made."

Briefly his wife was silent. When she resumed, her voice was choked and he knew she was close to tears. "Do you realize what you're doing to us, Malcolm?"

When he didn't answer, he heard a click as she hung up.

Dispirited, he switched off the cellular phone. He remembered guiltily the number of times he had disappointed Karen by putting official duty ahead of his family life. Karen's words of a week ago came back to him: *Malcolm, our life simply cannot go on like this.* He hoped desperately she didn't mean it.

Within the car a silence followed that Jorge had the good sense not to break. At length Ainslie said glumly, "My wife just loves being married to a cop."

Jorge rejoined warily, "Pretty mad, eh?"

"Can't think why." Ainslie added sourly, "All I did was screw up our vacation, all for the sake of having a chat with a killer who'll be dead by morning. Wouldn't any good husband do the same?"

Jorge shrugged. "You're a Homicide cop. Some things you just gotta do. Can't always explain them to outsiders." He added, "I'm never getting married."

Suddenly Jorge floored the accelerator, pulling out sharply to pass one car and cutting in ahead of another coming up behind. The second car's driver blasted his horn in protest.

Ainslie roared, *"For Christ's sake! Cool it!"* Then, turning in his seat, he waved to the car behind, hoping the driver would take it as an apology. He fumed, "It's Doil who's supposed to die tonight, not us."

"Sorry, Sergeant." Jorge grinned. "Got carried away with the need for speed."

Ainslie realized Leo Newbold was right. At times Jorge did drive like a madman, but his Cuban charm remained intact. His appeal clearly worked wonders on women as well—a series of beautiful, sophisticated women who accompanied Jorge everywhere, seemed to adore him, then, for reasons never explained, were periodically replaced.

"With the kind of arrangements you have, why *would* you get married?" Ainslie said.

"At my age I need to keep my options open."

"Well, you're certainly doing that. You're a regular prime-time Romeo. You remember yesterday—even Ernestine couldn't resist your charms."

"Sergeant, Ernestine's a hooker. Any guy with a wallet in his back pocket could charm her."

"I had forty-five dollars in my pocket, and she didn't come on to me."

"No. Well, it's just that . . . I don't know . . . people respect you. Those girls would feel like they were propositioning their uncle."

Ainslie smiled and said quietly, "You did well yesterday, Jorge. I was proud of you."

And he leaned back in his seat . . .

•   •   •

An elderly tourist, Werner Niehaus, was driving a Cadillac rental car when he got lost in Miami's maze of numbered streets—many of which had names as well, sometimes even two names. Getting lost happened often, even to locals. Unluckily, the bewildered German strayed into the notorious Overtown area, where he was attacked, robbed, and shot dead, his body then thrown from the rental car, which his attackers subsequently stole. It was a wanton, needless killing. Robbery—presumably the objective—could have been achieved easily without it.

A statewide BOLO—"be on the lookout"—was immediately issued for the missing car.

With the killing of foreign tourists already receiving international attention, pressure was building—from the mayor, the city commissioners, and the chief of police downward—for a speedy resolution. While nothing would undo the adverse publicity for Miami, a swift arrest might soften the negative edge.

The following morning, Jorge, accompanied by Malcolm Ainslie, cruised the Overtown area in an unmarked car in search of evidence or witnesses. Ainslie let Jorge take the lead, and near the corner of Northwest Third Avenue and Fourteenth Street he spotted two drug dealers, known to him by their street names, Big Nick and Shorty Spudman. There was an arrest warrant out for Shorty on an aggravated assault charge, a felony.

Jorge was quickly out of the car, followed by Ainslie. As the detectives approached from either side, cutting off any escape, Nick was stuffing something into his pants. He looked up casually.

Jorge set the tone. "Hey, Nick, how's it going?"

The response was wary. "Okay, what it is, man."

The druggies and detectives eyed each other. They all knew that if the police officers exercised their right to stop and frisk, they would find drugs, perhaps weapons, in which case the dealers, both with lengthy records, could face long prison terms.

Jorge asked Shorty Spudman, who was five feet two and pockmarked, "You hear about that German tourist murdered yesterday?"

"Heard on TV. Them punks doing shit to tourists people, they some real bad dudes."

"So there's talk on the street?"

"Some."

Ainslie picked up the exchange. "You guys can help yourself out if you give us names."

The invitation was clear: *Let's make a deal.* As Homicide detectives saw it, solving a murder took priority over most everything else. In return for information, lesser crimes would be ignored—even an arrest warrant.

But Big Nick insisted, "Ain't knowin' no fuckin' names."

Jorge motioned to the car. "Then we'd all better take a ride to the station." At Police Headquarters, as Nick and Shorty knew, a full-body search would be obligatory, and the arrest warrant could not be overlooked.

"Hold it!" Shorty offered. "Heard a coupla whores say last night there was a honky shot an' two dudes took his car."

Jorge: "Did the girls see it happen?"

Shorty shrugged. "Maybe."

"Give with their names."

"Ernestine Smart and one they call Flame."

"Where can we find them?"

"Ernestine's sleepin' at River an' Three. Dunno 'bout Flame."

Jorge said, "You're talking the homeless camp at Third and North River?"

"Yeah."

"If you've given us shit," Jorge told the pair, "we'll come back and find you. If it turns out okay, we owe you."

Jorge and Ainslie returned to their car. Locating one of the prostitutes took another hour.

The Third Street homeless camp was under I-95 and alongside the Miami River. Originally it had been a downtown parking area, and dozens of parking meters, unused, stood incongruously among countless cardboard packing cases and other flimsy shelters assembled from discarded junk—the whole crude, filthy mess resembling a hellhole in some fifth-rate country. Amid it all, human beings lived desperate, degraded lives. In and around the encampment, garbage was everywhere. Jorge and Ainslie left their car cautiously, knowing that at any moment they could step in a pile of excrement.

Ernestine Smart and Flame, they learned, jointly occupied a plywood box that, according to stencil marks, once had contained truck tires. It was now located on the river side of the former parking lot. A door had been cut in the box. It was padlocked on the outside.

Jorge and Ainslie moved on. Driving to "whore country"—Biscayne Boulevard and Northeast Eighth Street, Biscayne and Eleventh, East Flagler and Third Avenue—they questioned a few daytime prostitutes, asking about Ernestine and Flame. Neither had been seen that day, and eventually the detectives returned to the homeless shelters.

This time they found the roughly cut door of Ernestine and Flame's plywood box unlocked and open. Jorge put his head into the dark interior.

"Hey, Ernestine. It's your friendly neighborhood cop. How's tricks?"

A husky voice came back. "If I had more I wouldn't be livin' in this pigpen. You wanna fuck, copper? For you it's bargain day."

"Damn! Just can't take the time; got a murder to solve. Word on the street is you and Flame saw it."

From the interior gloom, Ernestine peered out. Jorge guessed she was about twenty, despite the jaded attitude of a woman twice her age. She was black and once beautiful, but now her face was puffy and etched with lines. Her figure was good, though. A white jumpsuit showed a slim body and firm breasts. Ernestine saw Jorge's eyes and seemed amused.

"We all see things," she told him. "Doan' always remember."

"But you'll remember if I help you?"

Ernestine smiled enigmatically. He knew the answer was yes.

That's the way it was with prostitutes, and it was why detectives cultivated them as friends and allies. Prostitutes were full of information and would reveal it if they liked the cop or liked the deal. But they never volunteered anything; you had to ask the right questions.

Jorge began tentatively. "Were you by any chance working Northwest Third and Twelfth Street last night?"

"I dunno. Maybe."

"Well, I was wondering if you saw two jitterbugs jump into a car driven by an older white guy, then shoot him and dump him out of the car."

"No, but I did see a brother an' this cheap-lookin' 'fay chick make some old guy stop his car, then do what you said."

Jorge glanced at Ainslie, who nodded, sensing pay dirt. "Let's get this clear," Jorge said. "It was a black male and a white woman?"

"Yeah." Ernestine eyed him directly. "Before I say any more, you gonna hit my skin, man?"

"If what you tell us isn't bullshit, it'll be worth a hundred."

"That's cool." She looked pleased.

"Do you know the names?"

"The black dude is Kermit the Frog. Looks like a frog; has funny bulgin' eyes. He's a bad one, always pullin' his piece."

"And the woman?"

"Heard her called Maggie, she's always with Kermit. They hang at the diner over on Eight Street, an' I saw them both get picked up for havin' smack."

"If I brought some photos, would you identify them?"

"Sure, sweetie, anything for you." Reaching out, Ernestine touched Jorge's cheek. "You're kinda cute."

He smiled, then pressed on. "What about Flame? Will she help us, too?"

"You'll have to ask him."

Jorge was startled. *"Him?"*

"Flame's a he-she," Ernestine said. "Name's Jimmy McRae."

Ainslie groaned audibly. "Not as a witness. No way!"

Jorge nodded. A he-she, a male who wanted to undergo a sex change and meanwhile dressed and lived as a woman, was common in the libidinous underworld. On top of that, it seemed, Flame paraded as a female prostitute. There was no way such a kink could be produced in court; the jury would be turned off, so forget Flame. Ernestine would be a good witness, and they might find others.

Jorge told Ernestine, "If what you've told us checks out, we'll stop by with your money in the next couple of days."

That kind of payoff—an informer's fee—was available from an expense account to which detectives had access.

At that moment Ainslie's portable police radio announced his unit number, 1910.

He responded, "QSK," meaning "Proceed with transmission."

"Call your lieutenant."

Using the same portable, which doubled as a phone, Ainslie gave Leo Newbold's number.

"We have a break in the Niehaus case," Newbold said. "State Police found the missing car with two suspects. They're being brought here now."

"Don't tell me, sir," Ainslie said, checking notes. "One black guy named Kermit, and a white girl, Maggie?"

"Right on! That's them. How'd you know?"

"Jorge Rodriguez has a witness. A prostitute. Said she'll make an ID."

"Tell Jorge, nice going. Better get over here. Let's wrap this up fast."

●   ●   ●

The facts slowly emerged. A sharp-eyed Florida state trooper, who had memorized the previous day's Miami Police BOLO, had spotted and stopped the wanted car and arrested its occupants—a black male, Kermit Kaprum, age nineteen, and Maggie Thorne, white female, twenty-three. They were carrying .38-caliber revolvers, which were sent for ballistics analysis.

They told uniform police that an hour or so earlier they had found the car abandoned, with the keys in the ignition, and had taken it for a joyride. It was a patently false story, though not contested by the uniforms, who knew that Homicide detectives would do the important questioning.

When Ainslie and Jorge reached Homicide, Kaprum and Thorne had already arrived and were being detained in separate interview rooms. A computer check revealed that both had criminal records, beginning at age eighteen. The young woman, Thorne, had served prison time for thefts and had misdemeanor convictions for prostitution. Kaprum had two convictions, for larceny and disorderly conduct. It was likely that both had records also as juvenile offenders.

•   •   •

Miami's Homicide department was totally unlike the noisy, frenetic detective divisions seen on TV, with their easy public access and anything-goes behavior. Located on the fifth floor of the fortresslike downtown Miami Police Headquarters building, Homicide was reached by elevator from the main lobby. However, the fifth-floor doors would open only with a special key-card. No one but Homicide detectives, civilian Homicide staff, and a few senior officers had key-cards. All other police personnel and the occasional visitor needed advance approval, and even then were accompanied by a key-card holder.

Prisoners and suspects brought to Homicide arrived via a guarded basement entrance and a secure elevator running directly up to the Homicide office. The result was a normally quiet, controlled environment.

Jorge Rodriguez and Malcolm Ainslie peered through one-way glass at the suspects seated in separate interview rooms.

"We need at least one confession," Ainslie said.

"Leave it to me," Jorge told him.

"You want to question both?"

"Yeah. I'll take the girl first. Mind if I do it alone?"

Normally, two detectives would interview a murder suspect together, but Jorge's previous successes solo were a persuasive argument, especially now.

Ainslie nodded. "Go ahead."

As the session with the twenty-three-year-old Maggie Thorne began,

Ainslie watched and listened through the observation window. The suspect looked pale and younger than her years, wearing stained, torn jeans and a dirty sweatshirt. If she put on a dress and washed her face, Ainslie thought, she'd be pretty. As it was, she seemed hard and edgy, rocking nervously in the metal chair to which she was handcuffed. When Jorge appeared she yanked on the cuffs, clanging them against the chair, and shouted, "Why the fuck do I have to wear these?"

Jorge smiled easily and moved to take them off. "How ya' doin', anyway? I'm Detective Rodriguez. Would you like some coffee or a cigarette?"

Thorne rubbed her wrists and muttered something about milk and sugar. She seemed a shade more relaxed, though her wariness persisted. A hard nut, Ainslie thought.

As usual, Jorge had brought a thermos, two Styrofoam cups, and cigarettes. He poured coffee for them both, talking at the same time. *So you don't smoke, eh? Me neither. Dangerous stuff, tobacco . . .* (Not as dangerous as the girl's .38, Ainslie thought.) *. . . Sorry, you'll have to drink it black . . . Hey, mind if I call you Maggie? I'm Jorge . . . See, I want to help you if I can. In fact, I think we can help each other . . . No, it's not a load of horseshit. The truth is, Maggie, you're in a lot of trouble and I'm trying to make things as easy for you as I can . . .*

Ainslie stood behind the one-way glass, tapping his foot. Get the Miranda over with, Jorge, he thought impatiently, knowing that Jorge could not move forward until he had advised Thorne of her rights, including the right to an attorney. Of course, the last thing an investigator wanted at this critical stage was the restrictive presence of a lawyer—a reason why Homicide detectives tried to present the Miranda caution in such a way that the answer came back, "No."

Jorge's skill in obtaining that answer had become legendary.

He started with a pre-interview—entirely legal—during which he gathered basics: the suspect's name, address, birth date, occupation, social security number . . . But Jorge proceeded with deliberate slowness, taking time for comments. *So you were born in August, Maggie? Hey, so was I. That makes us Leos, but I don't really believe in that zodiac crap. Do you?*

Despite the low-key approach, the girl was still wary, so Jorge let the pre-interview run on, though he had not yet mentioned the crime being investigated.

Maggie, just a few more personal details. Are you married? . . . No? Me neither. Maybe someday. Well, how 'bout a boyfriend? Kermit? Well, I'm afraid Kermit's in trouble, too, and not a lot of help to you right now. Maybe he's the one who got you here . . . How about your mother? . . . Wow! You never saw her? . . . Well, how about your father? . . . Okay, okay, no more questions about them.

Jorge sat close to Thorne, occasionally touching her arm or shoulder. With some suspects, he might hold their hand, even perhaps induce tears. But Thorne was tough, so Jorge held back. There were limits, though, to how long a pre-interview could last.

Is there anyone at all you'd like me to contact for you, Maggie? . . . Well, if you change your mind, be sure to tell me.

From outside, Ainslie waited tensely to witness the Miranda declaration. Meanwhile he watched the girl. There was something familiar about her face, but despite a facility for "flash recognition"—an identification system in which police were trained—he couldn't place her. The elusiveness puzzled him.

Okay, Maggie, there's a lot more to talk about, but I do have to ask you this: Are you willing to keep talking to me—just like we're doing now—without an attorney present?

Jorge was walking a hairline, though still within legal bounds.

Almost imperceptibly, Thorne nodded. *Good, 'cause I'd like to keep talking too. But there's something we need to get out of the way—you know how regulations are. So I have to tell you this, Maggie, for the record. You have the right to remain silent . . .*

The official formula continued, the wording more or less: *You need not talk to me or answer any questions . . . Should you talk to me, anything you say can be used as evidence against you . . . You have the right to an attorney at any time . . . If you cannot afford an attorney one will be supplied free of charge . . .*

Ainslie listened carefully. Although police interview rooms were mainly soundproof, voices could penetrate the one-way glass in front of him, so later he could testify, if needed, that the Miranda warning had been given. Never mind that Jorge's voice had become offhand and casual; the right words were what mattered, though Thorne seemed scarcely to be paying attention.

It was time for Jorge's second calculated gamble.

Now, we can either keep talking, Maggie, or I go back to work and you won't see me anymore . . .

On the girl's face a look of doubt: *What happens next if this guy disappears?*

Jorge recognized the signs. He was close to success.

Maggie, do you understand what I've just said? . . . You're sure? . . . Okay, so that's out of the way . . . Oh, just one thing! I need you to sign this piece of paper. It confirms what we've been saying.

Thorne signed the official release form, her handwriting scrawly but certifying that after having been informed of her rights she had chosen to talk to
Detective Rodriguez without a lawyer present.

Ainslie put away the notes he'd made. Jorge was in the clear, and Ainslie,
already convinced of the pair's guilt, believed there would be at least one full
confession within the hour.

As it turned out, there were two.

•   •   •

As Jorge's questioning continued—first of Thorne, then, in the other room,
of Kaprum—it became evident they had had no coherent plan to begin with,
a fact that caused a capital crime to be committed instead of simple robbery.
Then, afterward, they had seriously believed they could get away with it by
concocting a stew of lies, all of which seemed ingenious to them but ludi-
crous to anyone with crime-solving experience.

Jorge to Thorne: *About that car you and Kermit were in, Maggie. You told
the trooper you'd found it just a few minutes earlier, with the keys in it, and
took it for a ride . . . Well, what if I tell you we have a witness who saw both
of you in that car last night, saw the whole thing happen? Also, there were
a dozen or more empty drink cans in the car, food wrappers, too. It's all
been sent for fingerprinting. What if your prints, and Kermit's, are on that
stuff? . . . Actually, it will prove something, Maggie, because it will show you
were both in that car a whole lot longer than just the "few minutes" you say.*

Jorge sipped coffee and waited. Thorne drank some of hers.

*Something else, Maggie. When you were picked up and searched, you had
a lot of money on you—more than seven hundred dollars. Mind telling me
where you got that? . . . Working for whom and doing what? . . . Really! Must
have been a lot of odd jobs for all that cash. What were the names of the people who employed you? . . . Well, then, give me the names of one or two and
we'll check with them . . . You can't name anyone? Maggie, you're not helping
yourself here.*

*All right, let's move on. Now, mixed in with those dollars found on you
were some deutschemarks. Where did you get those? . . . Deutschemarks,
Maggie—German money. You been to Germany lately? . . . Oh, come on,
Maggie! How could you forget something like that? Did you get it from Mr.
Niehaus? . . . He's the gentleman who was killed. Did you shoot him with
that pistol of yours, Maggie? Tests are being done on the gun. They'll tell us
if you did.*

*Maggie, I'm talking to you as a friend. You're in trouble, big trouble, and I
think you know it. I'd like to help you, but before I can, you'll have to start*

telling the truth . . . Here, have more coffee . . . Think about it, Maggie. The truth will make everything easy—especially for you. Because when I know the truth I can start advising you about what to do . . .

And later, with the other, younger suspect, Kaprum—whose eyes did bulge like a frog's, Ainslie realized—the questioning was tougher: *Okay, Kermit, for the past half hour I've listened to you answer all my questions and we both know that everything you've told me is total bullshit. Now let's pack it in and have some facts. You and your girlfriend Maggie hijacked that car, robbed that old man, then killed him. Now, I may as well tell you that Maggie Thorne has confessed. I have her written confession in which she says the whole idea was yours, and that you fired the shot that killed Mr. Niehaus . . .*

The nineteen-year-old Kaprum leapt to his feet and shouted wildly, "That lying bitch! It was her who done it, her idea, not mine! I just went for—"

Hey, hold it! Stop right there, Kaprum! You hear me! Settle down!

It was like winning the lottery, Jorge thought. Kaprum, reacting to what he saw as Maggie Thorne's betrayal, was now eager to relate his own version of events. Ainslie might have smiled, but he remembered the poor dead German.

A Miranda warning had been given Kaprum earlier. No need to repeat it.

So are you ready to tell me, Kermit, what really happened—and this time the truth? If you are, you'll be helping yourself . . . Okay, let's begin when you and Thorne held up that car and took it over . . . All right, we'll put Thorne's name first if that's the way you want it . . . So where were you both when . . .

Jorge was scribbling on a pad as Kaprum spoke quickly, blurting out facts, heedless of consequences, failing to realize it made little difference, if any, who had done what, and what counted most was that the pair of them had killed in collusion. When asked by Jorge why any shot was fired at all, Kaprum answered, "The old bastard badmouthed us. Shouted a lot of crap we didn't understand. He wouldn't shut his goddam mouth, man."

When it was done, using a ballpoint pen that Jorge handed him, Kaprum initialed each page as having read it, then signed what had become a full confession.

A few hours later the ballistics report revealed that three bullets were found in the dead German's body. One had been fired from Kaprum's gun, two from Maggie Thorne's. The medical examiner's conclusion was that Kaprum's bullet would have wounded the victim. Either one of the two from Thorne would have caused immediate death.

Ainslie was called away, then returned in time to hear part of a second session between Jorge and Thorne. At the end the young girl asked a question, her expression serious. "What's gonna happen? Will we get probation?"

Jorge made no attempt to answer, and Ainslie knew why.

What could you say to someone who was so strangely ignorant about the gravity of what had transpired, and the inevitable consequences soon to come? How could Jorge tell a young girl, *No, there is not the slightest chance of your receiving probation, or even going temporarily free on bail, or for that matter ever getting out of jail again. What is a near certainty is that after the two of you have been tried before a judge and jury, you will be found guilty of murder and sentenced to die in the electric chair.*

●   ●   ●

In court, defense lawyers—going through the motions—would rant and rave, complaining that Thorne's and Kaprum's confessions had been obtained under duress. The word "trickery" might be used—not without some truth, Ainslie conceded.

But a judge, armed with testimony that proper Miranda warnings had been given and that the accused had knowingly signed their rights away, would dismiss the objections and the confessions would stand.

As to the "trickery," Ainslie had come to believe it was justified. With any capital crime, total, conclusive proof was hard to come by and because of guileful lawyers sometimes the guilty walked away. The O.J. Simpson case came inevitably to mind. But the Thorne and Kaprum confessions, however extracted, represented truth that would lead to justice, and from society's point of view—and Ainslie's—that was what mattered most.

●   ●   ●

The thought of confessions brought Ainslie's mind back to Elroy Doil and the reason for this interminable drive. He wondered, as he had since the phone call from Raiford earlier tonight: What kind of confession was he going to hear?

He peered out at lighted signs on the roadway. They had left I-95 and were on Florida's Turnpike, with Orlando—their first objective—two hundred miles away.

3

MALCOLM AINSLIE, WHO HAD dozed off soon after passing Fort Lauderdale, was awakened by a thump—perhaps a road bump or more likely a raccoon; their carcasses littered the highway. He stretched and sat up, then checked the time: ten minutes after midnight. Up ahead he could see an exit ramp to West Palm Beach, which meant they were a third of the way to Orlando. Jorge, he noted, was driving in the far left lane amid fairly heavy turnpike traffic.

Ainslie reached for the phone and punched in Lieutenant Newbold's number. When he answered, Ainslie announced, "Evening, sir. Miami's finest here."

"Hey, Malcolm. Everything okay?"

Ainslie glanced to his left. "The mad Cuban hasn't killed me yet."

Newbold chuckled, then said, "Listen, I checked some flights for you, and made reservations. I think we can get you up to Toronto by tomorrow afternoon."

"That's good news, Lieutenant. Thanks!" He jotted down the details: a 10:05 Delta flight from Jacksonville to Atlanta, connecting with Air Canada to Toronto.

He would be in Toronto only slightly more than two hours later than originally planned, and was relieved. The arrangement was not ideal because he knew that Karen's parents, who lived more than an hour's drive from Toronto's Pearson Airport, had some kind of party planned for lunchtime, which he would miss. But he would be at the family dinner in the evening.

Newbold continued, "Have Rodriguez drive you to Jacksonville. It's only sixty miles; you'll make it easily. And when you get back, we'll look at your extra expenses and work something out."

"That might appease Karen."

"Was she upset?" Newbold asked.

"You could say that."

Newbold sighed. "Devina's that way when I get lousy duty, and mostly I can't blame her. Oh, I called the State Prison. They've promised to waive formalities going in, so you'll get to Animal fast."

"Great."

"One thing they asked. When you're about twenty minutes from Raiford, phone Lieutenant Neil Hambrick. Here's the direct-line number."

Ainslie wrote it down. "Nice going, Lieutenant. Thanks again."

"Hey, have a good trip and enjoy Toronto."

Switching off the phone, Ainslie reflected on the excellent relations between Newbold and his white subordinates. Like most others in Homicide, Ainslie liked and respected Newbold, a twenty-four-year veteran of the force who had come to the United States with his immigrant Jamaican parents thirty years ago, at age fifteen. Young Leo had attended the University of Miami, where he majored in criminology, afterward joining the Police Department at twenty-two. Because he was black, affirmative action of the 1980s speeded his promotion to lieutenant, but unlike some other such promotions, because of Newbold's obvious ability, it was not resented by his white colleagues. Now he was in his eighth year as head of Homicide.

A great deal was being written nationally about racial disharmony in big-city police forces, notably the Los Angeles Police Department, where ugly discrimination against blacks, both on and off the force, had had semiofficial approval from the top over many years. Only now was some attempted balance and fairness taking shape in L.A., amid bitterness on all sides. By contrast, the Miami PD had gone through the same traumatic change more than a decade earlier, so that integration, with only minor hangovers from the past, was now a *fait accompli*. It worked, and the public was better served.

●   ●   ●

To Malcolm's surprise, Karen was sleeping when he phoned with the new flight information, which he gave her, then urged her to return to sleep. "I'll see you tomorrow about four," he finished.

She mumbled sleepily, but with some affection, "I'll believe it when I see it."

When Ainslie ended the connection and settled back, Jorge's voice broke into his thoughts.

"Sergeant, are you still Catholic?"

The question was unexpected. "Excuse me?"

Jorge eased the blue-and-white past one of the many tractor-trailers traveling the highway. When they were safely clear he continued, "Well, you used to be a priest, and now you're not. So I was curious—are you still a Catholic?"

"No."

"Well, I was wondering, as a Catholic, or ex, how you really feel about this trip—capital punishment, going to see Animal Doil before they strap him in the chair, knowing it was mainly you who put him there?"

"That's a heavy question this late at night."

Jorge shrugged. "It's okay if you don't want to talk about it, I understand."

Ainslie hesitated. When he'd quit the priesthood at thirty, after a seminary education and a Ph.D. degree, followed by five years as a parish priest, he simply walked away, abandoning religion entirely. As to motives, apart from confiding in a few close friends, he had stayed mainly silent, having no wish to influence others. As time passed, though, he grew more willing to answer questions.

"In some ways," he told Jorge, "there's not a huge difference between cops and priests. A priest tries to help people, strives for fairness and justice—or so he should. A Homicide cop wants to see murderers caught and, if found guilty, pay the penalty."

"Sometimes," Jorge said, "I wish I could talk about stuff, saying it perfectly, the way you do."

"You mean capital punishment?"

"Yeah, exactly. On the one hand I'm a cop. How many cops in this country are truly against capital punishment? Two? Maybe three? But then I'm also Catholic. And the Church opposes capital punishment."

"Don't be so sure, Jorge. Underneath, most religions are full of hypocrisy because they accept killing when it suits them. Oh, I know the beautiful theory. I was taught it. 'Life is a gift from God and no human being has the right to terminate life.' But that's only when it's convenient."

"When isn't it convenient?"

"During wars, when men, not God, take lives. And every country that goes to war, from the Old Testament Israelites through to modern America—they all assume God's on their side."

Jorge laughed. "Well, I sure as hell hope he's on *my* side."

"With some of your shenanigans, there's not much chance of that."

"Me?" Jorge said. "You're the one who turned in your dog collar. Can't imagine you're on the Pope's top-ten list."

Ainslie smiled. "Well, lately there haven't been too many popes on my list, either."

"How come?"

"Some of them have different rules for themselves than they do for others. Like Pope Pius XII—you've heard of him. He's the one who ignored Hitler's slaughter of Jews, making no protest when it could have saved Jewish lives? That's how religions condone murder without actually taking a stand."

"My parents were ashamed when that all came out," Jorge said. "Wasn't there talk a while back about the Church admitting guilt?"

"Yes, in 1994, and it lasted one day. A draft of a Vatican document surfaced in Israel; it described Catholic 'shame and repentance' over the Holocaust. But the next day the Vatican said, 'No way, not us. Maybe someday, not now.' They did a Galileo."

"Give me that again."

"In 1633," Ainslie explained, "Galileo was condemned for heresy and held under house arrest for the last eight years of his life—all because he showed that the earth revolves around the sun. That, of course, was contrary to Catholic doctrine, which said that the earth was the center of the universe and didn't move. Only in 1992, after what the Vatican called 'thirteen years of study,' did Pope John Paul II admit the Church was wrong—something science had confirmed centuries before."

"The Church did *nothing?* Between 1633 and almost now?"

"Three and a half centuries. Rome doesn't hurry its own confessions."

Jorge laughed. "But if I use a condom on Friday, I'd better confess on Saturday. Or else!"

Ainslie smiled. "I know; it's a crazy world. Getting back to your question— I didn't like any kind of killing when I was a priest, and still don't. But I believe in the law, so while capital punishment is part of the law, I'll go along."

Even as he spoke, Ainslie was reminded of the few dissidents—labeled by prosecutors as a lunatic fringe—who argued that Elroy Doil, because of his adamant denials, had not been proven guilty. Ainslie disagreed. He was convinced guilt *had* been proven, but wondered again about Doil's proposed confession.

"Will you stay to see Animal executed?" Jorge asked.

"I hope not. We'll see what happens when we get there."

Jorge was briefly silent, then he said, "Rumor around the station is that you wrote a book, some important religious thing. Sold millions of copies, I'm told. Hope you made millions, too."

Ainslie laughed. "You don't get rich co-authoring a book about comparative religions. I've no idea how many copies were sold, though it went into a lot of languages and you can still pick it up in a library."

·   ·   ·

The dashboard clock read 2:15 A.M. "Where are we?" Ainslie asked, realizing he'd dozed off again.

"Just passed Orlando, Sergeant."

Ainslie nodded, remembering other, more leisurely journeys along this way. On either side of them, he knew, was some of the more glorious countryside in Florida. From Orlando to Wildwood, fifty miles ahead, the turnpike was officially a scenic byway. Out there, hidden by darkness, were rolling hills adorned with wildflowers, stands of tall pines, tranquil lakes and flowering trees with multicolored blossoms, cows grazing on vast fields of farmland, orange groves, loaded with fruit this time of year . . .

Florida, Ainslie reflected, had become one of the chosen, coveted places of the world. It seemed that whatever was innovative, sophisticated, artistic, and exciting was to be found there, especially in greater Miami—a sprawling, bubbling, international cauldron of much that was best in modern living. It was also, he was somberly reminded, a hodgepodge of the worst.

He had read once how the explorer Ponce de León had named Florida in 1513, invoking the Spanish phrase *pascua florida*—"season of flowers." Still, that much was still as true now as then in the aptly named Sunshine State.

Ainslie asked, "Are you tired? Would you like me to drive?"

"No, I'm fine."

They had been on the road slightly more than three hours, Ainslie calculated, and were better than halfway. Allowing for inferior roads after Interstate 75, which they would shortly join, they could reach Raiford at about 5:30 A.M.

With the execution set for 7:00 A.M., that left almost no time to spare. Except for a last-minute reprieve—unlikely in Doil's case—there was no way a scheduled execution would be postponed.

•　　•　　•

Ainslie leaned back in the car in an effort to organize his thoughts. His memories of Elroy Doil and all that had occurred were like a file folder of jumbled notes and pages.

He remembered having seen Doil's name for the first time a year and a half ago when it appeared on a computer-generated list of potential suspects. Then, later, when Doil became a prime suspect, Homicide had made extensive inquiries going all the way back to Doil's early childhood.

Elroy Doil was thirty-two when the killings began. He had been born and raised in Miami's "poor white" neighborhood, known as Wynwood. Though the name does not appear on published maps, Wynwood comprises a sixty-block, half-square-mile area in mid-Miami with a mainly underprivileged white populace, plus a grim record of high crime, riots, looting, and police brutality.

Immediately southwest of Wynwood is Overtown, also not named on maps, with a mainly underprivileged black occupancy, plus a similarly dreary record of high crime, riots, looting, and police brutality.

Elroy Doil's mother, Beulah, was a prostitute, drug addict, and alcoholic. She told friends that her son's father "coulda been any one of a hundred fuckers," though she later advised Elroy that his most probable father was serving a life term in Florida's Belle Glade prison. Even so, Elroy encountered a long succession of other men who lived with his mother for varying periods, and remembered many of them from the drunken beatings and sexual abuse he received.

Why Beulah Doil had a child at all was unclear, having had several previous abortions. Her explanation: she "just never got around to getting rid of the kid."

Eventually Beulah, a shrewdly practical person, instructed her son in petty crime and how to avoid "getting your ass busted." Elroy learned fast. At ten he was stealing food for himself and Beulah, as well as filching anything else in sight. He robbed other boys at school. It helped that he was big for his age, and a savage fighter.

Under Beulah's tutelage, Elroy grew up learning to take advantage of the lenient laws affecting juvenile crime. Even though he was apprehended several times for assaults, thefts, and petty larcenies, he was always released back to his mother's custody with a virtual slap on the wrist.

At seventeen, as Malcolm Ainslie learned long afterward, Elroy Doil was first suspected of murder. He was caught running from the area where the crime had occurred, and detained for questioning. Because of his juvenile status, his mother was brought to the police station where he had been taken, and in her presence, Doil was questioned by detectives.

Had there been clear evidence against him, Elroy would have been charged with murder as an adult. As it was, Beulah knew enough to refuse to cooperate, and would not allow voluntary fingerprinting of her son, which might have linked him to a knife found near the murder scene. In the end, lacking sufficient evidence to hold him, the police released Doil and the crime remained unsolved.

Years later, when he became a suspect in a series of killings, his juvenile record remained closed and his fingerprints were not on file.

As it was, after Doil became an official adult at eighteen, he used his street smarts acquired as a juvenile to continue his criminal ways. He was never caught, and thus no adult criminal record existed. Only much later, when the Police Department delved into Doil's background, was crucial information produced that had been forgotten or hidden.

●   ●   ●

Jorge's voice broke in abruptly: "We need gas, Sergeant. Why don't we stop at Wildwood, just ahead." It was almost 3:00 A.M.

"Okay, but get this car filled like we're making a pit stop in a race. I'll run in and get some coffee."

"And potato chips. No, make it cookies. We need cookies."

Ainslie peered over fondly and realized why he sometimes looked upon Jorge as a son.

As they took the exit ramp, both men could see the beacons of several gas stations. Wildwood was a traditional highway interchange—in daytime an untidy conglomeration of junk-laden tourist stores, at night a refueling stopover for long-distance truckers.

Jorge chose the nearest gas station, a Shell. Beyond it was an all-night Waffle House with cars parked nearby. A half-dozen shadowy figures were huddled together around two of the cars. As the blue-and-white drove in, heads shot up and faces turned toward the new approaching headlights.

Then, with incredible speed, everything changed. The figures separated, some thrust aside, others running, the former close-knit scene a sudden melee of gyrating legs and arms. Doors of parked cars were flung open, figures hurled themselves in, and while doors were still closing the cars started up and drove away. Taking local roads, avoiding the main highway, they were quickly out of sight.

Jorge and Ainslie laughed.

"If we do nothing else tonight," Ainslie pronounced, "we just broke up a drug deal."

Both knew that I-75 was a dangerous route this late at night. As well as drug traffickers, there were thieves, prostitutes, and muggers, all looking for action.

But the sight of a police car had preempted everything.

Ainslie gave Jorge money for the gas, then, in the Waffle House, bought coffee and cookies, saving receipts for expense vouchers. As well as expenses, both men would receive overtime pay for this trip tonight.

They sipped their coffee through holes in the plastic tops of cardboard cups as Jorge pulled back onto I-75.

4

ANSLIE AND JORGE WERE 270 miles north of Miami now, with about a hundred miles to go. They were still moving quickly amid mostly commercial traffic. It was 3:30 A.M.

Jorge volunteered, "We'll make it, Sergeant. No problem."

For the first time since leaving Miami, Ainslie felt himself relax. He stared through the windshield into the darkness and muttered, "I just want to hear him say it."

He was speaking of Doil, and in some ways, he acknowledged, Karen was right. His interest in Doil *had* moved beyond the professional. After observing the carnage left behind at each murder scene, after hunting the killer down for months, after observing Doil's total lack of remorse, Ainslie honestly felt that the world needed to be rid of this man. He wanted to hear Doil confess to the murders, and then—despite what he had told Jorge earlier—he wanted to see him die. Now it looked as if he would.

At that moment Jorge's voice broke in. "Oh no! Looks like big trouble up ahead."

The I-75 northbound traffic had suddenly thickened and slowed. Ahead of them, trucks were rolling to a stop, as were lines of cars between them. Across the divider, on the southbound lanes going the opposite way, not a single vehicle was on the road.

"Damn! Damn!" Ainslie slammed a hand on the dashboard. The blue-and-white had slowed to a crawl, with a bright chain of red taillights up ahead. Flashing lights of emergency vehicles were visible in the distance.

"Take the shoulder," he commanded. "Use our lights."

Jorge turned on their blue, red, and white flashers and eased across traffic onto the right-hand shoulder. They moved steadily but cautiously, passing other vehicles now at a standstill. Doors of trucks and cars were opening, people leaning out, trying to see the cause of the blockage.

"Go faster!" Ainslie ordered. "Don't waste a minute."

Within seconds, several Florida Highway Patrol cars loomed ahead, their roof lights flashing, blocking all traffic lanes, including the shoulder on which the Miami Police car now approached.

A Highway Patrol lieutenant put up a hand, signaling them to stop, and walked toward the car. Ainslie stepped out.

The lieutenant said, "You guys are really off your turf. You lost?"

"No, sir." Ainslie held out his identification badge, which the other inspected. "We're on our way to Raiford, and we don't have much time."

"Then I have bad news, Sergeant. This road is closed. Big accident up ahead. A tanker tractor-trailer jackknifed and flipped."

"Lieutenant, we have to get around!"

The other officer's voice sharpened. "Listen! It's a mess up there. The driver's dead; so, we believe, are two people trapped in a car the tractor rolled onto. The tanker ruptured, and twenty thousand gallons of high-octane gas are pouring onto the highway. We're trying to clear traffic before some idiot lights a match. We've got fire trucks with foam on the way, but they aren't here yet. So no! There is no way you can get around. Excuse me."

Responding to a call from another officer, the lieutenant turned away.

Ainslie seethed. "We need another route."

Jorge already had a Florida road map spread out on the hood of the car, and shook his head doubtfully. "There's no time, Sergeant. We'd have to go back on I-75, then take side roads. We could easily get lost. Can't we ride over the foam?"

"No way. Triple-F foam is mostly liquid soap, and slippery as hell. Besides, there'd be gasoline underneath; a car as hot as ours could start an inferno. So there's no choice—we turn around. No time to waste. Let's go!"

As they climbed in the blue-and-white, the Highway Patrol lieutenant ran back. "We'll do our best to help you," he said quickly. "I just talked with Control. They know about you, and why you're going to Raiford, so here's the plan: From here, go back south to Micanopy; that's exit 73. Take that exit, go west to Highway 441." Jorge was scribbling notes as the lieutenant continued. "You'll reach 441 almost at once. When you get there, turn left, go north toward Gainesville; it's not a bad road, you should make good time. Just before Gainesville you'll intersect with Highway 331. There's a traffic light; when you reach it, turn right. On 331, one of our patrol cars will be waiting. Trooper Sequiera is in charge. Follow him. He'll escort you all the way to Raiford."

Ainslie nodded. "Thanks, Lieutenant. Okay to use our lights and siren?"

"Use everything you've got. And hey, all of us here know about Doil. Make sure that bastard fries."

Jorge already had the car in drive. He eased across a grass-and-shrubbery divider, swung sharply left, and headed south—emergency lights flashing, siren wailing, and the accelerator to the floor.

•   •   •

They were now critically short of time. Ainslie knew it. So did Jorge.

Their delay and rerouting would cost them the better part of an hour, possibly more.

The clock on the dashboard showed 5:34 A.M. Animal was to be executed in less than an hour and a half. What remained of the journey, assuming all went perfectly, would take roughly forty minutes, which meant they'd arrive at Raiford at 6:14. Allowing time for Ainslie to enter the prison and reach Doil, plus time at the end when the prisoner would be taken to the electric chair and strapped in, the longest time Ainslie could hope for with him was a half hour.

Not enough! Not nearly enough.

But it would have to do.

"Oh shit!" Ainslie muttered, tempted to urge Jorge to go faster. But there was no way they could. Jorge was driving superbly, his eyes riveted on the road ahead, his mouth set tightly, hands firmly on the wheel. He had passed the instructions to Ainslie, who used a flashlight to read them out when needed. Highway 441, which they were on now, was rougher than I-75, with frequent intersecting side roads and some cumbersome truck traffic. Still, Jorge was maneuvering around it, making every second count. The emergency lights and siren helped. Some of the truck drivers, observing them in rearview mirrors, moved over, giving way. But a light rain had begun and there were occasional patches of mist, both slowing them down.

"Damn!" Ainslie griped. "We're not going to make it."

"We have a chance." Jorge was sitting forward, his eyes glued on the road; he increased their speed a little. "Trust me!"

That's all I can do, Ainslie thought. *This is Jorge's moment; mine is coming*—maybe! *Anyway,* he told himself, *try to unwind, think of something else. Think about Doil. Will he spring any surprises? Will he finally tell the truth, the way he* didn't *at his trial?* . . .

• • •

The sensational murder trial of Elroy Doil prompted headlines in almost every newspaper in the country and was featured daily on network TV. Outside the courthouse some demonstrators paraded, their placards urging the death penalty. Journalists competed—many unsuccessfully—for the limited courtroom space allotted to the media.

Public outrage was compounded by the state attorney's decision to try Doil for the most recent crime only—namely the first-degree murders of Kingsley and Nellie Tempone, an elderly, wealthy, and respected black couple who were savagely tortured, then killed, in their home in Miami's exclusive Bay Heights.

As for the additional ten murders Doil was believed to have committed, if he was found guilty and executed for the Tempone killings, they would remain forever unresolved.

The controversial decision by State Attorney Adele Montesino, acting on advice of her senior prosecutors, produced an outcry from families of other victims who desperately wanted to see justice done in the names of loved ones they had lost. The media reported their indignation, providing an opportunity to link Doil's name publicly with the earlier killings. Newspapers and TV seldom worried about liability in such matters. As an editor expressed it, "When did you last hear of a serial killer suing for libel?"

Thus awareness and criticism grew.

Miami's chief of police was also known to have urged the state attorney to include at least one other double murder in the charges against Doil.

But Adele Montesino, a short, heavyset fifty-four-year-old, sometimes referred to as "the pit bull," remained adamant. She was serving her third four-year term, had already announced her intention not to seek another, and could afford to exercise her independence.

Sergeant Malcolm Ainslie had been among those attending a pretrial strategy meeting at which Ms. Montesino said, "With the Tempone case we'll have a cast-iron prosecution."

She used her fingers to tick off crucial points. "Doil was arrested at the scene with both victims' blood on him. We have the knife found in Doil's possession, identified by the medical examiner as the murder weapon, and also with both victims' blood. And we have a strong eyewitness to the murders, whom the jury will sympathize with. No twelve people in the world would let Doil off on this one."

The witness to whom she referred was the Tempones' twelve-year-old grandson, Ivan. The boy had been visiting his grandparents and was the only other person in the house when Doil broke in and attacked the elderly couple.

Young Ivan was in the next room, where he remained transfixed, watching with silent horror through a partially open door while his grandparents were continually cut and stabbed. Though terrified, knowing he would be killed if discovered, the boy had the sense and courage to go silently to a phone and call 911.

Although police arrived too late to save Kingsley and Nellie Tempone, they were in time to catch Elroy Doil, who was still on the victims' property, his gloved hands and clothing covered in their blood. Ivan, after being treated for shock, described the attack with such clarity and composure that Adele Montesino knew he would be convincing on the witness stand.

"But if we prosecute those other cases as well," the state attorney continued, "we do not, in any one, have the same positive, incontestable proof. Yes, there's circumstantial evidence. We can prove opportunity, and that Doil was close by when the killings happened, and that he has no alibis. From the first serial killing there's a partial palm print that is almost certainly Doil's, though our fingerprint technicians caution there are only seven matching points, instead of the nine or ten needed for a positive ID. Also, Dr. Sanchez said a bowie knife, which killed the Tempones, is *not* the same knife used on other victims. Oh, I know he could have had several knives, and probably did, but the police haven't found another.

"So you can be sure any defense lawyer would make the most of those weaknesses. And if the defense infused enough doubt into those other murders, a jury could begin wondering if our one airtight, certain case—the Tempones—is also questionable.

"Look, we're going to get a guilty verdict for the Tempones, which will send Doil to the chair. We can only kill the man once. Right?"

Despite the protests, the state attorney declined to alter her tactic. In the end, though, what Montesino had not foreseen was that her failure to charge Doil with at least one other double murder out of a presumed total of twelve serial killings would create a post-trial impression—especially among anti-capital-punishment crusaders—that some doubt existed overall, even extending to the one case where Doil was found guilty and sentenced to death.

Doil's eventual trial for the Tempone killings—as Malcolm Ainslie remembered—abounded with confrontations, stormy polemics, and even violence.

Since the defendant had no financial resources, the presiding judge, Rudy Olivadotti, appointed an experienced criminal trial attorney, Willard Steltzer, to represent Doil.

Steltzer was well known in Miami's legal community, in part for brilliance in court, but also for his eccentric appearance and manner. At forty he still refused to conform to the traditional lawyer's dress code, opting for antique suits and ties, generally from the fifties and bought at specialty shops. He also wore his long, coal-black hair in a braid.

True to form, Steltzer's first action as Doil's attorney rankled both the prosecution and Judge Olivadotti. Arguing that it would be impossible to find an impartial jury in Dade County, owing to widespread publicity, Steltzer filed a motion for a change of venue.

The judge, despite his irritation, ruled in favor of the motion and the trial was moved to Jacksonville, Florida—nearly four hundred miles north of Miami.

As another defense ploy, Steltzer sought to have his client declared insane. He cited Doil's fits of rage, the fact that he had been abused as a child, a ferocious violence demonstrated in prison, and his habitual lying, underscored by Doil's insistence that he was never anywhere near the Tempone home, despite evidence that even defense counsel admitted was conclusive.

They were all valid reasons for possible insanity, Steltzer believed, and again Judge Olivadotti reluctantly agreed. He ordered Doil to be examined by three state-certified psychiatrists, whose study lasted four months.

At the end, the psychiatrists concluded that, yes, all of the assessments of Elroy Doil's nature and habits submitted by his defense attorney were true. However, these did not make Doil insane. The crucial issue was that he knew the difference between right and wrong. The judge thereupon declared Doil to be mentally competent and ordered him to stand trial for first-degree murder.

Doil's presence at his trial was unlikely to be forgotten by anyone who attended it. He was an enormous man, standing six feet four and weighing two hundred and ninety pounds. His facial features were large, his chest broad and muscular, his hands immense. Everything about Elroy Doil was oversized, including his ego. Each day he moved into the courtroom with a superior, menacing swagger and a sneer. The combination made him seem indifferent, at times, to events around him—an attitude that persisted throughout his trial and beyond. One reporter wrote in a summation, "Elroy Doil might just as well have asked for his own conviction."

What might have helped him, as it had on past occasions, would have been the presence of his mother, who was wise in the ways of crime and the law. But Beulah Doil had died several years earlier of AIDS.

As it was, Doil remained abusive and hostile. Even during jury selection he blurted out such remarks to his counsel as, "Get that fucking grease monkey out of here!"—speaking of a garage mechanic whom Willard Steltzer had been on the verge of approving as a juror. Because a defendant's wishes count, Steltzer was forced to reverse himself, then use a precious peremptory challenge for dismissal.

Again, when a dignified black woman showed some empathy toward Doil, he shouted, "That dumb nigger couldn't see the truth if it ran over her." The woman was excused.

At that point the judge, who until now had refrained from comment, cautioned the accused, "Mr. Doil, you had better settle down and be quiet."

There was a pause while Willard Steltzer, visibly disturbed and clenching his client's arm, spoke seriously into Doil's ear. After that the interruptions ceased during jury selection, but resumed when the main trial proceedings began.

A Dade County medical examiner, Dr. Sandra Sanchez, was on the witness stand. She had testified that a bowie knife, bearing the victims' blood and found in Elroy Doil's possession, was the actual weapon that killed Kingsley and Nellie Tempone.

At that point Doil, his face twisted with rage, rose from the defense table and shouted, "You fucking bitch, why you tell them lies? All lies! It ain't my knife. I wasn't even there."

Judge Olivadotti, a martinet with lawyers but known for giving a defendant all the latitude he could, now warned sternly, "Mr. Doil, if you do not remain silent, I am going to have to take extreme measures to keep you quiet. This is a serious warning."

To which Doil responded, "Screw you, Judge. I'm tired of sitting here, listening to all this bullshit. This ain't no court of justice. You already made up your minds, so execute me, goddammit! Get it over with!"

Flushed with anger, the judge addressed Willard Steltzer: "Counsel, I order you to talk some sense into your client. This is my final warning. Court is adjourned for fifteen minutes."

After the adjournment, Doil was fidgety but silent while two crime-scene specialists testified. Then, when Ainslie took the stand and described the arrest at the Tempone murder scene, Doil exploded. Leaping from his seat, he raced across the court and hurled himself at Ainslie, screaming obscenities. "Crooked conniving cop . . . I wasn't even there . . . fucking priest, disgraced. God hates you! . . . Bastard, liar . . ."

As Doil pounded with his fists, Ainslie barely protected himself, raising one arm as a shield, and did not strike back. In seconds, two bailiffs and a prison officer threw themselves on Doil. Pulling him clear, they locked his arms behind him, wrestled handcuffs into place, then slammed him face forward to the ground.

Once more, Judge Olivadotti adjourned the trial.

When it resumed, Elroy Doil was tightly gagged, and handcuffed to a heavy chair. The judge addressed him sternly.

"Never before, Mr. Doil, at any court proceeding, have I ordered a defendant restrained as you are now, and I regret this action greatly. But your disorderly behavior and abusive language leave me no choice. However, if your counsel comes to me tomorrow, before this trial resumes, with your solemn promise of good behavior for however long these proceedings take, I will consider having the restraints removed. But I caution that if your promise is broken, there will be no second chance; the restraints will be reinstated for the remainder of this trial."

The next day, Steltzer did make the promise on behalf of his client, and Doil's gag was removed, though the handcuffs remained. Before the day's proceedings were an hour old, Doil leaped up in his chair and screamed at the judge, "Go fuck your mother, you asshole!" after which the gag was reinstated and remained in place for the duration of the trial.

On both occasions when the restraints were ordered, the judge cautioned the jury, "The restrictions I have placed upon the defendant must have no effect on your verdict. You are concerned here solely with the evidence presented."

Ainslie remembered thinking how impossible it was for the jurors to ignore the image of Doil's courtroom histrionics. But whether that influenced a decision or not, at the conclusion of a six-day trial, and after five hours of deliberation, the jury returned with a unanimous verdict: "Guilty of murder in the first degree."

A sentence of death inevitably followed. Subsequently, while still insisting on his innocence, Doil refused to cooperate in any appeal process and stubbornly denied others the right to appeal on his behalf. Even so, substantial paperwork was needed before the legal machinery ground out an execution date. The law's tedious process between sentencing and execution took a year and seven months.

But now, inexorably, the day had come, and with it the tantalizing question: What did Doil want to say to Ainslie in the closing moments of his life?

If they made it in time . . .

● ● ●

Jorge was still speeding north on Highway 441 in the mist and rain.

Ainslie checked the time: 5:48.

He reached for his notepad and the cellular phone, then tapped out the number. There was a curt answer on the first ring.

"State Prison."

"Lieutenant Hambrick, please."

"This is Hambrick. Is this Sergeant Ainslie?"

"Yes, sir. I'm about twenty minutes away."

"Well, you've cut it fine, but we'll do our best when you get here. You understand, though—nothing can be delayed?"

"I understand that."

"Do you have your escort yet?"

"No . . . Wait! I see a traffic light ahead."

Jorge nodded vigorously as two green lights came into view.

"Turn right at the light," Hambrick instructed. "Your escort is around the corner. We're alerting Trooper Sequiera now. He'll be rolling when you get there."

"Thanks, Lieutenant."

"Okay, listen carefully. Follow Sequiera closely. You're already cleared through our outer gate, the main gate, and two checkpoints after that. The tower will spotlight you, but keep moving. Stop at the front entrance to Administration. I'll be waiting. Got all that?"

"Got it."

"I presume you're armed, Sergeant."

"Yes, I am."

"We'll immediately enter the control room, where you'll hand over all weapons, ammunition, and police ID. Be ready. Who's driving you?"

"Detective Jorge Rodriguez. Plainclothes."

"We'll give him separate instructions when you get here. Listen, Sergeant. You've got to move fast, okay?"

"I'll be ready, Lieutenant. Thank you."

Ainslie turned to Jorge and asked, "Could you hear all that?"

"Got it all, Sergeant."

The traffic light ahead turned red, but Jorge ignored it. Barely slowing, he entered the four-way intersection and swung right. Directly ahead, a Highway Patrol black-and-yellow Mercury Marquis, bristling with roof antennae and flashing emergency lights, was already moving. The Miami blue-and-white fell in behind, and within seconds the two were a single eye-catching coruscation hurtling headlong through the night.

Later, when Ainslie attempted to recall that final portion of the four-hundred-mile journey, he found that all he could remember was a vague flashing montage. As best he could calculate later, they covered the last twenty-two miles of minor, twisting roads in less than fourteen minutes. Once, he noticed, their speed reached ninety-two miles per hour.

Some checkpoints were known to Ainslie from previous journeys. First the small town of Waldo, then Gainesville Airport to the right; they must have passed both so fast that neither registered. Then Starke, the dismal dormitory town of Raiford; he knew there were modest houses, prosaic stores, cheap motels, cluttered gas stations, but he saw none of them. Beyond Starke was an interval of gloom — an impression of trees . . . all lost in a miasma of haste.

"We're here," Jorge said. "There's Raiford, up ahead."

5

FLORIDA STATE PRISON LOOKED LIKE a mammoth fortress, and it was. So were two other prisons immediately beyond.

Paradoxically, the State Prison was officially in the town of Starke, not Raiford. The other two, which *were* in Raiford, were Raiford Prison and the Union Correctional Institute. But it was Florida State Prison that contained Death Row, and it was here that all executions took place.

Looming ahead of Ainslie and Jorge was an immense succession of high, grimly austere concrete structures, a mile-long complex punctuated by row after row of narrow and stoutly barred cellblock windows. A functional one-story building, jutting forward, housed the State Prison Administration. Another concrete mass to one side, three stories high and windowless, contained the prison workshops.

Three heavy-duty chain-link fences enclosed it all, each fence thirty feet high and topped with rolls of concertina barbed wire and a series of live electrical wires. At intervals along the fences, tall concrete towers, nine in all, were manned by guards armed with rifles, machine guns, tear gas, and searchlights. From there they could view the entire prison. The three fences created parallel twin enclosures. Within the enclosures, trained attack dogs roamed, among them German shepherds and pit bulls.

Approaching the State Prison, both the Highway Patrol and Miami Police cars slowed, and Jorge, who was seeing the complex for the first time, whistled softly.

"It's hard to believe," Ainslie said, "but a few guys have actually escaped from here. Most of them didn't get very far, though." He glanced at the dashboard clock—6:02 A.M.—and was reminded that Elroy Doil would be escaping in less than an hour, in the grimmest way of all.

Jorge shook his head. "If this were my home, I'd sure as hell try to escape."

The State Prison's outer gate and a large parking lot beyond were bathed in lights. The parking area was bustling—unusual for this time of day, but public interest in the Doil execution had lured many reporters to the scene, and at least a hundred others now milled around, hoping for a hint of the latest developments. Several TV mobile trucks were parked nearby.

As usual, demonstrators stood in small groups, chanting slogans. Some bore signs denouncing today's execution and capital punishment in general; others held lighted candles.

A new breed of protesters held placards reading YOUR TAXES ARE PAYING FOR THIS SUICIDE and STOP STATE-SPONSORED SUICIDE. These were mainly young lawyers or their supporters who objected to condemned murderers like Elroy Doil being allowed to decide against the prolonged process of appeal.

After every death sentence, one appeal went automatically to the Florida Supreme Court, but if that was rejected, as most were, further appeals could take ten years or more of legal effort. Now, instead, some prisoners accepted the death penalty for their crimes and let it happen. The state governor had wisely ruled that if a condemned prisoner made that decision, it was part of his or her freedom of choice and not "suicide." As to the objecting lawyers, the governor commented acidly, "They are less concerned about condemned prisoners having another day in court than about having *their own* day in court."

Ainslie wondered how much thought, if any, the demonstrators gave to the silent: a murderer's victims.

Driving past the parking lot, Ainslie and Jorge neared the main gate, a two-lane entranceway with uniformed figures standing guard. Normally at this point all arrivals were asked for identification documents and questioned about their business at the prison. Instead, uniformed guards in distinctive kelly green pants and white shirts waved both police cars through. At the same time a tower searchlight encompassed the two cars and tracked them toward the prison buildings. Ainslie and Jorge put up hands to shield their eyes.

They were similarly cleared through two other checkpoints and, within seconds, were approaching the Administration building. Ainslie had visited the prison several times before, usually to interview crime suspects, and once to arrest an inmate on new charges, but never had he reached the interior so quickly.

The Highway Patrol car stopped at the Administration entrance, and Jorge maneuvered the Miami blue-and-white alongside.

As Ainslie stepped out, he saw a tall, slender black man, wearing a prison guard's uniform with a lieutenant's rank badges, move forward. Probably in his mid-forties, he had a trim mustache and wore half-glasses over penetrating eyes. On one cheek was a long scar. His speech was brisk and confident as he put out his hand. "Sergeant Ainslie, I'm Hambrick."

"Good morning, Lieutenant. Thanks for the arrangements."

"No problem; let's just keep moving." The lieutenant led the way inside, walking quickly down a brightly lit hallway—a tightly controlled linkage between the strict security outside and the formidable cellblocks ahead. The two paused briefly for clearance through two separate sets of electrically operated steel gates, then a thick steel door opening to a main cellblock corridor, as wide as a four-lane highway and running the length of the prison's seven cellblocks.

Hambrick and Ainslie stopped outside a secure control room enclosed by steel and bulletproof glass. Inside were two male guards and a female lieutenant. The lieutenant approached the two men standing outside and slid a metal drawer outward; Ainslie inserted his Glock 9mm automatic pistol, a fifteen-round ammunition clip, and his police ID. The items were drawn inside the control room, where they would be placed in a safe until retrieved. No one had asked him about the recording device under his coat, which he had strapped on in the car. He decided not to volunteer the information.

"Let's move it," Hambrick said, but at the same moment a group of about twenty people emerged from the hallway behind and blocked their way. The newcomers were well-dressed visitors; all appeared intent and serious as prison guards hustled them through the corridor. Glancing at Ainslie, Hambrick mouthed the word "Witnesses."

Ainslie realized the group was headed for the execution chamber— "twelve respectable citizens" as required by law, plus others whose presence the prison governor had approved, though there were always more applicants for execution viewing than available seats. The limit was twenty-four. The witnesses would have been assembled not far away and brought to the prison by bus. It was a sign that events were moving on schedule as 7:00 A.M. approached.

Scanning the group of faces, Ainslie recognized a woman state senator and two men who were members of the state House of Representatives. Politicians were competitive about attending executions, hoping their presence at such weighty law-and-order scenes would garner votes. Then he was startled to see one face: Miami City Commissioner Cynthia Ernst, who had once been important in his life, but he realized why she would want to watch Animal Doil's execution.

For a moment their eyes met, and Ainslie felt a sharp intake of breath, the effect she invariably had on him. He sensed, too, that she was aware of his presence, though made no acknowledgment and, as she moved by, her expression remained cool.

Moments later the witnesses were gone and Lieutenant Hambrick and Ainslie moved on.

"The superintendent is letting you use his Death Facility office to talk with

Doil," Hambrick said. "We'll bring him to you there. He's already been through preparation." The lieutenant glanced at his watch. "You'll have about half an hour, not much more. By the way, have you ever watched an execution?"

"Yes, once." It had been three years ago. At the request of a bereaved family, Ainslie had accompanied a young husband and wife who chose to witness the death of a habitual criminal who had raped, then killed their eight-year-old daughter. Ainslie, who had solved the case, had gone as a duty, but had found the experience unsettling.

"You're going to see another," Hambrick said. "Doil asked for you to be a witness, and it's been approved."

"No one asked me," Ainslie rejoined. "But I suppose that's not relevant."

Hambrick shrugged, then said, "I've talked to Doil. He seems to have some special feeling about you. I'm not sure admiration is right; respect maybe. Did you get close to him in some way?"

"Never!" Ainslie was emphatic. "I arrested the son of a bitch for murder, and that's all. Besides, he hates me. At his trial he attacked me, called me 'perjurer,' 'crooked cop,' stuff like that."

"Nuts like Doil change moods like you and I shift gears. He doesn't feel that way now."

"Makes no difference. I'm only here to get some answers before he dies. Apart from that, my feelings for the guy are zero."

They continued walking while Hambrick digested what had been said. Then he asked, "Is it true you were once a priest?"

"Yes. Did Doil tell you?"

Hambrick nodded. "As far as he's concerned, you still are. I was there last night when he asked for you to come. He was spouting something from the Bible, about vengeance and repaying."

Ainslie nodded. "Yeah, it's from Romans: 'Give place unto wrath; for it is written, Vengeance is mine; I will repay, saith the Lord.'"

"That's it. Then Doil called you 'God's avenging angel,' and the message I got was that you meant more to him than a priest. Did the Father tell you all that when he phoned?"

Ainslie shook his head; already depressed by these surroundings, he wished he were at home, having breakfast with Karen and Jason. Well, at least what he had just learned explained Ray Uxbridge's antagonism on the phone and the priest's tirade about a "blasphemous charade."

They had reached the Death Facility, or "Death House," as it was usually called. It occupied all three floors of a cellblock building and contained Death Row, where condemned prisoners lived while exercising their appeal rights and later awaited their turn for execution. Ainslie knew of the other areas—an ultra-Spartan "ready cell" where a prisoner spent the final sixty-five hours of life continuously under observation; a preparation room, its centerpiece a decrepit barber chair where a condemned's head and right leg were shaved before execution in order to provide good electrical contacts; and finally the execution chamber containing the electric chair—"Ol' Sparky," as prisoners called it—where there were seats for witnesses and, shielded from view, the executioner's booth.

Within the execution chamber, Ainslie knew, preparations would have been going on for the past several hours. The chief electrician would have been first on the scene, to connect the electric chair with the power source and to check voltages, a fail-safe bar, and the ultimate control with which the black-robed, hooded executioner sent two thousand volts into a condemned prisoner's skull in automatic eight-cycle bursts. The massive electric charge brought death within two minutes, though unconsciousness was supposedly instant and painless. There were doubts about the painlessness, but they were unresolvable because no one ever survived to report on the experience.

Also inside the execution chamber, within sight of the electric chair, was a red telephone. Immediately before an execution, the prison warden spoke with the state governor on that phone, seeking final permission to proceed. Similarly, the governor could call the warden, even seconds before the death control was thrown, ordering a stay of execution, perhaps on the basis of last-minute evidence, a ruling from the U.S. Supreme Court, or some other judicial cause. It had happened, and could even happen today.

Though unwritten and unofficial, there was a rule that every execution was delayed by one minute—a precaution in case the red phone rang a few seconds late. Thus Doil's execution, though scheduled for 7:00 A.M., would not take place until 7:01.

"This is it," Hambrick announced. They had come to a sturdy wooden door that he opened with a key. Then, inside, he turned a switch, illuminating a windowless, boxlike room about twenty-four feet square. It was furnished with a plain wooden desk and tilt-back chair, a heavy metal chair bolted to the floor in front of the desk, and a small table to one side. Nothing else.

"The super doesn't use this much," Hambrick said. "Only when we have executions." He motioned to the chair behind the desk. "That's where you sit, Sergeant. I'll be back soon."

During the lieutenant's absence, Ainslie switched on the recorder concealed beneath his clothing.

In less than five minutes Hambrick was back, accompanied by two prison guards who were leading and partially supporting a figure whom Ainslie recognized. Doil was wearing leg irons and handcuffs, the latter secured to a tightly strapped waist belt. Behind the trio was Father Ray Uxbridge.

It was more than a year since Ainslie had seen Elroy Doil; the last occasion had been at the sentencing following his trial. In the meantime, the change had been dramatic. At his trial and sentencing he had been physically robust, tall and powerful, with matching aggressiveness; now he seemed pitifully the reverse. He was stooped, with sagging shoulders, his body thin, his face wan and gaunt. In place of aggression, his eyes showed nervous uncertainty. His head had been shaved for the execution, and the unnatural pink baldness added to his desolate appearance. At the last minute, conductive gel would be applied to his scalp, ready for the electric chair's metal death cap.

Father Uxbridge stepped forward; he was in clerical garb, a breviary in hand. A large, broad-shouldered man with patrician features, he projected a presence that Ainslie remembered from previous encounters. Ignoring Ainslie, he addressed Doil.

"Mr. Doil, I am willing to stay with you to provide God's comfort for as long as these circumstances allow, and I remind you again that you are not required to make any statement or answer questions."

"Just a moment," Ainslie said, springing up from the desk chair and moving closer to the others. "Doil, I've driven eight hours from Miami because you asked to see me. Father Uxbridge told me you had something to say."

Glancing down, Ainslie saw that Doil's hands were clenched tightly together, and that his wrists were raw where the handcuffs had chafed. He glanced at Hambrick and gestured. "Can you take those off while we're talking?"

The lieutenant shook his head. "Sorry, Sergeant, can't do it. Doil has beat up three of our people since he's been here. One had to be hospitalized."

Ainslie nodded. "Scratch that idea."

As Ainslie spoke, Doil lifted his head. Perhaps it had been the preceding humane thought about the handcuffs, or perhaps Ainslie's voice, but for whatever reason, Doil fell to his knees and would have tumbled face forward if the guards had not supported him. As it was, he brought his face close to one of Ainslie's hands and attempted, unsuccessfully, to kiss it.

His voice blurred, he mumbled, "Bless me, Father, for I have sinned . . ."

Father Uxbridge leapt forward, his face flushed with anger. "No, no, no!" he shouted to Ainslie. "This is blasphemy!" Turning toward Doil, he insisted, "This man is not—"

"Shut up!" Ainslie snapped. Then, to Doil, more quietly, "I am not a priest anymore. You know that. But if you want to confess anything to me, I will listen as a human being."

Uxbridge shouted again, "You can't take a confession. You have no right!"

Doil began speaking to Ainslie. "Father, it has been . . ."

Uxbridge shouted, "I have told you he is not a Father!"

Doil mumbled, and Ainslie caught the words, "He is God's avenging angel . . ."

"This is desecration!" Uxbridge roared. "I will not allow it!"

Suddenly Doil turned his head. He snarled at Uxbridge, "Fuck off!" Then, facing the others, he cried, "Get that asshole out of here!"

Hambrick advised Uxbridge, "I'm afraid you'll have to go, Father. If he doesn't want you here, that's his privilege."

"I will not go!"

Hambrick's voice sharpened. "Please, Father. I don't want to have to remove you by force."

At a signal from the lieutenant, one of the guards left Doil and seized Uxbridge's arm.

The priest jerked his arm away. "Do not dare! I am a priest, a man of God!" As the guard stood hesitantly, Uxbridge faced Hambrick. "You will hear more of this. I shall personally bring your behavior to the attention of the governor." He snapped at Ainslie, "The church was well rid of you." Then, with a final, all-encompassing glare, Uxbridge left.

Elroy Doil, who was still on his knees before Ainslie, began again, "Bless me, Father, for I have sinned. My last confession was . . . I don't fuckin' remember."

In other circumstances Ainslie might have smiled, but he was torn. His conscience troubled him. He wanted to hear what Doil had to say, but not as an impostor.

It was Hambrick who, glancing at his watch, added words of common sense. "If you want to hear it at all, better let him do it his way."

Ainslie still hesitated, wishing this moment could have happened in some other way.

But he wanted to *know*—to have answers and insights to so many events that had begun so long ago.

•   •   •

It was two years earlier, in Miami's Coconut Grove—a fresh January morning, shortly after 7:00 A.M.

Part Two

THE PAST

ORLANDO COBO, A MIDDLE-AGED security guard at Coconut Grove's Royal Colonial Hotel, was tired. He was ready to go home when he entered the eighth floor a few minutes before 7:00 A.M. on routine patrol. It had been an uneventful night, with only three minor incidents during his eight-hour shift.

Security problems relating to youth, sex, or drugs rarely occurred at the "Royal Colostomy," as it was sometimes called. The clientele comprised mainly middle-aged, staid, well-to-do people who liked the hotel's old-fashioned quiet lobby, its indoor profusion of tropical plants, and an architectural style once described as "brick wedding cake."

In a way the hotel matched its Coconut Grove locale—a sometimes jarring mix of past and present. Within the Grove, decrepit frame houses nudged once-exclusive, stylish homes; mom-and-pop trivia shops stood cheek-by-jowl with upscale galleries and boutiques; fast-food takeouts abutted gourmet restaurants; everywhere, poverty and wealth rubbed shoulders. Florida's oldest settlement—a historic village established twenty years before Miami—Coconut Grove seemed to have not one character but many, all untidily competing.

None of this troubled Cobo as he left an elevator and walked along the eighth-floor corridor. He was neither a philosopher nor a Coconut Grove resident, but drove to work each day from North Miami. At the moment nothing seemed amiss, and he began to anticipate the relaxing journey home.

Then, nearing a fire-exit stairway at the corridor's end, he noticed that the door of room 805 was slightly ajar. From inside he could hear the loud sound of a radio or TV. He knocked, and when there was no response, he inched open the door, leaned inside, then gagged in disgust at an overwhelming odor. Holding a hand over his mouth, Cobo moved forward into the room, and at the sight of what faced him, his legs weakened. Directly ahead, in a pool of blood, were the bodies of a man and a woman—with dismembered parts of their bodies around them.

Cobo hastily closed the door, composed himself with an effort, then reached for a phone clipped to his belt. He tapped out 911.

A woman's voice answered, "Nine-one-one emergency. Can I help you?" A beep indicated the call was being recorded.

•   •   •

At Miami Police Communication Center, a complaint clerk listened while Orlando Cobo reported an apparent double murder at the Royal Colonial Hotel.

"You say you're a security guard?"

"Yes, ma'am."

"Where are you?"

"Right outside the room. It's 805." As the complaint clerk spoke, she was typing the information on a computer, to be read moments later by a dispatcher in another section.

"Stay there," the complaint clerk told the caller. "Secure the room. Let no one in until our officers arrive."

A mile and a half away, a young uniformed policeman, Tomas Ceballos, in patrol unit 164, was cruising the South Dixie Highway when he received a dispatcher's urgent call. Immediately he swung his car hard right, tires screaming, and, with flashing lights and siren, headed for the Royal Colonial.

Minutes later, Officer Ceballos joined the security guard outside room 805.

"I just checked with reception," Cobo told him, consulting a note. "The room's registered to Mr. and Mrs. Homer Frost from Indiana; the lady's name is Blanche." He handed over the note and a room key-card.

Inserting the card, Ceballos cautiously entered 805. Instantly he recoiled, then forced himself to take in the scene, knowing he would need to describe it later.

What he saw were the bodies of an elderly man and woman, gagged and bound and seated facing each other, as if each had been witness to the other's death. The victims' faces had been beaten; the man's eyes and face were burned. Both bodies were a maze of knife cuts. In the background a radio was playing hard rock.

Tomas Ceballos had seen enough. Returning to the corridor, he used a portable radio to call Dispatch; his unit number would appear automatically on the dispatcher's screen. His voice wavered. "I need a Homicide unit on Tac One."

Tactical One was a radio channel reserved for Homicide use. Detective-Sergeant Malcolm Ainslie, unit number 1310, was on his way to work in an unmarked police car and had already checked in with Dispatch. Today Ainslie and his team were the on-duty hot unit.

The dispatcher alerted Ainslie, who switched to Tac One. "Thirteen-ten to one-sixty-four. QSK?"

"Two bodies at the Royal Colonial Hotel," Ceballos responded. "Room 805. Possible thirty-one." He swallowed, steadying his voice. "Make that a definite thirty-one. It's a bad one, real bad."

A 31 was a homicide, and Ainslie answered, "Okay, on my way. Secure the scene. Don't allow anyone in that room—including yourself."

Ainslie spun his car around on a two-way street and pushed hard on the accelerator. At the same time he radioed Detective Bernard Quinn, a member of Ainslie's team, instructing Quinn to join him at the Royal Colonial.

His remaining detectives were handling other murders and for the time being unavailable. The past few months had been rife with homicides; investigations were piling up. Today, it seemed, the grim reaping was continuing.

Ainslie and Quinn arrived at the hotel within moments of each other, and together headed for a bank of elevators. Quinn, with graying hair and a seamed, weathered face, was impeccably dressed in a navy sports jacket, immaculate gray slacks, and a striped tie. A Britisher by birth and an American by adoption, he was a Homicide veteran, his retirement at age sixty not far away.

Quinn was respected and liked by colleagues, in part because he was never a threat to anyone's ambitions. After becoming a detective and doing his job well, he had not sought promotion. He simply did not want to be responsible for others, and had never taken the sergeant's exam, which he could have passed easily. But Quinn was a good man to have as lead investigator at any crime scene.

"This will be your case, Bernie," Ainslie said. "I'll stay to help, though. Get you started."

As they passed through the spacious, foliage-lined hotel lobby, Ainslie saw two women reporters near the registration desk. Media people sometimes cruised the streets, listening to police radio, and got to crime scenes early. One of the two, recognizing the detectives, hurried toward an elevator they had boarded, but the door slid closed before she reached it.

As the elevator rose, Quinn sighed. "There must be better ways to begin a day."

"You'll find out soon enough," Ainslie said. "Who knows? You might even miss this in retirement."

At the eighth floor, as they emerged, the security guard, Cobo, stepped forward. "Do you gentlemen have business—" He stopped on seeing the Miami Police ID badges that Ainslie and Quinn had clipped to their jackets.

"Unfortunately," Quinn said, "we do."

"Sorry, guys! Sure glad you're here. I've been stopping everyone who has no—"

"Keep it up," Ainslie told him. "Stay on it. Lots of our people will be arriving, but don't let anyone by without identification. And we'll want this corridor kept *clear*."

"Yes, sir." With all the excitement, Cobo had no intention of going home.

From the doorway of room 805, Officer Ceballos approached, treating the Homicide detectives with respect. Like many young policemen, his ambition was to shed his uniform one day for a detective's plain clothes, and it did no harm to create a good impression. Ceballos handed over the security guard's note identifying 805's occupants, and reported that apart from the two brief inspections by Cobo and himself, the crime scene was undisturbed.

"Good," Ainslie acknowledged. "Remain on the scene and I'll get a two-man unit to assist you. The press is already in the hotel and pretty soon they'll be swarming. I don't want a single one on this floor, and don't give out any information; just say a PI officer will be here later. Meanwhile, no one else gets even close to room 805 without seeing me or Detective Quinn. You got all that?"

"Yes, Sergeant."

"Okay, let's see what we have."

As Ceballos opened the door of 805, Bernard Quinn wrinkled his nose in disgust. "And you think I'll miss this?"

Ainslie shook his head dismally. The odor of death was a sickening, rancid smell that permeated every homicide scene, especially where there were open wounds and seeping body fluids.

Both detectives recorded in notebooks their time of entry. They would continue making notes—about every action taken until the case was closed. The process was burdensome, but necessary in case their memories were later challenged in court.

Initially they stood stock-still, surveying the awful scene before them— twin pools of partially dried blood and the mutilated, already decomposing bodies. Homicide detectives learn early in their careers that once a human body has ceased to live, the process of decay is extraordinarily swift; when heartbeats stop and blood no longer flows, armies of microbes soon turn flesh and body liquids into rotting offal. Ainslie remembered a veteran medical examiner who was given to proclaiming, "Garbage! That's all a human corpse ever is, and once we've learned what we need to, the sooner we dispose of it the better. Burn cadavers! That's the best way. Then if somebody wants to spread the ashes over some lake, fine, no harm done. But cemeteries, coffins, they're all barbaric—a waste of good land."

Apart from the bodies in 805, the room was in a state of wild disorder, with chairs turned over, bedding disarrayed, and the victims' clothes scattered around. The radio, on a windowsill, continued to play.

Quinn turned to Ceballos. "That was on when you came in?"

"Yes, and when the security guy got here. Station sounds like HOT 105."

"Thanks." Quinn made a note. "My son listens. I can't stand the noise."

Ainslie was beginning a series of calls on his portable police phone. Room 805's telephone would not be used until after a fingerprint check.

His first call was to summon a Crime Scene ID detail—identification technicians who were part of a civilian arm of the Miami Police Department. The ID team would photograph the crime scene and all evidence, including minuscule items that untrained eyes might miss. They would seek finger-prints, preserve blood samples, and do whatever else the detectives needed. Meanwhile, until the ID crew arrived, the crime scene would remain "frozen in time"—exactly as when discovered.

One single blundering individual, merely walking or touching, could destroy a vital clue and make the difference between a crime being solved and a criminal going free. Sometimes even senior police officers, visiting a murder scene out of curiosity, compromised evidence; that was one reason why a Homicide lead investigator had total authority at any scene, no matter what his or her rank.

More calls by Ainslie: a report to Homicide's commander, Lieutenant Newbold, already on his way; a request for attendance of a state attorney; a plea to Police Headquarters for an information officer to handle the media people.

As soon as the ID team was finished with the victims' bodies, Ainslie would summon a medical examiner, whose first inspection should take place as soon as possible after death. ME's were touchy, however, about being called too soon and having to wait while the ID people completed their work.

Later still, after the medical inspection and the bodies' removal to the Dade County morgue, an autopsy would follow, which Bernard Quinn would attend.

While Ainslie was telephoning, Quinn used a rubber glove to unplug the loud radio. Next he began a detailed study of the victims' bodies—their wounds, remaining clothing, articles nearby—all the while still making notes. He observed several pieces of expensive-looking jewelry on a bedside table. Then, turning his head, he exclaimed, "Hey, look at this!"

Ainslie joined him. Incongruous and bizarre—laid out on the far side of the dead persons, and initially out of sight, were four dead cats.

The detectives studied the inert creatures.

At length Ainslie said, "This is meant to tell us something. Any ideas?"

Quinn shook his head. "Not offhand. I'll work on it."

In the weeks and months to come, every brain in Homicide would conjecture reasons for the dead cats' presence. While numerous exotic theories were advanced, in the end it was conceded that none made sense. Only much later would it be realized that an important matching clue was present at the Frost crime scene, within a few short inches of the cats.

Now Quinn leaned down, viewing more closely the crudely severed body parts. After a moment he gulped. Ainslie glanced across. "You all right?"

Quinn managed to say, "Back in a minute," and headed for the outer door.

In the corridor outside, Cobo pointed to an open doorway down the hall. "In there, Chief!"

Seconds later, Quinn disgorged into a toilet bowl the breakfast he had eaten an hour before. After rinsing his mouth, hands, and face, he returned to the murder scene. "Long time since I've done that," he said ruefully.

Ainslie nodded. The experience was one that Homicide officers shared from time to time, and no one criticized. What *was* unforgivable was vomiting at a murder scene and contaminating evidence.

Voices in the hall signaled the arrival of an ID crew. A lead technician, Julio Verona, stepped inside, followed by an ID technician grade one, Sylvia Walden. Verona, short, stocky, and balding, stood still, his piercing dark eyes moving methodically over the scene confronting him. Walden, younger, blond, and leggy, whose specialty was fingerprints, carried a black box resembling a weekend suitcase.

Nobody spoke while the two surveyed the room. Finally, Verona shook his head and sighed. "I have two grandkids. This morning we were having breakfast and watching this TV news story about a couple of teenagers who murdered their mother's boyfriend. So I tell the kids, 'This world we're handing you has become a pretty rotten place,' then right at that moment I got this call." He gestured to the mutilated bodies. "It gets worse every day."

Ainslie said thoughtfully, "The world's always been a savage place, Julio. The difference now is there are a lot more people to kill, and more who do the killing. And every day news travels faster and farther; sometimes we watch the horror while it's happening."

Verona shrugged. "As always, Malcolm—the scholar's viewpoint. Either way's depressing."

He began photographing the dead couple, taking three photos of several groupings: an overall shot, a medium, and a close-up. After the bodies he would photograph other areas of room 805, the corridor outside, stairwells, elevators, and the building exterior, the last including entrances and exits a criminal might have used. Such photos often revealed evidence originally overlooked.

As well, Verona would make a detailed sketch of the scene, to be transferred later to a specialized, dedicated computer.

Sylvia Walden was now busy, searching for latent fingerprints, concentrating on the doorway first, inside and out, where a perpetrator's prints were most likely to be found. When entering, intruders were often nervous or careless; if they took precautions about prints, it was usually later.

Walden was dusting wood surfaces with a black graphite powder mixed with tiny iron filings, and applied with a magnetic brush; the mix adhered to moisture, lipids, amino acids, salts, and other chemicals of which fingerprints were composed.

On smoother surfaces—glass or metal—a nonmagnetic powder was used, of differing colors to suit varied backgrounds. As she worked, Walden switched from one type of powder to another, knowing that prints varied depending on skin texture, temperature, or contaminants on hands.

Officer Tomas Ceballos had reentered the room and briefly stood watching Walden at work. Turning her head, she told him, smiling, "Finding good prints is harder than people think."

Ceballos brightened. He had noticed Walden the minute she arrived. "It always looks easy on TV."

"Doesn't everything? In real life," she explained, "it's surfaces that make the difference. Smooth ones like glass are best, but only if they're clean and dry; if there's dust, prints will smear—they're useless. Doorknobs are hopeless; the area's not flat, too small for good prints, and just turning a knob smears any prints made." Walden regarded the young officer, clearly liking what she saw. "Did you know fingerprints can be affected by what someone ate recently?"

"Is this a joke?"

"No joke." After another smile, she went on working. "Acidic foods cause extra skin moisture and clearer prints. So if you're planning a crime, don't eat citrus fruits beforehand—oranges, grapefruit, tomatoes, lemon, lime. Oh, and no vinegar! That's the worst."

"Or the best, from our viewpoint," Julio Verona corrected.

"When I make detective," Ceballos said, "I'll remember all that." Then he asked Walden, "Do you give private lessons?"

"Not normally." She smiled. "But I can make exceptions."

"Good, I'll be in touch." Officer Ceballos left the room looking pleased.

Malcolm Ainslie, who had overheard, commented, "Even at a murder scene, life goes on."

Walden grimaced, glancing toward the mutilated bodies. "If it didn't, you'd go crazy."

Already she had located several prints, though whether from the killer or killers, or the dead couple, or belonging to hotel employees on legitimate business would be determined later. For now the next step was to "lift" each print onto a transparent tape that was placed on a "latent lift card." The card, dated, signed, and the print's location noted, would then become evidence.

Julio Verona asked Ainslie, "Did you hear about our zoo experiment?"

Ainslie shook his head. "Tell me."

"We got permission from MetroZoo and took fingerprints and toeprints of their chimpanzees and apes, then studied them." He gestured to Walden. "Tell him the rest."

"Everything was exactly the same as with human prints," she finished. "The same characteristics—ridges, whorls, loops, arches, identical points, no basic difference."

"Darwin was right," Verona added. "We've all got monkeys in our family tree, eh, Malcolm?" The comment was pointed. Verona knew of Ainslie's priestly past.

There was a time when Ainslie—though never a fundamentalist— accepted the Catholic skepticism of Darwin's *Origin of Species*. Darwin had, after all, scoffed at divine intervention and denied mankind's superiority to the rest of the animal world. But that was long ago and Ainslie answered now, "Yes, I believe we came that route."

What they were all doing, he knew—Walden, Verona, Ceballos, Quinn, even he himself—was distracting themselves, however briefly, from the ghastly horror that faced them. Outsiders might have viewed their behavior as cold-blooded; in fact, it was the reverse. The human psyche—even a con- ditioned Homicide crew's—had limits on how much sustained revulsion it could handle.

Another male technician had appeared and was working on blood sam- ples. Using small test tubes, he collected samples of the pooled blood around each victim. Later these would be compared with blood taken at autopsy. If the blood groups differed, some of the pooled blood might be from the attacker or attackers. From appearances, though, it seemed unlikely.

The technicians took fingernail scrapings from the Frosts, in case one of them had scratched an assailant, causing minuscule fragments of skin, hair, cloth fibers, or other materials to lodge under their nails. The scrapings were placed in containers for lab technicians to examine later. Then the victims' hands were bagged for preservation, so that before autopsy they could be fin- gerprinted, and the bodies examined, too, for alien fingerprints.

The Frosts' clothing was inspected carefully, though it would remain in place until their bodies reached the morgue. Then, before autopsy, it would be removed, with each item sealed in a plastic bag.

By now, with the additional people, a buzz of conversations, and continuous phone calls, room 805 had become crowded, noisy, and even more malodorous.

Ainslie glanced at his watch. It was 9:45 A.M., and he suddenly thought of Jason, who, at that moment, would be in the school auditorium with the rest of his third-grade class, waiting for a spelling bee to begin. Karen would be in the audience with other parents, feeling anxious and proud. Ainslie had hoped to join her briefly, but it hadn't worked out. It so seldom did.

He turned his mind back to the homicide scene, wondering if the case would be solved quickly, hoping the answer was yes. But as the hours wore on, the biggest impediment emerged: despite a multitude of people moving within the hotel, no one had even glimpsed a possible suspect. Somehow the murderer or murderers had managed to get in and out of the room, and probably the hotel, without any attention being paid. Ainslie had police officers question all the guests on the eighth floor, as well as on the two floors above and below. No one had seen a thing.

During the seventeen hours Ainslie was at the murder scene that first day, he and Quinn considered motives. Robbery was possible; no money whatever was found among the victims' possessions. On the other hand, the jewelry left at the scene (and later appraised at twenty thousand dollars) could have been removed easily. And certainly a cash robbery could have been achieved without two people being murdered. Nor was the awful savagery explained, or the enigma of the dead cats. So a prime motive remained as elusive as a prime suspect.

Initial information about Homer and Blanche Frost, resulting from calls to police in South Bend, Indiana, their hometown, revealed them as well-to-do but innocuous people with no apparent vices, family problems, or unsavory connections. Even so, to make on-the-spot inquiries Bernie Quinn would fly to South Bend within the next few days.

Some facts and opinions did emerge from the medical examiner, Sandra Sanchez, who inspected the Frosts' bodies at the scene and autopsied them later.

After the two victims had been subdued, then gagged and bound, she believed they had been placed so that each could see the other suffer. "They were tortured while conscious," Sanchez suggested. She believed the bodily assaults were done "methodically and slowly."

While no weapon was found at the murder scene, the autopsies showed deep knife cuts on both bodies, producing distinctive flesh and bone markings. And a terrible detail: flammable liquid had been poured into Mr. Frost's eyes, then set alight, leaving charred cinders where the eyes had been and blackened skin around them. Beneath the woman's gag, part of her tongue had been bitten off, probably a reaction to her agony.

Dr. Sanchez, in her late forties, had a reputation for directness and an acid tongue. She dressed conservatively in navy or brown suits; her graying hair was pulled back into a ponytail. Among her scholarly interests—as Bernard Quinn knew—was Santería, the Afro-Cuban religion that flourished in Dade County, Florida, with an estimated seventy thousand adherents.

Quinn had once heard Sandra Sanchez affirm, "Okay, I'm not saying I believe in the orishas—the gods—of Santería. But if you believe those other tall tales—Moses parting the Red Sea, the virgin birth, Jesus multiplying loaves and fishes, and a whale regurgitating Jonah—there's at least equal logic in Santería. And what it does is offer soothing voodoo for troubled minds."

Quinn, aware that animal sacrifice was part of some Santería rites, wondered if the four dead cats were Santería-related.

"Positively not," Sanchez told him. "I've looked at those cats; they were killed by hand—almost certainly brutally. Santería animal-killing is done with a knife and with devotion, and dead animals aren't abandoned like those cats. They're often eaten at a feast, and cat is never on the menu."

Ainslie and Quinn concluded that initial results were far from promising. As Ainslie reported to Leo Newbold, "It's a classic whodunit."

A whodunit—which, oddly enough, was exactly what detectives called it—was the kind of murder Homicide teams liked least. It implied a total absence of information about an offender, and sometimes about the victim, too. In such cases there were neither witnesses nor anyone to suggest paths of inquiry. The two opposites of whodunits were an "easy rider"—a case in which a murder suspect was quickly apparent, along with evidence to convict; and a "smoking gun," easiest of all—where the guilty party was still at the murder scene when police arrived.

In the end, long after the tragic saga of Homer and Blanche Frost, it was a smoking-gun homicide that would provide an apparent solution and close the case of the Frost murders.

2

SHORTLY BEFORE EIGHT O'CLOCK on Friday morning, three days after the Royal Colonial Hotel murders, Bernard Quinn walked from the Homicide offices to the civilian-staffed Identification Unit, also on the fifth floor of Police Headquarters. In an interior office where a half-dozen ID technicians worked amid computers and printout-laden desks, Quinn approached the young fingerprint specialist who had searched for latent prints at the Royal Colonial crime scene. Sylvia Walden was tapping at a keyboard in front of a large computer screen and looked up as he approached. Her long hair, he noticed, was damp, perhaps from the heavy rain shower that had also caught Quinn on his way to work.

"Good morning, Bernard," she said, smiling.

"It isn't good so far," he told her glumly. "Maybe you can improve it."

"A shortage of clues from Tuesday?" Walden's voice was sympathetic.

"More like none. Which is why I'm here, mostly to ask why in hell a fingerprint report is taking so long."

"Three days isn't long," she answered sharply. "Not when I had a fistful of prints to check out and identify—as you should know."

"Sorry, Sylvia," Quinn said penitently. "This sick case has turned me into an ass. Manners out the window."

"Don't worry," she said. "We're all pretty frazzled over this."

"So what have you got?"

"Some prints came through this morning from New York. They belong to the guy who stayed in the hotel room just prior to the Frosts."

"Were they on file there?"

"No, no. He agreed to be fingerprinted by the NYPD to help us out. I'm just comparing them with those we found."

The computer that Walden faced was a state-of-the-art AFIS model—shorthand for Automated Fingerprint Identification System. The machine, after scanning a fingerprint from a crime scene, could accomplish in less than two hours what it would take a human being an estimated one hundred and sixty years to complete—a search through hundreds of thousands of fingerprints on record across the United States—and provide a matching print, with identification, if one existed. Fingerprints in the system were stored and retrieved by a digital code that worked at lightning speed. AFIS was often an instant crime-solver; also, since its arrival, many old investigations had been reopened, with bygone fingerprints identified and criminals charged and convicted. Today, though, Walden's task was simpler—comparing the set of prints from New York, transferred by modem, with unidentified prints she had lifted from room 805 of the Royal Colonial.

The computer did not take long to provide an answer. The New York prints matched those from 805.

Sylvia Walden sighed. "Not good news, I'm afraid, Bernie." She explained that the only fingerprints she had found at the murder scene proved to be from the dead victims, a hotel maid, and now the room's previous occupant.

Quinn ran his fingers through his tousled hair and grunted unhappily. There were days when he felt his retirement could not come soon enough.

"I'm not too surprised about the prints," Walden said. "I noticed some smudges in places where there might have been fingerprints—smudges that latex gloves leave. I'm pretty sure the killer wore them. I do have something, though."

Quinn's brows shot up. "What?"

"An unidentified palm print. It's only a partial, but it doesn't match palm prints from any of those people whose fingerprints we've identified—I asked for their palm prints specially. There's also a Police Department register of palm prints, but no match there, either." Walden, crossing to a desk, leafed through computer printouts and passed a single sheet to Quinn; it bore a black-and-white partial handprint. "There it is."

"Interesting." He turned the sheet around, viewing it sideways and upside down, then handed it back. "Nobody I recognize," he said laconically. "So what can *you* do with it?"

"What I can do is this, Bernie: If you locate a suspect and get his palm prints, I'll tell you—pretty close to a certainty—if he was at the murder scene."

"If we ever get that far," he told her, "I'll be here like a rocket."

Walking through the fifth-floor corridors on his way back to Homicide, Quinn felt slightly heartened. At least the palm print was a minor start.

From the outset there had been an unusual lack of evidence in the Frost case. The day after the murders were discovered, Quinn had returned to the Royal Colonial scene armed with a lengthy list of questions. First he took a fresh overview of the scene, then he and Julio Verona, the lead technician, discussed each item of discovery to assess its value. One of those items—

among others already removed as evidence—was a torn envelope from the First Union Bank. Later that day, Quinn visited First Union branches in the area and learned that the morning before their deaths, the Frosts had cashed eight hundred dollars in traveler's checks at a Southwest 27th Avenue branch near the hotel. The bank teller who had served them remembered the two older people well and was sure no one else was with them. Also, neither he nor the other tellers had noticed anyone following the Frosts when they left the bank.

Quinn ordered a further fingerprint search of room 805, in darkness, using fluorescent powder and laser lighting. The process sometimes revealed prints missed when a normal fingerprint powder was used. Again, nothing was found.

He obtained from the Royal Colonial manager a list of guests at the time of the murders, plus a second list of those who had stayed in the hotel during the preceding month. Each guest would be contacted by police, either by phone or in person. If anyone seemed suspicious or hostile, a closer follow-up would be made by an officer, or perhaps Quinn himself.

A sworn statement was taken from Cobo, the security guard. Quinn pressed hard with questions, hoping to jog Orlando Cobo's memory in case something small but significant had been overlooked. Other hotel staff who had known the Frosts also made sworn statements, but nothing new emerged.

Phone calls to and from room 805 during the victims' stay were checked by police. The hotel had a record of outgoing calls; the phone company was subpoenaed to provide a log of incoming calls. Again, no leads.

Quinn contacted several known informers, hoping for street gossip about the murders. He offered money for information, but there was none.

He flew to South Bend and inquired at the police department there if any police record existed involving the Frosts; the answer was no. To the victims' family members Quinn expressed condolences, followed by questions about the backgrounds of Homer and Blanche Frost. In particular, was there anyone who did not like the Frosts and might want to harm them? All responses were negative.

Back in Miami, both Ainslie and Quinn were surprised by the absence of phoned-in tips following the extensive media coverage of the murders. The main facts were released through Public Information, though a few were held back, as was normal with homicides, to ensure that certain details were known only to the investigators and the murderer. Those details, if alluded to by a suspect, either inadvertently or in a confession, would strengthen the prosecution's case at trial.

Among the information not released was the presence of dead cats, and that Homer Frost's eyes had been set on fire.

Thus, as time began to slip by—one week, two weeks, three—any solution seemed increasingly remote. In a homicide investigation the first twelve hours are most critical. If by then a strong lead or suspect has not emerged, the likelihood of success diminishes with each passing day.

A trio of essentials with any homicide are witnesses, physical evidence, and a confession. Without the first and second, the third was unlikely. But in the Frost investigation there continued to be a glaring absence of all three.

Inevitably, as other new homicides occurred, the Frost case lost its priority.

Months went by as crime in Florida kept on escalating. Every police force in the state, including homicide departments, was overwhelmed, many of their personnel exhausted. Part of the pressure was an unceasing Niagara of paper—external mail, internal mail, Teletypes, fax messages, local police reports, protocol reports, crime reports, lab reports on blood and drugs, reports and requests from other jurisdictions, BOLOs . . . the list seemed endless.

Out of necessity, priorities emerged. Urgent local matters came first, and other paper was supposedly handled in order of importance; sometimes it wasn't. Some reports or requests were glanced at, then put aside, becoming an ever-growing pile for later reading. At times it could be three, six, or even nine months before certain papers were dealt with, if at all.

Bernard Quinn had once dubbed those papers the Tomorrow Pile, and the name stuck. Typically, he'd quoted Macbeth:

> "Tomorrow, and tomorrow, and tomorrow
> Creeps in this petty pace from day to day . . ."

All of which was why a Teletype from the police department of Clearwater, Florida, dated March 15 and addressed to all police agencies in the state, received only cursory attention at Miami Homicide, then remained in the Tomorrow Pile—until five months after its arrival.

The Teletype was from a Detective Nelson Abreu, who, stunned by the brutality of a recent Clearwater double murder, asked for information about any similar murders that might have occurred elsewhere. Included in the Teletype was a note that "unusual items" were left at the murder scene, the victims' home. These were not described because Clearwater Homicide was limiting knowledge of that evidence for the same reason Miami Homicide had withheld information about the Frosts' murder scene.

Clearwater had a large population of elderly people, and the murder victims were a husband and wife, Hal and Mabel Larsen, both in their seventies. They had been bound and gagged, then, while facing each other, had been tortured, finally dying from loss of blood. The torture included a savage beating and mutilation by severe knife wounds. Inquiries revealed that the Larsens had cashed a thousand-dollar check a few days earlier, but no money was found at the crime scene. There were no witnesses, no unaccounted-for fingerprints, no murder weapon, no suspects.

While Detective Abreu received several replies to his Teletype, none proved helpful, and the case remained unsolved.

•　　•　　•

Two and a half months later, another scene:

Fort Lauderdale, May 23.

Again, a married couple, the Hennenfelds, in their mid-sixties and living in an apartment on Ocean Boulevard near 21st Street. Again the victims were found bound and gagged, and in seated positions, facing each other. Both had been beaten and stabbed to death, though their bodies were not discovered for an estimated four days.

On the fourth day a neighbor, aware of a foul odor coming from the adjoining apartment, called police, who made a forced entry. Broward Sheriff-Detective Benito Montes was sickened at the sight and stench.

At this crime scene no "unusual items" were left. However, a two-burner electric space heater had been lashed by wire to the feet of Irving Hennenfeld, then plugged into an electric outlet. The space heater's red-hot bars had burned out before the bodies were found, though not until the man's feet and lower legs were reduced to cinders. In this crime, too, any money the victims may have had was apparently taken.

Once more, no fingerprints, no witnesses, no weapon.

But this time Sheriff-Detective Montes remembered reading about the Coconut Grove murders of an elderly couple some three months earlier, which seemed similar. Following a phone call to Miami Homicide, Montes drove to Miami the next day, where he met with Bernard Quinn.

In contrast to the veteran Quinn, Montes was young, in his mid-twenties, with neatly trimmed hair. Like most Homicide detectives he dressed well—that day in a navy blue suit with a striped silk tie. During a two-hour discussion the detectives compared notes of the Frosts' and Hennenfelds' murders and viewed photos of both crime scenes. They agreed that the manner of the victims' deaths seemed identical. So did other factors, including placement of the bodies, and the killer's barbaric cruelty.

One small detail: When the bodies were found, a radio was playing loudly, presumably having been left that way by the killer.

"Do you remember what kind of music?" Quinn asked.

"Sure do. Rock, so goddam loud you couldn't hear yourself speak."

"Was the same way at the Frost scene." Quinn made a note.

"It's the same guy," Montes declared. "Has to be."

Quinn quizzed him. "You're sure it's a man—one man?"

"Yep. And the bastard's big, strong as an ox, and smart."

"Educated smart?"

"My instinct says no."

Quinn nodded. "Mine, too."

Montes added, "He enjoys it, wallows in it, slavers over it. We're looking for a sadist."

"Any thoughts about the dead cats at our scene?"

Montes shook his head. "Only that this prick loves killing. Maybe he did the cats to pass the time, and brought them along for kicks."

Quinn said, "I still think it's a message—in some code we haven't deciphered."

Before Sheriff-Detective Montes left, Bernard Quinn apologized for the absence of his sergeant. Quinn explained that Malcolm Ainslie would have liked to be present at their meeting since he, too, was involved. However, Ainslie was committed to attend a one-day police management seminar in another part of town.

Benito Montes said, "That's okay—there's time. I think what we've seen is only the beginning."

3

DURING THE SPRING AND SUMMER of that year, the residents of South Florida wilted in exceptionally high temperatures and steamy humidity, sustained by daily thunderstorms and drenching rain. In Miami itself a series of electrical outages, caused by heavy power demand, brought those who had air conditioning into the sticky world of those who did not. Another problem, exacerbated by heat-induced irritability and carelessness, was crime. Gang fights, crimes of passion, and domestic violence all flourished. Even among normally peaceful people, patience ebbed and tempers flared; in streets or parking lots, trivial disagreements resulted in total strangers coming to blows. With more serious disputes, anger turned to rage and even murder.

At Homicide headquarters, an entire wall was occupied by a white glazed board known to detectives as the "People-Dying-to-Meet-Us Board." Divided by neat lines and columns, it recorded the names of all murder victims during the current year and the year preceding, along with key details of investigations. All possible suspects were named on the board. Arrests were recorded in red.

At mid-July of the preceding year, the board showed seventy murders, of which twenty-five still remained unsolved. By mid-July of the current year, there had been ninety-six murders, with the unsolved figure a highly unsatisfactory seventy-five cases.

Both upward trends pointed to an increase in homicides accompanying otherwise routine robberies, carjackings, and everyday street holdups. Everywhere, it seemed, criminals were shooting and killing their victims for no apparent reason.

Because of wide public concern about the numbers, Homicide's commander, Lieutenant Leo Newbold, had been summoned several times to the office of Major Manolo Yanes, commander of the Crimes Against Persons Unit, which combined Robbery and Homicide.

At their last meeting Major Yanes, a heavily built man with bushy hair and a drill sergeant's voice, wasted no time after his secretary ushered Newbold in.

"Lieutenant, what the hell are you and your people doing? Or should I say *not* doing?"

Normally the major would have used Newbold's first name and invited him to sit down. This time he did neither, and simply looked up, glaring, from his desk. Newbold, suspecting that Yanes had received his own castigation from higher up, and knowing the down-through-the-ranks drill, took his time before answering.

The major's office was on the same floor as Homicide, and a large window overlooked downtown Miami, bathed now in brilliant sunshine. The desk was gray metal with a white plastic top, on which piles of folders and pencils were laid out in neat military order. Facing him was a conference table with eight chairs. As in most police offices, the effect was austere, relieved slightly by a few photographs of Yanes's grandchildren on a side table.

"You know the situation, Major," Newbold responded. "We're swamped. Every detective is working sixteen-hour days or more, following every lead we've got. These guys are near exhaustion."

Yanes waved an arm irritably. "Oh, for Christ's sake! Sit down."

When Newbold was seated, Yanes declared, "Long hours and exhaustion are part of this job and you know it. So however much work you're getting from everyone, drive 'em harder. And remember this—when people are exhausted they're apt to miss things, and it's our job to make damn sure they don't. So I'm telling you, Newbold, take a good, hard look at every case, right now! Make sure there's nothing undone that should have been done. Go over every detail—and look especially hard for connections between cases. If I learn later that something important has been overlooked, I promise you'll regret ever having told me your men are tired. Tired! For Christ's sake!"

Newbold sighed inwardly but said nothing.

Yanes concluded, "That's all, Lieutenant."

"Yes, sir." Newbold rose from his chair, turned smartly and went out, deciding that he would do exactly what Manolo Yanes urged.

It was less than a month after this confrontation that—as Leo Newbold would describe it later—"the whole goddam roof fell in."

• • •

The series of events began on August 14 at 11:12 A.M., when the temperature in Miami was ninety-eight degrees Fahrenheit and the humidity eighty-five percent. Detective-Sergeant Pablo Greene was heading that day's Hot Team when a radio call to Homicide headquarters, from a uniform patrol officer named Frankel, reported an apparent murder at Pine Terrace Condominiums on Biscayne Boulevard at 69th Street.

The victims were a Hispanic couple in their sixties named Urbina, Lazaro and Luisa. A male neighbor, after knocking on their door and getting no response, peered in through a window. Seeing two bound figures, he forced the door open, then moments later used the Urbinas' phone to call 911.

The dead husband and wife were in the living room of their four-room condominium. Both victims had been beaten, their bodies slashed by a knife, and cruelly mutilated. Blood had pooled on the floor around them.

Sergeant Greene, a twenty-year Miami Police veteran, tall, lean, and with a bristling mustache, told Frankel to secure the scene, then urgently looked around the office for someone to send.

Standing up and surveying all of Homicide, he could see that every other detective's desk was empty. The room was large, with a half-dozen rows of small, bureaucratic metal desks, set side by side and separated by shoulder-high dividers. Each desk contained a multiple-line phone, several file trays, overflowing, and in some cases a computer terminal. Every detective had his or her own desk, and most had tried to personalize their drab conformity with family photos, drawings, or cartoons.

In the entire room the only other people were two harried secretaries, busily answering phones. Today, as every day, the calls were from citizens, news media, members of victims' families asking for information about relatives' deaths, politicians looking for answers to the sudden rise in shootings, and countless other sources, rational and otherwise.

Greene knew that all available detectives were out working and, for most of the summer, Homicide headquarters had looked the way it did today. His own team of four was investigating eight murders, and other teams were under similar pressure.

He would have to go to Pine Terrace himself, Greene decided. Alone and quickly.

He looked down at the paperwork piled on his desk—two weeks' arrears of crime records and other reports that Lieutenant Newbold was urging him to complete—and knew he must put the work aside yet again. He slipped on his jacket, checked his shoulder holster, gun, and ammunition, and headed for the elevator. From his unmarked car he would radio one of his units and have someone join him, but, knowing everyone's workload, he doubted it would happen soon.

As to the burdensome, never-ceasing paperwork, Greene reasoned gloomily he would have to come back and move some more tonight.

●   ●   ●

Some fifteen minutes later Detective-Sergeant Greene arrived at Pine Terrace condominium number 18, where the condo and the surrounding area were cordoned off by official yellow display tape—POLICE LINE DO NOT

CROSS. Greene approached a uniform officer standing between the condo entrance and a small, curious crowd.

"Officer Frankel? I'm Sergeant Greene. What do you have?"

"Me and my partner were here first, Sergeant," Frankel reported. "We haven't touched a thing." He motioned to a heavily built, bearded man standing off to one side. "This is Mr. Xavier. He's the neighbor who called nine-one-one."

The bearded man joined them. He told Greene, "When I saw those bodies through the window I just broke down the door. Maybe I shouldn't have."

"Forget that. There's always a chance someone might be alive."

"The Urbinas sure weren't. Didn't know them well, but I'll never forget—"

Frankel interrupted. "Two things Mr. Xavier did—he used the phone inside to call nine-one-one, and he turned off a radio."

"It was so loud," Xavier said, "I couldn't hear on the phone."

Greene asked, "Did you do anything else to the radio, like change the station it was set to? Or touch anything else at all?"

"No, sir." Xavier looked crestfallen. "Do you think I messed up any fingerprints?"

Everybody's a crime expert, Greene thought. "Too early to tell, but we'd appreciate your letting us take your prints so we can separate them from any others. The print record will be returned to you." Greene told Frankel, "Stay in touch with Mr. Xavier. We'll need him later today."

When Sergeant Greene entered the Urbinas' condo, he knew at once that what he was seeing was no routine homicide, but a dire and crucial development in what was surely a sequence of ghastly serial killings. Greene, like most Homicide supervisors, kept himself informed of other teams' cases and was familiar with the Coconut Grove murders in January of Homer and Blanche Frost. He knew, too, of the Hennenfeld case in Fort Lauderdale almost three months ago that was so similar to the Frosts'. Now here— horribly and unmistakably—was a third matching atrocity.

Greene acted fast, reaching for his portable police radio secured to his belt, and made several calls.

First he called for an ID crew, the most pressing need in a case like this, where another serial killing could occur at any time. Every scrap of evidence had to be gathered fast, examined and assessed without delay. But a dispatcher informed Greene that all the ID crews were tied up on other cases, and one would not get to him for at least an hour. Pablo Greene seethed, knowing the delay might cause some evidence to deteriorate. But abusing the dispatcher would accomplish nothing, so he kept quiet.

He was far less patient when he made his second call, summoning a medical examiner to view the victims. No ME was available, he was told, though one would be sent "when possible."

"That's not good enough," he said, trying not to shout, but knowing there was nothing he could do. The next call yielded similar results: no state attorney was available; one presently in court would try to arrive within an hour.

So much was changing for investigators, he brooded. Not long ago, any summons to a murder scene produced immediate action, but obviously no more. He supposed it was all part of society's declining values, though certainly not declining murders.

Greene did manage to reach Lieutenant Newbold by radio and, while choosing his words carefully since others would be listening, conveyed the urgency for fast action at the Pine Terrace scene. Newbold quickly promised to do some phoning himself.

Greene also suggested that Sergeant Ainslie and Detective Quinn be notified, which Newbold agreed to do, adding that he would come to the scene himself within the next half hour.

Greene returned his attention to the two murder victims and the sadistic violation of their bodies, continuing the notes he had been scribbling since entering the building. Just as in the other two cases he had heard described, the man and woman had been positioned facing each other, bound and gagged. It seemed likely that each had been forced to watch in silent terror while the other was tortured.

Sergeant Greene sketched their positions, without disturbing anything before the ID crew's arrival. On a side table he observed an incoming addressed envelope from which a letter had been removed and left open. Moving the letter carefully with a penknife to avoid touching it, he was able to learn the Urbinas' full names, which he added to his notes.

On a small bureau near the bodies Greene spotted a portable radio—clearly the one that Xavier had switched off. Peering at the tuning dial, Greene noted the setting: 105.9 FM. He knew the station: HOT 105. Hard rock.

Then, still moving meticulously, stroking his mustache as he considered what he saw, he viewed the other rooms.

In both bedrooms the drawers had all been opened, presumably by an intruder, and left that way. The contents of a woman's purse and a man's wallet had been emptied onto a bed. There was no money, though some minor jewelry remained.

Each bedroom had a separate bathroom and toilet, and though the ID crew would go over both thoroughly, Greene saw nothing of significance. In what appeared to be the main bathroom, the toilet seat was raised, and there was urine in the bowl. Greene added both facts to his notes, even though he knew that neither urine nor stool could be linked to an individual for identification.

He returned to the living room and smelled something new—an addition to the putrid odor resulting from open wounds on dead bodies. As he moved closer to the victims, the smell grew stronger. Then he saw it. Alongside one hand of the dead woman was a bronze bowl containing what appeared to be human excrement, partly immersed in what was obviously urine.

There were occasional moments in his work when Pablo Greene wished he had chosen some other profession.

As he drew back, he reminded himself it was not unknown for criminals to defecate at crime scenes—usually during break-ins at well-to-do homes, presumably as a gesture of contempt for the absent owners. But he could not recall ever having seen this before at a homicide scene, especially given the nature of the awful killing of two old people. Greene, a good, decent family man, thought fiercely of the perpetrator: *What kind of vile piece of human garbage are you?*

"What was that, Pablo?" a voice from the outer doorway inquired. It was Newbold, who had just arrived, and Greene realized he had spoken aloud.

Still caught up by emotion that he rarely felt or showed, Greene gestured toward the two bodies, then pointed to the bowl he had just surveyed.

Leo Newbold stepped forward and inspected it all.

Then he said quietly, "Don't worry. We'll get the bastard. And when we do, we'll put this case together so goddam tight, we'll make sure the son of a bitch burns."

Newbold was also remembering Major Yanes's words, spoken not long ago: *Make sure there's nothing undone that should have been done. Go over every detail—and look especially hard for connections between cases.*

Well, Homicide knew of a probable connection between the Frosts' killings and the Hennenfelds' in Fort Lauderdale, and now, with this new double slaying so clearly aligned with those other two, inevitably the question would be asked: Could more have been achieved by combining the two earlier inquiries, accepting them as serial killings? Might they even have found a suspect?

Newbold didn't think so. Just the same, he was sure there would be some second-guessing, to which the media would contribute, almost certainly resulting in further pressure on Homicide and the Police Department generally.

But most essential at this moment was intensive focus on this latest case, coupled with reexamination of the other two. There was no question that Homicide was combating a bona fide serial killer.

"Were you able to get Ainslie and Quinn?" Greene asked.

Newbold nodded. "They're on their way. And I told Quinn to call his contact in Lauderdale."

A few minutes later an ID crew of four technicians arrived, followed almost at once by the ME, Sandra Sanchez. Whatever phoning Newbold had done after Greene's urgent call from the crime scene, he'd evidently pulled out all stops, probably by going much higher in the department.

Through the next five hours work progressed swiftly. Near the end of that time the remains of Lazaro and Luisa Urbina were placed in body bags and conveyed to the county morgue, where, later that night, they would be autopsied. Sergeant Greene would attend the autopsy, again putting off the paperwork on his desk for at least one more day, by which time still more would have been added.

While detailed study and analysis needed to be done on much of the evidence collected by the ID crew, one disappointment emerged early.

"Pretty certain the perp wore gloves," the fingerprint technician, Sylvia Walden, told Sergeant Greene. "There are quite a few smudges, the kind made by latex surgical gloves—same as we had at the Royal Colonial. Also, I think whoever did this knows enough to wear two pairs of latex gloves, because with one pair a print will come through after a while. There are some prints around, of course, and we'll check those out, but they're probably not the perp's."

Greene shook his head and mumbled, "Thanks."

"For nothing," Walden added.

Several hours earlier, Ainslie and Bernard Quinn had arrived at Pine Terrace and agreed with Newbold and Greene that a single serial killer was now their quarry.

On his way out, Ainslie walked around the scene a second time before the victims' bodies were removed, lingering over the bronze bowl still close to the dead woman's hand. There was something about that container and its contents that stirred an idea, a vague memory, an incomplete image he could not define. Ainslie returned to the object twice, hoping the elusive notion in his mind would clarify.

Maybe there was nothing at all, he decided, nothing except his own weariness with scenes of tragic death, and perchance some wishful searching for new leads. Perhaps what he needed now was to go home and spend an evening with his family . . . laugh around the dinner table . . . help Jason with his homework . . . make love to his wife . . . and possibly, by morning, some answers would have sprung to mind.

As it turned out, the next morning produced no new thoughts. It took four more days, when he least expected it, for Ainslie's memory to awaken with dramatic, shocking clarity.

4

FOUR DAYS AFTER THE PINE TERRACE murders, Lieutenant Leo Newbold held a formal Homicide Department conference. It included supervisors and detectives involved with the serial killings, ID technicians, a medical examiner, and a state attorney. Senior police officers were informed of the conference; two attended. It was at that conference, as Ainslie thought about it later, that the drama broadened and, like a Shakespearean plot mutation, a new cast of characters entered the scene.

Among the new characters—though not new to Homicide—was Detective Ruby Bowe, a member of Sergeant Ainslie's investigative team. Ruby, a petite, twenty-eight-year-old black woman with a penchant for glittering earrings and stylish clothes, was liked and respected, worked as hard as anyone in Homicide, sometimes harder, and expected no concessions because of her sex. She could be tough and tenacious, even ruthless. But at lighter times she displayed a sense of fun and mischief appreciated by her colleagues.

Ruby was the youngest of nine children born to Erskine and Allyssa Bowe, all of whom were raised in the crime-ridden ghetto of Miami's Overtown area. Erskine Bowe was a police officer who had been shot and killed by a fifteen-year-old neighborhood boy on drugs and in the process of robbing a local 7-Eleven store. Ruby was twelve at the time, devastatingly young to lose her father, but old enough to remember their special closeness.

Erskine Bowe had always believed there was something extraordinary about Ruby, and had said to his friends, "She's going to do something important. You just wait."

Ruby, even so long after her father's death, still missed him terribly.

Ruby had attended Booker T. Washington elementary school and Edison High, where she was a diligent student and volunteered for extracurricular activities, most aimed at social justice and change. She had fought especially hard against drug abuse, knowing it had been the real killer of her father.

Armed with an academic scholarship, Ruby attended Florida A&M University, majoring in psychology and sociology. She graduated with honors and, fulfilling a lifelong dream, immediately joined the Miami Police Department. Her father had been on the force for seventeen years; maybe in some positive way she could redress his death while "changing the world." And if not the world, perhaps in some significant way her own neighborhood.

No one was unduly surprised when Ruby graduated from the police academy at the top of her class. What did raise eyebrows was a decision by Lieutenant Newbold to accept Ruby immediately as a Homicide detective. The move was unprecedented.

Homicide, in any police force, was an apex. Homicide detectives were considered to have the best brains and the greatest resourcefulness, and their prestige made them the envy of most colleagues. Because of this, Ruby's appointment left a few older officers, who had hoped to join Homicide themselves, disappointed and resentful. But Newbold had a gut feeling about Ruby. "There are times," he confided to Malcolm Ainslie, "when you can just smell a good cop."

Ruby had now been a Homicide detective for four years, with an official rating of "outstanding."

As a member of Sergeant Ainslie's team, Ruby would automatically attend today's 8:00 A.M. conference, but while others were filing in, she was on the telephone, surrounded by a file of official papers. Newbold, walking past, called, "Wind it up, Ruby. We'll need you in there."

"Yes, sir," she acknowledged, and moments later she followed him, adjusting the large gold ear clip she had removed for the phone call.

Adjoining the general Homicide office were interview rooms for witnesses and suspects, a room with more comfortable couches and chairs where families of victims were sometimes received, a large file room with crime records going back ten years, and, beyond all of these, the conference room.

Malcolm Ainslie sat at the conference room's large, rectangular table along with two other sergeant supervisors, Pablo Greene and Hank Brewmaster, as well as Detectives Bernard Quinn, Esteban Kralik, José Garcia, and Ruby Bowe.

Garcia, born in Cuba, had been a Miami police officer for twelve years, including eight as a Homicide detective. Stocky and balding, Garcia looked ten years older than his actual thirty-three, prompting colleagues to refer to him as Pop.

The Homicide regulars were joined by the youthful Sheriff-Detective Benito Montes, who had driven to Miami from Fort Lauderdale in response to a phoned invitation from Bernard Quinn. In the matter of the Hennenfeld murders, Montes reported, there had been no progress since his previous visit to Miami Homicide.

The others included Dr. Sanchez, the medical examiner, ID technicians

Julio Verona and Sylvia Walden, and an assistant state attorney, Curzon
Knowles.

Knowles, who headed the state attorney's homicide division, had a formidable reputation as a criminal trial prosecutor. A soft-spoken, mild-mannered
man who dressed modestly in off-the-rack suits and knitted ties, he had once
been compared to an unassuming shoe clerk. During court trials, while cross-
examining uncooperative witnesses, he was sometimes hesitant, conveying an
impression of uncertainty when in fact nothing was further from the truth.
Many such witnesses, believing they could lie with impunity while answering
this unimpressive lawyer's questions, suddenly found they had been coaxed
into a spider's web and had incriminated themselves before realizing it.

His disarming manner and razor-sharp mind were reasons why Knowles,
during fifteen years with the state attorney's office, had achieved a remarkable eighty-two percent conviction rate at murder trials. Homicide detectives were always grateful to have Curzon Knowles handling their cases, just
as Newbold and the others were pleased to see him now.

Major Yanes was also present, as was a high-ranking assistant chief, Otero
Serrano, emphasizing the public importance of the new developments.

Lieutenant Newbold, at the head of the conference room table, opened
the meeting crisply. "We are all aware that two of our pending cases and a
third in Fort Lauderdale are now recognizable as serial double killings. It's
possible we should have reached this conclusion before the third one, and we
may take some heat for that as time goes on. But we'll deal with that later.
Right now we have urgent business.

"What I want, here and now, is a complete review of all three double murders, leaving absolutely nothing out. We must find *some connection* that can
lead us to—"

Ruby Bowe raised a hand. Newbold stopped abruptly, frowning. "Whatever it is, won't it keep until I've finished, Ruby?"

Detective Bowe answered, "No, sir. I don't think so." Her voice was nervous but controlled. She held a paper in her hand.

"This had better be good." Newbold's annoyance was clear.

"You said three double murders, sir."

"So? You questioning my arithmetic?"

"Not exactly, sir." Ruby raised the paper in her hand; she glanced toward
the others. "No one is going to like this, but you'd better make it four."

"Four! What do you mean?"

It was Ainslie, seated opposite, who asked quietly, "What have you
found, Ruby?"

She shot him a grateful glance, then returned to Newbold. "Couple of days ago, sir, you were worried about the size of the Tomorrow Pile. You asked me to work on it."

There were smiles at the reference to the Tomorrow Pile, Quinn's droll name for the perpetual inflow and accumulation of official paper.

Newbold acknowledged, "Yes, I did ask that. Obviously you've discovered something."

"I read it just this morning, sir. A BOLO from Clearwater."

"Let's hear."

Ruby Bowe's voice cut clearly through the silence in the room.

"BOLO to all police departments statewide. Double homicide of elderly man and woman occurred this city March twelfth. Exceptional brutality. Victims tied and gagged. Stabbed repeatedly and beaten savagely head and torso areas. Mutilation involved. Cash believed stolen amount unknown. Fingerprints other evidence nonexistent. Unusual items left at scene by offender or offenders. If any similar crime or crimes on record request contact Detective N. Abreu, Clearwater Police Department Homicide with all possible information."

Across the ensuing quiet, Major Yanes asked, "That date again, Detective?"

Bowe consulted her paper. "The murders were March twelfth, sir. The BOLO is stamped 'Received March fifteenth.' "

There was a collective moan. "Jesus Christ!" Hank Brewmaster said. "Five months ago!"

They all knew it could happen—shouldn't happen, but did. Some things slipped lower in the Tomorrow Pile and continued to escape attention. But this was an all-time disastrous example.

Besides official police communication, the Florida media often observed similarities in serious crimes separated by distance, and would note a resemblance and report it; such connections had proven helpful to police investigators in the past. But with so much crime happening everywhere, some similarities escaped attention all around.

Newbold covered his face with his hands, his anguish plain. Everyone knew the lieutenant would be held responsible for the communications breakdown that had resulted in Homicide's failure to deal promptly with the Clearwater BOLO.

Yanes said tersely, "For the time being, I suggest we move on, Lieutenant." It was obvious there would be more discussion, probably in private, later.

"There's a little more, sir," Bowe offered.

Newbold nodded. "Go on."

"Just before we came in, I phoned Detective Abreu in Clearwater. I men-

tioned that we have similar cases. He told me he and his sergeant would like
to fly here tomorrow and bring everything they have."

"All right." Newbold had recovered his composure. "Check their arrival
time and send a car to meet them."

"Lieutenant," Ainslie injected, "I'd like to ask Ruby a question."

"Go ahead."

Ainslie faced Ruby across the conference table. "Did Abreu mention anything about the items left at the Clearwater scene?"

"I asked what they were. One was an old, beat-up trumpet, the other a
piece of cardboard." She consulted her paper. "The cardboard was cut in the
shape of a half-moon and colored red."

Ainslie was frowning, concentrating, searching his memory, recalling again
the bronze bowl at the Pine Terrace condo. Addressing no one in particular,
he asked, "Have there been objects left at every scene? I remember there
were four dead cats in the Frosts' hotel room."

Without waiting, Ainslie turned to Bernard Quinn. "Was anything left at
the Hennenfeld killings?"

Quinn shook his head. "Not to my knowledge." He glanced at Sheriff-
Detective Montes. "Is that right, Benito?"

As a visitor Montes had remained quiet, but now, responding to Quinn's
question, he said, "Well, there wasn't something left that the perp brought
with him. But there was that electric space heater, though it belonged to the
Hennenfelds. We checked on that."

Ainslie asked, "What space heater? What about it?"

"It had been fastened with wire to Mr. Hennenfeld's feet, Sergeant, then
plugged in. When we found him, the space heater had burned out, but his
feet were completely charred."

Ainslie said sharply to Quinn, "You didn't tell me that."

Quinn looked embarrassed. "Sorry. I guess it was a detail I forgot."

Ainslie let it go, then turned to Newbold and asked, "Lieutenant, may
I go on?"

"All yours, Malcolm."

"Ruby," Ainslie said, "can we make a list of all the different objects found
at the scenes?"

"Sure. You want it on the computer?"

Newbold cut in. "Yes, we do."

Ruby moved to a small separate desk containing a computer terminal.
Since joining Homicide, she had become known to fellow detectives as "our
computer whiz," and even in other teams' cases she was often asked to lend
her skills. While Ainslie and the others waited at the conference table, Ruby

touched switches and ran her fingers nimbly over the keyboard. "Okay, shoot, Sergeant."

Referring to an open file in front of him, Ainslie dictated, "January seventh, Coconut Grove. Homer and Blanche Frost. Four dead cats."

Ruby's fingers moved swiftly. When they stopped, Ainslie continued, "March twelfth, Clearwater."

"Hold it!" The voice was Quinn's. Heads turned toward him. "At Coconut Grove there were Mr. Frost's eyes. Something flammable was poured in them, then set on fire. If we include the Hennenfeld burned feet . . ."

Ainslie told Ruby, "Yes, add Mr. Frost's eyes." He turned his head with the hint of a smile. "Thank you, Bernie. I forgot. Happens to all of us."

They completed the Clearwater listing with the old trumpet and cardboard moon, added Fort Lauderdale with the space heater and the male victim's burned feet, afterward moving on to Pine Terrace condominium number 18.

"There was a bronze bowl," Ainslie said.

Ruby's fingers paused. She asked, "Was there anything in it?"

Pablo Greene said sourly from his seat at the table, "Yeah, piss and shit."

Looking around, Ruby inquired innocently, "Is it okay if I write that as 'urine and feces'?"

The room erupted with laughter. Amid it, someone said, "Ruby, we love you!" Even Newbold, Yanes, and the assistant chief were laughing with the others. In an atmosphere where grisly death was an everyday occurrence, a sudden, unexpected flash of humor was like a cleansing rain.

And then . . . as the laughter died . . . swiftly, clearly, plainly, Ainslie had it. Now he knew. *All the pieces fit.*

It was as if an incomplete hypothesis, which had been forming tiresomely, vaguely in his brain, suddenly took shape. His excitement began to explode.

"I need a Bible," Ainslie said.

The others stared at him.

"A Bible," he repeated, his voice rising, its tone assuming the sound of a command. "*I need a Bible!*"

Newbold looked at Quinn, nearest the door. "There's one in my desk. Second drawer down, right side."

Quinn went to get it.

At Homicide the presence of Bibles was not unusual. A number of criminals, when brought in for arrest or questioning, asked for a Bible to read, some sincerely, others hoping their apparent religiosity might earn them a lighter sentence later on. There were precedents justifying that hope; certain offenders, notably white-collar criminals, had escaped heavy sentencing through religious "conversion" and claims of having been "born again." But at the investigating stage, Homicide detectives, while skeptical, were willing to oblige if a Bible would hasten a confession.

Quinn returned, Bible in hand. Reaching across the table, he handed it to Ainslie, who opened it near the back to the last book of the New Testament—Revelation, or, for Catholics, the Apocalypse.

For Newbold, a light dawned. "It's Revelation, isn't it?" he asked.

Ainslie nodded. "Every one of those objects is a message."

He motioned to Ruby, still at the computer. "Here's the first." Then, glancing around the table, Ainslie read out, "Revelation, chapter four, verse six: 'And before the throne there was a sea of glass like unto crystal: and in the midst of the throne, and round about the throne, were four beasts . . . ' "

Quinn breathed, "The cats!"

Ainslie flipped back two pages, searched with a forefinger, then read again, "Chapter one, verse fourteen: 'His head and his hairs were white like wool, as white as snow; and his eyes were as a flame of fire . . . ' " He glanced at Quinn. "Mr. Frost, right?"

Quinn added softly, "Those two things—the cats and Frost's burned eyes—were within inches of each other. But we never connected them . . . not in the way we should have."

The room was silent. Assistant Chief Serrano had leaned forward in his seat and was listening intently. Major Yanes had been scribbling notes but now paused. Everyone was waiting as Ainslie turned more pages. He asked Ruby, "A trumpet at Clearwater, right?"

She checked the computer screen. "A trumpet and a cardboard half-moon painted red."

"Here's the first. Chapter one, verse ten: 'I was in the Spirit on the Lord's day, and heard behind me a great voice, as of a trumpet . . . ' "

Ainslie turned pages again. "And I believe I remember the red moon. Right here. "Chapter six, verse twelve: 'And I beheld when he had opened the sixth sea, and, lo, there was a great earthquake and the moon became as blood . . . ' "

Looking at Benito Montes, Ainslie said, "Listen to this. Chapter one, verse fifteen: 'And his feet like unto fine brass, as if they burned in a furnace . . . ' "

"That's just the way Mr. Hennenfeld's feet were." Montes sounded awed.

Sergeant Greene spoke up. "How about the Urbinas, Malcolm?"

More page-turning. Then, "I think I have it. The dead woman was either touching that bowl or almost, wasn't she, Pablo?"

"One or the other, yes."

"Then this has to be it." Once more Ainslie read aloud from Revelation.

"Chapter seventeen, verse four: 'And the woman was arrayed in purple and scarlet color having a golden cup in her hand full of abominations and filthiness . . .' "

A murmur of appreciation rippled around the table. Ainslie waved for silence, protesting, "No, no!" While the others watched, he put both hands to his face and held them there for several seconds. When he removed them his expression had changed from high excitement to chagrin. His voice, when he spoke, was halting. "I should have got to it, I should have figured out those symbols sooner, even at the beginning. If I had, some of those people might still be alive."

Sergeant Brewmaster asked, "How could you have got it sooner? The rest of us didn't get it at all."

Ainslie was about to respond: *Because I have a doctorate in theology! Because for twelve interminable years I studied the Bible. Because all of those symbols stirred the past inside me, but I was slow and stupid, so it took until now to realize . . .* Then he decided to leave the words unspoken. What good would they do? But shame and self-reproach seethed deep within him.

Leo Newbold detected it. And understood. From the head of the table, his eyes met Ainslie's. "What matters most, Malcolm," the lieutenant said smoothly, "is that you've given us our first break, and it's an important one. I'd like to hear how you interpret it."

Ainslie nodded and said, "First, it's narrowed the field of investigation. Second, we know roughly the type of person we're looking for."

"Which is?" Yanes asked.

"An obsessed religious freak, Major. Among other things, he sees himself as an avenger from God."

"Is that the 'message' you spoke of, Sergeant? Is that the meaning of those symbols?"

"Yes, it is, keeping in mind that each symbol has been accompanied by two violent deaths. Most likely, as the killer sees it, he's delivering God's message, and at the same time fulfilling God's vengeance."

"Vengeance for what?"

"We'll know that better, Major, when we have a suspect and can question him."

Yanes nodded approvingly. "It looks like you've given us something to work with. Nice going, Sergeant!"

Assistant Chief Serrano added, "I'll second that."

Newbold resumed control. "Malcolm, you know more than the rest of us about this stuff from Revelation. Can you brief us on what else we ought to know?"

Ainslie considered before speaking, aware that he must draw on an amalgam of knowledge and ideas—his priestly past, his mindset since, his current role as a Homicide detective. Rarely, if ever, had all three overlapped as now.

He tried to keep his explanation simple.

"Revelation was originally in Greek, and is apocalyptic, which means it was written in code, with many symbolic words, so that only biblical scholars understand them. To many people it's a crazy hodgepodge of visions, symbols, allegory, prophecy—mostly incoherent."

Ainslie paused, then went on. "At times it makes some Christians, who don't understand it, uncomfortable. And the fact that Revelation can be used to prove or argue anything is why it's always attracted lunatics and fanatics. As those people view it, there's a ready-made prescription for any evil they choose. So what we need to know is how the guy we're looking for got to Revelation and adapted it to suit himself. When we have that answer, we'll go get him."

Lieutenant Newbold surveyed the conference table. "Anyone have anything to add?"

Julio Verona raised a hand. Perhaps to offset his small stature, the ID lead technician sat stiffly upright in his chair. At a nod from Newbold he said, "The fact that we know the kind of person who is committing these crimes is good, and my compliments to Malcolm. But I should remind you that even if you find a suspect, we have very little evidence right now—certainly not enough to convict." He glanced toward the assistant state attorney, Curzon Knowles.

"Mr. Verona's right," Knowles said. "So we need to recheck every item collected at the murder scenes to be sure nothing has been overlooked or misinterpreted. Obviously we are dealing with a psychotic killer, and the smallest minute detail left behind could be the factor we need."

"We do have a partial palm print from the Frost murders," Sylvia Walden pointed out.

Knowles nodded. "But as I understand it, there's not enough of the palm for positive identification."

"We could match six points on the print we have. For positive ID we need nine at least. Ten is better."

"So the partial would be only circumstantial evidence, Sylvia."

Walden conceded, "Yes."

Dr. Sanchez intervened. As usual, she was wearing one of her dark brown suits, and her graying hair was fastened back into a ponytail. "As reported earlier, the knife cuts on four bodies—the Frosts and Urbinas—are identifiable," she stated. "They were made by the same bowie knife, ten inches long, with distinctive notches and serrations. I have photos of the wounds, showing in detail the notches on bones and cartilage."

Everyone in the meeting knew about a bowie knife, sometimes called an "Arkansas toothpick." The hunting knife, invented in the mid-nineteenth century by one of two Texas brothers, either James or Rezin Bowie, has been used widely ever since for hunting both animals and humans. The knife, distinctive and deadly, has a wooden handle and a strong, single-edge blade, the back of the blade straight for most of its ten-to-fifteen-inch length, then curving concavely to join the cutting edge at a single sharp point. For a century and a half the bowie knife has inflicted vicious wounds, often as an instrument of death.

"Dr. Sanchez," Knowles asked, "could you match those wounds to a particular bowie knife?"

"If someone produced the right knife, yes."

"And you'd testify to that?"

"If I'm telling you now, of course I'd testify." Sanchez added sharply, "That kind of evidence has been accepted before."

"Yes, I know. Just the same . . ." Knowles seemed indecisive. To those at the conference table who knew him well, he had slipped into the hesitant, unsure role he adopted so often in court. "Assume I'm a defense attorney and I ask you this question: 'Doctor, I have testimony certifying that knives of this type are manufactured in batches of several hundred at a time. Can you be absolutely sure that this one knife, among hundreds—perhaps thousands— of its kind, produced the wounds you are describing? And when you answer the question, Doctor, please remember that a man's life is at stake here.' "

Deliberately, Knowles turned away as Sanchez hesitated.

She began, "Well . . ."

The attorney turned back toward her. He shook his head. "Never mind."

Sanchez flushed, her lips tightening as she realized precisely the point that Knowles had skillfully made. Instead of answering with her usual confidence, she had hesitated, acknowledging there might be a doubt—something that a jury would note and that a defense attorney would make the most of with succeeding questions.

Sanchez glowered at Knowles, who smiled. "Sorry, Doctor. Only a practice run, but better here than on the witness stand."

"For a moment," she said ruefully, "I thought that's where I was."

The attorney turned to Julio Verona. "None of that means we won't make the most of the knife evidence if the opportunity arises. There could be a limit, though, as to how far I'd take it."

"We don't have the knife, of course," the ID lead technician said, "and whether or not we get it will depend on you guys." He motioned to the Homicide detectives, including Newbold. "And now that Sylvia and I know that two of the cases are connected, we'll go over every bit of evidence for similarities."

Dr. Sanchez said, "And I'll do the same with the medical records; maybe I can find an unsolved murder with similar wound patterns or some kind of religious connotation." She added thoughtfully, "There's always a possibility that what we're looking at now is a repeat of something in the past that's been overlooked. I heard once of a serial killer who waited fifteen years before resuming his killing spree."

"All of that's good," Newbold said. "Now . . ." He glanced toward his superior, Manolo Yanes, commander of the Crimes Against Persons Unit. "Major, would you like to add anything?"

"Yes." Typically, Yanes wasted no time with preamble. Steely-eyed and speaking with his usual sharp-edged voice, he declared, "Everyone here needs to make a much bigger effort—an all-out effort. We've simply got to stop these killings before any more occur."

Yanes's eyes swung to Newbold. "For the record, Lieutenant, you and your people now have carte blanche to take whatever measures are necessary, including creating a special task force. When you decide exactly what you need and what kind of task force, I'll get you extra detectives from Robbery. As to costs, you have my approval to charge whatever's needed, including overtime."

Yanes glanced around the room, then added, "So now, with those logistics in place, the objective of all of you is clear—find this guy! I want results. And keep me informed."

"All of that noted, sir. As everyone heard, we will form a task force right now to work solely on these cases. Task force members will be relieved of other duties. I've already asked Sergeant Ainslie to head the team."

Heads turned toward Ainslie as Newbold told him, "Sergeant, you'll work with two teams of six detectives. I leave it to you to name another sergeant to head the second team."

"Sergeant Greene," Ainslie said. "Assuming he's agreeable."

Pablo Greene waved a hand airily. "You betcha!"

Newbold told Greene, "You'll report through Sergeant Ainslie. That's understood?"

"QSL, sir."

Ainslie added, "For my team I'll definitely want Detectives Quinn, Bowe, Kralik, and Garcia. Pablo and I will decide on the rest later today." Ainslie faced Major Yanes. "We have a lot of ground to cover, sir, and a great deal of

detail work. So we'll need at least two extra detectives from Robbery, probably four."

Yanes nodded. "Tell Lieutenant Newbold when you know exactly, and
you'll have them."

Curzon Knowles intervened. "If that isn't enough, I can arrange for a
couple of state attorney investigators. Either way, we'd like to stay in the
picture."

"We want that too, Counselor," Ainslie said.

Newbold reminded everyone, "The task force, of course, will work closely
with Fort Lauderdale and Clearwater; I want those detectives kept
informed."

The talk continued for a few minutes more, after which Newbold turned
to Assistant Chief Serrano. "Chief, anything you wish to add?"

Serrano, formerly a detective himself, and with a distinguished record on
the Miami force, spoke clearly but quietly. "Only to say that all of you have
the support of the entire Police Department in this matter. Obviously, as
these serial killings become widely known, there will be tremendous publicity, which will generate a lot of public and political pressures. We'll try to protect you from that so you can continue doing whatever is needed to bring this
maniac in. At the same time, work fast. *And never stop thinking.* Good luck
to us all!"

5

A S THE HOMICIDE CONFERENCE broke up, the newly formed task force gathered around Ainslie, along with the assistant state attorney, Curzon Knowles. Twenty years earlier Knowles had been a police officer himself—the youngest sergeant on the New York City force. Later he had become a lieutenant, then resigned to study law in Florida. Knowles felt comfortable with detectives and they with him.

Now he asked Ainslie, "Since we'll be working together, Sergeant, do you mind telling me your first move?"

"A short one, Counselor—to the computer. You're welcome to join me." Ainslie looked around him. "Where's Ruby?"

"Wherever you need her." Detective Bowe's bright voice emerged from a group.

"I need your dancing fingers." Ainslie motioned to the computer she had just used. "Let's search some records."

Seating herself, Ruby switched on and typed LOGON.

A query appeared: GIVE IDENTIFICATION.

Ruby asked Ainslie, "Yours or mine?"

He told her, "Eight-four-three-nine."

The screen responded: ENTER YOUR CODE.

Ainslie reached over and tapped in CUPCAKE, an affectionate name he sometimes used for Karen. The code name did not appear on the screen, but CIC—abbreviation for Criminal Investigation Center—did.

As the other detectives and Knowles watched silently, Ruby said, "We're in the magic kingdom. *Quo vadis?*"

Someone murmured, "What in hell's that?"

" 'Whither goest thou?' " Bernard Quinn answered.

"Took Latin in kindergarten," Ruby quipped. "Us ghetto kids are smarter than you think."

"Prove it," Ainslie said. "Find 'Criminal Records.' After that, a category called 'Oddities.' "

A series of typed commands, then the heading ODDITIES appeared. "There's a whole raft of subfiles," Ruby announced. "Any ideas?"

"Look for 'Religion' or 'Religious.' "

Fingers moved swiftly. Then, "Hey, here's one: 'Religious Freaks.' "

Ainslie raised his eyebrows. "That should do the trick."

If they had been expecting a harvest of names, the result was disappointing. Only seven appeared, each accompanied by an abridged personal history, along with charges and convictions. Ainslie and Ruby read through names and information; the others peered over their shoulders.

"You can eliminate Virgil," Quinn said. "He's in prison. I put him there." The computer listing showed a Francis Virgil as imprisoned for the past two years with another six to serve. A similar status applied to two more of the seven names, leaving four.

"Strike Orneus," Ainslie said. "It says here he's dead." As the detectives knew, a deceased offender's criminal record was not removed until two years after death.

"I guess we can eliminate Hector Longo," Ruby suggested. The entry showed Longo as age eighty-two, almost blind, and with a withered right hand.

"Amazing what the handicapped can do these days," Ainslie said. Then, "Okay, delete."

The remaining two names were "possibles," but the search had produced neither the numbers nor choices they had hoped for.

Knowles asked, "How about trying 'Modus Operandi'?"

"We already did that with the individual cases," Ainslie said. "Came up with nothing." He added thoughtfully, "The further we get into this, the more I believe we're after someone who has no record."

It was Ruby who suggested, "Why don't we try FIVOs?"

Ainslie was doubtful, but told her, "Why not? We've nothing to lose."

FIVOs—Field Intelligence and Vehicle Occurrence reports—contained information gathered by police officers who witnessed behavior in a public place that was peculiar, raunchy, or eccentric, though not illegal. A similar report was made if someone was seen in a suspicious circumstance, especially late at night, but was not breaking the law.

A FIVO report was supposedly written at the scene, on an official printed card. Officers were instructed to include as much information as possible, including a person's full name, home address, occupation, detailed physical description, facts about a vehicle if any, and the circumstances of the encounter. Most of those stopped and questioned were surprisingly cooperative, especially after learning they would not be arrested or ticketed. Anyone with a criminal record, however, usually didn't mention it.

The FIVO cards were turned in at Police Headquarters and eventually loaded into a computer bank. During the process an automatic cross-check added any criminal convictions to the FIVO report.

For a while FIVO records were in bad repute within the Miami force. It happened after several police officers clogged the system with bogus reports—in hopes of gaining attention and perhaps promotion. Some FIVO cards even bore names copied from graveyard tombstones. Eventually, after a few officers were caught and disciplined, the practice ceased. But many in the force distrusted FIVOs long afterward, including Ainslie.

Computer procedure to access FIVOs was similar to Criminal Records, and Ruby quickly found ODDITIES within the new category, followed by RELIGIOUS FREAKS. Suddenly the screen came alive with names, dates, and paragraphs of information. Ainslie leaned forward, his attention sharpened. Behind him a voice said, "Hey, look at that!" Someone else emitted a long, low whistle.

As before, they reviewed the names and details, eliminating some, then added those that remained to a new computer file already containing the two possibles from criminal records. At the end, Ruby printed out a half-dozen copies of the combined list and passed them around.

The printout contained six names:

JAMES CALHOUN, w/m AKA "Little Jesus." DOB 10 Oct 67. 5'11" 200lbs. LKA 271 NW 10 St, Miami. Has tattoo of a cross on upper chest. Talks about the coming end of world and claims to be Christ making second coming. Has a past for manslaughter, assault, armed burglary.

CARLOS QUINONES, l/m AKA "Diablo Kid." DOB 17 Nov 69. 5'6" 180lbs. Heavyset. LKA 2640 SW 22 St, Miami. Claims to be only Messiah and preaches the word of God. Has extensive violent past for assault, rape, armed robbery with violence.

EARL ROBINSON, b/m AKA "Avenger." DOB 2 Aug 64. 6'0" 180lbs. LKA 1310 NW 65 St, Miami. Lean build, former heavyweight boxer, very aggressive. Preaches on street corners, quotes from Bible, always Revelation, says he is God's judgment angel. Has extensive past for armed robbery, second degree murder, numerous assaults with a knife.

ALEC POLITE, h/m AKA "Messiah." DOB 12 Dec 69. 5'11" 180lbs. LKA 265 NE 65 St, Miami. Talks about the scriptures to anyone who will listen, says he talks with God. Gets aggressive if doubted, questioned. Could be violent but no record. Been in U.S. since 1993.

ELROY DOIL, w/m AKA "Crusader." DOB 12 Sep 64. 6'4" 290lbs. LKA 189 NE 35 St, Miami. Claims to be a disciple of God, knows God's wishes. Preaches in public. Not believed dangerous. Works as part-time truck driver.

EDELBERTO MONTOYA, l/m, DOB 1 Nov 62. 5'9" 150lbs. LKA 861 NW 1 St, Apt #3, Miami. Has thick dark mustache and beard. Claims to be a born-again Christian, quotes from Bible, prays for end of the world. Has past for rape, felonious assault and sexual assault.

As Ainslie, Knowles, and the others studied the names and descriptions, the sense of excitement grew.

Sergeant Greene expressed it. "Malcolm, I think we're on to something."

Detective Garcia looked up eagerly. "Robinson's our man! He has to be. Look at that stuff about Revelation! And he's known as Avenger; that fits. A boxer too, which means he's strong!"

Ruby Bowe added, "Not to mention the 'assaults with a knife.' "

"Okay, okay," Ainslie said. "Let's not jump to conclusions. We'll take a look at them all."

Sheriff-Detective Montes asked, "Will you pull anyone in?"

Ainslie shook his head. "Not enough to go on. We'll use surveillance."

Curzon Knowles cautioned, "Sergeant, you've got to be very, very careful that those people don't catch on." Knowles scanned the room, taking in all the detectives. "Please, everyone remember how very little evidence we have so far. And if one of those six is our man, and he suspects we're on to him, he could go totally inactive, leaving us nothing to use against him."

"A little inactivity would do no harm, though," Pablo Greene commented. "We sure as hell don't want him killing someone else."

"If your surveillance is tight, that won't happen." Knowles paused, considering. "The ideal thing would be to catch him in the act."

"Ideal for a prosecutor," Ruby Bowe said. "Risky for a victim."

Ainslie joined in the laughter, then quieted the group with a wave of his hand.

"Ruby's right, though," Quinn insisted. "Surveillance will pose a risk. We know this guy is smart, and he knows we're looking for him."

Ainslie turned to Leo Newbold, who had rejoined the group a few minutes earlier. "What do you think, Lieutenant?"

Newbold shrugged. "It's your call, Malcolm. You're the task force leader."

"Then we'll take the risk," Ainslie said. "And I assure you, Counselor, he'll never see us watching." He turned to Greene. "Pablo, let's plan a surveillance schedule now."

It was agreed that, to begin, Sergeant Ainslie's team would put surveillance on Earl Robinson, James Calhoun, and Carlos Quiñones. Sergeant Greene's team would watch Alec Polite, Elroy Doil, and Edelberto Montoya. In every case the surveillance would be total, twenty-four hours a day.

Ainslie informed Newbold, "We need those extra bodies from Robbery right away, sir—two to start with, and I'll work them into the schedule."

The lieutenant nodded. "I'll talk to Major Yanes."

Then, as the group prepared to leave, the conference room door was suddenly flung open. Sergeant Hank Brewmaster, who had left when the department conference officially broke up, stood breathlessly in the doorway, his face contorted with shock and disbelief. Brewmaster was heading that day's Homicide Hot Team, so they all knew what was coming.

Newbold stepped forward. "A bad one, Hank?"

"The worst, sir." Brewmaster drew in a breath. "It's City Commissioner Gustav Ernst. And his wife. Both dead, murdered. Call just came in. From the description, it's another just like—"

Ainslie cut in. "Oh God! The kind we—"

There was no need to finish as Brewmaster nodded. "Apparently it's exactly the same."

He turned back to Newbold. "My team is moving on it now, sir. I thought you should know." His gaze took in the others. "Thought all of you should know because the media's on the scene, and the way I hear it, all hell is breaking loose."

●   ●   ●

In the days to follow, media and public outrage blazed through the city like a three-alarm fire; the Ernst murders had become a *cause célèbre*.

As for the Police Department, the savage killing of a city commissioner and his wife was bad enough—Commissioner Ernst was one of three commissioners who, along with the mayor, deputy mayor, and city manager, governed Miami. But for Ainslie, Newbold, and everyone else in the force, the crime hit even closer to home because the daughter of the dead couple was Major Cynthia Ernst, a senior Miami police officer.

When the murders occurred, Cynthia Ernst was in Los Angeles on a police business trip combined with a personal visit. She was contacted through the L.A. Police Department, then, "stunned and grieving," as the six o'clock news described her, was flown back to Miami, becoming the focus of attention in a tightly strung, tumultuous city.

6

THE HASTY FIRST REPORT THAT the slayings of Miami City Commissioner Ernst and his wife were apparently identical with the savage murders of three other elderly couples—the Frosts in Coconut Grove, the Hennenfelds of Fort Lauderdale, and the Urbinas in Miami—proved discomfitingly true. Meanwhile the matching killings of Hal and Mabel Larsen in Clearwater—the subject of the five-month-old BOLO uncovered by Ruby Bowe—were publicly added to the list.

The now-burgeoning investigation centered on the Ernsts' Mediterranean-style mansion in the exclusive Bay Point subdivision—enclosed and security protected—located on the western shore of Biscayne Bay.

It was there that the battered and bloody bodies of Gustav and Eleanor Ernst had been found by their maid. The maid had arrived before anyone in the house was stirring, and as usual she prepared morning tea, which she carried on a tray to the Ernsts' bedroom. On seeing the couple bound and facing each other in a pool of their own blood, she screamed, dropped the tray, and collapsed from shock.

The screams were heard by the Ernsts' elderly majordomo, Theo Palacio, who, with his wife Maria, managed the house and cooked. Both Theo and Maria had slept unusually late, having been out—with their employers' approval—until after 1:00 A.M. the night before.

On reaching the bedroom death scene, Palacio reacted quickly, going to the nearest phone.

When Sergeant Brewmaster arrived, uniform police were stationed outside the house and, inside, paramedics from Fire Rescue were treating the maid for shock.

Detectives Dion Jacobo and Seth Wightman from Brewmaster's Homicide team had preceded him. Brewmaster had named Jacobo his co–lead investigator, thereby giving Jacobo some extra authority, which, in view of the importance of the case, he was likely to need.

Jacobo, sturdy, heavily built, and with a dozen years of Homicide experience, had already instructed the uniform officers to cordon off the entire house and garden with yellow tape.

Moments later Julio Verona and Dr. Sandra Sanchez arrived. Verona had traveled in a crime-scene van, accompanied by three colleagues. The chief of police was reportedly on the way.

The media, alerted by an exchange of urgent calls on police radios, were assembled in force outside the main gate of Bay Point, where they were being restricted from entering by security guards, also acting on Detective Jacobo's orders. Reporters were already debating how the murderer or murderers had penetrated Bay Point's security system and entered the Ernst house.

Brewmaster, on arrival, had been stopped briefly by three television reporters, holding microphones to the open window of his car while TV cameras shot closeups. The shouted questions overlapped. "Detective, are there any suspects yet?" . . . "Is it true the Ernsts have been murdered in the same way as others?" . . . "Has their daughter, Major Ernst, been informed?" . . . "Is she on her way back to Miami?" But Brewmaster had shaken his head and continued driving, stopping outside the Ernst house to instruct a uniform officer, "Call PIO and tell them we need someone here to deal with the press."

In some police jurisdictions the murder of a prominent official or celebrity was categorized as a "red ball" homicide or, less officially, a "holy shit" case. Once given that label, the case received priority attention. In Miami, supposedly, no such category existed and all murders and murderers were deemed "equal under the law." But the slaying of City Commissioner Ernst and his wife was already proving this untrue.

Part of the proof was the immediate arrival of Chief of Police Farrell W. Ketledge Jr., in an official car, driven by his sergeant aide. The chief was in uniform, his four stars of rank clearly displayed—the equivalent of a full general in the United States Army. As Detective Wightman observed quietly to one of the uniform men, "In any given year you can count the number of times the chief shows up at a homicide on the fingers of one hand."

Lieutenant Newbold, who had arrived a few minutes earlier, met the chief at the main doorway to the house, with Brewmaster beside him.

The chief ordered crisply, "Show me the scene, Lieutenant."

"Yes, sir. This way."

With Newbold leading, the trio climbed a broad stairway, then walked along a landing to a bedroom, the doorway open. Inside they paused as the chief looked around.

The ID technicians were already at work. Dr. Sanchez was standing to one side, waiting for a photographer to finish. Detective Jacobo and Sylvia Walden were discussing possible fingerprint sites.

"Who found the bodies?" the chief asked. "How much do we know?"

Newbold signaled to Brewmaster, who described the maid's arrival, her morning tea duty, and her screams, all of which he had learned about from the majordomo, Theo Palacio. Palacio had explained that he and his wife were away from late afternoon the day before until early that morning—which happened every week when they visited Maria Palacio's invalid sister in West Palm Beach. The maid, too, had left the house at 5:00 P.M. the day before.

"We don't know the time of death yet," Newbold added, "but it seems pretty likely it happened when Mr. and Mrs. Ernst were in the house alone."

Brewmaster told the chief, "Of course, sir, we'll double-check the Palacios' whereabouts."

The chief nodded. "So we could be looking for someone who knew the house routines."

The conclusion was so obvious that neither Newbold nor Brewmaster made a comment. As both knew, Chief Ketledge had never been a detective and had risen to his high rank through police administration, at which he excelled. Occasionally, though, like everyone else in law enforcement, the chief savored a taste of the detective process.

The chief moved farther into the room to get a better view. He walked beside, then behind, the recumbent bodies on which the ID crew was working. Then, as he was about to move again, the voice of Dion Jacobo rang out.

"Stop! Don't go there!"

The chief wheeled, incredulity and anger in his eyes. In an icy voice he demanded, "And who—"

Without waiting, Jacobo answered smartly, "Sir! Detective Jacobo, Chief. I'm co-lead investigator here."

The two men faced each other. Both were black. Their eyes met squarely.

Jacobo volunteered, "Sorry to shout, sir, but it was urgent."

The chief was still glaring, clearly weighing his next move.

Technically, the peremptory order Jacobo had given was appropriate and correct. As co-lead investigator he had authority over everyone else at the scene, irrespective of rank. But it was an authority seldom pushed to its limits, especially when the officer being spoken to was seven ranks higher than the detective.

As the others watched, Jacobo swallowed. He knew that, correct or not, he had probably gone too far, and by this time tomorrow he could be back in uniform on a midnight walking beat in downtown Miami.

It was then that Julio Verona coughed discreetly and addressed the chief. "If you'll excuse me, sir, I think the detective was just trying to preserve what's here." He pointed to an area behind both bodies.

Lieutenant Newbold asked, "What is it?"

"A dead rabbit," Verona said, looking down. "It may be significant."

Brewmaster looked up, startled. "Damn right, it's significant! It's another symbol. We need Malcolm Ainslie."

The chief asked Verona skeptically, "You're suggesting that Detective Jacobo knew the animal was there?"

"I don't know, sir," the ID supervisor said mildly. "But until we've searched the area we have to assume there's evidence everywhere."

The chief hesitated, plainly exercising control. He had a reputation as a rigid disciplinarian, but also for being fair.

"Very well." More composed, he regarded everyone at the crime scene. "I came here to make it clear how important this case is. Right now a lot of eyes are watching us. Work hard. We need a solution soon."

Moving back to the doorway, Chief Ketledge paused before Newbold. "Lieutenant, see to it that a commendation is recorded in Detective Jacobo's file." The chief smiled slightly. "Let's say, 'for tenaciously preserving evidence in difficult circumstances.' "

A moment later the chief was gone.

About an hour afterward, as evidence was still being collected, Julio Verona reported to Sergeant Brewmaster. "There's a wallet among Mr. Ernst's effects with his driver's license and credit cards. No money, but the shape of the wallet looks like there usually was some."

Brewmaster promptly checked with Theo Palacio, who, with his wife, had been instructed to remain in the kitchen and not disturb anything in the house. The majordomo was close to tears and had trouble speaking. His wife, seated at the kitchen table, had clearly been crying too. "Mr. Ernst always had money in that wallet," Theo said. "Mostly big bills, fifties and hundreds. He liked having cash."

"Do you know if he recorded the numbers of those big bills?"

Palacio shook his head. "I doubt it."

After pausing to let Palacio compose himself, Brewmaster continued, "Let me ask something else." He flipped through several pages of his notebook, referring to notes made earlier. "You told me that when you came into the Ernsts' bedroom this morning, you realized there was nothing you could do to help Mr. and Mrs. Ernst, and you went immediately to a phone."

"That's the way it was, sir. I called nine-one-one."

"But did you touch anything in the bedroom? Anything at all?"

Palacio shook his head. "I knew that until the police got here, everything had to stay the same." The majordomo hesitated.

Brewmaster prompted, "What is it?"

"Well, there was one thing I'd forgotten until now. The radio was playing very loudly. I turned it off. I'm sorry if I—"

"Never mind. But let's go look at it."

In the Ernst bedroom, the two men walked toward a portable radio. Brewmaster asked, "When you turned this off, did you change the station?"

"No, sir."

"Has anyone used the radio since?"

"I don't think so."

Brewmaster slipped a rubber glove over his right hand, then turned the radio on. The song, "Oh, What a Beautiful Mornin' " from Rodgers and Hammerstein's *Oklahoma!* filled the room. The detective peered at the radio's dial, set to 93.1 FM.

"That's WTMI," Palacio said. "It was a favorite of Mrs. Ernst. She often listened to it."

Soon afterward, Brewmaster took Maria Palacio to the murdered couple's bedroom to ask another question. "I advise you not to look at the bodies," he told her. "I'll stand between them and you. But there's something else I want you to see."

The "something else" was jewelry—a sapphire and diamond ring with matching earrings, another gold ring, a pearl necklace with a pink tourmaline clasp, a gold bracelet set with diamonds—all of it obviously valuable and left in plain view on a bedroom dressing table.

"Yes, that's Mrs. Ernst's," Maria Palacio said. "At night she never bothered to put it away, just left it out, then put it in the safe the next morning. I warned her once . . ." The woman's voice broke.

"That's all, Mrs. Palacio, thank you," Brewmaster said. "You've told me what I needed to know."

Still later, replying to another Brewmaster question, Dr. Sanchez affirmed, "Yes, essentially the facial and head beatings and body mutilations of Mr. and Mrs. Ernst are similar to those in the Frost and Urbina cases—and probably, from reports I've received, in the Fort Lauderdale and Clearwater cases too."

"And the knife wounds, Doctor?"

"I won't be sure, of course, until after autopsy. But superficially I'd say the knife wounds on both bodies are from the same kind of bowie knife used on the others."

As to the dead rabbit, Dr. Sanchez asked the owner of a pet store, Heather Ubens, with whom she had worked before, to come to the Ernst house.

Ubens, an authority on small animals, identified the creature by its commercial name, a Lopear rabbit. Many of them, she said, were sold locally as pets. Since there was no sign of injury to the rabbit, in Ubens's opinion it had been killed by asphyxiation—simply deprived of air.

After the rabbit had been photographed, Dr. Sanchez had it sent to the medical examiner's office to be preserved in formaldehyde.

Sergeant Brewmaster checked with Theo Palacio to see if the rabbit had been a pet at the Ernst house. "Absolutely not. Mr. and Mrs. Ernst didn't like animals," the majordomo told him, adding, "I wanted them to have a guard dog because of all the crime; I even offered to take care of it myself. But Mr. Ernst said no, with him being a city commissioner, the police would always look out for his safety. But they didn't, did they?"

Brewmaster chose not to answer.

Subsequently police made inquiries at other Miami pet stores, using crime-scene photos in an attempt to find the rabbit's purchaser. But since so many rabbits were sold, sometimes in litters of seven or eight, and since few stores kept detailed records, the search proved fruitless.

Hank Brewmaster told Malcolm Ainslie about the dead rabbit and asked, "Is there something in Revelation that fits—the way those other things did?"

"There's no rabbit in Revelation, or in any other part of the Bible; I'm sure of that," Ainslie said. "It could still be a symbol, though. Rabbits as a species are very old."

"Any religious connotation at all?"

"I'm not sure." Ainslie paused, recalling a lecture series—*Life Origins and Geologic Time*—that he had attended soon after his religious faith began to wane. Details came back; he sometimes surprised himself by how much his memory retained. "Rabbits are Lagomorpha—that's rabbits, hares, and pikas. They originated in North Asia near the end of the Paleocene." He smiled. "Which is fifty-five million years before the Genesis version of creation."

"You think our guy—an obsessed religious freak, you called him—knows all that?" Brewmaster asked.

"I doubt it. But who knows what he thinks, or why?"

That night at home Ainslie went to Karen's personal computer, on which he kept a King James version of the Bible. The next day he told Brewmaster, "I did a computer search for any Bible reference to 'lagomorph,' 'hare,' or 'pika.' No lagomorphs or pikas, but 'hare' appears twice—once in Leviticus, once in Deuteronomy, though not at all in Revelation."

"Do you think our rabbit could have been intended as a hare, and that way be a Bible symbol?"

"No, I don't." Ainslie hesitated, then said, "I'll tell you what I *do* think,

after a lot of thought last night. I don't believe that rabbit is a Revelation symbol at all. It doesn't fit. I reckon it's a fake."

As Brewmaster looked at him curiously, he went on, "All those other symbols left at murder scenes fitted something specific. Like the four dead
cats—'four beasts'—and the red moon—'the moon became as blood'—and
the trumpet—'a great voice, as of a trumpet.' "

"I remember." Brewmaster nodded.

"Oh, sure, a rabbit could be a 'beast'—Revelation's full of beasts." Ainslie
shook his head. "Somehow I don't think so."

"So what are you suggesting?"

"I guess it's mostly instinct, Hank. But I think we need to keep an open
mind about whether the Ernst murders were really another serial killing, or
whether someone else did them and tried to make them look that way."

"Aren't you forgetting? We withheld those earlier crime-scene details."

"But some were published. Reporters have sources; always happens."

"Well, all that's startling, Malcolm, and I'll try to keep it in mind. But I
have to tell you, after seeing that Ernst scene, I reckon your thoughts are
way out."

They left it there.

•   •   •

Soon afterward, Sandra Sanchez announced her findings following the
autopsies of both victims. Yes, they had been killed by a bowie knife, as her
first inspection of the wounds suggested. However, the distinctive notches
and serrations in the bodies differed from those at the other killings, so a different knife was used—which proved nothing, because bowie knives could
be purchased readily and a serial killer might easily own several.

Thus, as days went by, and despite Malcolm Ainslie's doubts, it seemed
increasingly certain that the Ernst killings had been committed by the same
hand as the eight preceding unsolved murders. The basic circumstances
were identical, and so were the supplementals: the dead rabbit, still possibly
a Revelation symbol; removal of all money; the highly visible jewelry left
untouched; and the loud playing radio. Also, as with the earlier murders,
there was no fingerprint evidence.

The investigators were troubled, however, by the speed with which the
Ernst killings had followed the Urbina/Pine Terrace Condo murders only
three days earlier. The previous killings had been spaced two to three months
apart. The media and public were curious about that fact, and asked perti-
nent questions: Had the killer speeded up his deadly mission, whatever it
might be? Did he have a sense of invincibility, of being "on a roll"? Was there

special significance in a Miami city commissioner being a victim? Were other commissioners or officials in danger? And what were the police doing, if anything, to anticipate the killer's next moves?

While the last question could not be answered publicly, the special task force surveillance of six suspects had begun, with Sergeant Ainslie in charge.

The Ernst murders, too, were quickly assigned as a task force responsibility. Sergeant Brewmaster, while continuing to lead the Ernst investigation, became a task force member, reporting to Malcolm Ainslie, as did the detectives from Brewmaster's team—Dion Jacobo and Seth Wightman.

But even before all task force duties were fully in effect, a meeting took place that Ainslie knew was inevitable.

A T 8:15 A.M., TWO DAYS AFTER the mutilated bodies of Gustav and Eleanor Ernst were discovered, Malcolm Ainslie arrived at Homicide headquarters, having already met Sergeant Brewmaster at the murder scene for an update. Disappointingly, nothing more had emerged since the day before. A canvass of the neighborhood, during which residents were asked about recent strangers in the Bay Point area, had produced, as Brewmaster said, "*Nada.*"

In Homicide, Lieutenant Newbold was waiting alongside Ainslie's desk. He pointed and said, "Someone's waiting for you in my office, Malcolm. You'd better hustle!"

Moments later, as Ainslie stood in the Homicide commander's office doorway, he saw Cynthia Ernst, seated in Newbold's chair.

She was dressed smartly in police uniform and looked stunning. How ironic, Ainslie thought, that severely cut masculine clothes could become so sexy on the body of a woman. The tailored, square-shouldered jacket bearing her gold oak leaves of major's rank only emphasized the perfect proportions of her figure. Dark brown hair, trimmed to the regulation inch and a half above the collar line, framed her pale, creamy skin and penetrating green eyes. Ainslie caught the scent of a familiar perfume and was suddenly overwhelmed by memories.

Behind the desk, Cynthia had been perusing a single sheet of paper and now glanced up, her face expressionless.

"Come in," she said. "Close the door."

Ainslie did so, noticing that her eyes were red, presumably from crying.

Standing before the desk he began, "I'd like to say how truly sorry I am—"

"Thank you," Major Ernst said quickly, then continued, in a businesslike manner, "I'm here because I have some questions for you, Sergeant."

He matched her tone. "I'll try to answer them."

Even now, despite her coolness toward him, the sight and sound of Cynthia Ernst excited him, as it had so often when they were lovers. That erotic, arousing, provocative interlude now seemed long ago.

Their affair had begun five years earlier, while they were both Homicide detectives. Cynthia had been beautiful and desirable then, at thirty-three—three years younger than Malcolm. Now, he decided, she was even more alluring. Also, in a strange way, her unyielding coldness since their breakup, a year after the affair began, made her seem even more tempting and exciting than before. Cynthia transmitted her sexuality like a beacon—always had—and to Ainslie's embarrassment he felt, even in this unromantic setting, an erection stirring.

She motioned to a chair that faced the desk and said, unsmiling, "You may sit down."

Ainslie allowed himself the slightest smile. "Thank you, Major."

He sat, realizing that already with their brief exchange, Cynthia had made their relationship clear—a matter of relative ranks, with hers now much senior to his own. Well, fair enough. There was nothing wrong with knowing where you stood. He wished, though, that she would allow him to express his genuine sympathy over her parents' ghastly deaths. But Cynthia returned her gaze to the paper she had been reading, then, taking her time, she put it down and faced him.

"I understand you are in charge of the investigation of my parents' murder."

"Yes, I am." He began explaining the special task force and its reasons, but she cut him off.

"I know all that."

Ainslie stopped and waited, wondering what Cynthia was after. One thing he was sure of: she was deeply and genuinely grieving. Her red eyes proclaimed it and, to his personal knowledge, the relationship between Gustav and Eleanor Ernst and Cynthia, their only child, had been exceptionally close.

In different circumstances he would have reached out and put his arms around her, or simply touched her hand, but knew better than to do so now. Apart from their having gone their separate ways for four years, he knew Cynthia would instantly raise the inviolable, protective barrier she used so often, eliminating the personal while she became the impatient, hard-driving professional he had known so well.

Cynthia had also exhibited some less admirable traits while Ainslie was working with her. Her hard-line directness made her reject subtlety, even though subtlety could sometimes be a useful investigative tool. She favored shortcuts in police inquiries, even if it meant crossing a line to illegality—making deals with criminals outside of official plea bargaining, or planting evidence to "prove" some known offense. While he was her Homicide supervisor, Ainslie occasionally questioned Cynthia's methods, though no one

could quarrel with her results, which, at the time, reflected favorably on him
as well.

Then there was the wholly unprofessional, intimate, abandoned, wildly
sensual Cynthia—the side of her he would not see today, or ever again. He
pushed the thought away.

She leaned forward on the desk and said, "Get to the point. I want to hear
what you're really doing, and don't hold anything back."

This scene, Ainslie thought, was a replay of so much that had gone before.

•   •   •

Cynthia Ernst had joined the Miami Police Force when she was twenty-
seven, one year before Malcolm Ainslie. She had progressed rapidly—some
said because her father was a city commissioner, and certainly that connection did her no harm, nor did the fact that minorities' and women's rights
were creating new priorities and opportunities. But the real reasons for Cynthia's success, as all who knew her well conceded, were her innate abilities
and drive, coupled with hard work for as long as needed.

Right from the beginning, during the obligatory ten-week police academy
course, Cynthia excelled, demonstrating a retentive memory and a quick
mind when confronting problems. She was outstanding at weapons performance, described by the course firearms instructor as "remarkable." After
four weeks, during which she fired with the proficiency of a marksman and
was able to strip and reassemble her weapon at lightning speed, her score
was never below 298 out of a possible 300.

Following the academy course, Cynthia proved herself a highly competent
police officer, becoming valued by superiors for her initiative and ingenuity,
and for her speed in making decisions—the last an essential talent when
enforcing law, and notable especially in a woman. All of those talents, plus a
flair for getting noticed, prompted Cynthia's transfer to Homicide after only
two years on uniform patrol.

In Homicide her record of success continued, and it was there she
encountered Malcolm Ainslie, also a detective, with a growing reputation as
an outstanding investigator.

Cynthia was assigned to the same Homicide team as Ainslie, then headed
by a long-service detective-sergeant, Felix Foster. Soon after Cynthia's
arrival, Foster was made a lieutenant and moved to another department.
Ainslie, promoted to sergeant, took his place.

But even before that, Ainslie and Cynthia had worked together and were
mutually attracted—an attraction that simmered briefly, then exploded.

Cynthia was lead investigator in a triple murder, aided at times by Ainslie.
While following several promising leads, the two of them flew to Atlanta for

two days. The leads promised to pay off, and at the end of the first grueling but successful day, they checked into a suburban motel.

Then, over dinner that night in a small, surprisingly good trattoria, Ainslie looked at Cynthia across the table and, with instinct telling him what was coming, he asked, "Are you very tired?"

"Tired as hell," she answered. Then, reaching for his hand, "But not too tired for what you and I want most—and it's not dessert."

In the car, as they drove back to their motel, Cynthia leaned over and brushed her tongue across his ear. "I'm not sure I can wait," she breathed. "Can you?" Then she teased him with her hand, causing him to groan and swerve.

At the door to his room, he leaned over and kissed her gently. "I gather you want to come in."

"Just as badly as you want me to," she answered playfully.

It was all Ainslie needed. Opening the door, he pushed her inside. The door slammed and the room was dark. Easing Cynthia against a wall, he let his weight press into her. He felt her breathing quicken, her body pulsate with eagerness. Breathing into her hair, kissing the back of her neck, Ainslie slipped his hand around her waist and into her pants.

"Oh Jesus," Cynthia whispered, "I want you now."

"Shhh," Ainslie said, his finger wet and tantalizing. "Don't say anything. Not a word."

She turned then—quickly and without warning—so she faced him but was still flattened against the wall. "Screw you, Sergeant," she said, breathless, then smothered him with her lips.

They struggled out of their clothes as the kissing grew more desperate. "You're beautiful," Ainslie muttered several times. "Christ, you're beautiful."

Finally Cynthia pushed him onto the bed and crawled on top of him. "I need you now, my love. Don't you dare make me wait one more second."

Afterward they rested, then made love again, continuing all through the night. Amid the chaos of his thoughts, it came to Malcolm that Cynthia had become their sexual leader and, surprising him, he had a sense of being dominated and possessed, though he didn't mind.

In the months to come, with Ainslie's promotion from detective to detective-sergeant, he was able to arrange duty schedules so that he and Cynthia were frequently together—both in Miami and on occasional overnight assignments outside the city. Either way their affair continued.

There were many moments when Ainslie reminded himself, with a semblance of guilt, of his marriage to Karen. But Cynthia's explosive hunger and his own wild pleasure in satisfying her seemed to eclipse all else.

Like their first sexual encounter, each subsequent romp began with the long, continuous kiss as they undressed and, as time went by, their magical, exhilarating game continued.

It was during one of their disrobings that Ainslie discovered a second gun Cynthia carried in an ankle holster beneath the trousers that, like most women detectives, she wore on duty. The usual police weapon both Ainslie and Cynthia carried was a 9mm Glock automatic with a fifteen-shot clip and hollow-point bullets. But this small one Cynthia had purchased herself—a tiny, chrome-plated Smith & Wesson five-shot pistol.

She murmured, "It's for anyone other than you who attacks me, darling." Then, inserting the tip of her tongue in his ear, "Right now yours is the only weapon I'm interested in."

The extra gun—known on the force as a "throw-down"—was legal for a police officer, providing it was registered and the owner had qualified in its use at the shooting range. In both cases Cynthia fulfilled the requirements.

Her extra gun, in fact, would be put to use in a way that Malcolm Ainslie remembered gratefully.

●   ●   ●

Cynthia Ernst was lead detective, Ainslie her supervising sergeant, in a complex whodunit investigation in which a male employee of a Miami bank was believed to have witnessed a murder, but had not come forward voluntarily. Cynthia and Ainslie had gone together to the bank—a large downtown branch—to question the potential witness and, upon entering, found a robbery in progress.

The time was near noon; the bank was crowded.

Barely three minutes earlier the robber, a tall, muscular white man armed with an Uzi automatic machine pistol, had confronted a woman teller and ordered her to put all the cash from her till into the cloth bag he pushed toward her. Few people knew what was happening until a bank guard noticed the man and rushed forward. With his pistol drawn, the guard commanded, "You at the counter! Drop that gun!"

Instead of obeying, the robber swung around, firing a burst from his Uzi at the guard, who fell to the floor. As panic and screams ensued, the intruder shouted, "This is a robbery! Nobody move, and no one else will get hurt!" Then he reached over, seized the teller by the neck, and, dragging her across the counter, caught her in a choke-hold.

It was during this confusion, then sudden silence, that Cynthia and Ainslie walked into the bank.

Ainslie unhesitatingly reached into the holster beneath his jacket and produced his 9mm Glock. Using both hands, maintaining a steady stance, he aimed it at the robber, shouting in a strong voice, "I'm a police officer. Let the woman go. Put your gun on the counter and raise your hands, or I shoot!"

At the same time, Cynthia eased away from Ainslie, though making no sudden move that might attract the man's attention. Held casually in her hands was a small, inconspicuous purse.

The robber tightened his grip on the teller and pointed his gun at her head. He snarled at Ainslie, "*You* drop the gun, scumbag, or the broad gets it first. *Do it! Drop it!* I'll count to ten. One, two . . ."

The teller, her voice thin and stifled, called, "Please do what he says! I don't want—" Her words were cut off as the choke-hold tightened.

The robber continued, "Three . . . four . . ."

Ainslie called out, "I tell you again, put the damn gun down and give up."

"Bullshit! Five . . . six . . . *You* drop the fucking gun, shitbag, or I nix this bitch at ten!"

Cynthia, off to one side, her mind cool and calculating, weighed the fields of fire. She knew that Ainslie would have guessed what she was doing and was trying to stall and gain time, though without much chance of success. The robber was a loser, knew he would never get away, and therefore didn't care . . .

His count continued. "Seven . . ."

Ainslie, unyielding, held his firing position. Cynthia knew he was relying on her totally now. There was no sound in the bank; everyone was still and tense. By this time, presumably, silent alarms had been tripped. But it would be several minutes before more police arrived, and even then, what could they do?

She could see there was no one immediately behind the robber. He now faced Cynthia almost directly, though seemingly unaware of her as his focus remained on Ainslie. The teller, with the gun still aimed at her head, was dangerously close, too close for safety, but there was no choice. Cynthia would get one shot only, and it had to be dead-on, a killing shot . . .

"Eight . . ."

With a single swift movement, Cynthia released a fall-away seam of her specialized purse—a new, efficient substitute for an ankle holster. Letting the purse drop, she grasped the tiny Smith & Wesson pistol from inside, the chrome-plated gun gleaming as she raised it.

"Nine . . ."

Instantly taking aim, bracing herself, she fired.

The sharp sound of the shot caused heads to turn. Cynthia ignored the stares, her eyes locked on the man who slumped over as a single red hole near the center of his forehead began oozing blood. The woman teller quickly freed herself from the man's arm, then fell to the ground sobbing.

Ainslie, his gun still trained on the robber, walked toward him, looked carefully at the body, now motionless, then put the gun away. As Cynthia joined him, he said with a grin, "You cut it fine. But thanks."

Within the bank a buzz of conversation rose; then, as realization dawned, applause broke out, changing almost at once to spontaneous cheers directed at Cynthia. Smiling, she leaned against Malcolm and, sighing with relief, whispered, "I think you owe me a week in the sack for that one."

Ainslie nodded. "We'll have to be careful. You're going to be famous." And over the next few days, as a widely acclaimed media heroine, she was.

• • •

Long after, when Malcolm Ainslie looked back on his affair with Cynthia, he wondered if his own unbridled lust was a delayed reaction to those long years he had spent in unnatural priestly celibacy. True or not, his priority throughout what he thought of still as Cynthia's Year was his personal, exquisite carnal satisfaction.

Occasionally during that time he had asked himself, *Should my conscience trouble me?* Then reminded himself there were aeons of precedents—the year 1000 B.C., or thereabouts, as an example. His scholarly recall (would he ever escape it?) brought back the Bible's King David and the Second Book of Samuel, chapter 11:

> *In an eveningtide . . . David arose from off his bed . . . and from*
> *the roof he saw a woman washing herself; and the woman was very*
> *beautiful to look upon.*

It was Bathsheba, of course, the wife of Uriah, who was away fighting—as the Old Testament described it—one of God's wars.

> *And David sent messengers, and took her; and she came in unto*
> *him, and he lay with her . . . And the woman conceived, and sent*
> *and told David, and said, I am with child.*

Unfortunately for David, all of that was before condoms, which Ainslie used with Cynthia. Nor did Ainslie have a paramour's husband to contend with—like the warrior Uriah, whom King David had ordered killed . . .

Surprisingly, through all of that time with Cynthia, Malcolm Ainslie's love for Karen did not diminish. It was as if he had two private lives: one, his marriage, representing security and permanence, the other a wild adventure he always knew must one day end. Ainslie never seriously considered leaving Karen and their son Jason, then three and growing up into a delightful little guy.

Occasionally, during that period, there were moments when Ainslie wondered if Karen was aware of, or even suspected, the affair. A word or attitude could leave him believing uneasily that she did.

Meanwhile, as the Year of Cynthia progressed, some aspects of Cynthia's nature began to make Ainslie uncomfortable, at times professionally uneasy. She would periodically switch moods—for no discernible reason—from free-flowing, amorous warmth to sudden and icy coldness. At such moments Ainslie would wonder what had happened between them, then realize after several experiences that nothing had; it was simply Cynthia's way, a facet of her character, more visible and frequent as time went on.

But that mood shift was manageable, the professional unease less so.

Ainslie, throughout his police career, had believed in ethical behavior, even when dealing with habitual criminals who disregarded ethics totally. Sometimes minor tradeoffs were acceptable in exchange for information, but that was Ainslie's limit. Some in police work, though, held differing views and would make illegal deals with criminals, or lie when making statements, or plant evidence when there seemed no other way to get it. But Ainslie would have no part of such tactics, either for himself or those who worked with him.

Cynthia apparently had no such scruples.

As Cynthia's superior, Ainslie had suspected that some of her investigative successes might be morally questionable. But nothing came to his direct attention, and his questions about her rumored freewheeling methods produced strong denials from Cynthia, and once indignation. One matter did surface, though, in a way he could not overlook.

It concerned a con artist and thief named Val Castellon, recently released from prison on parole. Cynthia was lead investigator in a murder, and while Castellon was in no way a suspect, it was believed he might have information about another ex-con who was. Brought in for interrogation, Castellon denied any such knowledge, and Ainslie was inclined to believe him. Cynthia did not.

In a subsequent private session with Castellon, Cynthia threatened to plant drugs on him if he failed to testify for her, then have him arrested, in which case his parole would be revoked and he would go back to prison, as well as face stiff new charges. Planting drugs in a suspect's pocket, then appearing to discover them, was a simple tactic for police and all too frequently used.

Ainslie learned about Cynthia's threat through Sergeant Hank Brewmaster, who had been told of it by one of his regular informants, a crony of Castellon's. When Ainslie asked Cynthia if the report was true, she admitted it was, though the drug plant had not yet been done.

"And it won't be," he told her. "I'm responsible, and I won't allow it."

"Oh, bullshit, Malcolm!" Cynthia said. "That prick will wind up back in jail anyway. I'd just be sending him there sooner."

"Don't you get it?" he asked incredulously. "We're here to enforce the law, which means we have to obey it, too."

"And you're being as stuffy as this old pillow." Cynthia threw one at him from the bed of a motel where they had rented a room on a rainy afternoon. At the same time she fell back on the bed. She spread her legs wide and asked, "Is what you want legal? After all, we're both on duty." She laughed quietly then, knowing precisely what would happen next.

Ainslie's face changed. He went to her and threw his jacket and tie on the bed. Cynthia said suddenly, sharply, "Hurry, hurry! Slide your lovely big illegal cock inside me!"

As he had at other times, Ainslie felt powerless, melting into her, and yet diffident, even embarrassed by Cynthia's raunchy language. Yet it was part of her sexual aggressiveness, and each time made their coupling more exciting.

By then they had abandoned the subject of Val Castellon, which Ainslie intended to bring up later, though he never did. Nor did he learn how the missing information in Cynthia's murder inquiry was supplied, except that she obtained it, resulting in one more investigative triumph for Cynthia—and himself.

What Ainslie did make sure of was that Castellon was not charged with drug possession, and his parole was not revoked. In one way or another, it seemed, Ainslie's warning to Cynthia had been heeded.

•　　•　　•

Something else bothered Ainslie. Unlike most other police officers, Cynthia seemed comfortable, even happy, in the company of criminals, mingling with them at bars in an easy, friendly way. She and Ainslie also differed in their attitudes to lawbreaking. Ainslie viewed crime-solving, particularly of homicides, as moral high ground. Cynthia didn't, and once told him, "Face reality, Malcolm! It's a contest, with crooks, police, and lawyers all competing. The winner depends on how clever each lawyer is and how rich the defendant is. Your so-called moral issues don't stand a chance in this game."

Ainslie was not impressed. Nor was he happy to learn eventually that a regular companion of Cynthia's at bars and restaurants was Patrick Jensen, a successful novelist and Miami bon vivant, but with an unsavory reputation, particularly among police.

Jensen, a former TV newsman, had written a succession of best-selling crime novels, published worldwide, and by the age of thirty-nine he had amassed what was rumored to be twelve million dollars. Some said the success had gone to his head, and Jensen had evolved into a rude and arrogant womanizer with a violent temper. His second wife, Naomi, from whom he was divorced, made several spousal battery complaints to police, then withdrew them before official action could begin. Several times after their divorce, Jensen tried to reconcile with Naomi, but she would have no part of it.

Then Naomi Jensen was found murdered, with a .38-caliber bullet through her throat. Beside her lay a young musician, Kilburn Holmes, whom she had been dating, killed by a bullet from the same gun. According to witnesses, earlier that day Naomi and Jensen had had a bitter argument outside Naomi's house, during which she insisted he leave her alone and told him she intended to remarry.

Patrick Jensen was an obvious suspect, and inquiries by Miami Homicide showed he had opportunity and no alibi. A handkerchief near the bodies matched others owned by Jensen, though there was nothing on the handkerchief to prove it was his. However, a fragment of paper in Holmes's hand did match another fragment, found in Jensen's garbage. Detectives then discovered that two weeks before the murders Jensen had purchased a Smith & Wesson .38-caliber revolver, but he claimed to have lost the gun, and no murder weapon was found.

Despite intensive effort by Sergeant Pablo Greene's Homicide team, no other evidence was obtained, and what little they had was insufficient to take to a grand jury.

Patrick Jensen knew it, too.

Detective Charlie Thurston, the lead investigator, told Sergeants Greene and Ainslie, "I went to that arrogant dickhead Jensen today to ask a few more questions, and the fucker just laughed and told me to beat it." Thurston, a seasoned detective, normally mild-mannered and patient, was still burning from the encounter.

"The bastard knows we know he did it," he went on, "and he's telling us, 'So what, you'll never prove it.' "

"Let him laugh now," Greene said. "It may be our turn later."

But Thurston shook his head. "Won't happen. He'll put it all in a goddam book and make a pisspot full of money."

To an extent Thurston was right. Nothing more emerged to connect

Jensen with the murders of Naomi and her friend Kilburn Holmes, and he did write a new crime story in which the homicide detectives were incompetent buffoons. But the book did not do well, nor did one more which followed, and it appeared that Patrick Jensen's best-seller days had ended, as so often happens when fresh young writers ascend into literary orbit and older ones decline. At the same time there were rumors that, through bad investments, Jensen had lost a major part of his millions and was looking around for other sources of income. Another rumor was that Jensen and Detective Cynthia Ernst had, for a long time, been having an affair.

Ainslie dismissed the second rumor. For one thing, he did not believe Cynthia would be so foolish, in view of Patrick Jensen's status as a murder suspect. Second, he found it inconceivable that she could conduct two intense affairs at the same time, particularly since Cynthia's relationship with Ainslie frequently left the two of them drained.

Just the same, Ainslie did raise Patrick Jensen's name with Cynthia, trying to make the reference casual. Cynthia, as usual, wasn't fooled.

"Are you jealous?" she asked.

"Of Patrick Jensen! That'll be the day." He hesitated, then added, "Do I have reason to be?"

"Patrick's nothing!" she asserted. "It's you I want, Malcolm—and all of you. More of your time, all of your time! I don't want to share you, not with anyone." They were in an unmarked police car, Cynthia driving. The last few words rang out like a command.

He was startled and asked, scarcely thinking, "Are you saying we should get married?"

"Malcolm, get free. Then I'll consider."

The answer, he thought, was typical Cynthia; in the past year he had come to know her well. If he were free, the probability was that she would use him, squeeze him dry, and then discard him. No permanence for Cynthia; on that point she had made herself quite clear.

So there it was. Ainslie had known something like this was inevitable and that a moment of decision had arrived. He knew Cynthia would not like what he would say next, and knew too that her anger could erupt like Vesuvius.

For a moment, postponing the confrontation, he thought back again to David and Bathsheba, the lovers who married after Bathsheba's husband Uriah was disposed of in battle as King David prearranged. But God—according to the Bible—was personally upset by David's perfidy.

> . . . the thing that David had done displeased the Lord. And the
> Lord sent Nathan unto David . . . And Nathan said to David . . .

Thus saith the Lord, Behold, I will raise up evil against thee out of thine own house, and I will take thy wives before thine eyes, and give them unto thy neighbor, and he shall lie with thy wives . . .

Like so much else in the Bible, it was—as scholars saw it—highly implausible folk legend, told around the campfires of semi-nomadic Israelites, then two hundred years later written down with a core of reality, plus myths from ten thousand retellings. But the extent of truth and fiction didn't matter; what did was that in human relations there was nothing new under the sun, but only variations of old themes. One variation now—Ainslie wasn't going to marry Cynthia and didn't want to "get free" of Karen.

They had been driving on a quiet suburban street. As if anticipating what was to come, Cynthia pulled the car to the curb and stopped.

She looked at him. "Well?"

Reaching out to take her hand, he said gently, "My love, what's happened between us has been magical, wonderful. It's something I never expected, and as long as I live I'll be grateful. But I have to tell you—I can't go on, we have to end it."

He had expected an outburst. But it didn't happen. Instead she laughed. "I presume you're joking."

"No," he answered firmly.

She sat silently for a few moments, staring out of the passenger window. Then, without turning, she said with eerie calm, "You'll regret this, Malcolm, I promise—regret it for the rest of your miserable life."

He sighed. "That may be true. I guess I'll have to take that chance."

Suddenly she looked at him with tears on her cheeks and rage in her eyes. Her fists were clenched and shaking. "You bastard!" she screamed.

From that point onward they saw little of each other. One reason was that Cynthia became a sergeant a few days later. She had taken the promotion exam a few weeks earlier and placed third on a list of six hundred.

Upon her promotion she was transferred from Homicide to Sexual Battery as a supervisor. She was put in charge of a team of five detectives investigating rapes, attempted rapes, sexual harassment, peeping toms; the coverage was wide, and Cynthia became outstandingly successful. As in Homicide, she proved adept at developing leads through a web of contacts and informants. A dedicated, natural leader, she worked her team hard, as well as herself, and early on made a notable arrest that resulted in the sentencing of a fifteen-count serial rapist who, over two preceding years, had terrorized women in the city.

In part because of this and an excellent rating in one more promotion exam, Cynthia was made a lieutenant two years later and moved to a new department—Community Relations—as second-in-command. There she liaised with the public, appeared at town meetings, lectured community groups and sometimes other police forces, and generally put forward a convincingly positive image of the Miami force.

All of this brought her to the attention of Police Chief Farrell Ketledge, and when Cynthia's department head died unexpectedly, the chief appointed her to take over. At the same time, because of the prominence and increasing importance of Community Relations, Chief Ketledge decided it should be headed by a police major. Thus Cynthia attained that senior rank without ever having been a captain.

Meanwhile, Ainslie was still a sergeant, to some extent penalized by the fact that he was a white male at a time when affirmative-action promotions of minorities and women were disproportionately—and many thought unfairly—large. However, he had passed the examination for lieutenant with distinction and expected to move up soon. From a practical point of view, a promotion would increase his annual sergeant's salary of $52,000 by a welcome $10,400.

With financial pressures eased, he and Karen would be able to travel more, go to more concerts—they loved jazz and chamber music—dine out more often, and generally improve the quality of their lives. Since he'd ended his affair with Cynthia a belated sense of guilt had grown, making Ainslie more determined then ever to be a loyal, devoted husband.

Then he received a call from Captain Ralph Leon, who was in Personnel Management. Ainslie and Leon had been recruits together, and in the same police academy class, where they became friends, frequently studied in tandem, and otherwise helped each other. Leon was black and well qualified—and therefore affirmative action had not delayed his upward progress.

On the phone Leon merely said, "Malcolm, meet me for coffee." He named a day and time and a small café in Little Havana—a long way from Police Headquarters.

Outside the restaurant they smiled at the sight of each other and shook hands warmly. Leon, who wore a sports jacket and slacks instead of his uniform, opened the door and led the way to a quiet booth. He was a trimly built man, studious and methodical, and becoming serious, he weighed his words before speaking. "Malcolm, this conversation is not taking place."

His eyes posed a question, to which Ainslie nodded. "Okay. I understand."

"There are things I hear in Personnel . . ." Leon stopped. "Oh, hell, Malcolm. Here it is. If you stay a Miami cop, you're never going anywhere. You'll never make lieutenant or any rank higher than you have now. It isn't fair, I hate it, but out of friendship I had to let you know."

Ainslie, stunned by what he had heard, sat in silence.

Leon's voice became more emotional. "It's Major Ernst. She's bad-mouthing you everywhere, blocking your promotion. I don't know why, Malcolm; maybe you do. But if you do know, don't tell me."

"Blocking it on what grounds, Ralph? My record's clean and officially . . . well, outstanding."

"The grounds are trivial, and everybody knows it. But a major—that one especially—has a lot of influence, and in our shop, if you have a powerful enemy, you usually can't win. You know how it is."

Ainslie did know. But curiosity made him ask, "What am I accused of ?"

"Neglect of duty, laziness, careless work habits."

In other circumstances, Ainslie might have laughed.

Leon said, "She must have searched through every goddam file." He spelled out some details. There was an occasion, for example, when Ainslie had failed to make a scheduled court appearance.

"I remember that. I was on the way to court when I got a radio call—a freeway killing. There was a chase, we got the guy, and afterward a conviction. Later that day I saw the judge, explained, and apologized. He was fine about it and rescheduled."

"Unfortunately the court documents just show your absence. I checked." Leon pulled a folded paper from his pocket. "Several times you were late for work, missed meetings."

"Jesus!—that happens to everybody. There isn't anyone in the Department who doesn't get that kind of stuff—emergency calls, so you respond and let the office wait. I don't even remember."

"Ernst remembered *and* found the records." Leon looked at his paper. "I said it was trivia. Want more?"

Ainslie shook his head. Quick changes of plan, fast decisions, dealing with the unexpected, were a normal part of police work, especially in Homicide. Sometimes, administratively, the results were messy; it was part of the job. Everyone, including Cynthia, knew it.

But he knew the answer, too; there was nothing he could do. Cynthia had the rank and the influence, and held all the cards. He remembered her threatening words to him. Well, she had kept her promise in spades.

"Damn it," Ainslie muttered, staring through a window at the street outside.

"I'm sorry, Malcolm. It's really a bum rap."

Ainslie nodded. "I appreciate your telling me, Ralph. And no one will ever know we talked."

Leon looked down at the table in front of him. "That doesn't seem so important now." He raised his eyes. "Will you stay on?"

"I think so." Mainly, he reasoned, because there were few alternatives. And in the end he did.

•   •   •

Following the exchange with Ralph Leon, one other thought came back to Malcolm: the memory of a brief, unexpected conversation several months earlier with Mrs. Eleanor Ernst, Cynthia's mother.

Police sergeants normally do not meet city leaders or their spouses socially, but this happened at a small retirement dinner given for a senior officer with whom Ainslie had worked, and Commissioner and Mrs. Ernst attended. Ainslie knew Mrs. Ernst by sight; she had always seemed a demure woman, expensively dressed but slightly shy. Therefore he was surprised when, holding a wineglass, she approached him during the reception preceding the dinner.

Speaking softly, she asked, "You're Sergeant Ainslie, aren't you?"

"Yes, I am."

"I believe that you and my daughter are no longer—how shall I put it?—meeting each other. Is that correct?" Seeing Ainslie hesitate, she added, "Oh, don't worry, I won't tell anyone. But sometimes Cynthia isn't the most discreet person."

He answered uncertainly. "I rarely see Cynthia at all these days."

"This may seem strange, coming from a mother, Sergeant, but I was sorry to hear that. I think you were a good influence on her. Tell me, was the ending friendly or otherwise?"

"Otherwise."

"A pity." Mrs. Ernst lowered her voice still more. "I shouldn't do this, I suppose, but I want to tell you something, Sergeant Ainslie. If Cynthia thinks she's been wronged, she never forgets, never forgives. Just a warning you should bear in mind. Good evening."

Still holding her wineglass, Mrs. Ernst melted away.

Thus, in due course, the predictive words of Eleanor Ernst were confirmed. Captain Ralph Leon had become the messenger, and Ainslie—permanently it seemed—had paid Cynthia's price.

•   •   •

Now, long after so many events, so much maneuvering, and so many changes for them both, Malcolm Ainslie and Cynthia Ernst faced each other in Leo Newbold's office.

"Get to the point," Cynthia had said about her parents' murders. "I want to hear what you're really doing, and don't hold anything back."

"We've compiled a list of suspects for surveillance. I'll have a copy sent—"

"I already have it." Cynthia touched a file folder in front of her. "Is there anyone on that list who's number one?"

"Robinson seems a probability. Several things fit, but it's too early to tell. Surveillance should give us more information."

"Are you convinced the same person did all of the murders?"

"Just about everybody is." His own doubts, Ainslie thought, were unimportant.

More questions followed, and as far as he could, Ainslie tried to convey sympathy with his answers, despite Cynthia's coldness. At the same time he was very much on guard. Cynthia had that effect on him, knowing from experience that she would make use of any information in any way she chose.

Toward the end she said, "I understand you associated some things found at the murder scenes with Biblical references."

"Yes, mostly Revelation."

"Mostly?"

"Nothing is exact. As you know, it's impossible to be sure of a source, or of a criminal's reasoning, which can be inconsistent. What those references did was point us toward the group of people we're now watching."

"I want you to inform me of every new development. Daily reports by phone."

"Excuse me, Major, but you should clear that with Lieutenant Newbold."

"I already have. He has my instructions. Now I'm giving them to you. Please see that you follow them."

Well, he thought, Major Cynthia Ernst had the rank to get away with such instructions, even though, strictly speaking, they were outside her own departmental field. It didn't follow, though, that she should receive every last scrap of information, even about her parents' murders.

Standing, Ainslie moved closer to the desk and looked down at Cynthia. "Major, I will do my best to keep you informed, but as head of this task force my first duty is to solve the case." He waited until she looked up, then continued. "*Nothing* will come before that."

She seemed about to say something, then evidently thought better of it. Ainslie moved back, his gaze fixed on hers. Yes, she outranked him and could order him to do virtually anything in the line of duty. But on a personal level, he decided, he would not be pushed around by her. Ever.

The plain fact was, he didn't trust Cynthia and scarcely liked her anymore. He knew there were things she was not revealing, though what they were and how they might relate to the serial murder investigations, he had no idea. What he did know from his own sources in the Department was that Cynthia

Ernst continued to cut corners, and to keep dubious company, especially with the author Patrick Jensen.

Jensen was still being watched by Miami police. There had been rumors of a connection between Jensen and a drug distribution gang, the same gang that was suspect in a Homicide investigation by Metro-Dade Police into what had become known as the Wheelchair Murder. The victim, a paraplegic and a valued police informant, had been wheeled at night, bound and gagged, into tidewater in a remote area south of Homestead. His wheelchair had been secured by a chain and weights to a lonely offshore islet, and the man left to drown as the tide rose.

Of course, it was all a long way from Major Cynthia Ernst . . .

She nodded slightly. "That will be all, Sergeant. You may go."

8

"OF ALL THE JOBS COPS ARE asked to do," Detective Charlie Thurston said, "surveillance has to be the shittiest."

"It sure ain't my favorite," Bradford Andrews acknowledged. "And this damn rain's not helping, either."

· Thurston from Homicide and Andrews from Robbery were sitting in a Florida Power & Light van, their temporary undercover vehicle. They were assigned to keep track of Carlos Quiñones, one of the six computer-generated suspects in the serial killings.

The Police Department owned a variety of vehicles for surveillance use. They included taxis, phone, gas, and electrical service trucks, store delivery vehicles, and even postal vans. Some were given or sold to police by the organizations that owned them. Others, confiscated during drug raids, were awarded through the courts. The type of vehicle used to watch any particular subject, such as Quiñones, was changed from day to day.

The two detectives, both in their early thirties, had been parked for nearly two hours outside Quiñones's apartment—one of a series of squalid residences in the unofficially named Liberty City area.

The time was approaching 7:00 P.M., and Brad Andrews yawned with boredom. Andrews liked action. All detectives did, which is why many had become detectives. Yet, much of the time, surveillance was the reverse. It involved sitting in a vehicle for several hours, peering out the windows, with nothing happening. Even in good weather it was hard to concentrate on an assignment without thoughts turning to that night's dinner, sports, sex, an overdue mortgage payment . . .

The heavy rain had persisted for an hour, making it impossible for the detectives to see clearly what was going on outside, but to turn on the wipers would only advertise that someone was being watched. The patter of water droplets didn't help, either; it was like a soporific drumbeat, lulling the men to sleep.

Thurston, seeing Andrews yawn, cautioned, "Wake up, man!"

"I'm trying," Brad Andrews said, sitting up straight. A seasoned officer, he was one of the detectives borrowed from Robbery for surveillance duty. Andrews was formerly with Homicide, but in an effort to stabilize his family life, he had transferred to Robbery, where the hours were more reasonable. Now, temporarily, he was back.

The special surveillance force comprised twenty-four people: the two sergeants from Homicide, Ainslie and Greene, their two teams of four detectives, plus twelve other detectives from Robbery. Two investigators from the state attorney's office were also sharing the surveillance duty.

"Hey!" Andrews said. "Here's our guy, and would you believe he's combing his hair again?"

Quiñones, an olive-complexioned Hispanic, was tall and lean, with a narrow face and thick, wavy hair that he must have combed two dozen times during the two and a half days Thurston and Andrews had been observing him. Quiñones's extensive criminal career included assault, rape, and armed robbery with violence.

Now, accompanied by an unknown bearded male, he entered a yellow, beat-up '78 Chevrolet and drove away. The two detectives, in their Florida P&L van, followed, with Andrews at the wheel.

Quiñones went directly to Highway 836, a busy expressway. There, after heading west toward Miami International Airport, he began driving erratically, bumping several cars in the rear—an obvious attempt to stop and rob them.

Watching, Thurston griped, "Shit! I'd love to arrest those two bastards."

Andrews nodded. "Yeah, well, maybe we'll have to."

They faced a dilemma, both detectives knew. Their mission was to observe Quiñones as a possible serial killer, but if any of the bumped cars stopped, the detectives had a duty to protect their occupants from danger. None of the cars did stop, however, undoubtedly because of the many police and media warnings about that specific danger.

After a while, to the detectives' relief, the bumping ceased and Quiñones appeared to have given up.

The yellow Chevy left the expressway at Northwest 57th Avenue, turned south into the western end of Little Havana, and stopped at a 7-Eleven store, where the bearded man got out. Quiñones then drove on alone to the south campus of Miami-Dade Community College, at Southwest 107th Avenue and 104th Street. It was a long, tedious ride, taking most of an hour, and Andrews, still driving the undercover van, dropped back as much as possible without losing sight of the Chevy.

By now it was 8:30 P.M., and Quiñones stopped in the college parking lot within sight of students walking to and from evening classes. The detectives saw some women students abruptly turn their heads as they passed Quiñones's car. Apparently he had called out, though none of the women stopped.

Thurston leaned forward and muttered, "This dude has assaults and a rape on his sheet. You don't think . . ."

As he spoke, Quiñones left his car and began following a young blond woman to another portion of the parking lot.

"Let's go!" Thurston jumped from the van, with Andrews behind.

Quiñones was within twenty feet of the young woman when she reached her car—a red Honda—jumped in, started the engine, and pulled away. Quiñones ran to his own car, still unaware of the detectives, who were also darting back to their van.

As the blond woman's car passed Quiñones's, he drove out behind it. The detectives were now following both cars.

"Don't let that son of a bitch out of your sight," Thurston warned. "If this is our guy, we don't want another corpse."

Andrews nodded. He was staying closer to the yellow Chevy now, reasoning that Quiñones's attention was focused on the red Honda ahead. The three vehicles moved north on Southwest 107th Avenue amid light traffic until, without warning, the Honda swung abruptly right onto Southwest Eighth Street, the Tamiami Trail. Quiñones, clearly not ready for a turn, braked, skidded well into the wide intersection, then turned sharply to follow.

"She's on to the bastard," Thurston said.

Quiñones's pursuit of the Honda was further delayed by another car about to turn out of Eighth Street. He reversed a few feet more, then, with tires squealing, made the right turn. Andrews, who had held back through the last block, followed.

Then, as traffic cleared, the detectives saw the blond woman leave her car, which was now in a parking area of a high-rise apartment complex. She walked quickly to the lobby, using a key to open a main doorway. Almost at once she was inside, the door closed behind her.

Moments later, Quiñones's yellow Chevy pulled up near the Honda. Andrews drove the van into the parking lot and pulled into a space where the detectives could both see Quiñones, still seated in his car, and the apartment building directly ahead. After a few minutes they saw lights go on in one of the lower-floor apartments, with the blond woman clearly visible through a window. Only for a moment, though. Crossing the room, she pulled draperies across the window.

"She knows he's out there," Thurston said.

"Yeah, and he may have tailed her before. Probably knows the apartment."

Suddenly Thurston shouted, "Shit! He's gone." While they had been looking up at the window, Quiñones had left his car and moved to the apartment
building doorway, where he was entering behind another figure.

Both detectives flung their van doors open and raced to the door. Andrews
wrenched at it, but it was securely closed. By now no one was visible inside.
Thurston immediately started pressing buttons on the residents' speaker system. "Police officers!" he cried out. "We're chasing a suspect. Open the front
door, please."

Many, he knew, would be suspicious, but someone might . . .

Someone did. A loud buzz sounded. Andrews called over, "It's open!" and
they both rushed in.

"What floor was she on?" Andrews queried. "I'd say the third."

Thurston nodded. "Get up there!"

A hallway contained two elevators, both closed. Andrews hit a call button,
then abruptly the doors of one opened and an elderly woman slowly
emerged, with a Pekingese on a leash. The dog seemed reluctant to move.
Thurston settled the matter by picking it up and dumping it outside. As the
woman opened her mouth to protest, both detectives were already inside the
elevator, Andrews jabbing the third-floor button, then a lower button to close
the doors. But the machinery was unhurried; only after a pause, while the
two men fumed, did the doors slide together.

At the third floor they hurried out, turning right toward where they judged
they had seen the blond woman through her window. But the corridor was
silent, and no door was open. Thurston knocked at two doors without
response.

"Nothing here!" he pronounced. "Has to be the fourth floor. Use the
stairs!" He headed for a doorway marked FIRE EXIT, Andrews following. They
bounded up concrete steps, then through another door, emerging on a corridor matching the one below. A few yards away an apartment door was open,
with part of the door splintered. At the same moment two loud blasts, clearly
gunshots, sounded through the apartment doorway. As both detectives
paused, drawing their guns, they heard four more shots in quick succession.

Thurston, his face set grimly, moved against the wall on the same side of
the corridor as the open door. Motioning Andrews to stay behind him, he
whispered, "I'll take this one. Cover me."

Small sounds could be heard through the open doorway—light footsteps
briefly, then several indistinct thuds—while Thurston approached carefully.
Then, with gun extended, he put his head cautiously around the doorway.
Almost at once he lowered the gun and stepped inside.

Beyond a small hallway, in what appeared to be a living room, Quiñones was facedown on the floor, unconscious, in a pool of blood. His right arm was extended, a sharp-edged, gleaming knife close by. It was a pearl-handled switchblade, Thurston noted. The woman, who looked older than she had from a distance, was seated on a circular ottoman. She held a gun pointed downward; her body was slumped, hair a mess, face dazed.

Thurston approached her. Pointing to the gun, he said, "I'm a police officer. I'll take that." He observed it was a .22 Cal Rohn automatic pistol that held six shots, the number he had heard fired. Obediently she held the gun out to him. Taking a pen from his shirt pocket, he placed it in the trigger guard, handling the weapon so no contamination of fingerprints would occur, and, for the time being, put it on a table to the side.

Andrews entered cautiously, then went straight to Quiñones's body and checked for vital signs. "He's gone," he pronounced. Then, moving the body slightly, he asked Thurston, "Did you see this, Charlie?" He pointed to the trousers front, where the zipper was down and Quiñones's penis protruded.

"No, but it figures." As the detectives knew, rapists often exposed themselves, believing the sight would turn women on. Thurston added, "Better get Fire-Rescue here to confirm he's dead."

On his portable police radio, Andrews transmitted, "Nineteen-thirty-one to dispatcher."

"QSK."

"Send me Fire-Rescue to 7201 Tamiami Canal Road, apartment 421, to check a possible forty-five. Also send a two-man unit for crowd control, and dispatch an ID unit, too."

"QSL."

Within less than a minute, approaching sirens could be heard outside as uniform police and Fire-Rescue medics responded to the call. An ID team, though traveling with less urgency, was undoubtedly on the way.

Thurston made a radio call to Sergeant Malcolm Ainslie, as head of the special task force, informing him of developments.

"I'm close by," Ainslie said. "Be with you in minutes."

Andrews, meanwhile, had begun crime-scene routine, making notes, then questioning the woman, still seated.

"Your name, miss, please?"

With an effort she seemed to collect her thoughts, though her hands were shaking. "Dulce Gomez."

She was single, she reported, thirty-six years old, and lived in this apartment. She had been in Miami ten years. She was attractive, Andrews thought, though with a certain hardness to her.

She was employed by Southern Bell as a phone-repair technician, Gomez told him. In the evenings she attended classes at Miami-Dade Community College, where she was majoring in telecommunications. "I want to get a better job."

Thurston, who had joined them, motioned toward Quiñones's body. "Do you know this man, Dulce? Had you seen him before he followed you today?"

She shuddered. "Never!"

"We've been watching him. It's possible he might have done this before without your knowing."

"Well . . . now you ask, couple of times I did have a feeling someone was . . ." She stopped, remembering. "That *pendejo* sure knew the apartment number, must have come straight up."

Andrews prompted, "And broke down the door?"

She nodded. "He stormed right in like a crazed dog, his dick hanging out, and swinging a knife."

Thurston said, "And that's when you shot him?"

"No. I didn't have the gun then, so I gave him a karate kick. He dropped the knife."

"You do karate?"

"Black belt. I let him have it to the head and torso and he went down. Then I got the gun and shot him."

"Where was the gun?"

"In another room. My bedroom, in a drawer."

Thurston was startled. "You mean you already had the guy down, but you still got a gun and shot him—emptied it into him—six shots?"

The woman hesitated. "Well, I wanted the shit to stay down. He had the knife and was wriggling around. That's why, even after I shot him, I kicked him in the head some."

It explained the sounds—light footsteps and thuds—that both detectives had heard while approaching the apartment. Andrews said, "But he wasn't wriggling after you shot him."

Gomez shrugged. "I guess not. But I was still pretty scared."

During the detectives' questioning, the paramedics had arrived; it took them only a few seconds to confirm that Quiñones was dead. And two uniform officers were now on duty in the corridor outside. They had sealed off apartment 421 with yellow POLICE LINE tape and were assuring a crowd of assembled tenants: "All the excitement's over, folks," and "Everything's being taken care of."

Malcolm Ainslie had arrived in time to hear the later stages of the questions. Now he said carefully, "Let's be clear about this, Ms. Gomez. You had the man down because you do karate, and he was still on the ground when you got back and put six bullets in him?"

"I already told you that."

"May I see your gun permit, please?"

For the first time the young woman seemed uneasy. "I don't have one. My boyfriend gave me the gun last Christmas. It was under my tree, gift-wrapped. I didn't think—"

Thurston said softly as an aside, "Guy's gotta be in the NRA. Only that kind of mind would put a gun under a Christmas tree."

Among police officers, who saw so many deadly shootings and frequently faced death themselves from easily purchased assault weapons, the National Rifle Association did not rate highly.

Andrews asked, "What's your boyfriend's name, Dulce?"

"Justo Ortega. Except he isn't my boyfriend anymore."

Ainslie touched Brad Andrews's arm. "This is getting complicated. I think you should advise the lady of her rights."

"I was thinking that, too, Sergeant." Andrews faced the young woman. "Dulce, there's a Miranda law. Under it I have to advise you that you do not have to talk to me or answer questions. If you do talk from this point on, it's possible something you say might be taken down and used as evidence—"

Gomez said testily, "I know all about my rights. None of it applies, because I didn't ask that shithead to break in, and what I did was self-defense."

"All the same, I'm required to finish telling you, so please listen."

When Andrews had concluded, Ainslie added, "We don't usually do this, Ms. Gomez, but I strongly recommend you call your lawyer now."

"Why?"

"I'm not saying it will happen, but someone might argue you didn't have to shoot this man, that you'd already protected yourself enough—"

"That's bullshit!" Gomez shouted, then abruptly stopped. "Well, I guess I see what you're saying, even though—"

"We're simply advising you to get a lawyer."

"Look, I'm a working girl; I don't need a lot of big lawyer bills. Leave me alone for a while. I'll sit here and think about it."

Ainslie asked Thurston quietly, "Did you call for a state attorney?"

"Not yet."

"Get one here soon. We need a decision on this."

Thurston nodded and reached for his radio.

The ID crew had arrived and was working quickly. The .22 Cal Rohn pistol retrieved from Dulce Gomez had been sealed in a plastic bag after Thurston had noted the weapon's serial number. He used the apartment telephone, now cleared for use, to talk with Police Headquarters—Communications. "I would like a gun check, please." He described the weapon and serial number, then, responding to a question, "Start with Dade County, then go wider if you have to." Communications had computer access to gun registrations locally, nationally, and, if need be, worldwide.

Thurston waited silently, then was suddenly alert. "No shit! Hey, give me that again." He wrote swiftly in a notebook. "Yeah, I got it all. Thanks a lot."

He made another call, this time to Miami Homicide; it lasted ten minutes. Throughout, Thurston's voice was low but excited. Afterward, he signaled Ainslie and Andrews. The trio huddled in a corner of the apartment living room.

"You won't believe this," Thurston said. "Remember an old case—the Isham murder? Year and a half ago?"

Ainslie said thoughtfully, "Yes, I do. Victim was killed with a bullet from his own gun, but the gun was missing. It was Dion Jacobo's case. Dion had a suspect but, without a weapon, no proof. It's still unsolved."

"Not anymore. We just found the missing weapon."

"Hers?" Andrews gestured to Dulce Gomez.

Thurston nodded, looking pleased. "Communications identified the gun, its original owner, everything. And guess the name of Dion's suspect in the Isham case."

It was Andrews who offered, "Ortega?"

"You got it—one Justo Ortega, the idiot who gave a hot gun to his girlfriend, Dulce. Anyway, I just talked with Dion Jacobo. He knows where Ortega is, and he's getting a warrant to bring him in. With the gun, Dion says, that case is now solid."

"Win some, lose some," Ainslie said. "Nice going, Charlie." He pointed to the body of Quiñones, now covered with a sheet, still lying on the apartment floor. "How do you guys feel about bringing in the girl?"

"Personally I'd hate to tangle with her," Thurston said. "She's as tough as old boots. Just the same, I wouldn't want to see her charged with killing Quinones. In my opinion the creep asked for what he got."

Andrews added, "I go with that."

"I mostly agree with you," Ainslie told them, "though we have to remember that a karate expert's hands and feet are considered deadly weapons. That's why some black belts—which Gomez says she is—are registered with police. So prosecutors might want to go for manslaughter, proving negligence. Anyway, we'll soon know." He nodded toward the outer doorway, where a short, doughty woman in her mid-fifties had just come in and was surveying the scene.

The newcomer, dressed casually in a blue linen skirt and bright yellow blouse, was Mattie Beason, an assistant state attorney and a favorite of Ainslie's. He respected her consistent toughness in court in support of good police work and testimony, though she could be cruelly severe with detectives prior to trial if their preparation and evidence were incomplete or sloppy.

Beason asked, "So what do we have?"

It was Thurston who laid out the details: his and Andrews's surveillance of Quiñones, their quarry's pursuit of Dulce Gomez, the detectives' chase through the apartments, and the death scene discovered in apartment 421.

"Pretty slow in getting after him, weren't you?" Typically, the attorney put her finger on the crucial flaw in Thurston's statement.

He grimaced. "What else can I say except yes?"

"That's honest, anyway. And, fortunately for you, you won't be on trial."

Andrews asked, "Will anybody?"

Ignoring the question, the attorney glanced at Dulce Gomez, still seated by herself, apparently waiting for whatever would happen next. Beason turned to Ainslie. "I suppose you've weighed the karate deadly weapon postulate."

"We were discussing it when you came in."

"Always so thorough, Malcolm." She turned, confronting Andrews. "Before I answer your question, Detective, answer this one. If we charge this young woman with manslaughter in view of her karate skills, what do you see as being in her favor?"

"Okay, counselor." Andrews touched off points on his fingers. "She has a full-time job and attends night school to get ahead—good-citizen stuff. She was minding her own business when that scumbag with an assault and rape record stealthily tailed her. He trespassed in the apartment building and broke down the door to her place when she was alone. Then he came at her with his cock hanging out and a lethal knife in his hand. So what happened? She panicked and, in defending herself, went—maybe legally—too far. But tell all that to a jury and not only will they never convict, they'll fall over themselves to acquit her."

The state attorney permitted herself a smile. "Not bad, Detective. Maybe you should study law." She turned to Ainslie. "You concur?"

He nodded. "Makes sense to me."

"Sure does. So I have two words for you, Malcolm. Forget it! For the record—excusable homicide."

•   •   •

One postscript followed the drama of Carlos Quiñones's death.

A search of his tenement apartment by police revealed he could not have been the serial killer, since he had been out of town when three of the killings occurred and there was nothing to connect him with the others.

Thus, Quiñones was the first to be eliminated from the surveillance suspect list.

•   •   •

Detective-Sergeant Teresa Dannelly and Detective José Garcia did not have murder to contend with during their surveillance. It was the second duty week, and they were observing Alec Polite, a Haitian male living on Northeast 65th Street in Miami's Little Haiti.

Sergeant Dannelly, one of the Robbery detectives assigned temporarily to Homicide, was a tall, thirty-five-year-old brunette with ten years of service and considered a resourceful supervisor. She was sometimes known as "Big Mamma" because of her large bosom, a sobriquet she herself used good-naturedly. Dannelly and José Garcia of Homicide, usually called "Pop," had known each other for eight years and had worked together before.

As for Alec Polite, his FIVO card described him as a fervent Bible-quoter who claimed to talk with God. He was considered aggressive and sometimes violent, though he had no criminal record. His home, a two-story concrete-block house, was shared with four families, including six or seven children.

This was the first time during the surveillance duty that Dannelly and Garcia had been assigned to cover Polite. Until now they had been watching Edelberto Montoya, who had made no suspicious moves.

Their vehicle was parked close to the Northeast 65th Street house, and to the frustration of both detectives, it had already attracted the attention of people on the street as well as curiosity from several children gathered alongside.

As their supposedly "undercover" transport, Dannelly and Garcia had drawn a fancy, bright blue GM Lumina Minivan. The interior was crammed with technical gear, including cameras, telephones, sound recorders, and state-of-the-art transmitters and receivers, their antennae hidden in the van's paneling. The windows were tinted black, so it was impossible for anyone outside to see if the vehicle was occupied. The minivan was experimental and intended for specialized missions, but no other vehicles were available.

"For Christ's sake!" Garcia had groaned when he first saw the sparkling new Lumina and its high-tech contents. "I love the toys, but in Little Haiti we'll stick out like shit on a wedding cake."

Teresa Dannelly had laughed. "More likely the other way around, Pop.

When I saw what we'd drawn, I tried to get it changed, but today there's nothing else. We take this or walk."

Now, at the surveillance site, even more attention was being directed at the Lumina as several people emerged from the two-story house and approached the bright blue vehicle.

"We're gonna have to take off," Garcia said. "This damn thing's like a beacon."

"Let's try something first." On her portable police radio Dannelly selected a secure channel set up for the surveillance operation, and called, "Thirteen-twenty-one to station."

At police headquarters a special dispatcher took the call. "QSK."

"Send a zone car to 265 Northeast Sixty-fifth Street. Instruct unit to stay low-key, no lights or siren, but disperse the small crowd assembled near the building. Ignore blue Lumina van parked nearby."

"QSL." And a moment later, "I am dispatching unit three-two-four to your location."

Two men who had come from the brick house peered in the van windows but obviously could see nothing.

Inside, Garcia whispered, "This is crazy!"

Outside, a third man, gaunt and balding, had joined the others. Dannelly checked an identification photo and announced, "That bald guy is our suspect."

Garcia muttered, "Trouble is, he's surveying us."

The first man who had reached the van tried the door handle. When it wouldn't open he reached into a pocket and produced a heavy screwdriver. His voice, muffled but audible inside, said, "Ain't nobody in there." All three men outside were grouped around the door; the children had moved back.

"I don't believe this," Garcia said. "They're gonna break in."

"If they do, they're in for a surprise." Dannelly had a hand on her service revolver.

It could have become the ultimate paradox if the man with the screwdriver had not looked around to make sure there were no witnesses. What he saw was an approaching police car.

Dannelly said triumphantly, "There's my zone car."

Simultaneously, all three men jumped back and moved away. The newcomer whom Dannelly had identified as their suspect, Alec Polite, slipped while leaving, but managed to support himself briefly on the minivan's hood. Then he, too, disappeared.

The police car stopped and two officers got out and walked around. As usual in Little Haiti when police appeared, everyone scrambled in different directions. One officer glanced at the blue Lumina, then looked away. Moments later the police car left.

"Are we staying or going?" Garcia asked.

"Tell you in a minute." Dannelly used her radio to reach an emergency number for direct contact with the head of the special task force. When Sergeant Malcolm Ainslie answered, she told him, "It's Teresa Dannelly. I have a question."

"Okay, Terry. Shoot."

"At the first serial scene—the Royal Colonial—didn't you have a partial palm print, unidentified?" Typically, Dannelly had taken the trouble to read reports of the serial cases ahead of her surveillance duty.

"Yeah, and it still isn't matched."

"Well, we've got a palm print of Alec Polite, I think. It's on the outside of our van, and it may rain here soon. If we drive somewhere fast, can you arrange to have it checked?"

"Sure can," Ainslie answered. "Drive to the Impound Area and get your van under cover. I'll have someone from ID meet you."

"QSL. Thanks, Malcolm." Then, to José Garcia, who was now seated behind the Lumina's wheel, "Let's get out of here!"

"Hooray for that."

•   •   •

The Miami Police Impound Area, located under the I-95 Freeway near Police Headquarters and protected by a high steel fence, was where vehicles seized by police in raids—especially drug raids—were impounded as evidence. On the way, Garcia said, "That was smart of you to think of the palm print. I didn't see it happen. Was it a good one?"

"I'm pretty sure." Dannelly pointed forward. "It's right about there."

At the Impound Area the detectives were joined by Sylvia Walden. "I took the partial palm print at the Royal Colonial scene," she said. "I understand you may have a match."

"Either that or we'll eliminate a suspect." Dannelly led the way to the parked Lumina and indicated the area she had seen Alec Polite touch. Walden produced her brushes and powders and began work.

An hour later Malcolm Ainslie received a phone call at Homicide headquarters.

"It's Sylvia Walden. I've compared the print from Sergeant Dannelly's van—a good full palm print, by the way—with the partial palm we have from the Royal Colonial scene. There is no resemblance whatever. Sorry."

"Don't be," Ainslie said. "It means we have one less suspect, which helps."

He telephoned Dannelly and reported the result, adding, "Good observation. So we'll stop the surveillance of Alec Polite. He was never a strong candidate anyway. Take a rest, Terry; we'll advise you and José of your next target later today."

• • •

Proving the belief held by detectives that surveillance duty was invariably a gamble, capable of producing results ranging from high drama to slapstick comedy, across town Detectives Hector Fleites and Ogden Jolly had an experience like no other.

Both were on loan from Robbery. Fleites, young and energetic, had ambitions to start a private security business after a few years of learning police work firsthand. On hearing of the special surveillance detail, he had immediately volunteered. Jolly was competent, but more laid-back and with a better sense of humor than Fleites.

The pair's surveillance subject was James Calhoun, known as "Little Jesus" because of a tattooed cross on his chest and his claim to be the second-coming Christ, who would soon be heading back to heaven.

"Meanwhile he's been busy," Detective Jolly had joked. Calhoun had accumulated a criminal record for manslaughter, assault, and armed burglary, and had served two terms in prison. Now on parole, he lived in the Brownsville Projects—one more unofficial name, for a mostly black and Hispanic community adjacent to the Northside Shopping Center. The area was outside the City of Miami and thus beyond the jurisdiction of Miami police. For undercover work, however, official niceties such as informing local police were ignored, which was why Detectives Fleites and Jolly were seated in a Southern Bell phone-repair truck outside a popular disco called the Kampala Stereophonic.

This was the third night they had trailed Calhoun to the same bar, where he apparently joined cronies and drank steadily through the evening. By 9:00 P.M. the detectives had finished their store-bought sandwiches and gulped down several cups of coffee, and were weary and bored, Fleites regretting having volunteered for what he now labeled "a fat-nothing waste of time."

Then they spotted several prostitutes sauntering up the street and looking provocatively around before entering the Kampala. Both detectives recognized the women from their days in uniformed patrol. At the same time a Cadillac quietly pulled into a dimly lit parking lot nearby; it was almost certainly occupied by a pimp who would keep an eye on his girls while farming them out for business. Prostitution rings changed locales and bars from night to night to avoid police interference. The pattern was familiar to detectives.

Evidently word had been sent out to would-be clients, since a series of cars soon arrived. The drivers would enter the Kampala, then reappear with one of the prostitutes, each pair moving to the nearest dark corner, where their shadows merged—though not for long. Clearly this was no high-class boudoir operation.

"Shit!" Fleites said. "If those broads see us they'll go back in and blow our cover."

"Sit way back," Jolly advised. "They won't see us."

"I got to take a leak. Too much coffee, can't wait." Picking a moment when none of the couples was in sight, Fleites left the Southern Bell truck and went down an alley to the rear. When he was finished, he zipped up his trousers and headed out. At the same moment, approaching him in the alley, was a prostitute he had recognized, accompanied by her "trick." Fleites quickly turned back, but the alley dead-ended at a brick wall a few yards away.

Though there was little light, he spotted a Dumpster in the corner. Instinctively Fleites headed for it, pulled himself up, and dropped down inside. A second later, to his disgust, he discovered the Dumpster was filled with some kind of soggy, putrid mess. While he listened for the couple, who had stopped beside the Dumpster, he tried to scrape off what felt like wet potato peelings, fried chicken bones, banana skins, rotten tomatoes, and a soft, rancid-smelling, slimy substance he preferred not to attempt identifying.

Unlike the other couples, the two outside took their time, their sex accompanied by heavy breathing, theatrical "yes, yes"-es, some satisfied sounds, and finally soft conversation. Neither partner seemed in a hurry to move away, and knowing the ways of the business, Fleites guessed that whatever money had been paid by the man was more than usual. Seething with impatience, Fleites wondered if they would ever leave. Finally, after about twenty endless minutes, they did.

When Hector Fleites opened the phone truck door and climbed back in, Jolly looked up, then clapped a hand over his nose and mouth. "Jesus, man— you stink!" Then, peering more closely and seeing the garbage clinging to his colleague from head to foot, Jolly broke into peals of laughter.

Fleites nodded unhappily—about his condition, and knowing there were two things he could not change. First, there were still six hours of surveillance to be endured. Second, Ogden Jolly would forever recount to fellow detectives the story of Fleites going undercover.

•   •   •

At the beginning of the third week of surveillance, Detectives Ruby Bowe and Bernard Quinn met with Malcolm Ainslie at Homicide headquarters. Bowe and Quinn had shared, with two detectives from Robbery, the surveillance of Earl Robinson.

From the beginning Robinson had been a major suspect; everything about his record appeared to fit the nature of the serial killings. His FIVO card described him as "very aggressive." He was a former heavyweight boxer; he preached on streets—always from Revelation—and claimed to be God's judgment angel. His a.k.a. was "Avenger." Robinson's record included armed robbery, second-degree murder, and assaults with a knife.

It was therefore a surprise to Ainslie when Ruby Bowe announced, "All four of us think you should drop Robinson. We're convinced he's harmless. He spends all his free time helping out at a homeless shelter, the Camillus House."

"It's true," Bernard Quinn echoed.

As Bowe described it, all of Robinson's criminality occurred before his adoption of religion a year earlier. From then on he had become a peaceful citizen, holding a regular job and volunteering for civic and charitable causes.

Quinn continued, "In my experience most religious 'conversions' are phony. But I'm convinced this one is genuine."

"We talked to the director of the homeless shelter, David Daxman," Ruby Bowe reported.

"I know him," Ainslie said. "Good man."

"Daxman says he's known Robinson for years and that nowadays he's totally changed." Ruby glanced at her notes. " 'A gentle person who wants to help people' is how Daxman described him. He said Robinson is loved by all the guys at the shelter."

"Okay, cancel Robinson's surveillance," Ainslie instructed. "Scratch him from our list." He leaned back in his chair and sighed.

9

LOOKING BACK LONG AFTERWARD, Malcolm Ainslie remembered those three weeks of surveillance as a kaleidoscopic time when circumstances, most of them unforeseen, conspired to disrupt and complicate the work of everyone involved, especially Ainslie himself.

During the first day of group surveillance Ainslie learned that, as a member of the Miami Police Honor Guard, he was required to spend the next two days on duty at the wake and funeral of City Commissioner Gustav Ernst and his wife, Eleanor. The honor guard, commanded by Captain Warren Underhill, a twenty-year Police Department veteran and former U.S. Army major, comprised a roster of sixty handpicked officers—men and women—chosen for their exemplary police records, physical fitness, and outstanding deportment.

There was seldom a need to activate the honor guard, and the duty normally was not a burden. But for Ainslie it could not have come at a worse time. However, there was no escaping the obligation, as Captain Underhill told him on the phone. "I haven't called on you in quite a while, Malcolm, and I need a senior sergeant as my number two. Also I know you're in charge of the Ernst murder investigation, so it's appropriate for you to be there. Now, I'm sure you're busy as hell, but so is everyone else, and you won't waste your time or mine by offering a bunch of excuses, will you, Sergeant?"

Ainslie chuckled. "If you'd give me a clue, sir, as to which one would work, I'd sure give it a try."

"So you'll be there," Underhill answered crisply.

Ainslie said resignedly, "You know I will."

"Thank you, Sergeant; I appreciate your attitude. There will, of course, be overtime pay."

The Ernst wake, with both bodies in closed coffins, was held at the Klamerus Funeral Home in downtown Miami from noon until 8:00 P.M. Throughout that time six honor guard police in ceremonial uniforms stood at parade rest around the coffins; there were two shifts of guards, each relieved after two hours. Ainslie, who stood every other shift himself, was responsible for the changeovers. It was therefore impossible for him to leave the funeral home, but he kept in touch with surveillance developments as best he could by phone and police radio.

During the wake Ainslie periodically watched Cynthia Ernst as she moved among the flow of some nine hundred viewers throughout the day. She exchanged words with many people and accepted sympathy graciously. Cynthia, too, was in uniform, and must have seen Ainslie, but chose to ignore him.

When the wake finally ended, Ainslie changed out of uniform, then drove to Homicide, where he studied reports of that day's surveillance.

Through most of the next day he had even less time for the investigation.

At 9:00 A.M. the honor guard assembled at Klamerus Funeral Home, where, with military precision, guard members loaded the two coffins into motorized hearses. A procession led by two dozen police motorcycle units and accompanied by thirty patrol cars, all using flashing lights, wended its way to St. Mary's Church, where a funeral service was scheduled for 10:00 A.M.

The enormous church, at North Miami Avenue and 75th Street, was filled to capacity by 9:30 A.M., so that latecomers were obliged to sit on chairs outside, where, through a PA system, they listened to eulogies from the mayor, the governor, Florida's senior U.S. senator, and the church's own archbishop.

Inside, Ainslie watched and listened with waning patience. Yes, he thought, traditionally a city commissioner received an opulent send-off, but surely enough was enough.

Following the service the procession re-formed and headed to Woodlawn Cemetery. By now the train of vehicles included innumerable mourners in limousines, plus additional escorts from other police departments in the county and the Florida Highway Patrol. The procession's total length was an estimated three miles.

At the cemetery the honor guard lowered the coffins into a common grave, to the accompaniment of prayers. Near the ceremony's conclusion, Cynthia Ernst was presented with the two American flags that had draped the coffins.

From beginning to end the funeral proceedings lasted seven hours.

Any Miami city commissioner who died while in office would, as a matter of course, be given an elaborate funeral. But in the case of Commissioner and Mrs. Ernst the occasion was, as a skeptic expressed it later, as if Holly-wood, Disney World, and the Miami Police Department had combined to produce an extravaganza. And as for the large-scale police involvement that created most of the spectacle, perhaps—as a *Miami Herald* columnist theorized the next day—the force had a consciousness of guilt for not having better protected Commissioner Ernst and his wife, plus a further culpability because the Ernsts' killer was still at large and apparently unknown.

The columnist echoed a query that was circulating widely: What are the police doing to solve what they now acknowledge to be serial killings, and why is it taking so long?

That last question was on Malcolm Ainslie's mind throughout the long hours of the wake and funeral. Each time his gaze drifted over the pair of coffins, he remembered the bodies inside, so cruelly mutilated, and asked himself somberly, *Who? Why? Where next?*

●   ●   ●

Two days after the Ernst funeral an announcement was made on behalf of the Miami City Commission, which, bereft of Gustav Ernst, now consisted of the mayor, the vice-mayor, and two commissioners. Under the city's charter, the announcement pointed out, in the event of the death of a city commissioner, the remaining commissioners would, within ten days and by majority vote, appoint a successor to serve out the ex-commissioner's remaining time. In the case of Gustav Ernst this was two years, half the full term.

The announcement further stated that by unanimous vote the commission had named the deceased's daughter, Cynthia Ernst, to complete her father's term. A second accompanying announcement reported that Major Ernst had accepted the appointment and would resign immediately from the Miami police force.

After completing her father's term, Ms. Ernst would have to stand, if she chose, for public reelection. But as Detective Bernard Quinn said, during a discussion within Homicide on the subject, "Of course she'll run. And how can she possibly lose?"

Ainslie had mixed feelings about Cynthia's status change. On the one hand he was relieved that in terms of police rank she would no longer have authority over him, nor would he report to her about the serial killings. But on the other, instinct told him that her influence in the Police Department could conceivably increase.

●   ●   ●

Ainslie knew better than to expect quick results from the surveillance program. By the beginning of the third week, however, he was concerned that the only progress—if it could be called that, he mused gloomily—was the elimination of suspects Carlos Quiñones, Alec Polite, and Earl Robinson.

During the following week there was some doubt about the viability of
Elroy Doil as a suspect. According to Detectives Dan Zagaki and Luis
Linares, and confirming his FIVO report, Doil was working regularly as a
free-lance truck driver; he appeared increasingly unlikely to be the serial
killer. Zagaki had gone further and recommended that Doil be dropped as a
suspect, but Ainslie had disagreed.

Beyond that there were James Calhoun and Edelberto Montoya, still possibles but not yet probables, the whole picture raising doubts among the
increasingly bored detectives—doubts that Ainslie silently shared. Was the
computerized search for suspects, which originally seemed an excellent idea,
actually a misguided waste of time? Eventually he shared the thought with
Lieutenant Newbold, adding, "It's easy to give up now, maybe too easy, which
is why I hate to do it. My inclination is to go one more week, then, if there's
nothing conclusive, quit."

The lieutenant leaned back in his office chair, tilting it precariously, as he
often did. "I've been backing you, Malcolm, because I trust your judgment
and knew you'd come to me with any problems. You know I'll support you if
you feel we really should go on. But I'm getting pressure from Robbery. They
want their guys back."

Ainslie had twice seen Lieutenant Daniel Huerta, Robbery's commander,
in Newbold's office, and the reason was easy to guess. It would be Christmas
soon—a time when robberies increased by as much as fifty percent—and the
Robbery Department's case load would be building. In Homicide, too,
where, because of the surveillance program, every detective was working
heavy overtime, there were similar pressures.

Between them, Ainslie and Newbold decided on a compromise. The third
week of surveillance would continue, though because of the elimination of
three suspects, four detectives from Robbery, including the two sergeants,
would be released. Then, at the end of the third week, Ainslie would decide
whether or not to go for a fourth, and whatever the decision, Lieutenant
Newbold would support it. He told Ainslie, "Major Yanes committed the
extra troops to us. If I have to, I'll beat down his door and remind him."

Those arrangements, as agreed, continued for two more days. Then an
event occurred that swept everything else aside.

It began shortly before noon on Thursday.

At Coral Way and 32nd Avenue, outside a Barnett Bank branch, a Wells
Fargo armored truck pulled into a parking lot alongside the bank to make a
cash delivery. Moments later one of two security guards inside the truck
opened the side door and was confronted by three males—one black and two
Hispanic, according to witnesses—all armed with automatic weapons.

At that precise moment a Miami Police patrol car rounded a corner and directly faced the robbery scene. The robbers saw the police first and opened fire before the officers were even aware a crime was taking place. One police officer died instantly in the hail of bullets; the second, his gun partly drawn, was wounded as he attempted to leave the car. The robbers shot and killed the Wells Fargo security guard and grabbed a bag of money he was carrying. Then they rushed to their own car and sped away. The entire episode lasted less than a minute.

As the robbers left, a bystander named Tomas Ramirez—a tall, athletic young man, no more than twenty—rushed to the now-unconscious policeman. Observing a portable radio protruding from the wounded officer's gun belt, Ramirez grabbed it and pressed a button at the side.

In the police Communication Center his first message was received and logged.

"Hello, hello. This is Tom Ramirez. Is anybody there?"

A woman dispatcher responded calmly, "Yes, I am. Where did you get the police radio? Is everything all right?"

"No, my God, it isn't! There's been a robbery and shooting here at the bank. Two policemen are shot. Send some help, please."

"Okay, sir. Do not push the button at the side while I am talking. Where are you? Please give me your location." The dispatcher was typing into a computer while she talked, her report repeated on the computer screens of six other dispatchers in the communication center.

"Uh, I'm at Coral Way and Thirty-second Avenue, in the parking lot of the Barnett Bank. One policeman and the guard look dead, I think the other policeman's dying. Hurry, please."

Other dispatchers, reading their computer monitors, were already summoning help.

The first dispatcher replied, "Sir, we are on the way. Have the suspects left?"

"Yes, they jumped into their car—a gray Buick Century. There were three of them. They all had guns. They really shot up the policemen. They look dead."

"Okay, sir. Try to calm down. We need your help."

Another dispatcher had turned switches, opening the way for a BOLO. It would reach all county and state police and every other law enforcement agency. The call was preceded by a five-second loud continuous tone, signaling its importance and priority. The tone and message following would override all other transmissions everywhere.

"Attention all units. A three-two-nine just occurred at Coral Way and

Thirty-second Avenue, Barnett Bank. There are reports of at least two officers down. Suspects left the scene in a gray Buick Century."

The number "three" in the message indicated emergency; the "two-nine"
was a signal code for robbery.

From every part of the city, police units began converging at high speed
on the Barnett Bank at Coral Way. As a TV reporter commented soon after,
"When a cop gets shot, everyone heads for the scene. There are no holds
barred. All hell breaks loose."

By now another dispatcher had summoned Fire-Rescue—ambulances
and paramedics.

The first dispatcher: "Mr. Ramirez, are you still there?"

"Yes. I can hear sirens. Thank God they're coming."

"Sir, were you able to get any description of the suspects?"

"I got the license. NZD six-two-one, a Florida plate."

The dispatcher, quickly transferring the information to her computer,
thought, *This guy is one good citizen!*

Another dispatcher promptly sent a second BOLO, again preceded by the
five-second priority tone, with the license number of the suspects' car.

"Mr. Ramirez, did you see what the suspects looked like?"

"I got a pretty good look. Yes, I can describe them."

"That's excellent, sir. Please stay there until a unit arrives, and give them
that information."

"They're all arriving now. Thank God!"

●   ●   ●

Homicide's Lieutenant Newbold, driving with his radio on channel three,
heard the Ramirez call for help. Newbold immediately switched his radio to
the special surveillance channel and called Ainslie, whose voice, also from a
car, came back promptly.

"QSK, Lieutenant."

"Malcolm, take all your people off surveillance. Get them to Coral Way
and Thirty-second Avenue. Two policemen and a security guard have been
shot in an armored truck robbery, one policeman and the guard reported
DOA. I want you to handle it. Assign whoever you want to lead."

Ainslie permitted himself a silent *Damn!*—knowing this unexpected new
priority meant the surveillance program was going down the tubes. Aloud, he
transmitted, "Okay, Lieutenant. I'll take my units."

The surveillance teams, monitoring the same channel, should have
heard the exchange, but Ainslie called, "Thirteen-ten to all units. Did you
hear that?"

"Thirteen-eleven to thirteen-ten. Heard it." The other teams on duty made identical reports.

"Then go to Coral Way and Thirty-second, guys. I'll meet you there."

Switching channels, Ainslie called, "Thirteen-ten to dispatcher. Ask any unit on the shooting scene to go to Tac One for me." Tac One was the Homicide channel.

A familiar voice responded from the Barnett Bank scene: "Thirteen-ten, this is one-seven-zero. QSK."

Ainslie asked, "Is this Bart?" Bartolo Esposito was a uniform patrol sergeant, but last names were never used on radio, mainly because the media was listening.

"Sure is, Malcolm. We got big trouble here. What do you want me to do?"

"Rope off the scene, as big an area as you can, and keep everyone away."

"It's being cleared now, except for Fire-Rescue. They're trying to stabilize the wounded officer before transporting."

"Thanks, Bart. I'll be there shortly."

Ainslie returned to channel three and asked the dispatcher to get ID to the scene.

"Doing that now, thirteen-ten."

On another channel Ainslie summoned a state attorney.

•   •   •

On arriving at the Barnett Bank, Malcolm Ainslie appointed Detective Ruby Bowe as lead investigator. She immediately began questioning several witnesses, including Tomas Ramirez, who supplied a surprisingly good description of the three gunmen, now widely sought fugitives. Despite that information, and the earlier description of the getaway car and license number, the suspects had not been seen, so it seemed likely they had gone into hiding, probably not far away.

Only minutes after Lieutenant Newbold reached the crime scene, Lieutenant Daniel Huerta of Robbery arrived, too. His first words to Newbold were, "I know this is now your scene, Leo, but I need all my people back immediately."

"You got 'em," Newbold told him.

They agreed that Robbery could probably help in identifying the suspects, who most likely had previous robbery records.

Though no one said so, there was always a competitive edge between Robbery and Homicide. Neither side, however, was foolish enough to let rivalry impede an investigation.

As all leads were followed, evidence and information accumulated, including positive identification of the three killers by several witnesses who had pored over mug shots from police files. The charges would now be triple murder, because the wounded second policeman had since died.

Tips from informants about possible hideaways resulted in raids—unproductive until two of the offenders were spotted going into a first-floor apartment, part of an abandoned residential complex in the Deep Grove area, a seedy adjunct to Coconut Grove. Local residents who had seen the suspects called police.

Shortly before dawn on the third day after the robbery and murders, a SWAT team converged on the apartment, where all three men were sleeping. Though still heavily armed, the men were taken by surprise, handcuffed, and their weapons seized. The bag of money stolen from the armored truck was recovered, and the Buick Century used in the robbery was found two blocks away.

●   ●   ●

Ainslie now knew there was no chance of reviving the surveillance, and wasn't sure it was such a bad thing, given the disappointing results so far. Instead he concentrated on reviewing all the serial crimes. Contrary to his hopes, no leads or fresh ideas developed.

Then the unexpected happened.

Three days after the armored truck perpetrators were arrested, when routines in Homicide were beginning to return to normal, the Dade County assistant medical examiner phoned Malcolm Ainslie.

Sandra Sanchez said, "When we last met, Malcolm, I promised to look among old autopsy records for any unresolved deaths with similar wound patterns. Well, I have, and I'm sorry it took so long, but what I've been searching through is old stuff, papers that aren't computerized—"

"Don't apologize," Ainslie said. "The point is, have you found anything?"

"Yes, I think so. It's in a file with a lot of other material, and I've sent the whole lot over to you by messenger. The case is an old, unsolved killing seventeen years ago, with two elderly victims named Esperanza—Clarence and Florentina."

"Are any suspects named?"

"There's one. But look, I don't want to tell you any more because you must read through the file. Call me when you're finished."

The file arrived a short time later. As Sanchez had indicated, it contained a lot of paper. Without expecting too much, Ainslie opened the now-faded cover and began to read.

The Esperanzas were both in their early seventies and lived in the Happy

Haven Trailer Park in West Dade. Their bodies, discovered by a neighbor, were gagged and bound and in seated positions, facing each other. Both the man and woman had been brutally beaten and had suffered deep knife cuts. The official cause of both deaths was exsanguination—loss of blood resulting from wounds.

Ainslie skipped through the remaining medical papers, then found a copy of a police report that revealed the Esperanzas were comfortably off, though not wealthy. They had three thousand dollars in a bank account and, according to a nephew who lived nearby, the couple usually had several hundred dollars in cash on hand for their immediate needs. After the murders, no cash whatever was found.

At the back of the file, as Ainslie flipped more pages, he saw a familiar Form 301—a Homicide investigation report. It concerned a juvenile suspect who had been interrogated concerning the Esperanzas' deaths, then released for lack of evidence.

A name on the 301 leaped out at him. Elroy Doil.

10

I N CONFORMITY WITH FLORIDA LAW, Elroy Doil's juvenile crime record had been sealed when he reached the age of eighteen. At that point it became inaccessible to investigators except with a judicial order, which was rarely granted. Similar laws existed in most other states.

In Malcolm Ainslie's opinion, shared by many in law enforcement, the procedure was a legal anachronism, absurdly out of date, and a brazen disservice to law-abiding citizens. During a meeting with Lieutenant Newbold the morning after the discovery of Elroy Doil's name on the old Form 301, Ainslie spread out papers on the lieutenant's desk, his anger barely contained.

"This is insane! There are things here we should have known a year ago."

An hour earlier he had unearthed a file on the unsolved Esperanza killings from a storeroom containing old records. It was not a complete accounting because the crime occurred outside Miami, in Metro-Dade territory. But inquiries had extended across borders, and Miami Homicide opened its own Esperanza file, which included some Metro-Dade memos about the crime. It was among the latter that Ainslie found reference to the interrogation of Doil, which Sandra Sanchez had reported. But without the Sanchez tip there would have been no reason to disinter the long-ago file.

"Of course," Newbold pointed out, "Doil was never arrested or charged."

"Because his mother was smart enough not to let Elroy be fingerprinted. A knife was found near the murder scene with fingerprints on it, and both victims' blood. A bowie knife. Metro-Dade Homicide wanted to compare those prints with Doil's, and they were pretty sure they'd match. But because there wasn't enough evidence for an arrest, plus Elroy being a juvenile, it never happened."

Newbold agreed, "That's sure a lot of coincidence."

"Coincidence? The Esperanza MO at that trailer camp was the same as we're seeing now. The way the bodies have been found—gagged, facing each other—then the beatings, knife cuts, stolen money. If we'd had Doil's early records, those MO's would have been matched and we'd have been all over him long ago." Ainslie leaned forward staring fiercely. "Do you know how many lives we might have saved?"

Newbold stood up and glared back. "Hey, Sergeant, they're not *my* laws! Now back off!"

Ainslie slumped into the chair behind him and sighed. "Sorry. But, Leo, our whole juvenile system is crazy, not just in Florida but everywhere. There *isn't* just juvenile crime anymore; at whatever age, it's plain, simple crime— you know it as well as I do. Every day we see murders committed by kids— fourteen, fifteen, sixteen, for God's sake! Or younger. Of all weapons arrests, more than half involve teenagers. In Detroit a woman was murdered by boys of eleven and fourteen. Two twelve-year-olds in Chicago threw a kid of five from a high-rise. In England two ten-year-old boys killed a two-year-old. It's the same with robberies, assaults, rapes, carjackings, you name it. Yet here we are, policemen, law enforcers, handcuffed by this ridiculous, archaic system that should have been thrown out years ago."

"You're suggesting that juvenile records shouldn't be sealed at all?"

"Damn right I am! Every crime should go on record, stay there, and be available to investigators from that point on. If parents and the ACLU don't like it, screw 'em! You break the law, it goes on your record. That's the price to be paid—that *should* be paid—no matter what your age."

"There's been talk in the Department about petitioning state government along those lines," Newbold said. "Send me a memo with the details about Doil, plus your opinions, and I'll pass it on. Then, if there's a public hearing, I'll recommend you as a witness, and you can sound off all you want."

"I'll write the memo," Ainslie said. "But I doubt they'd want me to appear."

Newbold said sharply, "Don't write that off, or yourself, either." His eyes met Ainslie's directly. "My influence isn't as great as that of some other people we know. But I have friends, upstairs and upstate, who listen to me."

So, Ainslie thought, Newbold knew about Cynthia Ernst blocking his promotion, and had probably guessed the rest. None of it surprised Ainslie. The Police Department could be a small place, where rumors and gossip ran rampant, leaping departmental barriers and every rank.

"So what do you plan next?" Newbold asked. "You'll seek an order to have Doil's record opened, I presume."

"I'm working on that now. I've phoned Curzon Knowles; he's drafting the affidavit. I'll take it to Judge Powell. We don't want this talked about yet, and he won't ask too many questions."

"Your buddy Phelan Powell?" Newbold smiled. "As I recall, His Honor has obliged you often. If I asked what you've got on him, you wouldn't tell me, of course."

"I'm his illegitimate son," Ainslie deadpanned.

Newbold laughed. "That would mean he knocked up your mother when he was what? Twelve? So it's something else, but never mind. In this game we all accumulate our debits and credits."

On that score, of course, Newbold was right.

•   •   •

Many years before, when Detective Ainslie was new on plainclothes duty, he and his partner, Ian Deane, drove into an alley one night and saw a light blue Cadillac ahead. As they drew closer, a partially naked white male emerged from the driver's side, hurriedly pulling on trousers, and from the other side appeared a scantily dressed young black girl. The detectives recognized both. The girl was a prostitute named Wanda, the man a circuit court judge, Phelan Powell, before whom both detectives had appeared as witnesses on numerous occasions. Powell was tall and athletically built and normally had a commanding personality. This moment was an exception.

He and Wanda shielded their eyes from the headlights, trying desperately to recognize the figures emerging from the car behind them.

As Ainslie and Deane moved closer, momentarily blocking the lights, Wanda emitted a resigned, "Oh fuck!" The judge, in contrast, looked dazed. Then, slowly, the reality of his predicament crystallized.

"Oh my God! Detectives." His voice was desperate and strained. "I beg of you—please, please overlook this! I've been an idiot . . . gave in to sudden temptation. This isn't my way, but if you report it, I'll be disgraced, finished!" He paused and the three men exchanged awkward glances. "Officers, if you'll just let this pass, this one time, please! . . . I'll never forget . . . And whatever I can do for you, I will."

Fleetingly, Ainslie wondered how the judge would have responded to his own plea.

In fact, if an arrest had been made by Ainslie and Deane, or a citation issued, the charges against Powell would have been "soliciting a prostitute" and "loitering and prowling." Both were misdemeanors, for which, assuming this was a first offense, the penalty at most would be a fine; the charge might even be dismissed. But the judge's judicial career would be over.

Ainslie, who was the senior officer, hesitated. He knew the principle of law: justice should be blind, never drawing distinctions. On the other hand . . .

Without analyzing, or consciously debating a decision, Ainslie said to Deane, "I think I heard a radio call. We should get back to the car."

And so, the detectives left.

Over the years that followed, nothing was ever said, by Ainslie or Judge Powell, about that incident. Ainslie told no one, and Detective Ian Deane was killed soon afterward in a shootout during an Overtown drug raid.

But the judge kept his promise. Whenever Ainslie appeared before him as arresting officer or witness, he was treated with utmost courtesy and consideration. There were also times when Ainslie had gone to Judge Powell, seeking quick judicial action in a matter of investigative importance, and he invariably received it—as he hoped to do now.

Before leaving Homicide, Ainslie phoned the judge's office. Across the years, Phelan Powell had advanced in the judiciary and was now a member of the Third District Court of Appeals. Ainslie explained the situation to a secretary and after a short wait was told, "The judge is about to begin a hearing. But if you come to the court he'll call a recess and see you in chambers."

* * *

On the way, Ainslie stopped at the state attorney's office, where Curzon Knowles had prepared the required form. When signed by Judge Powell, it would unseal the juvenile record of Elroy Doil. The whole procedure was complicated and time-consuming—another reason why it seldom happened.

* * *

A bailiff in the Third District courtroom had obviously been given orders, and the moment Ainslie appeared he was escorted to a front-row seat. Judge Powell looked up, nodded, and almost at once announced, "Let us take a fifteen-minute recess. An urgent matter has come up that requires my attention."

Everyone in court then rose, the judge retired through a door behind him, and the same bailiff escorted Ainslie to the judge's chambers.

Judge Powell, already at his desk, looked up, smiling. "Come in; it's good to see you, Sergeant." He motioned Ainslie to a chair. "Let me guess—Miami Homicide is still in business."

"For all eternity—the way it looks, Your Honor." Seated, facing Phelan Powell, Ainslie described his mission. The judge was still an imposing figure, though over the years he had put on weight and his hair was almost white. Along with the signs of age were symptoms of strain; Ainslie supposed it went with the job. Appeal courts nowadays were heavily burdened, and even high rankers like Powell could be reversed by another appeal level above them— supporting the view, some said, that little had changed since Dickens wrote, "The law is a ass."

At the end of Ainslie's spiel, Powell nodded. "Okay, Sergeant, happy to help you out. Just to make everything regular, I should ask why you want this juvenile record unsealed."

"The record was sealed twelve years ago, Your Honor. Mr. Doil is now a suspect in a serious crime, and we believe some earlier details will help our investigation."

"So be it. Let's break that seal. I see you've brought the papers."

Ainslie passed them across.

In front of any other judge, he knew, the answer he had given to the single question would be dismissed as inadequate. And there would be other questions, more intense, perhaps even combative. Judges loved their prerogatives; many insisted on a verbal fencing match before approving anything. But what Ainslie wanted was a minimal number of people to know that Elroy Doil was now a prime suspect in the serial killings. The fact that Ainslie had not had to explain more details meant there was less chance that the opening of Doil's record would be talked about, or that Doil himself would find out he was under suspicion.

"All this looks in order," Judge Powell said. "Now the ritual is, I have to swear you in, but since we've known each other so long, let's take that for granted. You know the terms of the oath, and I've sworn you in. Okay?"

"I'm duly sworn, Your Honor."

A fast signing by Powell and it was done.

"I'd like to stay longer and talk," the judge said, "but they're waiting for me out there, and the lawyers are on metered time. You know how it is."

"Yes, Judge. And thank you."

They shook hands. At the doorway Powell turned back.

"Any other time you need my help, don't hesitate to come. You know I mean that—any time."

As the judge disappeared through his private doorway to the bench, Ainslie heard the bailiff's call: "All rise!"

•   •   •

Criminal Records was in the Metro-Dade Police Department Building, west of Miami International Airport. There, after more form filling and signing, the juvenile file of Elroy Doil was produced and opened in Ainslie's presence. He was free to study the file in a private room down the hall. He could make whatever copies he needed, but not take any part of the file away.

The file was bulkier than he'd expected. When he examined the papers, it became evident that Doil's skirmishes with the law were far greater than even Ainslie had believed.

He counted thirty-two apprehensions by police (with juveniles the word "arrest" was not used), resulting in twenty misdemeanor convictions, undoubtedly a mere sampling of the total number of offenses Doil had committed in his young life.

The record began when Elroy was ten years old—a charge of shoplifting a Timex watch. At eleven he was panhandling on a street corner, begging for money at his mother's instigation, and was taken home by police. At twelve he assaulted a woman teacher, inflicting bruises and a cut lip that required stitches. After questioning by the police, Elroy was released to his mother, Beulah Doil—a pattern that continued for years and was common with juvenile offenders. A few months later, Elroy was involved with a street gang specializing in purse snatching, and again he was apprehended, then "released to mother." Another purse snatching at thirteen was accompanied by an assault on an elderly woman—with the same outcome.

What the Doil file demonstrated, Ainslie thought, was that most juvenile crime was simply not taken seriously, either by police or the courts. He knew from his own experience that a police officer could "apprehend" a juvenile at 9:00 A.M. and before the officer went off duty at 3:00 P.M. the same offender would be back on the streets. In the meantime the parents would have been called to Police Headquarters, where the juvenile was released to their custody—incident closed.

Even when a juvenile was taken to court, penalties were minor—usually a few days' detention at Youth Hall, a not-unpleasant place where the kids stayed in fairly comfortable rooms, played video games, and watched TV.

Many believed the overall system, or lack of it, spawned lifelong criminals who became convinced, as minors, that crime was incredibly easy to get away with. Even the counselors of juveniles shared that belief and confirmed it in reports.

Counselors were assigned to juvenile offenders after two apprehensions. These were underpaid, overworked individuals with little or no special training, and of whom a college degree was not required. Each counselor, burdened with an impossibly large caseload, was expected to give advice to juveniles and parents—advice that was largely ignored.

Elroy Doil apparently had the same counselor, one Herbert Elders, throughout his juvenile crime career. The file contained several single-page sheets headed INFORMATION REPORT ONLY, all written by Elders, who seemed to have done his best in difficult circumstances. One report, written when Doil was "thirteen, but big for his age and very strong," warned of "a probability of long-term violence." The same report noted "indifference" from Doil's mother when confronted with the problem.

Ainslie was especially interested in an episode in which Doil, then thirteen, was caught torturing a cat to death. He had cut off the cat's legs one by one, then its tail, using a knife that, according to the report, he habitually carried. He was caught watching the cat writhe in agony as it died. This produced a charge of "cruelty to an animal," resulting in a fine of a hundred dollars. The record did not say who paid it.

Another "Information Report Only," also by Elders, referred to Elroy's involvement at age twelve in Operation Guidance, a city-sponsored program for underprivileged kids. Father Kevin O'Brien directed the program at Miami's Gesu Church; it included meals, sports, and Bible study every Sunday in the church's fenced-in grounds. Elders referred hopefully to Elroy's "awakening interest in religion and the Bible."

However, another report a year and a half later recorded dismally that religion had not curbed Doil's misdemeanors, nor had his religious-biblical fervor, which, according to Father O'Brien, was "erroneous and incoherent."

Ainslie scribbled down Father O'Brien's phone number and address.

Across the remaining years until Doil reached eighteen, the record showed an orgy of offenses, none of which had ever required Doil to be fingerprinted. A juvenile's fingerprints could only be taken after an arrest for a felony or with a parent's permission, which, according to the file, Beulah Doil consistently refused to give.

It was that absence of fingerprints that left Homicide hamstrung in the final report in the file, where Doil was a strong suspect in the murders of Clarence and Florentina Esperanza. But without prints or other supporting evidence, no charge was laid.

The Homicide detectives' frustration at that time was easy to envisage, Ainslie thought, as he closed the file and headed for a copy machine.

• • •

Using a phone at Metro-Dade headquarters, Ainslie called the number he had written down, and Father O'Brien answered personally. Yes, he told Ainslie, he remembered Elroy well, and would be willing to talk about him. In fact, if the sergeant wished to drive to Gesu Church now, the priest was in his office and available.

• • •

Father Kevin O'Brien, a bright-eyed Irishman, now middle-aged and balding, gestured to the wooden chair facing his desk.

Ainslie sat down, thanked the priest for seeing him, then briefly described his interest in Doil, adding, "I'm not here for evidence, Father. I simply wonder if you could tell me a bit about him."

O'Brien nodded thoughtfully. "I remember Elroy as if I'd seen him yesterday. I think, initially, he enrolled in our program because he needed the meals, but after a few weeks he seemed to become mesmerized by the Bible—much more than any of the other kids."

"Was he intelligent?"

"Extremely. But in his own way. And a voracious reader, which surprised me, given his marginal education. Now that I think about it, I remember he had a fascination with crime and violence—first in the newspapers, then later in the Bible." O'Brien smiled. "It was the Old Testament that absorbed him, with all its 'holy wars' and God's wrath, pursuit, revenge, and killing. Are you familiar with all that, Detective?"

Ainslie nodded. "Yes, I am." In fact, from memory, he thought, he could have put together the kind of passages that would have attracted Doil.

"I saw great possibilities in young Doil," O'Brien said, "and for a while I thought we had real communication, but in the end we didn't. We talked about the Bible, but he twisted words, including mine, to mean whatever he wanted. He lusted to be an avenger for God, though redressing, I suspect, what he saw as life's offenses against himself. I tried reasoning, pointing out God's love and forgiveness. He didn't listen; more and more he became incoherent. I wish I'd done better."

"I think you did all you could, Father," Ainslie said. "Do you think Doil has some mental disorder? Is insanity too strong a word?"

"Probably." The priest considered. "We all have aberrations; they come in differing packages, and experts decide where aberrations end and madness begins. Thinking back, one thing I'm sure of is that Elroy was a pathological liar. He lied when he didn't have to. He'd tell lies to me, for example, even when he knew I was aware of the truth. It's as if he had an aversion to the truth about anything, no matter how benign."

O'Brien concluded, "I'm not sure I can give you much more. He was simply a boy on the wrong track, and I gather, from the fact that you're here, he hasn't changed course."

"I'm not sure," Ainslie answered. "Father, I have one more question. Did you ever have reason to believe Doil carried a gun? Or any other weapon?"

"Yes," O'Brien said at once. "I remember that very well. Most of the boys in my program talked constantly about guns, though I forbade them to bring any here. But Doil disdained guns and said so. I don't know why, though I was told he did carry a knife—something big, I believe, which he boasted about to his friends."

"Did you ever see the knife?"

"Of course not. I would have confiscated it if I had."

Shaking hands with Father O'Brien as he left, Ainslie said, "Thank you for your help. Elroy Doil is an enigma, but you've helped put a few pieces in place."

• • •

Ainslie returned to Homicide headquarters in the early afternoon, having driven some thirty miles to various ports of call in his quest for information. He immediately summoned a meeting of selected members of the special task force for 4:00 P.M. that day. The list, which he handed to a secretary, comprised Sergeants Pablo Greene and Hank Brewmaster, as well as Detectives Bernard Quinn, Ruby Bowe, Esteban Kralik, José Garcia, Dion Jacobo, Charlie Thurston, Seth Wightman, Gus Janek, and Luis Linares. Each of them had been involved in the surveillance duty.

Dan Zagaki, another Homicide detective who had been part of the surveillance, was not included on the list. When Zagaki showed up in Homicide during the afternoon, Ainslie took the young detective to an empty office for a private talk. Zagaki was clearly uneasy as he sat down.

A comparative newcomer, Zagaki had been promoted to detective and assigned to Homicide two months earlier, moving up from uniform patrol duty, where his two-year record since recruitment had been excellent. He was from a distinguished military family, his father a U.S. Army general, an older brother a Marine lieutenant colonel. Since his Homicide arrival, Zagaki had demonstrated eagerness and energy—perhaps too much of both, Ainslie reflected now.

"When we were doing our surveillance," Ainslie said, "you reported to me that Elroy Doil was probably not our killer. You recommended we eliminate him as a suspect and discontinue surveillance. Is that correct?"

"Well, yes, Sergeant. But my partner, Luis Linares, felt the same way."

"Not entirely. When I talked with Linares he said he agreed with you that Doil was an unlikely candidate, but he wasn't in favor of ending his surveillance. His words were, 'I wouldn't go that far.' "

Zagaki looked crestfallen. "I was wrong, wasn't I? I guess you're about to tell me that."

Ainslie's voice sharpened. "Yes, very wrong—dangerously wrong, in fact. Recommendations by detectives are taken seriously here, though fortunately I didn't act on yours. Now I want you to read these." He handed Zagaki a sheaf of papers. They included the Form 301 from Sandra Sanchez, a report from the seventeen-year-old Homicide file on the Esperanza murders, with Doil named as the principal suspect, and three copied pages from Doil's juvenile file.

At length Zagaki looked up, his expression anguished. "Oh boy, how wrong can you get! What will you do, Sergeant—have me thrown out of Homicide?"

Ainslie shook his head. "This is between us; it goes no further. But if you want to stay in Homicide, you'd better learn from what's happened. You've got to take your time making these kind of judgments; you can't come to conclusions solely on appearances. Be a skeptic—always. Remember that most of the time, everywhere in life, things are seldom the way they seem."

"I sure will remember, Sergeant. And thanks for not taking this further."

Ainslie nodded. "One other thing you should know: I've called a meeting this afternoon to revive the surveillance on Elroy Doil. You will probably hear about it, but I've taken you off the list."

Zagaki looked pained. "Sergeant, I may be out of line, because I know I'm getting what I deserve. But is there any way I could persuade you to give me another chance? I won't screw up this time, I promise."

Ainslie hesitated. His judgment told him to stay with his decision. He still had doubts about Zagaki. Then Ainslie remembered his own early days in the force when he had made mistakes, and he supposed there was a forgiveness factor—a canon from his past that had never entirely left him.

"All right," he conceded. "Be here at four o'clock."

I **TAKE IT WE ALL AGREE ON OUR** prime suspect," Ainslie said.

There was a murmured chorus of assent from the twelve other members of the special task force crowded into Newbold's office. The lieutenant stood against the back wall, having told Ainslie to take over his desk and chair.

The task force of three sergeants, including Ainslie, and ten detectives sat in chairs or perched on window ledges and tabletops, or simply leaned against the wall. As the meeting progressed, Ainslie sensed the team's excitement, revived by the crucial information revealed through Sandra Sanchez and Elroy Doil's now-exposed juvenile crime record.

On hearing of Doil's criminal past, Sergeant Greene had exploded. "That goddam system! It's insane, a public menace—"

Ainslie cut him off. "The lieutenant and I have been over that, Pablo. We agree with you; a lot of people do, and we hope to see some changes. But for the time being, we have to work with the system as it is. In any case, we have Doil's record now."

Greene, though still simmering, muttered, "Okay."

"The first thing," Ainslie informed the group, "is to resume the surveillance of Doil immediately. So I'd like you, Pablo, and Hank to make up a duty schedule. I suggest you work out the next forty-eight hours right here, so you can tell us before we leave. I'll take my turn with the rest of you. Pair me with Zagaki."

Brewmaster nodded. "Got it, Malcolm."

"We need to remember two things about the surveillance," Ainslie continued. "One is to be damn careful Doil doesn't catch on to us. At the same time, we have to stay close enough that we don't lose him. It'll be a balancing act, but we all know what's at stake here.

"Oh, one other thing," Ainslie instructed the sergeants. "Don't put Detective Bowe on the duty schedule. I have some other work for her."

He turned to Ruby Bowe, who was standing near the door. "I want you to check on Elroy Doil's employment record, Ruby. We know he's a truck driver and works for different companies. We want to know which ones. Also, who was employing him, where was he, and what was he doing during the days of each serial killing? You'll have to be low-key because we don't want anyone telling him we're asking questions."

"It will help," Ruby said, "if I can get all the information we have on Doil, including the surveillance reports so far."

"I'll have copies made for you right after this meeting." Ainslie faced the others. "Is there any discussion? Any questions?"

When there was none, he pronounced, "Then let's get on with it."

•   •   •

The surveillance of Elroy Doil lasted three weeks and two days. Much of the continuous twenty-four-hour vigil by detectives was, as always, uneventful and often boring. At other times it was challenging, particularly when they were trying not to be spotted by the suspect. And throughout that time the weather proved the most miserable of the entire year. Shortly before the watch program began, a cold front moved eastward from Texas into southern Florida and sat in place for two straight weeks. It brought high winds and intermittent, drenching rain that made the task of following Doil, who drove trucks much of the time, unusually difficult. If the surveillance vehicle stayed too close for too long, Doil might notice it in his rearview mirror. On the other hand, in heavy rain with poor visibility, there was an equal danger of losing him if he got too far ahead.

In part the dilemma was solved by using two surveillance vehicles, and occasionally three, each communicating with the others by radio. After staying close to Doil for a while, one vehicle would drop back while another moved forward, taking its place. In police parlance, leapfrogging.

The three-vehicle mix, usually a commercial undercover unit and two innocuous-looking cars, was used for several out-of-town journeys Doil made for trucking companies that employed him as a temporary driver. On a journey to Orlando the six trailing detectives, two in each vehicle, all lost sight of him just after entering that city amid pounding rain. The three vehicles scoured downtown streets, cursing the poor visibility. Finally Detectives Charlie Thurston and Luis Linares, using an undercover Postal Service van, caught up with Doil. They spotted him through the window of a pizza bar, where he was eating alone, his massive shoulders hunched over a plate of food. The truck was parked nearby.

After Thurston had reported to the others by radio, Linares grumbled, "Hell! This caper ain't getting us nowhere. Could go on for years."

"Tell you what, Luis," Thurston told him. "You walk over to old Doil and tell him that. Just say, 'Hey, stupid, we're tired of this shit. Stop fucking around and get on with the next killing.' "

"Funny, funny," Linares said. "You should be on switched-off TV."

Apart from the long journeys, most of the surveillance took place near Doil's home, and that, too, presented problems.

When Elroy Doil's mother, Beulah, was alive, the two of them had lived in a two-room wooden shack alongside the railroad tracks at 23 Northeast 35th Terrace, in the Wynwood area. Elroy still lived alone in the same dilapidated shack, and kept an ancient pickup truck for his own use in the front yard.

Because an unfamiliar vehicle might draw attention if parked for too long, surveillance trucks and cars were switched frequently, though less so after dark or during heavy weather. All the vehicles had tinted windows, so there was never a problem about the detectives being seen.

During some evenings the surveillance teams spent long hours outside Doil's favorite local haunts. One was the Pussycat Theater, a bar and strip joint, another the Harlem Niteclub. Both were well known to police as hangouts for drug dealers and prostitutes.

"Christ!" Dion Jacobo complained after three successive rainy nights parked across the road from the Pussycat. "Couldn't the bastard go to a *movie* just once? At least one of us could sit a coupla rows behind." The detectives never followed Doil into bars or any other lighted place, aware that their faces might be known.

After nearly three weeks of round-the-clock surveillance, none of the detectives had spotted anything incriminating or even out of the ordinary. Ainslie, aware that most of his men were growing bored and frustrated with the assignment, tried to buoy their spirits with new information, most of which came from Detective Ruby Bowe.

•   •   •

Bowe had begun her research at the Social Security office in downtown Miami, where she received complete access to Elroy Doil's work records. Concentrating on the preceding two years, she found that Doil had been employed by five Miami-area businesses: Overland Trucking, Prieto Fast Delivery, Superfine Transport, Porky's Trucking, and Suarez Motors & Equipment. Most of the employment was for short periods. Doil appeared to move back and forth among employers. Bowe visited the companies one by one, her umbrella and raincoat barely protecting her from the continual downpours.

She found Mr. Alvin Travino, owner of Overland Trucking, especially helpful. He was a tiny, wizened man in his late sixties who apologized several times for "my poorly kept records," when in fact they were impeccable. With no trouble at all he produced details of Elroy Doil's assignments for the past two years, including logs with dates, times, mileages, and expenses, covering each trip. To save Ruby Bowe the trouble of taking notes, he called in a secretary to make copies.

Travino also talked about Elroy Doil. "From things I heard, I reckoned he'd been in trouble, but figured it was no business of mine unless he got up to some malarkey here, and he never has. Oh, there was an incident or two, but nothing much that affected his work. The main point is, he's one helluva good driver. Can whip a tractor-trailer rig in and out of the tightest spots, never hesitating, and that ain't easy—can't do it half as well myself. He's safe, too. Never had an accident, never brought back one of my rigs damaged."

"Those 'incidents' you mentioned," Bowe prompted. "What were they?"

Alvin Travino chuckled. "Weird stuff; almost sorry I mentioned 'em. Well, now and then we'd find a few things in the cab after he'd been driving—maybe six or seven dead birds, another time a coupla dogs, once a dead cat."

Ruby's eyes widened. "Wow, that *is* strange. What did you say to Doil?"

"Well . . ." The diminutive trucking boss hesitated. "We did have a real brawl one time."

"Really? What happened?"

"At first I thought those dead creatures might have something to do with religion, the way Haitians are with goats. Then I decided, hey, I don't want that crap in my cabs anyway, and I told Elroy."

"And?"

Travino sighed. "Wish I didn't have to tell you this, because I'm beginning to get an idea of what you're after. Fact is, the son of a gun went into a rage. Got red in the face, then pulled out this huge knife and waved it around, cursing like hell at me. Don't mind saying I was scared."

"Do you remember what the knife looked like?" Ruby asked.

Travino nodded. "The darned thing was sharp and shiny, with a long curved blade."

"Did he attack you?"

"No. Because I stood up to him, looked him straight in the eyes, and said loud and clear that he was through. Told him to get out and never come back. He put the knife away, and went."

"But he did come back?"

"Yep. Phoned after a week or two, said he'd like to work a bit. I let him. Had no trouble after that. As I said, he's a good driver."

The secretary returned with a pile of copied trip logs. Travino glanced through the pages, then passed them to Detective Bowe.

"You've been very helpful," she said. "I'd appreciate it if you didn't tell Doil I was here."

A final chuckle. "Not a chance. If I did, he might pull out that knife again."

•　　•　　•

At Superfine Transport, Ruby Bowe talked with the general manager and two employees who knew Elroy Doil. There, as with all the companies she visited, they answered questions readily, making it clear they wanted no problems with police.

A thoughtful, articulate black supervisor named Lloyd Swayze expressed what seemed to be a general view of Doil. "The guy's a loner. Doesn't want friends. But leave him alone, let him do a job—which he's mostly good at— and everything's okay. Has a savage temper, though; saw it explode once when another driver tried to kid him. Doil was ready to kill the guy, I swear."

"Was there a fight?"

"Would have been, except we don't allow that stuff here. I sent the other guy back to work, then told Doil unless he cooled down he'd get his walking papers pronto. For a minute I was sure he was gonna hit me, then he thought better. But the guy could be dangerous, all right, if that's what you're asking."

"Thanks," Bowe said. "You saved me the question."

A burly, rough-tongued Superfine driver, Mick Lebo, confirmed most of Swayze's words, adding, "The guy's a louse. I wouldn't trust him for one goddam second."

Was there anyone among the other drivers, Bowe asked, whom Doil talked to a lot, or might have confided in? It was a standard question, because many murderers were caught after talking about their crimes to supposed friends who later informed or testified against them.

"The bastard never talks!" Lebo scoffed. "Not a word to nobody. If you stood beside him to piss, he wouldn't give you the time o' day—'course, he might piss on your foot." Lebo roared at his own joke, knocking Ruby's arm with his elbow.

As at Overland Trucking, Detective Bowe left Superfine Transport with copies of Elroy Doil's journey records covering the previous two years, and promises from each of her informants that their conversation would remain confidential.

•　　•　　•

Unlike the other companies on the list, Suarez Motors & Equipment was not in the trucking business, but repaired automobiles and small trucks, and sold automotive parts. Elroy Doil had been employed there from time to time as a mechanic. However, about a month before, he had quit suddenly and not come back, even to collect his last paycheck from the young owner, Pedro Suarez. When he showed Bowe the check, she asked for a copy.

"Is he a good mechanic?" she asked Suarez.

"Pretty good, and works fast, but what a troublemaker! Picks fights all the time. I was planning to fire him when he quit."

"Would you say Elroy Doil is smart?"

"Yeah. He's smart because he's a quick learner. Explain something or show him how to do it, and he's got it. But he can't control himself."

Suarez went on to explain that the business operated a local delivery service as a sideline. Some of the automotive parts trade was handled that way, and Suarez Motors used two panel trucks to make deliveries for several retail stores in the area with no transport of their own.

"Did Doil ever do those deliveries?" she asked.

"Oh, sure. Sometimes when one of the regulars was off."

"Do you have a record of when that was and where he went?"

Suarez grimaced. "Afraid you'd ask that. I guess we do, but it'll take some digging."

He led Bowe to a small, dusty room at the rear of the building, with overflowing shelves, a half-dozen file cabinets, and a copying machine. Suarez pointed to two of the cabinets. "You want to cover two years? It'll all be in there. 'Fraid you'll have to search through yourself."

"That's fine. If it's okay, I'd like to use the copier."

"Be my guest." Suarez grinned. "If Doil drops by for his check, shall I bring him in?"

"No, please!" Bowe quickly repeated the need for confidentiality.

The search, which involved checking and relating invoices, delivery records, vehicle service schedules, and payroll sheets, took her most of a day. But she left with a complete history of Elroy Doil's work at Suarez Motors.

• • •

Prieto Fast Delivery and Porky's Trucking were similarly cooperative, and the four combined visits revealed other facets of Doil's character, including the fact that he disliked regular work. When he felt like working, probably because he needed money, he would phone one of the companies, and if work was available, he was taken on temporarily. He was obviously smart enough not to cheat or steal at any of those places, but he clearly could not control his turbulent, aggressive nature.

For Ruby Bowe, the next step was to compare the information with dates of the various killings.

Back at her desk at Homicide, Bowe dealt with the out-of-Miami murders first. On March 12, Hal and Mabel Larsen were murdered in Clearwater, 260 miles northwest of Miami. On that same day, while working for Overland Trucking, Elroy Doil drove a tractor-trailer load of furniture from Miami to Clearwater, where, according to a driving log and expense record, he arrived during mid-afternoon and stayed overnight at the Home Away From Home Motel. Bowe, her excitement growing, phoned the motel and learned that it was four blocks from the address of the murder victims. Doil returned to Miami the following day with a load of coiled steel and plastic pipe.

Also, Doil had made a previous trip to Clearwater for Overland only two weeks before and had stayed at the same motel. The first trip, Bowe reasoned, could have allowed him to pinpoint his victims, the second to murder them.

Next were the Fort Lauderdale killings of Irving and Rachel Hennenfeld, reported on May 23, though it was estimated the victims had died four days earlier, on May 19.

During May, Doil had made two trips to Fort Lauderdale, this time for Porky's Trucking, the first on May 2, and again on the nineteenth. A log for the second date showed he had left Miami at 3:30 P.M., made three deliveries in Fort Lauderdale, and returned a few minutes before midnight. Since the distance between the two cities was only twenty-five miles, eight and a half hours seemed a long time to be away. However, the earlier trip, on May 2, which included four deliveries in Fort Lauderdale, had taken only five hours. Again Bowe reasoned that finding the right victims probably took less time than the gory business of slaying them.

While the three Miami serial killings did not have quite the same close connections, each one displayed linkages too apposite to be dismissed as coincidence.

During the morning that preceded the killings of Homer and Blanche Frost in the Royal Colonial Hotel, Doil had made eight deliveries and four pickups in Coral Gables while working for Prieto Fast Delivery. Two of the deliveries were to businesses on Southwest 27th Avenue, the same location as the First Union Bank branch where the Frosts had gone that same morning to cash eight hundred dollars in traveler's checks.

It was entirely possible, Bowe thought—indeed probable—that Elroy Doil saw the elderly couple, perhaps even in the bank, and followed them back to their hotel. It would then be a simple matter to ride with the Frosts in an elevator to their floor and, while appearing to be just another hotel guest, note the number of their room, then return late that night. All conjecture, of course, but combined with the previous crimes and linkages, it was too credible to ignore.

Then there were the additional Miami killings—of Lazaro and Luisa Urbina at Pine Terrace Condominiums, and of Commissioner Gustav Ernst and his wife, Eleanor, at Bay Point. In both cases the records for both Prieto Fast Delivery and Suarez Motors & Equipment showed that Doil made deliveries near the victims' homes.

The Prieto records copied by Detective Bowe noted two Doil deliveries close to the Urbinas'—on separate days and within the three weeks preceding the Urbina murders. As for the walled-in, security-guarded Bay Point subdivision, Doil had made two small deliveries there for Suarez Motors—not to the Ernsts, but to other houses. The last occasion was more than a month before the Ernst killings, but that, Bowe reminded herself, could be because Suarez employed Doil as a mechanic and only occasionally used him as a driver. The two trips he had made into Bay Point, however, would have familiarized him with the security setup and probably enabled him to talk his way in again with phony delivery papers.

Something else caught Bowe's attention. Her copy of the Suarez Motors paycheck that Elroy Doil had not collected indicated that he had abruptly quit work the day after the murders of Gustav and Eleanor Ernst.

Did Doil quit, Bowe wondered, because he thought he might be a suspect in the serial killings by now and therefore wanted to disappear?

•   •   •

At the end of her research and analysis, an eager Detective Bowe communicated what she had learned to Sergeant Ainslie. He was buoyed by her news and, while holding a few details back, passed along most of the information to the special task force members, telling them, "Doil's our guy, no doubt of it, so be patient and stay alert despite this lousy weather. Sooner or later he'll slip up and we'll be there to grab him."

Ainslie also kept the assistant state attorney, Curzon Knowles, informed. Knowles's reaction, though, was unenthusiastic.

"Sure, Ruby's been resourceful in getting all that stuff. And, yes, it tells us that Doil had the opportunity to knock off all those people and probably did. But proving it is something else, and among the whole *schmeer* there's not one scrap of solid evidence. You don't even have enough for an arrest warrant."

"I know that, counselor, but I simply wanted to keep you in the picture. There *is* a positive side, though. We're sure enough about Doil not to waste time on anyone else."

"Yes, I can see that."

"So we'll keep working at it," Ainslie said. "There'll be a break somewhere, soon. I truly believe it."

The attorney chuckled. "I perceive, Malcolm, that you are, after all, still in the faith business."

12

ALONG WITH THE MISERABLE weather accompanying the more than three-week surveillance of Elroy Doil, an intestinal flu epidemic swept through Miami. Many in the Police Department were affected, including two detectives from the special task force, José Garcia and Seth Wightman. Both men were sent home, with instructions to stay in bed, creating even more problems for the surveillance process.

As a result, Malcolm Ainslie and Dan Zagaki were now working a double shift. They had been on duty for nine hours; another fifteen lay ahead. It was 4:20 P.M. and they were parked in a Burdines Department Store delivery van on Northeast 35th Terrace, half a block from Elroy Doil's two-room wooden shack.

Again, it had been raining throughout most of the day. Now, accompanying the rain, the sky was darkening.

Earlier in the day, beginning at 7:00 A.M., Doil had driven an Overland Trucking tractor-trailer rig from Miami to West Palm Beach, then to Boca Raton, returning to Miami at 3:00 P.M. after an approximately 140-mile haul in difficult weather. A trio of surveillance teams, including Ainslie and Zagaki, had monitored Doil's journey. Apart from continuous rain, nothing out of the ordinary happened except for one observation Zagaki made during the drive: "There's something different about Doil today, Sergeant. Not sure what it is . . ."

"He's tense," Ainslie agreed. "You can see it in his driving, and every time he stops he seems restless, like he has to keep his body moving."

"Does it mean anything, Sergeant?"

Ainslie shrugged. "Could be drugs, though he has no history of drugs. Maybe he's nervous. Only he knows why."

"Maybe we'll find out."

"Maybe." Ainslie left it there, but was aware of his own tension, a familiar sense that events were somehow moving toward a climax.

Now, having followed Doil from Overland Trucking's Miami depot to his home, Ainslie and Zagaki were waiting for whatever happened next.

"Mind if I doze off for a while, Sergeant?" Zagaki asked.

"No. Go ahead." It made sense to take some rest if possible on a long double shift, particularly since Doil, after his eight-hour truck journey, was inside and probably sleeping.

"Thanks, Sergeant," Zagaki said as he leaned back and closed his eyes.

Ainslie, though, had no intention of sleeping. He was still not totally confident of the young detective, and the reason he had paired himself with Zagaki was to keep an eye on him throughout the surveillance. To be fair, though, Ainslie reminded himself, Zagaki's performance so far could not be faulted. He had done everything required of him, including long spells of driving. Just the same . . .

It was Zagaki's manner that made him uneasy, and while it was difficult to point to anything specific, Ainslie's finely honed instincts told him that Zagaki's studied respectfulness, which he overdid by saying "Sergeant" a few times too often, was wafer-thin and bordering on fawning.

Or was he himself, Ainslie wondered, being excessively critical?

"Thirteen hundred to thirteen-ten." The call came crisply through his portable police radio.

It was Lieutenant Leo Newbold.

Ainslie answered, "Thirteen-ten. QSK."

To help out during the task force personnel shortage, Newbold had filled in on several shifts, pairing with Dion Jacobo. The two served as backup to Ainslie and Zagaki, and were now positioned a few blocks away in an eight-year-old Ford sedan with dented fenders, peeling paint, and a supercharged engine that enabled it to keep up with anything on the road.

Newbold's voice came back, "Is anything happening?"

"Negative," Ainslie said. "Subject is—" He stopped abruptly. "Hold on! He's just come out of the house, heading for his pickup." He reached over and shook Zagaki, who opened his eyes and sat up straight, then started the van's motor.

Outside, Doil lumbered across the yard, his hands pushed deep into the pockets of his jeans, his eyes downcast.

After a few moments Ainslie continued, "Subject now in pickup, pulling away, moving fast. We're following."

Doil's departure was unexpected. But Zagaki already had the Burdines delivery van in gear and was pulling out into the road, keeping the battered pickup truck in sight.

"We're rolling," Newbold responded. "Will be behind you. Advise direction of travel."

Ainslie transmitted, "Subject has reached North Miami Avenue, now turning south." And soon after, "He is crossing Twenty-ninth Street."

From Newbold: "We are on Second Avenue, parallel with you. Continue advising cross streets. Ready to cross and take over when you want."

Two surveillance vehicles traveling on parallel streets and switching periodically was a regular, though sometimes tricky, surveillance technique.

The rain was heavier now and the wind rising.

Newbold again: "This is your show, Malcolm. But do you think we should call in a third team?"

Ainslie answered, "Not yet. Don't believe he'll go out of town again . . . He is now crossing Eleventh Street; we are a block behind. Let's switch at Flagler."

"QSL."

Ainslie again: "Approaching Flagler Street. Subject continuing south. You take him, Lieutenant. We'll drop off."

Newbold: "We are on Flagler facing west, making a left turn onto South Miami Avenue . . . Yes, we see him. He's behind us . . . has now passed us . . . two vehicles between us; we'll keep it that way." A few minutes later: "Subject crossing Tamiami Trail, seems to know where he's going, probably west. Suggest we switch again at Bayshore."

"QSL. Closing on you now."

Thus it happened that Ainslie and Zagaki were in the lead car when Elroy Doil's pickup truck, after driving briefly west on the heavily traveled Bayshore Drive, slowed near Mercy Hospital, then turned right into the wealthy residential area of Bay Heights.

Ainslie reported, "Subject has left Bayshore Drive, entered Halissee Street, driving north, very little traffic." He told Zagaki, "Stay well back, but be sure not to lose him." It was becoming harder to see, though. While the rain had eased, the light was going, and it would soon be night.

Halissee, like most of Bay Heights, was a street of large, elegant residences, the whole area thickly wooded. A two-way cross street appeared ahead; Ainslie knew it was Tigertail Avenue, with similar style homes. But before reaching Tigertail, the pickup pulled over to the right and stopped under a large, overhanging ficus tree fronting one of the spacious houses. The pickup's headlights went out as Zagaki stopped the Burdines van and switched off his headlights, too. They were about five hundred feet behind, with several parked cars between, but were high enough to see over their roofs and observe the head and shoulders of Doil in the pickup, outlined by a streetlight.

"Subject has stopped on Halissee near Tigertail," Ainslie reported. "He is still in pickup cab. No sign of moving out."

Newbold responded, "We are a block behind you. Have stopped, too."

They waited.

Ten minutes passed and Doil had not moved.

"He doesn't seem so restless anymore, Sergeant," Zagaki said.

After a few more minutes the police radio came alive and Newbold asked, "Anything going on?"

"Negative. Pickup still stopped, subject in cab."

"I've received a message, Malcolm. I need to talk to you. Can you walk back? If anything happens, we can get you back fast."

Ainslie hesitated. He was not happy about leaving Zagaki alone to watch Doil, and his inclination was to stay. But he knew the lieutenant would have good reason for wanting him.

"I'm coming now," he transmitted, then said to Zagaki, "I'll be as fast as I can. Don't take your eyes off Doil, and use your radio to call me if he gets out or drives on, or if anything else at all happens. If he does move, follow him closely and above all keep in touch."

"Don't worry, Sergeant," Zagaki said brightly. "My mind will be on nothing else."

Ainslie left the van, noticing as he stepped down that the rain had stopped. In near darkness he walked briskly back the way they had come.

Watching him go, Dan Zagaki thought, *Christ, what a fucking bore you are, Sergeant, don't hurry back!*

From the start, Zagaki had wished he was paired with someone more with-it and exciting. Ainslie, in Zagaki's opinion, was an overly cautious plodder, and not very smart. If he were, he'd be a lieutenant by now, maybe captain— ranks that Zagaki had his eye on. He knew he had the smarts to go right to the top—hadn't he made it quickly out of uniform to become a Homicide detective? The main thing in any kind of force, police or military, was to think *promotion, promotion, promotion*, remembering that advancement didn't just happen; you had to *make it happen!* Coupled with that, it was essential to be *noticed*, frequently and favorably, by the brass above you.

Dan Zagaki had absorbed those rules and tactics by watching his father get promotion after promotion in the U.S. Army, and then his big brother Cedric move up similarly in the Marines. Cedric, like their father, was going to be a general someday—he made no secret of it. Cedric had also been contemptuous of young Dan's choice when he joined the Miami Police—a "pissant outfit," he had called it. The general hadn't been quite so blunt, but Dan sensed he was disappointed in his younger son's decision. Well, he would show them both.

He smiled, remembering how skillfully he, Detective Dauntless Dan, had buttered up Ainslie these past two weeks, calling him "Sergeant" with almost every other breath, and still the dimwit hadn't noticed. He'd even finagled his way back onto the serial killings caper by pretending to eat humble pie. And Ainslie ate it up. Fool.

"Oh damn," Zagaki muttered, still sitting in the driver's seat of the van. "I've gotta go again. How many times is that today?"

Like several hundred others in Miami, including the absent Detectives Wightman and Garcia, Dan Zagaki had intestinal flu. True, he didn't have an intense fever so far, but the other symptoms, especially an upset stomach and acute diarrhea, were very much in evidence. Unlike others, however, he had kept quiet about it, determined to soldier on at any cost. He just couldn't miss the chance to help break this case. He had managed to take care of his problem during several earlier stops today, but at this moment he had to, *simply had to*, find a sanctuary—and he could see one, a clump of bushes over to the right—where he could let nature take its urgent course.

Looking ahead, through the Burdines van windshield, he could still see the silhouette of Doil. If the bastard had stayed still this long, he sure as hell wasn't going to move in the few seconds he needed—*right now!*

Should he call Ainslie by radio to let him know? Nuts to that! Dauntless Dan could make his own decisions.

Moving quickly, Zagaki got out from the van and, closing the door quietly, moved to the bushes. Moments later, *Oh, what a relief! But hurry up!* He didn't have all night.

•   •   •

"I'll make this quick, Malcolm," Leo Newbold said. Ainslie had reached the backup surveillance car moments earlier and slipped into the backseat. The lieutenant continued, "I just took a call from Homicide in Philadelphia. We put out a nationwide 'detain and hold' BOLO on a Dudley Rickins. Right?"

"Yes, sir, I okayed it. It's Bernie Quinn's case, and Rickins is the hot suspect. If we question him, we think we can close it."

"Well, they have Rickins in Philadelphia and can hold him seventy-two hours, but someone goofed by not calling us sooner, and there's only twelve hours left before they must let him go. I know you need all the bodies here . . ."

"Just the same, we should fly Bernie up immediately."

Newbold sighed. "That's what I thought."

As both knew, they could ill afford the loss of one more from the surveillance detail, but would have to manage somehow.

"Okay, Malcolm. I'll get word to Bernie and send him on his way. Thanks. Now, you'd better get back. Doil still hasn't moved?"

"Not yet. If he had, we'd have heard from Zagaki."

Ainslie left the backup car and returned the way he had come.

•   •   •

Goddammit! Zagaki thought, adjusting his clothes. *That took too damn long!* He hurried back to the van.

As he arrived, so did Malcolm Ainslie.

Ainslie said incredulously, "Where the hell have you been?"

"Well, Sergeant, I just had to—"

Livid, Ainslie stormed, "Cut that crap out! Do you think I can't see through you? Didn't I tell you not to take your eyes off Doil, and if *anything* happened, to call me by radio?"

"Yes, Sergeant, but—"

"But nothing! When we finish tonight, you are through with this detail."

Zagaki pleaded, "Sergeant, if you'll only let me explain. I wasn't well—"

Ainslie was not listening, but looking around the vehicles ahead toward the pickup truck. Then he shouted, "Oh Jesus, he's gone!"

From the pickup's cab, Elroy Doil's silhouette had disappeared.

Briefly, confusion reigned. Ainslie ran toward the truck, peering into the darkness for any sign of Doil. There was none—nor were there any pedestrians in sight. From the pickup he ran the short distance to Tigertail Avenue. The streets were only faintly lit. Doil, Ainslie realized, could easily hide out in any of the shadows.

Dan Zagaki ran up behind him, panting. "Sergeant, I'm—"

Ainslie spun around. *"Shut the fuck up!"* He snarled at Zagaki, "How long were you away from the van?"

"Only a minute or two, I swear."

"Don't lie to me, you little bastard!" Ainslie grabbed the younger man by his lapels and shook him. "How long was it?" Seething, he pulled Zagaki toward him until their eyes were close. "Was it the whole time I was gone?"

Zagaki, close to tears, conceded, "Most of it."

Pushing him away in disgust, Ainslie calculated that Doil's head start could be ten minutes, maybe twelve. Even assuming he had remained in the area, he could be anywhere, and there was no way of finding him without help, which left only one choice. He reached for his police radio.

"Thirteen-ten to dispatcher."

A woman's calm voice answered, "Thirteen-ten QSK."

"Send me several units into the area of Tigertail Avenue . . ." Ainslie paused to read the nearest street number. "Number 1611. We have lost a white male who was under surveillance. Height six feet four, weighs about two hundred and ninety pounds, is wearing red shirt and dark pants. He is armed and dangerous."

"QSL."

Within seconds, Ainslie could hear the approaching sirens, responding to a swiftly transmitted 315—3 for "Emergency," 15 for "Officer needs help."

Newbold and Jacobo would have overheard his transmission, Ainslie knew, and would also be on their way. For the moment there was nothing he could do.

Then he received a radio phone call from the communications sergeant in charge of dispatchers and radio traffic who spoke quickly but calmly.

"Malc, just caught your call. I have a boy on the phone who says his grandparents are being beaten and stabbed by a big man in their house."

"That's Doil, Harry! Give me the address fast."

"I'm getting it, hang on. Kid has to whisper." Ainslie could hear the communications sergeant asking patient questions, addressing the caller as "Ivan." The sergeant came back. "Says his grandparents' name is Tempone, their house is on Tigertail. Doesn't know the number, we're looking it up . . . We have it! It's 1643 . . . I've called for paramedics, Malcolm, and am changing that 315 to a 331." Meaning, "Emergency—homicide in progress."

Ainslie scarcely heard. He was already running eastward down Tigertail Avenue. Dan Zagaki ran beside him, though Ainslie was long past caring.

As both drew near, they could see the number 1643 on the gate of a large two-story house fronted by several pillars and a wide paved path leading to a carved doorway. A high iron fence surrounded the entire property, with six-foot-high shrubbery on both sides. The double gate in the fence provided access from the street; one side of the gate was slightly open.

As Ainslie and Zagaki arrived, two squad cars with flashing lights and fading sirens pulled up, tires screeching. Four officers leapt out, guns drawn. Two more squad cars were speeding down Tigertail from both directions.

Ainslie identified himself and quickly described Doil. "We think he's inside, maybe killing *right now.*" He motioned to two of the officers. "You two come with me." And to the others, "Gendry, take charge and set up a perimeter four blocks each way. Don't let anyone in or out until you hear from me."

One of the officers called out, "Sergeant, over there!" He pointed to the side of the house, where a shadowy figure was creeping along a small path. Another officer directed a powerful flashlight. It lit up the back of a large man wearing a red shirt and brown pants.

"That's him!" Ainslie shouted. With his own gun drawn, he raced through the gate and across the lawn, the others following fast behind him. Doil was running now, and Ainslie shouted, "Freeze, Doil, or I'll blow your fucking head off!"

The figure stopped and turned. Doil snarled, "Fuck you!"

Moving closer, Ainslie could see a knife in Doil's right hand, and noticed that both of his hands were encased in rubber gloves.

With his gun raised, Ainslie ordered fiercely, "Drop that knife. *Now!*" Then, as Doil hesitated, "And peel off those gloves. Let them fall beside the knife."

Slowly, Doil complied. When he had done so, Ainslie bellowed, "Now down on your stomach, you son of a bitch, hands behind you. *Move!*"

Again slowly, Doil obeyed as Ainslie held his gun steady. Then Zagaki moved in and seized Doil's wrists, quickly handcuffing him behind his back. As he did so, a brief flash from behind lit up the scene.

Instinctively, Ainslie swung around, his gun still raised, but a woman's voice called out. "Sorry, Chief. But it's what the papers pay me for."

"Dammit," Ainslie muttered, lowering his gun. He knew the news media monitored police radio and moved fast with a breaking story, but he was still dismayed to see them so soon. He turned to the uniform officers. "One of you cordon off this area with tape—about fifty feet around the entire house—and keep everyone behind it."

The yellow POLICE LINE DO NOT CROSS tape, which all squad cars carried, was promptly wrapped around anything handy—trees, streetlights, fence posts, and the mirrors of two parked police cars—creating a visual barrier between detectives and a fast-assembling crowd of spectators and media people.

Zagaki, kneeling beside Elroy Doil, called out, "This guy is covered in blood! So are the knife and gloves."

"Oh no!" Ainslie groaned, knowing instinctively that what he had feared most had happened. Composing himself for the moment, he addressed the increasing number of uniform officers. "Two of you strip this guy down to his underwear; shoes and socks off, too. Keep the clothes off the ground; don't smear any blood, and get everything in plastic bags as soon as possible—especially that knife and the gloves. And don't let up; guard his every move. He's violent and dangerous."

The reason for stripping Doil was to preserve the blood on his clothing in its present state. If DNA testing showed it to be a victim's, any case against him could be conclusive.

Within the past few minutes Leo Newbold and Dion Jacobo had appeared. The lieutenant asked Ainslie, "Have you been inside?"

"No, sir. Just going."

"We'll come, too, okay?"

"Of course."

Ainslie instructed one of the officers who had been early on the scene, "I want you to come with us. Walk where we do, and stay alert." To Zagaki he added curtly, "You stay right here. Don't move a fucking inch."

Led by Ainslie, the four moved toward the house.

A side door was open—probably where Doil had come out. Inside was a dim corridor; Ainslie snapped lights on. They moved forward, the corridor connecting with a paneled hallway and, on the hallway's far side, a wide carpeted and balustraded stairway. Sitting on the bottom step was a small boy— about twelve, Ainslie guessed—who was staring blankly into space and trembling violently.

Ainslie knelt down and put his arms around the boy, asking gently, "Are you Ivan?" He told the others, "He called nine-one-one." The boy made the slightest movement of his head.

"Can you tell us where . . ."

The boy seemed to shrink into himself, but turned his body, looking up the stairway, then began shaking even more.

The uniform officer said, "Excuse me, Sergeant, he's in shock. I know the signs. We should get him to a hospital."

"Can you carry him out?"

"Sure can."

"Paramedics were called for," Ainslie told him. "They should be outside by now. If they take the boy to Jackson Memorial, go with him and report back where you are. Do not, on any account, leave the boy; we need to talk with him later. Is that clear?"

"All clear, Sergeant." The officer put out his arms and lifted the boy. "Let's go, Ivan." And as they moved away, "It's gonna be okay, son. Just hang on to me."

Ainslie, Newbold, and Jacobo ascended the stairs. As they reached the first landing they spotted an open door directly ahead, the room inside lighted. A few steps inside the room, the trio paused to view the scene they faced.

Dion Jacobo, a veteran who had seen many homicides, made a choking sound, then, with a loud groan, burst out, "Oh my God! Oh my God!"

It was, as Ainslie had feared the moment he saw Doil's bloodstained clothes, a reenactment of the earlier killings—this time with an elderly black couple the tragic victims. The only difference was that Doil had obviously acted more hastily and less precisely, probably because he heard the approaching police sirens.

The dead couple were bound, gagged, and facing each other; they had also been brutally beaten around their faces and skulls. One of the woman's arms was twisted and broken; the man's right eye had been pierced by a sharp instrument, leaving the eyeball split. Compared with the earlier killings, the knife slashes on both bodies were more random and deeper. It was as if everything had been done hurriedly, with the killer aware that his time was limited.

Ainslie stood transfixed, fighting to control his deep, despairing anguish, knowing that as long as he lived he would never forget this scene or his own terrible guilt. He must have remained motionless for nearly a minute before being brought back to reality by Leo Newbold's voice. "Malcolm, are you all right?"

With an effort he nodded. "Yes. I am."

"I know what you're thinking," Newbold said softly, "and I'm not going to let you carry this alone. We'll talk about it soon, but for now, would you like to go home and sleep? You're exhausted. Dion can take charge here."

Ainslie shook his head. "I'll see this through, Lieutenant, though I'd like Dion to stay and help. But thanks."

He reached for his portable police radio, beginning the standard procedures.

·   ·   ·

It was a few minutes after 1:00 A.M. when Malcolm Ainslie at last reached home, where Karen, whom he had managed to phone a few hours earlier, was waiting up, wearing a pale green cotton robe. When she saw him, she held out her arms and hugged him tightly. After a while she eased back, looking upward, and touched his face.

"It's been bad, hasn't it?"

He nodded slowly. "Pretty much."

"Oh, sweetheart, how much more can you take?"

Ainslie sighed. "Not too many like tonight."

She snuggled closer. "It's so good to have you home. Do you want to talk?"

"Tomorrow, maybe. Not right now."

"Malcolm, dear, go straight to bed. I'll bring you something."

The "something" was hot Ovaltine, a drink from childhood that he liked at night. When he had finished it, and fallen back on his pillow, Karen said, "That should help you sleep."

"And keep the nightmares away?"

Climbing into bed beside him, she held him tightly again. "I'll take care of those."

But while Malcolm slept soundly and deeply, Karen lay awake thinking. How long, she wondered, could they survive this kind of life? Sooner or later Malcolm would have to choose between his home and family and the demons of his work. Like so many other wives, past and present, of Homicide detectives, Karen could not foresee indefinitely a harmony between their marriage and her husband's present career.

●   ●   ●

The next day brought an ironic postscript.

A professional photographer with ties to syndicated photo services lived in Bay Heights, a short distance from the Tempone murder scene. It accounted for her immediate presence at the house and the flash photo she had taken while Doil was being subdued.

The dramatic action shot showed Doil facedown and struggling, and Detective Dan Zagaki securing him with handcuffs. Distributed by the Associated Press, the picture appeared in major U.S. newspapers with the caption:

POLICE HERO

Following a dramatic chase, Detective Dan Zagaki of the Miami Police captures and subdues a suspect, Elroy Doil, who is charged with the murders of an elderly black couple and is being questioned about other serial killings. Asked about his work and its dangers, Zagaki replied, "It's risky sometimes. You just do the best you can." He is the son of General Thaddeus Zagaki, Commander, First Army Division, Fort Stewart, Georgia.

13

ELROY DOIL WAS ARRESTED, CHARGED with the first-degree murders of Kingsley and Nellie Tempone, and imprisoned in Dade County Jail. As required by law, a bond hearing was held at the adjoining Metro Justice Building within twenty-four hours of his arrest. Doil was not required to plead; that would come at a preliminary hearing two to three weeks later. Instead, a court-appointed attorney perfunctorily asked for bail, which was just as perfunctorily refused.

Doil showed little interest in the proceedings, refused to speak with his defense attorney, and yawned in the judge's face. However, when he was due to be removed from court and a bailiff grasped his arm, Doil punched the man in the stomach so hard that he doubled up. Instantly two other bailiffs and a prison officer leapt on Doil, pummeled him, shackled him with chains, and removed him from the court. Outside, in the prisoners' holding cell, they hammered him again with their fists until he was gasping and subdued.

While official decisions in the case now rested mainly with state prosecutors, a team of ID technicians and Homicide detectives continued to accumulate evidence.

The weapon—a bowie knife—which Elroy Doil had been holding when apprehended, had blood on the blade and handle that matched the blood of both murder victims. Further, Sandra Sanchez was prepared to testify that that particular knife, identifiable by distinctive notches and serrations, was the actual weapon that killed Kingsley and Nellie Tempone.

According to Sanchez, however, it was not the bowie knife used to kill the Frosts, the Urbinas, or, more recently, the Ernsts. The wound details from the Clearwater and Fort Lauderdale murders had not yet been received in for comparison.

Talking with detectives and the ID crew, the ME added, "That isn't to say Doil didn't do those other murders. Judging by the type of wounds, I think he did. But maybe he bought more than one of those knives, and you'll find others when you search his stuff."

But, to the disappointment of detectives and prosecutors, who had hoped for conclusive solutions to the earlier killings, no knives were found among Doil's skimpy possessions, nor, for that matter, was any other evidence.

Solid evidence in the Tempone case, though, continued to pile up. The blood found on Doil's clothing and shoes matched blood samples from both victims; so did blood on the rubber gloves he had worn—obviously to avoid leaving fingerprints. Shoe prints discovered at the crime scene—a few with traces of the victims' blood—were identical with the sneakers Doil was wearing.

And then, on top of everything, there was the testimony of twelve-year-old Ivan Tempone. Having recovered from his shock, he proved a self-possessed, convincing eyewitness. First to Detective Dion Jacobo, and later to a state attorney, he described how, peering through a barely open door, he had seen Doil torture and kill his grandparents.

"We've simply never had a stronger case," State Attorney Adele Montesino declared when announcing her controversial decision to prosecute Doil for the Tempones' murders only.

●   ●   ●

While the prosecution took more than six months to review evidence and prepare for trial, within the Miami Police Department an evaluation moved more quickly. At issue was the bungled surveillance of Elroy Doil that had resulted in the Tempones' needless deaths, though full knowledge of those events was restricted as far as possible to a few high-ranking officers. Homicide detectives, in particular, were warned not to discuss the subject with anyone, including their families, and especially not with the media.

For several days following the Tempone killings the Police Department, in effect, held its breath, wondering if some enterprising reporter would dig deeper than the surface news, dramatic though it was. An added concern was that Kingsley and Nellie Tempone were black. Though there was nothing racist about the police blunder—the victims could just as easily have been white—there were always activists eager to turn any opportunity into a racial confrontation.

Then, remarkably—almost incredibly—what had been feared did *not* happen; the information dam held. The media, including national newspapers and network TV, gave prominence to the grisly crime and concentrated on the fact that an apparent serial killer had finally been caught. Another factor helped. Young Ivan Tempone, who, as one news writer put it, "courageously summoned police at the risk of attracting the murderer's attention and being killed himself," became an instant folk hero.

There was neither air time nor column inches for much more.

During it all, quietly and behind the scenes, penalties against the officers involved in what was privately described as "the homicide that shouldn't have" were being debated. Because of potential public-relations damage if the truth should ever emerge, the discussion went as high as the chief of police. Final decisions, though, were left to Major Mark Figueras, commander of the Criminal Investigations Section, which ruled all detective branches.

Figueras made his intentions clear: "I want to know everything, every last little detail, with not the smallest bit of fly-shit left out." The instruction reached Lieutenant Newbold, who conducted separate hour-long, tape-recorded interviews with Malcolm Ainslie and Dan Zagaki.

Ainslie, while holding nothing back about Zagaki's actions, still blamed himself for reversing his original judgment about the young detective. He told Newbold, "I made a mistake. The responsibility was mine, and I accept it. No excuses."

Zagaki, on the other hand, tried to talk his way out of any wrongdoing, at one point accusing Ainslie of failing to issue explicit orders—a statement that Newbold did not believe, and went on record to that effect.

Newbold delivered his report and tape recordings to Major Manolo Yanes, commander of the Crimes Against Persons Unit, who passed them upward to Major Figueras. A few days later the decisions were quietly announced.

Detective Zagaki would receive a reprimand for "neglect of duty," forfeit sixty hours of pay, and be removed as a detective and returned to uniform. Figueras commented to Yanes, "I'd like to throw the son of a bitch out altogether. Unfortunately, under Civil Service rules, neglect isn't a terminating offense."

Sergeant Ainslie would receive a reprimand for "poor judgment." When informed, Ainslie accepted it as his due, even though it would remain like an albatross on his record through the remainder of his police service.

Lieutenant Newbold, however, had other ideas.

Going to the office of Major Yanes, he requested an immediate interview with Yanes and Figueras.

Yanes looked up from his desk. "You sound pretty formal, Leo."

"This *is* formal, sir."

"Subject?"

"Sergeant Ainslie."

Yanes regarded Newbold curiously, then picked up a phone and spoke quietly. Replacing the phone, he nodded. "Okay, right now."

The two walked silently down a corridor and were escorted by a secretary into Major Figueras's office. The secretary closed the door as she left.

Figueras said sharply, "I'm busy, Lieutenant, so whatever's on your mind, make it short."

"I'm asking you, sir, to reconsider the reprimand of Sergeant Ainslie."

"Has Ainslie asked for this?"

"No, sir. I'm asking. Ainslie doesn't know I'm here."

"A decision has been made. I see no reason to change it. Ainslie was at fault."

"He knows that. He's his own biggest critic."

"Then why the hell are you here?"

"Because Sergeant Ainslie is one of our finest officers, Major. His record is exemplary, his crime solving and his leadership outstanding. You know that, I believe. So does Major Yanes. And . . ." Newbold hesitated.

Figueras snapped, "Get on with it!"

Newbold looked both senior officers in the eye. "Recently Ainslie has had a goddam unfair deal, as just about everybody in the PD knows. I think we owe him something."

There was a momentary silence as Figueras and Yanes looked at each other, understanding exactly what Newbold meant. Then Yanes said quietly, "I support the lieutenant, sir."

Figueras glared at Newbold. "What do you want?"

The lieutenant answered, "A ninety-day reprimand."

Figueras hesitated, then said, "Do it. Now get out!"

Newbold did.

What Ainslie would now receive was a reprimand that would go into his file for ninety days, after which the reprimand and all copies would be destroyed.

●   ●   ●

As succeeding weeks and months went by, Elroy Doil and the crimes attributed to him ceased to be at the forefront of either Homicide's concerns or public curiosity. For a while, during his trial, public attention came back when Ainslie, Dr. Sanchez, Ivan Tempone, and others appeared as witnesses, followed by a jury's guilty verdict and the judge's sentence of death. Several months later, there was some cursory interest as Doil's automatic appeal was rejected, followed by the news that Doil himself refused to allow further appeals, and an execution date was set.

Then, once more, Doil was almost forgotten until the night when Sergeant Malcolm Ainslie received a telephone call from Father Ray Uxbridge at Raiford prison.

The message was puzzling. Elroy Doil, who would go to the electric chair in eight more hours, had asked to see Malcolm Ainslie before he died.

Part Three

1

I N THE AUSTERELY FURNISHED, windowless room to which Elroy Doil
had been brought, Malcolm Ainslie's thoughts were pulled back from
the past by the pale, emaciated figure facing him. The man wearing leg
irons and handcuffs secured to a waist belt and flanked by prison guards
seemed so much in contrast to the physically powerful and aggressive Doil
of the past that Ainslie found it hard to believe this really was the condemned prisoner he had come to see. But Doil's behavior had quickly left
no doubt.

The room was quiet now that the priest, Father Ray Uxbridge, had left
under protest, after Doil's insistent demand, "Get that asshole out of here!"

Doil was still kneeling before Ainslie, and the words of the prison officer,
Lieutenant Hambrick—*If you want to hear it at all, better let him do it his
way*—hung in the air.

"Whenever your last confession was," Ainslie told Doil, "doesn't matter now."

Doil nodded, then waited in silence. Ainslie knew why, and reluctantly,
hating himself for the charade, recited, "May the Lord be in your heart and
on your lips so that you may rightly confess your sins."

Doil said immediately, "I killed some people, Father."

Ainslie leaned forward. "Which people? How many?"

"There was fourteen."

Instinctively, Ainslie felt a surge of relief. The small but vocal group who
had been arguing Doil's innocence would be squelched by the statement
he'd just made. Ainslie glanced at Hambrick, who was a witness, remembering, too, that his own concealed tape recorder was running.

Miami Homicide, which conducted investigations into four double serial
killings, and collaborated with Clearwater and Fort Lauderdale police concerning two more, would have their judgments confirmed. Then a thought
struck Ainslie. "Who was the first you killed?"

"Them Ikeis—coupla Japs in Tampa."

"*Who?*" Ainslie was startled. It was a name he had not heard before.

"Two old farts. I-k-e-i." Incongruously, as Doil spelled out the name, he
chuckled.

"You killed them? When?"

"Don't remember . . . Oh, 'bout a month, maybe two, before I done them spics at the trailer place."

"The Esperanzas?"

"Yeah, them."

On hearing Doil admit to fourteen murders, Ainslie had assumed that number included Clarence and Florentina Esperanza, murdered seventeen years ago in West Dade's Happy Haven Trailer Park. As a juvenile, Doil was never charged, though recent evidence had shown him to be guilty—as he had just admitted.

And yet, if the Ikeis were included—a crime that, so far as Ainslie knew, Miami Homicide had never heard of—something was wrong with the numbers.

Ainslie's mind was racing. *Would* Doil admit to a murder of which he *wasn't* guilty, especially now, when he was about to die? *Inconceivable.* So if he had killed the Ikeis and admitted to fourteen murders altogether, that left two victims unaccounted for.

But everyone—police, state attorneys, news media, the public—were convinced that Doil had committed *fourteen* murders: the Esperanzas, Frosts, Larsens, Hennenfelds, Urbinas, Ernsts, and Tempones.

If Doil was telling the truth, had some murders been committed by someone else? And if so, which ones?

Inevitably, Ainslie remembered his own instinct, first expressed to Sergeant Brewmaster, that the Ernst murders might not have been the work of the same serial killer they were after. But for the moment he brushed the thought away; this was no time to indulge personal theories. Earlier, his colleagues had all disagreed with him and he had not contested the consensus view. But now, somehow—representing everyone, all viewpoints, including his own—he had to wring the truth from Doil.

Ainslie glanced at his watch. *So little time!* Less than a half hour to Doil's execution, and they would take him away ahead of time . . . He steeled himself and his voice to lean hard on Doil, remembering Father Kevin O'Brien's words: *Elroy was a pathological liar. He lied when he didn't have to.*

Ainslie hadn't wanted to assume the priestly role; now it was time to drop it. "That's a crock of shit about the Ikeis and the Esperanzas," he scoffed. "Why should I believe you? Where's the proof?"

Doil thought briefly. "In the Esperanzas' trailer I musta dropped a gold money clip. Had 'HB' on it. Got it in a robbery, coupla months before I knocked off them slants. Missed it when I got away."

"And the people in Tampa. What proof there?"

Doil smiled aberrantly. "There's a cem'tery near where the Ikeis lived.

Had ta get rid o' the knife I used, hid it in a grave. Know what was on the marker? Same last name as mine. Saw it, knew I'd remember if I wanted the fuckin' knife back, but I never got it."

"You buried the knife in a grave? Was it deep?"

"No, not deep."

"Why did you always kill old people?"

"They had it good too long, were fulla sin, Father. I did it for God. Watched 'em first, though. All fat cats."

Ainslie let the answer go. All of it made as much sense, or as little, as most of Doil's tortured mind. But how much of the truth was he telling, even now? Some for sure, but Ainslie disbelieved the knife-in-the-grave story; probably the money clip, too. And there was still the problem about numbers. He became specific.

"Did you kill Mr. and Mrs. Frost at the Royal Colonial Hotel?"

Doil nodded several times.

"You nodded your head. If that meant yes, please say so."

Doil looked at Ainslie sharply. "Gotta tape on, ain't you?"

Annoyed that he had given himself away, Ainslie said, "Yes."

"Don't matter. Yeah, I done them people, too."

At the mention of a tape, Ainslie had glanced toward Lieutenant Hambrick, who shrugged. Now Ainslie continued.

"I want to ask about other names."

"Okay."

Ainslie went through the list—Larsen, Hennenfeld, Urbina. In each case the answer was yes, Doil admitted having killed them.

"Commissioner and Mrs. Ernst."

"No, I never done them. That's what—"

Not letting him finish, Ainslie said sharply, "Wait!" He went on, speaking for the consensus viewpoint he was representing, "Elroy, at this time, because of what's soon to happen, you *must* tell the truth. The Ernsts were killed in the same way as all the others—exactly the same way. And you knew about Bay Point, where they lived. You went there when you worked for Suarez Motors; you know the security system and how to get in. And the day after the murders, you left your job at Suarez and never went back, even to collect your paycheck."

Doil's voice was frantic. "That's 'cause I heard about them killings, watched the fuckin' TV an' figured, because of them others, they might think it was me. But it wasn't. Father, I swear! That's what I want forgiveness for. *I didn't do it!*"

Ainslie persisted, "Or is it because you think the Ernsts were important people and—"

Doil cut in, shouting, his face flushed. "No! No, no! It ain't fuckin' true. I done them others, but I don't wanna die blamed for what I never done."

Was it a lie or the truth? Superficially, Doil was convincing, Ainslie thought, but it was like flipping a coin for the answer.

He pressed on. "Let's clear up something else. Do you admit you killed the Tempones?"

"Yeah, yeah. I done that."

Throughout his trial, despite overwhelming evidence against him, Doil had insisted he was innocent.

"About all those killings—the fourteen you admit to. Are you sorry for those?"

"Fuck 'em all! I don't give a shit! If you wanna know, I enjoyed doin' 'em. Just forgive me them others I never done!"

The demand made no sense, and Ainslie wondered if Doil should, after all, have been declared insane before his trial.

Still trying to reason, Ainslie said, "If you didn't murder Mr. and Mrs. Ernst—as you claim—then you don't need forgiveness. In any case, without contrition and penance for *all* you've done, a priest could not give you absolution, and I'm not a priest."

Even before the words were finished, Doil's eyes were pleading. When he spoke, his voice was choked with fear. "I'm gonna die! Do somethin' for me! Gimme somethin'!"

It was Lieutenant Hambrick who moved first. The young, black prison officer confronted Ainslie. "There's less than five minutes left. Whatever you were or weren't, or are now, doesn't matter. You still know enough to do something for him. Put your goddam pride in your pocket and *do it!*"

A good man, Hambrick, Ainslie thought. He also decided that, true or false, nothing would persuade Doil now to change his story.

He groped in his memory, then said, "Repeat after me: 'Father, I abandon myself into Your hands; do with me what you will.' "

Doil reached out as far as his belt-secured handcuffs would allow. Ainslie moved forward, and Doil placed his hands on Ainslie's. Doil repeated the words clearly, his eyes locked on Ainslie.

Ainslie continued, " 'Whatever You may do, I thank You: I am ready for all, I accept all.' "

It was Foucauld's *Prayer of Abandonment*—left for all sinners by the French nobleman Viscount Charles-Eugène de Foucauld, once a soldier, then a humble priest remembered for his life of study and prayer in the Sahara Desert.

Ainslie hoped his own memory would last. He took it line by line.

> *"Let only Your will be done in me,*
> *and in all Your creatures—*
> *I wish no more than this, O Lord,*
> *Into Your hands I commend my soul."*

There was a second of silence. Then Hambrick announced, "It's time." He told Ainslie, "Mr. Bethel is waiting outside. He'll take you to your witness seat. Let's all move quickly."

The two prison guards had already raised Elroy Doil to his feet. Strangely composed, as compared with his mood of a few moments earlier, he let himself be led, walking awkwardly in his leg irons, toward the door.

Ainslie preceded Doil. A waiting guard outside, with the name tag BETHEL, said, "This way, sir." At a fast pace now, they moved back the way Ainslie had come, through concrete corridors, then circuiting the execution area and pausing at a plain steel door. Beside it a sergeant guard held a clipboard.

"Your name, please?"

"Ainslie, Malcolm."

The sergeant checked off the name on the clipboard. "You're the last. We saved a hot seat for you."

Behind him, Bethel said, "You'll make the man nervous, Sarge. It's not *the* hot seat, Mr. Ainslie."

"No, not that one," the sergeant agreed. "That's reserved for Doil, but he said to give you a good view." He regarded Ainslie curiously. "Also said you are God's avenging angel. That true?"

"I helped get him convicted, so maybe that's the way he sees it." Ainslie did not enjoy the conversation, but he supposed that if you worked in this grim place, a light touch now and then was needed.

The sergeant opened the door; Ainslie followed him inside. The scene ahead, with only minor variations, was as it had been three years earlier. They were at the rear of the witness booth, and immediately in front of them were five rows of metal folding chairs, most already filled. There would, Ainslie knew, be the twelve official witnesses whom he observed soon after his own arrival today, about the same number from the news media, and perhaps a few special visitors approved by the state governor.

Surrounding the witness booth on three sides was an expanse of reinforced and soundproof glass. Visible through the glass and directly ahead was the execution chamber, its central feature the electric chair—made of solid oak, with only three legs, and once described as "rearing back like a bucking horse." The chair, built by convicts in 1924 after Florida's legal form of execution changed from hanging to electrocution, was bolted to the floor. It had a high back and a broad seat covered with thick black rubber. Two vertical wooden posts formed a headrest. Six wide leather straps were designed to secure a condemned prisoner so tightly that any movement was impossible.

Five feet from the chair, and also visible through the glass, was the executioner's booth, a walled enclosure with a rectangular slit for the executioner to peer through. By this time the executioner would already be in place—hooded and robed, his identity a guarded secret. At the exact moment he received a signal from outside, the executioner would turn a red switch inside the booth, sending two thousand volts of electricity into the electric chair and its occupant.

In the execution chamber a few figures were milling around. A prison officer studied his watch, comparing it with a large wall clock with a sweep second hand. The clock showed the time as 6:53.

Within the witness booth a faint hum of conversation ceased, most of the assembled people watching curiously as the guard sergeant led Ainslie to the front row and pointed to an empty central chair. "That's for you."

Ainslie had already noticed that Cynthia Ernst was in the seat immediately to his left, though she neither acknowledged him nor looked at him, keeping her eyes directed forward. Glancing beyond, Ainslie was startled to see Patrick Jensen, who did look over and gave the slightest smile.

2

ABRUPTLY, THE EXECUTION CHAMBER came alive. Five of the men who had been waiting in the chamber formed a line. A prison lieu - tenant in charge stood in front; behind him were two guards, a doctor carrying a small leather medical bag, and a lawyer from the state attorney's office. The prison electrician, surrounded by thick, heavy cables that he would shortly connect, was behind the electric chair.

In the witness booth a guard called out, "Silence, please! No talking." What little conversation there had been ceased entirely.

Seconds later a side door in the execution chamber opened and a tall man with stern features and close-cropped, graying hair entered. Ainslie recognized him as the prison warden, Stuart Foxx.

Immediately behind the warden was Elroy Doil, staring fixedly at the ground as if unwilling to face what he knew must lie ahead.

Ainslie noticed that Patrick Jensen had reached out and was holding Cynthia's hand. Presumably consoling her, he thought, for the murders of her parents.

His eyes went back to Doil, and Ainslie was reminded again of the difference between the once robust, powerful figure of the past, and the pathetic, tremulous creature he had since become.

Doil was still restricted by leg irons, which allowed him to take only small, awkward steps. A prison guard was on each side of him, a third guard in the rear. Each of Doil's hands was secured to one of the guards alongside by an "iron claw" manacle device—a single handcuff with a horizontal metal bar that enabled each guard to totally control one hand, so that any kind of resistance was impossible.

Doil was wearing a clean white shirt and black trousers. A jacket matching the trousers would be placed on him for burial. His shaved head shone where electrically conductive gel had been applied moments earlier.

The small procession had come down what was known as the "death watch corridor," passing through two armored doors, and Doil, when he chose to look up, would see for the first time the electric chair and the audience that had come to watch him die.

Finally he did, and at the sight of the chair, his eyes widened and his face froze with terror. He halted impulsively, averting his head and body as if to bolt away, but it was a split-second gesture only. The guards on both sides instantly twisted the iron claws, causing Doil to yelp with pain. All three guards then closed in on him, propelling him to the chair, and while he struggled in vain, they lifted him into it.

In his helplessness, Doil looked intensely at the red telephone on a wall to the right of the electric chair. As every condemned prisoner knew, it represented the only chance of a last-minute reprieve from the state governor. Doil stared at the phone, as if pleading for it to ring.

Suddenly he turned toward the glass separating him from the witness booth and began shouting hysterically. But because the glass was soundproof, Ainslie and the others could hear nothing. They simply watched Doil's face contort with rage.

He's probably ranting about Revelation, Ainslie thought grimly.

In earlier days the sounds within the execution chamber were transmitted to witnesses through microphones and speakers. Now, all that witnesses heard was the warden's reading of the death warrant, his prompting of the condemned for any last words, and whatever brief statement followed.

Then for a moment Doil stopped and scanned the faces in the witness booth, causing several to fidget uncomfortably. When his eyes fell on Ainslie, Doil's expression changed to pleading, his lips framing words that Ainslie understood. "Help me! Help me!"

Ainslie felt beads of sweat break out on his forehead. *What am I doing here?* he asked himself. *I don't want to be involved in this. Whatever he's done, it's wrong to kill anyone this way.* But there was no means of moving. In a bizarre fashion, within this prison Ainslie and the others with him were prisoners, too, until Doil's execution was concluded. Then, when a guard on the execution floor moved, blocking Doil's view, Ainslie felt a flood of relief, while reminding himself that Doil had just confessed to fourteen vicious murders and dismemberments.

For a moment, he realized, he had fallen into the same warped trap as the mawkish protesters outside the prison—caring about the murderer while forgetting his dead, savaged victims. Still, if cruelty was an issue, Ainslie thought, these last few minutes were probably the cruelest of all. No matter how fast the prison staff worked, the final procedures all took time. First, Doil was pulled back into the chair by the guards on either side and held there while a wide chest strap was cinched and secured; now, whatever else he did, he could no longer move his body. Next his feet were seized and pulled down into T-shaped wooden stocks, then secured by ankle straps so that neither foot could shift at all. More conductive gel was applied—this time to his previously shaved right leg; after that a lead-lined leather ground pad was put around the leg four inches above the ankle and laced tightly. Meanwhile the remaining straps had been cinched and tightened, including a chin-strap that held Doil's head immovably against the two upright wooden posts at the back of the chair. The brown leather death cap, resembling an ancient Viking helmet, which held a copper conductive plate inside, was poised above the chair like a Damoclean sword about to be lowered . . .

●   ●   ●

Ainslie wondered if electrical execution really was as savage and barbaric as so many claimed. What he was now seeing certainly seemed so, and there were other instances to support that belief. He knew of one—a case nearly a decade ago . . .

On May 4, 1990, in Florida State Prison, a condemned prisoner named Joseph Tafero, convicted of killing two police officers, received an initial two thousand volts. Flames and smoke erupted at once as his head and a supposedly wet sponge beneath the death cap caught fire. The executioner immediately turned the current off. Then, for four minutes, the current was repeatedly turned on and off again, and each time more flames shot out and smoke poured from under a black mask covering Tafero's face. Through it all, Tafero continued to breathe and slowly nod his head until, after three voltage surges, he was finally declared dead. Witnesses were sickened; one fainted. Later an official statement admitted "there was a fault in the headpiece." Another claimed Tafero "was unconscious the minute the current hit him," though few witnesses believed it.

Some people, Ainslie was reminded, argued that execution *should* be barbaric, given the nature of the crime preceding it. The gas chamber, still used in the United States, killed a prisoner by suffocation with cyanide gas, and witnesses said it was a terrible, frequently slow death. There seemed a consensus that death by lethal injection was more humane—though not in the case of former drug users with collapsed veins; finding a vein to administer the dose could take an hour. A bullet to the head, used in China, was probably swiftest of all, but the prior torture and degradation was undoubtedly the world's most bestial.

Would Florida adopt some other form of execution, perhaps lethal injection? Ainslie speculated. It seemed unlikely, given the public mood about crime, and widespread anger that criminals had brought the Sunshine State into international disrepute, thereby frightening away tourists, so vital to Florida's livelihood.

As to his own feelings about capital punishment, he had been opposed to it as a priest and was against it now, though for different reasons.

Once upon a time he had believed all human life to be divinely inspired. But not anymore. Nowadays he simply believed that judicial death morally demeaned those who administered it, including the public in whose name executions were carried out. Also, whatever the method, death was a release; a lifetime in prison without parole was a greater punishment by far . . .

*　　*　　*

The warden's voice interrupted Ainslie's thoughts, this time transmitted to the witness booth, as he read aloud the black-bordered death warrant, signed by the state governor.

" 'Whereas . . . Elroy Selby Doil was convicted of the crime of murder in the first degree, and thereupon . . . sentenced for said crime to suffer the pains of death by being electrocuted by the passing through his body of a current of electricity . . . until he be dead . . .

" 'You the said Warden of our State Maximum Security Prison, or some deputy by you to be designated, shall be present at such execution . . . in the presence of a jury of twelve respectable citizens who shall be requested to be present, and witness the same; and you shall require the presence of a competent practicing physician . . .

" 'Wherefore fail not at your peril . . . ' "

The document was lengthy, burdened by pompous legalisms, and the warden's words droned on.

When he was finished, a prison guard held a microphone before Doil, and the warden asked, "Do you have any last words?"

Doil tried to wriggle but was too tightly secured. When he spoke, his voice was choked. "I never . . ." Then he spluttered, trying vainly to move his head while managing only a feeble "Fuck you!"

The microphone was removed. Immediately the pre-execution procedures resumed, and again Ainslie wished he were not watching, but the process was hypnotic; none of the witnesses turned their eyes away.

A tongue pad was forced between Doil's teeth, so he could no longer speak. Beside the chair, the prison electrician dipped his hand into a five-gallon bucket containing a strong salt solution and retrieved the copper contact plate and a natural sponge. He inserted both in the death cap poised above Doil's shaven head. The contact plate was a perfect conductor of electricity; the salt-soaked sponge, also a good conductor, was intended to prevent the burning of Doil's scalp and the resulting sickly stench of seared flesh that had offended witnesses in the past. Mostly the sponge worked; occasionally, as in the Tafero execution, it didn't.

The death cap was lowered onto Doil's head and secured in place. At the front a black leather strip served as a mask, so that Doil's face could no longer be seen.

Ainslie sensed a collective sigh of relief from the witnesses around him. Had it, he wondered, become easier to watch now that the victim had, in a sense, become anonymous?

Not anonymous, though, to Cynthia in the seat beside him. Ainslie saw now that Cynthia and Patrick Jensen had their hands entwined so tightly that Cynthia's knuckles were white. She must hate Doil fiercely, he thought, and in a way he could understand why she was here, though he doubted that watching Doil die would ease her grief. And should he tell her, he wondered, that while Doil had confessed to fourteen murders, he had denied killing Gustav and Eleanor Ernst—something Ainslie himself considered might be true? Perhaps he owed that information to Cynthia, if only because she was a former police officer and colleague. He wasn't sure.

On the execution floor, all that remained was the connection of two heavy electric feed lines, one to the top of the death cap, the other to the lead-lined ground pad around Doil's right leg. Both were attached quickly and locked down with heavy wing nuts.

At once the guards and electrician stepped back, well clear of the chair, though making sure not to block the warden's view.

In the witness booth, some of the media people were scribbling notes. One woman witness had grown pale and held a hand to her mouth as if she might be sick. A man was shaking his head, clearly dismayed by what he saw. Knowing the intense competition for seats, Ainslie wondered what motivated people to come. He supposed it was a universal fascination with death in all its forms.

Ainslie returned his attention to the warden, who had rolled up the death warrant and now held it, poised like a baton, in his right hand. He looked toward the executioner's booth, from where, through the rectangular eye slit, a pair of eyes peered out. In a single gesture the warden lowered the rolled warrant and nodded his head.

The eyes disappeared. An instant later a heavy *thunk* reverberated throughout the execution chamber as the red death switch was turned on and heavy circuit breakers engaged. Even in the witness booth, where microphones and speakers were again cut off, a softer thud was audible. Simultaneously the lights all dimmed.

Doil's body convulsed, though the initial effect of two thousand volts surging through him was largely suppressed because, as a reporter wrote for the next day's edition, Doil was "strapped in tighter than a fighter pilot." The same effect, however, was repeated during a two-minute automatic killing cycle, the voltage falling to five hundred, then rising back again to two thousand, eight times in all. At some executions the warden would signal the executioner to override the automatic control and switch off if he believed the first cycle had done the job. This time he let the full cycle run, and Ainslie suddenly smelled the rancid odor of burning flesh, which had seeped into the witness booth through the air conditioning. Others nearby wrinkled their faces in disgust.

When safety clearance had been given, the doctor moved to the chair, opened Doil's shirt, applied a stethoscope, and listened for a heartbeat. After about a minute he nodded to the warden. Doil was dead.

The rest was routine. Electric lines, belts, and other fastenings were quickly undone. Doil's released body slumped forward into the arms of the waiting guards, who swiftly transferred it to a black rubber body bag. The bag was zipped up so quickly that it was impossible to see from the witness booth if the body was burned. Then, on a gurney, the remains of Elroy Doil disappeared through the same doorway that only minutes earlier he had entered alive.

By this time most witnesses were on their feet, preparing to leave. Without waiting, Ainslie turned toward Cynthia and said quietly, "Commissioner, I feel I should tell you that shortly before his execution, I talked to Doil about your parents. He claimed—"

Instantly she swung toward him, her expression blank. "Please, there is nothing I want to hear. I came to watch him suffer. I hope he did."

"He did," Ainslie said.

"Then I'm satisfied, Sergeant."

"I hear you, Commissioner."

But what did he hear? Following the others, Ainslie left the witness booth wondering.

Immediately outside, where witnesses were gathered, waiting to be escorted from the prison, Jensen broke away and approached Ainslie.

"Just thought I'd introduce myself. I'm—"

"I know who you are," Ainslie said coolly. "I wondered why you were here."

The novelist smiled. "I have a scene in a new novel about an execution and wanted to see one firsthand. Commissioner Ernst arranged to get me in."

At that moment Hambrick appeared. "You don't have to wait here," the lieutenant told Ainslie. "If you'll follow me, we'll get your gun, then I'll take you to your car."

With a cursory nod to Jensen, Ainslie left.

3

"I SAW THE LIGHTS DIM," JORGE SAID. "I figured Animal was getting the juice."

Ainslie said quietly, "He was."

It was their first exchange since leaving the prison ten minutes earlier. Jorge was driving the Miami Police blue-and-white and handled outward clearance through the prison checkpoints. They passed the inevitable demonstrators on the way; a few still held lighted candles, but most were dispersing. Ainslie had been silent.

He had been deeply affected by the grim process by which Doil had died. On the other hand, there was no denying Doil got what he deserved, though of course that took into account Ainslie's knowledge that Doil was guilty not only of the two killings for which he had been charged and sentenced, but for at least twelve others.

He touched his suit jacket pocket, where he had put the crucial recording of Doil's confession. When and how the taped information would be released, or if it would be made public at all, would be someone else's decision. Ainslie would turn over the tape to Lieutenant Newbold, and the Police Department and the state attorney's office would handle it from there.

Jorge began, "Was Animal—"

Ainslie interrupted. "I'm not sure we should call him Animal anymore. Animals only kill when they have to. Doil did it for—" Ainslie stopped. Why *did* Doil kill? For pleasure, a religious mania, uncontrollable compulsion? He said aloud, "For reasons we'll never know."

Jorge glanced sideways. "Anyway, did you find out anything, Sergeant? Something you can tell me?"

Ainslie shook his head. "I have to talk with the lieutenant first."

He checked his watch: 7:50 A.M. Leo Newbold was probably still at home. Ainslie picked up the phone from the seat beside him and tapped out the number. Newbold answered on the second ring.

"I thought it was you," he said moments later. "I presume it's all over."

"Well, Doil's dead. But I doubt very much if it's over."

"Did he tell you anything?"

"Enough to know the execution was justified."

"We were certain anyway, but it's a relief to know for sure. So you got a confession?"

Ainslie hesitated. "I've quite a bit to report, sir. But we don't want this going out over the wire services."

"You're right," the lieutenant acknowledged. "We should all be so careful. Okay, not on a cell phone."

"If there's time," Ainslie told him, "I'll call you from Jacksonville."

"Can hardly wait. Take it easy, Malcolm."

Ainslie switched off the cellular.

"You'll have plenty of time; the airport's only sixty miles," Jorge volunteered. "Maybe enough for breakfast."

Ainslie grimaced. "The last thing I feel like is eating."

"I know you can't tell me everything. But I gather Doil must have confessed to at least one murder."

"Yes."

"Did he treat you like a priest?"

"He wanted to. And I guess, to a degree, I let him."

Jorge asked quietly, "Do you believe Doil is in heaven now? Or is there some other fiery spot called hell that's run by Satan?"

Ainslie chuckled and asked, "Why, are you worried?"

"No. Just wanted your opinion—*is* there a heaven and a hell?"

You never leave your past behind totally, Ainslie thought. He remembered parishioners asking him much the same question, and he was never certain how to answer honestly. Now, turning toward Jorge, he said, "No, I don't believe in heaven anymore, and I never did believe in hell."

"How about Satan?"

"Satan's as fictional as Mickey Mouse—invented as an Old Testament character. He's fairly harmless in Job, then in the second century B.C. he was demonized by an extremist Jewish sect called the Essenes. Forget it."

For years after leaving the church, Malcolm Ainslie had been reluctant to discuss his beliefs, disbeliefs, and religion's sophistry, even though he was sometimes sought out as an expert because of his book on comparative religions. *Civilization's Evolving Beliefs*, he learned from time to time, was still widely read. Lately, though, he had become more up front and honest about religion, and now here was Jorge, who so clearly wanted guidance.

They were well clear of Raiford by this time and in open countryside, the grimness of the prison and its dormitory towns behind. The sun was shining brightly, the beginning of a beautiful day. Directly ahead was a four-lane highway, Interstate 10, which they would take into Jacksonville, where Ainslie would catch his flight. He was already happily anticipating his reunion with Karen and Jason and the family celebration.

"Mind if I ask another question?" Jorge said.

"Ask away."

"I always wondered how you got to be a priest to begin with."

"I never expected to be a priest," he said. "It was something my older brother wanted. Then he was shot and killed."

"I'm sorry." Jorge was startled. "Do you mean murdered?"

"The law saw it that way. Though the bullet that killed him was intended for someone else."

"What happened?"

"It was in a small town just north of Philadelphia. That's where Gregory and I grew up . . ."

• • •

New Berlinville was a small borough incorporated near the end of the nineteenth century. It had several steel mills and ironwork factories, as well as producing ore mines. The combination provided work for most local residents, including Idris Ainslie, the father of Gregory and Malcolm, who was a miner. He died, however, when the boys were babies.

Gregory was only a year older than Malcolm, and they were always close. Gregory, big for his age, took pride in protecting his younger brother. Victoria, their mother, never remarried after the death of Idris, but brought up her sons alone. She worked at unskilled jobs, her income aided by a small annuity inherited from her parents, and spent all the time she could with Gregory and Malcolm. They were her life and they, in turn, loved her.

Victoria Ainslie was a good mother, a virtuous woman, and a devout Catholic. As time went by, it became her greatest wish that one of her sons become a priest, and, by precedence and his own willingness, Gregory was chosen.

At eight, Gregory was an altar boy at the community's St. Columkill Church, and so was his close friend, Russell Sheldon. In some ways Gregory and Russell were an unlikely, contrasting combination. Gregory, as he grew, was tall and well built with blond good looks, his nature warm and outgoing; he was also devoted to the church, especially its rituals and theatrics. Russell was a short, tough bulldozer of a boy with a flair for mischief and practical jokes. On one occasion he put hair dye in Gregory's shampoo bottle, turning him temporarily into a brunette. On another he placed an ad in the local paper offering Malcolm's new and beloved bicycle for sale. He also placed

Playboy pinups in both Gregory's and Malcolm's bedrooms for their mother to find.

Russell's father was a police detective in the Berks County sheriff's department, his mother a teacher.

A year after Gregory and Russell became altar boys, Malcolm was recruited, too, and, through succeeding years, the trio were inseparable. And just as Gregory and Russell had differing natures, so did Malcolm. He was an unusually thoughtful boy who took nothing for granted. "You're always asking questions," Gregory once said irritably, then conceded, "But you sure get answers." Malcolm's questioning, combined with decisiveness, sometimes put him—though younger than the other two—in a leadership role.

Within the Church the three were obedient Catholics, their minor sins confessed weekly and consisting mainly of Indecent Sexual Thoughts.

The trio were all good athletes and played for South Webster High's football team, where Russell's father, Kermit Sheldon, was a part-time coach.

Then, toward the end of the trio's second football year, there arose—expressed in biblical terms, as Malcolm Ainslie would remember it—"a little cloud out of the sea, like a man's hand." Unbeknownst to school authorities, *Cannabis sativa* was procured and used by a few senior members of the football team. Before long, other team members learned of marijuana's pleasurable, exciting highs, and soon, inevitably, almost the entire football team was smoking pot. In some ways it was a preview of how cocaine use would expand, more seriously, in the 1980s and 1990s.

The Ainslie brothers and Russell Sheldon were latecomers to cannabis, and tried the "weed," as the players called it, only after being harassed by their peers. Malcolm tried it once, then asked innumerable questions—where the substance came from, what it was, its lasting effect. The answers convinced him cannabis was not for him, and he never used it again. Russell, though, continued using it occasionally, and Gregory more intensively, having convinced himself it was not a religious sin.

Malcolm at first was inclined to question Gregory's growing habit, then let it go, believing his brother was indulging in a fad that would shortly disappear. It was a lapse in judgment that Malcolm would regret for the rest of his life.

The marijuana came mostly in "nickel bags"—plastic bags containing a small quantity of pot and selling for five dollars on the street—meaning the area around South Webster High. However, the total amount consumed by the football players and, by now, other students consistently increased, prompting greater trafficking and competition.

Even in those times, drug gangs were beginning to proliferate, and initially one such gang, the Skin Heads, based in Allentown, supplied the New

Berlinville students' needs. Then, as demand expanded and with increasing cash flow, a gang in nearby Reading, the Krypto-Ricans, looked covetously at the territory. One day they decided to take it over.

It was the same afternoon Gregory and Russell left school and headed for a seedy part of town. Gregory, having been there before, knew exactly where to go.

At the doorway of an abandoned house a burly white male with a shaven head confronted him. "Where you headed, punk?"

"You got four bags of weed?"

"Depends if you got the green, man."

Gregory produced a twenty-dollar bill, which the other snatched, adding it to a bulging roll pulled briefly from his pocket. From behind, another man handed over four nickel bags, which Gregory stuffed beneath his shirt.

At that precise moment a car pulled up outside and three members of the Krypto-Ricans emerged, their guns drawn. The Skin Heads saw the others coming and dived for their guns, too. Moments later, as Gregory and Russell headed for the street to get away, bullets were flying.

Both ran hard until Russell realized that Gregory was no longer at his side. He looked back. Gregory was lying on the ground. By then the wild shooting had stopped, and the members of both gangs were vanishing. Soon after, police and paramedics were called. The paramedics, arriving first, quickly declared Gregory dead, the result of a gunshot wound to the left side of his back.

By chance, because he was driving nearby and heard the dispatcher's radio call, Detective Kermit Sheldon was the first police officer on the scene. Taking his son aside, he spoke sternly. "Tell me everything fast. And I mean *everything*, exactly as it happened."

Russell, still in shock and in tears, complied, adding at the end, "Dad, this will kill Greg's mother, not just him dying, but the marijuana. She didn't know."

Russell's father snapped, "Where is the stuff you bought?"

"Greg hid it in his shirt."

"Do you have any at all?"

"No."

Kermit Sheldon put Russell in his official car, then walked to Gregory's body. The paramedics had finished their examination and covered the body with a sheet. Uniform police hadn't arrived yet. Detective Sheldon looked around. He lifted the sheet, groped inside Gregory's shirt, and found the marijuana packets. He removed and put them in his own pocket. Later he would flush them down a toilet.

Back at his car he instructed Russell, "Listen to me. Listen carefully. This is your story. The two of you were walking when you heard the shooting, and ran to get away. If you saw any of the people with guns, describe them. But nothing more. Stick with that and do not vary it. Later," Russell's father added, "you and I will have a serious talk, which you're not gonna enjoy."

Russell followed the instructions, with the result that subsequent police and press reports described Gregory Ainslie as an innocent victim caught in the crossfire of an out-of-town gang war. Several months after Gregory's death, the bullet that killed him was matched with a gun owned by a Krypto-Ricans gang member, Manny "Mad Dog" Menendez. But by that time Mad Dog was also dead, having been killed in another shootout, this time with police.

Not surprisingly, Russell Sheldon never used marijuana again. He did, however, confide in Malcolm, who had already half-guessed the real story. The confidence they thus shared—as well as grief and a shared sense of blame—made their friendship stronger, a bond that would last across the years.

Victoria Ainslie suffered terribly because of Gregory's death. But the cover-up contrived by Detective Kermit Sheldon left her with a comforting belief in Gregory's innocence, and at the same time, her religious faith consoled her. "He was such a wonderful boy that God wanted him," she told friends. "Who am I to question God's decision?"

Malcolm was impressed by what Russell's father had done—at some risk to himself—to protect the memory of Gregory for their mother's sake. It had not occurred to Malcolm before that police officers could be figures of benevolence in the community as well as enforcers of the law.

It was shortly after Gregory's death that Victoria said to her son, "I wonder if God knew that Gregory was going to be a priest. If He had, He might not have taken him."

Malcolm reached for her hands. "Mom, maybe God knew that I would follow Gregory into the Church."

Victoria looked up with surprise. Malcolm nodded. "I've decided to go to St. Vladimir Seminary with Russell. We've talked about it. I'll take Gregory's place."

And so it happened.

The Philadelphia seminary, which Malcolm Ainslie and Russell Sheldon attended through the next seven years, was an old but renovated turn-of-the-century building, conveying serenity and erudition, an atmosphere in which both young men were immediately at home.

From the beginning, Malcolm's decision to seek religious orders entailed no sacrifice for him. He was happy and composed when it was made. In what he saw as their order of importance, he believed in God, the divinity of Jesus, and the Catholic Church, which brought system and discipline to those other beliefs. Only years later would he realize that, as an ordained priest, he would be expected to reorient that precedence subtly, so that, as in Matthew 19:30, the "first shall be last; and the last shall be first."

The seminary education, strong on theology and philosophy, was the equivalent of college, followed by three more years of theology, producing, at the end, a doctoral degree. Thus, having graduated at ages twenty-five and twenty-six respectively, Fathers Malcolm Ainslie and Russell Sheldon were appointed associate parish priests—Malcolm at St. Augustus Church in Pottstown, Pennsylvania, Russell at St. Peter's Catholic Church in Reading. The two parishes were in the same archdiocese and only twenty miles apart.

"I suppose we'll be visiting each other all the time," Malcolm said cheerfully, and Russell agreed, their closeness having persisted through the seminary years. But in fact, because of heavy workloads and a shortage of Catholic priests worldwide, which would continue and worsen, their meetings were few and hurried. That is, until several years later, when a natural catastrophe brought them, once more, close together.

• • •

"And that," Ainslie told Jorge, "is pretty much how I became a priest."

Several minutes earlier, in the Miami blue-and-white, they had passed through Jacksonville. Now the airport was visible directly ahead.

"So how come you left the Church and became a cop?" Jorge asked.

"It's not complicated," Ainslie told him. "I lost my faith."

"But how'd you lose your faith?" Jorge persisted.

Ainslie laughed. "That *is* complicated. And I have a plane to catch."

4

I DON'T BELIEVE IT," LEO NEWBOLD SAID. "The bastard probably thought he was being cute, leaving some phony clue so we'd bash our brains together and get nowhere."

The lieutenant was responding to Malcolm Ainslie's report, made from a pay phone at Jacksonville Airport, that while Elroy Doil had admitted to fourteen murders, he had denied killing Commissioner Gustav Ernst and his wife, Eleanor.

"There's too much evidence against Doil," Newbold continued. "Just about everything at the Ernst killings matched those other scenes, and because we held back so much of the information, no one but Doil knew enough to put all that together. Oh, I know you have doubts, Malcolm, and I respect them, but this time I think you're wrong."

A moment of obstinacy seized Ainslie. "That damn rabbit left beside the Ernsts didn't make sense. It didn't fit the other Revelation signs. Still doesn't."

"But that's *all* you have," Newbold reminded him. "Right?"

Ainslie sighed. "That's all."

"Well, when you get back, I guess you should check out that other name Doil gave you. What was it?"

"Ikeis, in Tampa."

"Yeah, and the Esperanza thing, too. But don't take too much time, because we've got two new whodunits here and more pressures every day. As far as I'm concerned, the Ernst case is closed."

"How about the tape of Doil? Should I FedEx it from Toronto?"

"No, bring it back with you. We'll have copies and a transcript made, then decide what to do. For now, have a good trip with your family, Malcolm. You've all earned it."

•   •   •

With ample time to spare, Ainslie boarded his Delta flight for Atlanta en route to Toronto. A light passenger load allowed him a three-seat economy section to himself, where he leaned back and relaxed, enjoying the luxury of being alone.

Despite his efforts to sleep, Jorge's words kept ringing through his mind: *But how'd you lose your faith?*

It was impossible to answer simply, Ainslie realized, because it had happened almost without his awareness as incidents along the way, subtly and over time, contrived to steer him in a new direction.

The first effect occurred during his seven-year education at St. Vladimir Seminary, shared with Russell Sheldon. Malcolm, then twenty-two, was recruited by Father Irwin Pandolfo, a Jesuit priest-professor, to assist him in researching and writing a book about ancient and modern comparative religions. Malcolm accepted eagerly, and thus, for the next two years, slaved over the book project as well as completed regular studies. The result was that by the time *Civilization's Evolving Beliefs* was ready for press, with a publisher hovering, it was hard to tell how much Pandolfo and Malcolm Ainslie had each contributed. Pandolfo, a small man physically but with a large intellect and sense of fairness, then took an extraordinary step. "Your work's been exceptional, Malcolm, and you'll get equal author billing. No discussion. Both our names in the same size type, but mine comes first. Okay?"

Malcolm was so overwhelmed that for once he could not speak.

The book brought both men a great deal of acclaim. But it also made Malcolm, now an acknowledged scholar on the origins of all religions, question aspects of the single religion to which he planned to dedicate his life.

He recalled one occasion—a conversation with Russell near the end of their seminary years. Looking up from some lecture notes, Malcolm asked, "Who was it that wrote, 'A little learning is a dangerous thing'?"

"Alexander Pope."

"He might also have written, 'A *lot* of learning is a dangerous thing, especially for priests-in-training.' "

No need to ask what Malcolm meant. Portions of their theology studies had involved the history of the Bible, both Old and New Testaments. In recent years—mainly since the 1930s—historians and theologians had uncovered facts about the Bible previously unknown.

The Old Testament, for example, still considered by many—especially lay people—as a single, unified text, was perceived nowadays by scholars as a dubious miscellany of independent documents from many sources, much of it "borrowed" by Israel—at the time a small, backward power—from the religious creeds of ancient neighbors. The Old Testament, it was generally agreed, covered a thousand years, from about 1100 B.C.E.—the beginning of the Iron Age—to after 200 C.E.

Historians preferred the terms "Before the Common Era" and "Common Era" to B.C. and A.D., though in numbers of years the meaning was the same.

As Malcolm once joked, "You don't have to work it out like Fahrenheit and Celsius."

Malcolm said to Russell, "The Bible isn't holy, or 'God's word,' as zealots claim. Those who believe that just don't understand—or maybe don't want to know—how the Bible was put together."

"Does any of that lessen your faith?"

"No, because real faith isn't built on the Bible. It stems from our instinct that everything around us didn't happen accidentally, but was an act of God, though probably not God as portrayed by any Bible."

They discussed another scholarly acceptance—that no record or writing about Jesus is known to have existed until fifty years after his death, and then by Paul in First Thessalonians, the New Testament's oldest writing. Even the four gospels—Mark's was first—were all written later, between 70 and 110 C.E.

On another level, until 1933, Catholics were forbidden by papal decree to engage in what was labeled "Bible probing." But in that year the enlightened Pope Pius XI lifted the ban, and Catholic scholars were now as well informed as any in the world, generally agreeing with Protestant researchers in Britain, America, and Germany about Bible authorships and dates.

"They took off the blindfolds," was how Malcolm put it to Russell, "though churches are still concealing those facts about the Bible from the laity. Look, there isn't any question Jesus existed and was crucified; that's in Roman history. But all those stories about him—the virgin birth, the star in the east, shepherds and a neon angel, wise men, the miracles, the Last Supper, even the Resurrection—they're simply legends, passed down by word of mouth for fifty years. As to accuracy . . ."

Malcolm stopped. "Consider this: How many years is it since President Kennedy was killed at Dallas?"

"Nearly twenty."

"And the whole world saw it—television, radio, news reporters, the Zapruder tape, playbacks of everything, then the Warren Commission."

Russell nodded. "And there still isn't agreement about how it happened and who did what."

"Exactly! So go back to New Testament times—*without* communication systems, no surviving records—if any existed—during *fifty* years, and imagine the invention and distortion in all that intervening time."

"Don't you believe those stories about Jesus?"

"I'm doubtful, but it doesn't matter. Whether by legend or fact, Jesus had more effect on the world than anyone else in history, and left behind the purest, wisest teaching there has ever been."

Russell asked, "But was he the Son of God? Was he divine?"

"I'm willing to believe so. Yeah, I still believe it."

"Me too."

But did they really? Even then—at least for Malcolm—faint glimmerings of doubt arose.

Later, during a discourse on Church doctrine by a visiting archbishop, Malcolm stood and asked, "Why is it, Your Excellency, that our Church never shares with parishioners the expanded knowledge we now have about the Bible's origins, and the fresh light it sheds on the life and times of Jesus?"

"Because doing so could undermine the faith of many Catholics," the archbishop responded quickly. "Theological debates are best left to those with the intellect and wisdom to handle them."

"Do you not believe, then, in John 8:32?" Malcolm shot back. " 'Ye shall know the truth, and the truth shall make you free'?"

The archbishop replied tartly, "I would prefer young priests to concentrate on Romans 5:19—'By the obedience of one shall many be made righteous.' "

"Or perhaps Ephesians 6:5, Your Excellency," Malcolm returned, " 'Be obedient to them that are your masters.' "

The lecture hall exploded with laughter. Even the archbishop smiled.

•　•　•

After their seminary graduations, Russell and Malcolm went their separate ways as associate priests, their views about religion and the contemporary scene growing and changing as time moved on.

At St. Augustus Church in Pottstown, Malcolm was second-in-command to Father Andre Quale, who, at sixty-seven and suffering from emphysema, almost never left the rectory and often ate alone in his room.

"So you basically run the show," Russell commented one day over a shared rectory dinner.

"I don't have as much freedom as you think," Malcolm said. "I've already had two reprimands from Old Iron-ass."

"Our lord and master, Bishop Sanford?"

Malcolm nodded. "Some of the old brigade here told him about two of my homilies. He wasn't happy."

"What were they about?"

"One was on overpopulation and family planning; the other on homosexuals, condoms, and AIDS."

Russell burst out laughing. "You sure went for the jugular."

"I guess so. But some obvious things the Church won't recognize exasperate me. Okay, so the physical idea of homosexuality makes my skin crawl, but there are well-known professionals in science and medicine who insist homosexuality is mainly a matter of genes, and that those people can't change, even if they want to."

Russell filled in. "So you ask, 'Who made those people that way?' And if God made us all, didn't he make homosexuals, too?—maybe even for a purpose we don't understand?"

"Our stand on condoms infuriates me even more," Malcolm added. "How can I look my parishioners in the eye and forbid them to use something that helps prevent the spread of AIDS? But the Church doesn't want to hear what I think. They only want me to shut up."

"Are you going to?"

Malcolm shook his head slowly. "Wait till you hear what I'm planning for next Sunday."

•   •   •

The 10:30 A.M. mass began with a surprise. Bishop Sanford arrived, without warning, only minutes before the mass was due to begin. The elderly, wizened prelate was accompanied by an aide, and today was walking with a cane. He had a reputation as a disciplinarian who followed rigidly the Vatican line.

After the opening procession Malcolm publicly welcomed the bishop. Internally he felt his anxiety mounting. The sudden arrival had startled him, since he knew that the remarks he planned to deliver would inevitably meet with Sanford's disapproval. Malcolm had expected word to filter through to the bishop after his homily, and was prepared for that, but having him listen directly was another matter. But it was too late to change, even if he wanted to.

When the time came he leaned forward in the pulpit and spoke forthrightly. "Absolute faith in the reality of God and Jesus Christ is essential to us all. But, equally, we must have strength to retain our faith when it is tested, as occurs so often in our lifetimes. I intend to test your faith right now."

Surveying the crowded pews facing him, he continued, "True faith needs nothing whatever to support it, nothing materialistic, no proof of any kind, because if there were proof we would have no need of faith. And yet at times we do prop up our faith, we support it with a material object, usually the Bible."

Malcolm paused, then asked, "But what if you found out that parts of the Bible, supposedly important parts, and particularly concerning Jesus, were untrue, or distorted, or exaggerated? Could you still hold on to your faith, with the same conviction?"

Half smiling, he asked, "Do I see puzzled faces? Well, I assure you my question is very real. Real because modern scholarship has shown that parts of the Bible *are* almost certainly inaccurate for one simple reason: They were passed down through generations, not by written words, but by word of mouth—a notoriously unreliable means of communication, as we all know.

"This is not news. Historians and Bible scholars have known it for a long time, as have the upper echelons of our Church."

By now there was some stirring among the congregation, a few questioning glances exchanged, and the bishop was frowning and shaking his head.

But Malcolm continued, "Let's take specifics. Did you know that after the crucifixion of Jesus, a gap of fifty years passed before there was any written record about Jesus' birth, his life, his teachings, his disciples, and the Resurrection? Half a century, and if anything *was* written during that time, not a trace remains."

Despite the restiveness of a few in the church, the majority stayed focused on Malcolm as he summarized what was known but so seldom talked about: The gospels were written separately, for varying purposes . . . Matthew's and Luke's gospels were almost certainly copied from Mark's . . . All four are by unknown authors, despite the names on them . . . The New Testament was not assembled until the fourth century C.E. . . . And none of the original text—in Greek, on papyrus scrolls—still exists.

"Papyrus," Malcolm explained, "was made from a reed growing by the Nile and was the only form of paper at that time. But papyrus disintegrated quickly, so all of the original writing was lost. Of course, copies were written, but the Canon copier, if you'll pardon the pun. . . . " He paused, smiling. "Copying machines were still three thousand years away, so changes inevitably occurred. There were other changes in the New and Old Testaments—during translations from Greek and Hebrew to Latin, then to other languages, including English . . . So all we can be sure of is that the Bible as it exists today is neither accurate nor a true copy of what was first set down."

He added thoughtfully, "I tell you all this not to influence your thinking or alter your faith, but simply to relay the facts. I don't believe in withholding the truth—not for any reason."

·   ·   ·

After the mass, as the clergy moved outside to shake hands with departing parishioners, positive words could be heard from those around Malcolm. "Most interesting, Father" . . . "Never heard all that before" . . . "You're right, it should be known more widely."

Bishop Sanford was gracious and smiling as parishioners shook his hand.

When everyone had gone he waved his cane peremptorily, motioning Malcolm aside.

His warmth replaced with glacial coldness, the bishop ordered, "Father Ainslie, you will preach no further homilies here. I am once more reprimanding you, and you will shortly receive orders about your future. Meanwhile I urge you to pray for humility, wisdom, and obedience, qualities you clearly lack and sorely need." Unsmiling, he raised a hand in formal benediction. "May God guide your penance and move you in more virtuous ways."

That night on the phone Malcolm repeated the conversation to Russell, adding, "We're ruled by too many sour old men."

"Who are completely sex-starved. What do you expect?"

Malcolm sighed. "We're all sex-starved. This life is perverse."

"Sounds like another homily in the making."

"No way. Sanford's put a muzzle on me. He thinks I'm a rebel, Russell."

"Has he forgotten Jesus was a rebel? He asked questions just like yours."

"Tell that to Iron-ass."

"What sort of penance do you think he'll give you?"

"Who knows?" Malcolm said. "To tell the truth, I'm not sure I care."

But the answer came quickly.

Bishop Sanford's decision was relayed to Malcolm two days later by Father Andre Quale, who received the news in an archdiocesan letter. Malcolm was to be transferred immediately to a Trappist monastery in the Pocono Mountains of northern Pennsylvania, a lonely place where he would remain indefinitely.

"I've been sentenced to silence in Outer Mongolia," Malcolm reported to Russell. "You know about the Trappists?"

"A little. They live hard and never speak." Russell recalled an article he had read. The Catholic Order of Cistercians of the Strict Observance, the Trappists' official name, had a doctrine and way of life that were penitential—little food, no meat, arduous manual labor, and strict silence. Founded in France in 1664, the Trappists had seventy monasteries worldwide.

"Penance is what old Sanford promised," Malcolm said, "and he kept his word. I'm to stay there and keep praying—silently, of course—until I'm ready to toe the Vatican line."

"Will you go?"

"I have to. If I don't, they'll unfrock me."

"Which might not be the worst thing for either of us." The impulsive words tumbled out, surprising Russell himself.

"Maybe not," said Malcolm.

•   •   •

He went to the monastery and, to his surprise, found himself at peace. The hardships he simply shrugged off. The silence, which he had expected to be a burden, wasn't, and later, when he returned to the outside world, he found it full of senseless chatter. People, Malcolm realized, were compulsive about filling a silence with their voices. But silence, accompanied by quickly learned hand signals, he discovered in the Poconos, was in many situations more desirable.

Malcolm disobeyed only one condition of his banishment. He did not pray. While the monks around him presumably did so in their silence, he used the time to think, imagine, dip into accumulated knowledge, and assess his past and future.

At the end of a month of introspection he reached three conclusions. He no longer believed in any god, the divinity of Jesus, or the mission of the Catholic Church. While the reasons were multiple, most important was that all religions had a background of, at maximum, a mere five thousand years. Compared with the vast unknown aeons of geological time through which the universe had existed—Earth being a relative pinhead—the duration of religion's presence equaled, perhaps, a single sand grain from the whole Sahara Desert.

It was also increasingly conclusive that mankind, *Homo sapiens*, evolved from hominids—apelike creatures—millions of years ago. The scientific evidence had become increasingly irrefutable, evidence that most religions chose to ignore because accepting it would put them out of business.

Therefore all the many gods and religions were simply *recent*, made-up fantasies.

Then why did so many people choose to believe, Ainslie often asked himself. One answer: It was mainly their subconscious urge to escape oblivion—the dust-to-dust concept, which, ironically, Ecclesiastes spelled out so well.

> *That which befalleth the sons of men befalleth beasts . . . a man*
> *hath no preeminence above a beast; for all is vanity. All go unto one*
> *place; all are of the dust, and all turn to dust again.*

Should the practice of religion be discouraged? Absolutely not! Those who found solace in it should be left alone and, if need be, protected. Malcolm vowed that he would never, of his own accord, disturb the genuine beliefs of others.

As for himself, what came next? Clearly he would quit the priesthood. In retrospect he saw his choice of vocation as a mistake from the beginning—a reality easier to confront because of his mother's death, a year earlier. At their final meeting, and knowing the end was near, Victoria Ainslie had held his hand and whispered, "You became a priest because I wanted it. I'm not sure you really did, but I was full of pride and had my way. I wonder if God will hold that against me as a sin." Malcolm had assured her that God would not, nor did he regret his choice. Victoria died peacefully. But, without her, he felt free to change his mind.

•   •   •

A flight attendant's voice on the PA system broke into Malcolm's thoughts. "The captain advises we will shortly begin our approach into Atlanta. Please make sure your seat belts are fastened, tray tables stowed, and seat backs restored . . ."

Tuning out those familiar words, Malcolm drifted back into the past.

•   •   •

He stayed at the monastery for another month, allowing time for his mind to change. But his convictions only deepened, and at the end of the second month, he wrote a letter of resignation as a priest and simply left.

After walking several miles, carrying all that he wanted from his past in a single suitcase, he was given a ride by a truck driver into Philadelphia. Taking a bus to the city's airport and undecided where to go, he impulsively bought a ticket on the next flight out—a nonstop to Miami. There his new life began.

•   •   •

Soon after Malcolm's arrival he met Karen, a Canadian on vacation.

They were in line at Stan's Dry Cleaners. Malcolm, leaving some shirts for laundering, had been asked by a clerk if he wanted them folded or on hangers. He was hesitating when a voice behind him prompted, "If you travel a lot—folded. If you don't, have hangers."

"I'm all through with traveling," he said, turning to face the attractive young woman who had spoken. Then to the clerk, "So make it hangers."

After Karen had left a dress for cleaning, she found Ainslie waiting at the doorway. "Just wanted to say thanks for your help."

"Why are you through with traveling?" she asked.

"Not the best place to tell you. How about over lunch?"

Karen paused for only a moment, then answered cheerfully, "Sure. Why not?"

Thus their romance began, and they quickly fell in love, leading to Ainslie's proposal of marriage two weeks later.

At about the same time, Malcolm read in the *Miami Herald* that the city police force was recruiting. Spurred by the memory of Russell's father, Detective Kermit Sheldon, who had befriended the Ainslie family, Malcolm applied. He was accepted, and enrolled in the Police Department Academy's ten-week course, emerging with distinction.

Karen not only had no objection to living in Florida instead of Toronto, but loved the idea. And having by now learned about his past, she was perceptive concerning Malcolm's work choice. "In a way you'll be doing the kind of thing you did before—keeping humanity on the straight and narrow."

He had laughed. "It will be a lot more gritty, but a hell of a lot more practical."

In the end, it turned out to be both.

•   •   •

After a gap of several months, Malcolm learned that Russell Sheldon, too, had left the official Catholic Church. Russell's first objective was simple: he wanted to marry and have children. He wrote in a letter to Malcolm:

> *Did you know there are seventeen thousand of us, more or less, in the United States—priests who left the Church by their own decision, and most in their thirties? That's a Catholic figure, by the way.*

Russell, however, neither lost his beliefs nor abandoned religion, and joined an independent Catholic group in Chicago, where he was accepted as a priest, his unfrocking ignored. In the same letter Russell wrote:

> *We worship God and Jesus, but regard the Vatican and Curia as power-obsessed, inward-looking pachyderms which eventually will self-destruct.*
>
> *And we are not alone. All over America are about three hundred parishes of Catholics who've cut their ties to Rome. There are more here in Illinois, five we know of in South Florida, others in California. Don't have a full list because there's no central authority and may never be. Our feeling is that some "infallible" HQ, staffed by deputy-gods, is the last thing we need.*
>
> *Oh yes, we do certain things Rome wouldn't like. We let all who wish take Communion, believing we don't have to protect God from anyone. We'll marry divorced Catholics, and those of the same sex if that's their choice. We do our utmost to persuade against abortion; on the other hand, we believe in a woman's right to choose.*
>
> *We've no elaborate church, no fancy robes, statuary, stained*

glass, or gold ornaments, and won't be buying any. Whatever spare
money there is we use to feed the homeless.
    From time to time we're attacked by the Roman Catholic
Church, and as our numbers grow, it happens more often. They're
increasingly nervous, we think. An RC archbishop told a newspaper
reporter that nothing whatever that we do has God's blessing. Can
you believe that! Rome has the holy ointment; no one else.

Malcolm still heard from Russell occasionally. He continued to be an independent priest, happily married to a former Catholic nun; at last report they
had two children.

•　　•　　•

The Delta flight touched down smoothly at Atlanta and taxied in. All that
remained now was the two-hour flight to Toronto.

Gratefully, Malcolm turned his mind from the past to pleasant thoughts of
the next few days ahead.

5

OUTSIDE IMMIGRATION AND customs at Toronto airport Malcolm was confronted by a raised card reading AINSLIE, held by a uniformed limousine driver.

"Mr. Ainslie from Miami?" the young man inquired pleasantly as Malcolm stopped.

"Yes, but I wasn't expecting—"

"I have a car here with the compliments of General Grundy. It's right outside. May I take your bag, sir?"

Karen's parents, George and Violet Grundy, lived in Scarborough Township, near the eastern limits of Metro-Toronto. The journey there took an hour and a quarter—longer than usual because of a heavy snowfall the previous night, only partially cleared from the transprovince Highway 401. The sky was gloomily gray and the temperature near freezing. Like many Floridians heading north during the winter months, Malcolm realized he was dressed far too lightly, and if Karen had not brought him some warm clothes, he would have to buy or borrow some.

His reception at the Grundys' modest suburban home, however, was exceedingly warm. The moment the limousine stopped outside, the front door flew open and a flock of family members streamed out to greet him— Karen in front, Jason close behind. Karen kissed and hugged him tightly, whispering, "It's so good to have you," which was unexpected and reassuring. Jason was tugging at his coat, shouting, "Daddy! Daddy!" Ainslie lifted him with a joyous "Happy birthday!" and the three were locked together in each other's arms.

But not for long. Karen's younger sister, Sofia, tall, slim, and sexy, eased herself in to give Malcolm an affectionate kiss, followed by her husband, Gary Moxie, a Winnipeg stockbroker who gripped Malcolm's hand, assuring him, "The whole family's proud of what you do, Malc. Want to hear a lot about it while you're with us." The Moxies' two daughters, Myra, twelve, and Susan, ten, joined the noisy, fond welcome.

Violet Grundy, elegant and motherly, with large eyes and a sweet smile, was next, embracing her son-in-law. "We're all so happy you could come. A little delay doesn't matter; what's important is you're here."

As the others turned back toward the house, George Grundy, white-haired, erect, and not an ounce overweight at seventy-five, put an arm around Malcolm's shoulders. "Gary's right, we're proud of you. Sometimes people forget how important it is to put duty first; nowadays so many don't." George lowered his voice. "I gave them all—especially Karen—a little lecture on the subject."

Ainslie smiled; the brief confidence explained a lot. Karen adored her father, and whatever he had said clearly had a strong effect. "Thank you," he said appreciatively. "And a very happy birthday."

Brigadier General George Grundy, an active-duty soldier for most of his life, had served in the Canadian Army in Europe through World War II, where he was commissioned from the ranks, survived some of the heaviest fighting, and received the Military Cross. Later he'd fought in the Korean War. Since retiring at age fifty-five he had been a college lecturer, specializing in international affairs.

"Let's get inside before you turn into a pillar of ice," George Grundy said. "They've planned a full program for both of us."

•   •   •

The welcoming continued through the day. The double-birthday dinner for George and Jason included an additional twelve people, a total of twenty, crammed into the Grundys' modest house. The newcomers included Karen's older brother, Lindsay, from Montreal, who, like Malcolm, had been delayed by his work. With him was his wife, Isabel, their grown son, Owen, and Owen's wife, Yvonne. The other seven guests were longtime friends, mainly ex-military, of George and Violet.

Amid it all, Malcolm found himself the center of attention. "It's like having a real detective from TV," twelve-year-old Myra said after plying him with questions.

Jason sat up, suddenly alert. "My dad's a lot neater than those guys on TV."

Others wanted to hear a description of the execution Malcolm had just attended, of the murders that preceded it, and how they were unraveled. Malcolm answered as honestly as he could, though he left out his final confrontation with Elroy Doil.

"One reason for our interest," George Grundy said, "is the big increase of violent crime in Canada. Time was when you could walk out of your house and feel safe, but not anymore. Now we're almost as gun-crazy here as you are in the States." There were murmurs of agreement.

During a discussion about homicides, Malcolm explained that most murderers were caught either because they did stupid things or failed to realize the forces they were up against.

"You'd think," Sofia Moxie said, "that with so much information—in newspapers and novels, and on TV—about crime and punishment, they'd know the odds are against them."

"*You* would," Malcolm acknowledged. "But the murderers out there are often young and not well informed."

"Maybe they're not informed because they don't read much," Owen Grundy said. He was thin and wiry, an architect with a passion for oil painting.

Malcolm nodded. "Lots of them don't read at all. Some probably *can't* read."

"But they must watch television," Myra said. "And TV criminals get caught."

"Sure they do," Malcolm agreed. "But the crooks on TV seem like big shots. They get *noticed*, and that's what kids—especially deprived kids—want. The consequences come later, when it's usually too late."

To Malcolm's surprise, most of the group favored the death penalty for murder, even crimes of passion. It was an opinion-swing evident in the United States, and now perhaps in Canada, where capital punishment had been abolished nationally in 1976. Isabel Grundy, a homemaker and physics teacher, with a brusque no-nonsense manner, was vehement. "We should bring back capital punishment. Some people say it isn't a deterrent, but common sense says it has to be. Besides, those who get executed are usually the scum of the earth. I know that's not fashionable to say, but it's true!"

Out of curiosity, Malcolm asked, "What kind of death penalty would you favor?"

"Hanging, electrocution, injection—I don't care which, as long as we're rid of those people."

There was an awkward silence, because Isabel had spoken heatedly. Just the same, Malcolm noted, no one contradicted her.

●   ●   ●

For the birthday dinner, a partition between the living and dining rooms had been opened to accommodate a fifteen-foot table with colorful streamers and party hats. While caterers prepared to serve a four-course meal, George and Jason took their places of honor, side by side.

George looked around and commented, "I have a feeling something should be said . . ."

Karen told her father, "Let Malcolm!"

Heads turned toward him. Gary Moxie said, "Ball's in your court, Malc."

Raising his head, Malcolm said, smiling, "A few unrehearsed thoughts for this historic occasion . . ."

He continued, looking around and speaking clearly, "At this table, where we join for food and fellowship, we reaffirm our belief in ethics, truth, love, and—especially today—the best ideals of family life. We celebrate this family's unity, its achievements, good fortune, and—for our youngest clan here—their promise, dreams, and hopes. On this sunny occasion for George and Jason we pledge our mutual loyalty, promising to support each other in difficult times, however and wherever these occur. And as well as family, we welcome those treasured friends who share our celebration and affections."

Malcolm concluded, aware of bilingual Canada, with a robust *"Salut!"*

Amid appreciative murmurs, the toast was echoed. One of the guests said, "I'm a churchgoer, but I like that better than a lot of conventional graces that I've listened to."

The meal proceeded—roast turkey as its centerpiece—followed by more toasts and responses, including a simple but heartfelt "Thanks a lot!" from Jason.

●   ●   ●

The following morning Malcolm, Karen, and Jason walked together through the residential lakeside streets of Scarborough. From high bluffs they could see clearly across Lake Ontario, though neighboring New York State, some ninety miles away, was beyond their sight. It had snowed again during the night, and the trio threw snowballs at each other. After three tries, Jason finally found his target: Malcolm's head. "Wish we had snow in Miami!" he shouted happily.

He was a sturdy boy, square-shouldered, with long, well-shaped legs. His eyes were wide and brown and often looked serious and questioning, as if aware that there was much to discover, though the means of doing so was at times unclear. But now and then his face would light up with a radiant smile—as if to remind the world that life was sunny after all.

Brushing the powdery snow from each other, they resumed walking. These moments were all too few, Malcolm realized, draping his arms around his wife and son.

After a while, as Jason skipped ahead, Karen said, "I guess this is as good a time as any to break some news. I'm pregnant."

Malcolm stopped, his eyes wide. "I thought . . ."

"So did I. It shows sometimes doctors can be wrong. I've had two examinations, the second yesterday; didn't want to tell you sooner and raise both our hopes. But, Malcolm, think about it—we're going to have a baby!"

For the past four years they had wanted another child, but Karen's gynecologist had told her it was unlikely to happen.

Karen went on, "I'd planned to tell you on the airplane coming here . . ."

Malcolm clapped a hand to his head. "Now I understand how you felt yesterday. Darling, I'm sorry."

"Don't be. I know you did the right thing. Anyway, here we are, and now we know. Are you happy?"

Instead of answering, Malcolm swept Karen into his arms and kissed her.

"Hey!" Jason said, and laughed. "Look out!" Then, as they turned, a snowball hit them, perfectly aimed.

• • •

"We gotta do this more often," Gary Moxie said early on the fourth day when the family rendezvous was breaking up with affectionate farewells. They had risen before dawn for a quick breakfast, then departed in several cars, all heading for the Toronto airport and early flights.

George Grundy drove Karen, Malcolm, and Jason. On the way, Jason chatted happily. He said, "Gramps, I'm sure glad we have the same birthday."

"Me too, son," the general told him. "I hope when I'm not around anymore, you'll celebrate for both of us. Think you can do that?"

"Oh yes."

"He'll do it," Karen said. "But you're talking a long way off, Dad. How about having next year's birthdays in Miami? We'll invite the family."

"A done deal!" Her father turned to Malcolm, who was seated behind. "If that's okay with you?"

Malcolm looked startled. "Sorry! What was that?"

Karen sighed. "Hello! Anyone home?"

George Grundy laughed. "Never mind. Used to be that way myself; I know the signs. Were you sorting out tomorrow's problems?"

"To tell the truth, I was," Malcolm acknowledged. He had been wondering: What was the best way to deal with the still unanswered questions arising from the final dialogue with Elroy Doil? And how quickly could it be done?

6

AS IT TURNED OUT, MALCOLM Ainslie had no chance whatever to think about Doil during most of his first day back at work. Upon reaching his desk in Homicide, he found the entire surface covered with files and paper accumulated during the four days he was away.

The first priority was a pile of detectives' overtime slips. Ainslie pulled them toward him. At the next desk, Detective José Garcia greeted him with, "Nice to have you back, Sergeant," then, seeing the overtime slips, "Glad to see you're getting to the important stuff first."

"I know how you guys operate," Ainslie said. "Always out to make an extra buck."

Garcia feigned outrage. "Hey, we got to make sure our kids get fed."

In truth, overtime pay was critical to detectives' livelihood. Paradoxically, while a promotion to detective was coveted and went only to the best and brightest, on the Miami police force no extra pay accompanied the advancement.

Until 1978 Miami detectives received an extra hundred dollars a month in recognition of their specialized duties, skills, and risks. But that year the Fraternal Order of Police union, in which detectives were an oft-ignored minority, needed a bargaining chip and gave away the bonus—a sellout, as detectives saw it, making overtime earnings a necessity. Now, on average, a detective working a regular forty-hour week earned $880, from which taxes took a hefty bite. An additional twenty hours' overtime produced another $660. However, there was a price: any hours left for the detective's normal home life were virtually nil.

Every hour of overtime, though, was reported in detail, then certified by a sergeant in charge of a detective team—a time-consuming chore that Ainslie impatiently completed.

After that came semiannual personnel evaluations—one was now due for each detective on his team, handwritten for a secretary to type. Then still more paper—a review of detectives' reports on investigations in progress, including new homicides—all for memorizing, signature, and action where needed.

"Sometimes," Ainslie complained to Sergeant Pablo Greene, "I feel like a clerk in a Dickens novel."

Greene replied, "That's because we're all busting our butts for Scrooge."

Thus, it was not until late afternoon of his initial day back that Ainslie had time for the Doil matter. Carrying the tape recording, he headed for Newbold's office.

"What kept you?" Leo Newbold asked. "On second thought, don't tell me."

While Ainslie set up a tape recorder, Newbold told his secretary, "No calls unless it's urgent," and closed his office door. "I've been looking forward to hearing this."

Ainslie let the tape run from the beginning—when he had switched it on in the small, austere office near the execution chamber. There was a short silence, then the sound of a door opening as the young prison officer, Hambrick, returned with Elroy Doil, manacled, his head shaved, along with two prison guards, the grim procession trailed by the chaplain, Father Ray Uxbridge. Ainslie murmured an explanation of the sounds.

Newbold listened intently to the exchanges that followed: the chaplain's oleaginous voice . . . Doil's blurred tones addressing Ainslie, *"Bless me Father . . . "* Uxbridge shouting, *"Blasphemy!"* . . . Doil shouting, *"Get that asshole out . . . "*

Newbold shook his head, his face incredulous. "I can't believe this."

"Wait, there's more."

The recording was quieter as Ainslie went through the charade of hearing Doil's "confession."

"I killed some people, Father" . . .

"Who was the first?"

"Coupla Japs in Tampa" . . .

Newbold, his attention riveted, began making notes.

Soon, Doil's affirmation of his other killings . . . *Esperanzas, Frosts, Larsens, Hennenfelds, Urbinas, Tempones . . .*

"The numbers don't add up," Newbold said. "You told me so, though I was hoping . . ."

"That my math was wrong?" Ainslie smiled faintly, shaking his head.

Next came Doil's frantic plea concerning the Ernst murders: *"Father, I swear . . . I didn't do it . . . ain't fuckin' true . . . don't wanna die bein' blamed for what I never done . . . "*

The outpouring continued, then abruptly Newbold exclaimed, "Stop it!" Ainslie pressed the black PAUSE key. In the glass-paneled office there was silence.

"Jesus! It's so goddam real." Newbold rose from his chair, took an impulsive turn around the room, then asked, "How far away was Doil from being dead when he said all this?"

"Ten minutes, maybe. Not much more."

"I don't know, I just don't know. I was sure I wouldn't believe him . . . But when death is that close . . ." The lieutenant faced Ainslie directly. "Do *you* believe what he said?"

Ainslie answered carefully. "I've always had doubts about that one, as you know, so . . ." He left the sentence incomplete.

Newbold finished it. "You find it easier to believe Doil."

Ainslie was silent. There seemed nothing more to say.

"Let's hear the rest of it," Newbold said.

Ainslie pressed PLAY.

He heard himself ask Doil, *"About all those killings—the fourteen you admit to. Are you sorry for those?"*

"Fuck 'em all! . . . Just forgive me them others I never done."

"He's insane," Newbold said. "Or was."

"I thought so, too; still do. But the insane aren't lying every minute."

"He was a pathological liar," Newbold reminded them both.

They stopped, listening again as Ainslie told Doil, *". . . a priest could not give you absolution, and I'm not a priest."*

Then Lieutenant Hambrick, confronting Ainslie: *"You know enough . . . Do something!"*

Newbold's eyes were on Ainslie during Foucauld's *Prayer of Abandonment*, which Ainslie intoned and Doil repeated. The lieutenant passed a hand across his face, seemingly moved, then said softly, "You're a good man, Malcolm."

Ainslie switched off the recorder and rewound the tape.

Back at his desk, Newbold sat silently, clearly weighing what he had believed against what he had just heard. After a while he said, "You were in charge of the task force, Malcolm, so to that extent it's still your case. What do you suggest?"

"We check everything Doil claimed—the money clip, a robbery, the Ikeis, the knife he talked about, and a grave. I'll give it to Ruby Bowe; she's good at that kind of thing. At the end we'll know how much Doil was lying, or if he was lying at all."

"And if, just for once," Newbold queried, "Doil wasn't lying?"

"There isn't any choice. We take a fresh look at the Ernsts."

Newbold looked glum. Few things in police work equaled the frustration of reopening a closed murder case that everyone believed was solved, especially one so public and celebrated.

"Do it," Newbold said finally. "Get Ruby started. We have to know."

7

CHECK OUT THOSE THINGS IN whatever order you want, Detective,"
Ainslie told Ruby Bowe. "But at some point you'll have to go to
Tampa."

It was shortly after 7:00 A.M. the morning following Ainslie's session with
Lieutenant Newbold, and they were in the Homicide offices, Bowe in a chair
alongside Ainslie's desk. The previous evening he had given her a tape deck
and a headset, telling her to take both home and listen to the State Prison
recording. When he first saw her this morning she had shaken her head in
dismay. "That was heavy shit. I didn't sleep much afterward. But I *felt it*.
Closed my eyes and I was *there*."

"So you heard the things Doil said, the stuff we need to check?"

"I wrote them down." Bowe handed Ainslie a notepad, which he glanced
at. Typically, she had listed every point requiring follow-up.

"It's all yours," he told her finally. "I know you'll get it right."

Ruby Bowe left, and Ainslie returned to the accumulated paper that confronted him—though unaware he would have only a few fleeting minutes in
which to work on it.

●   ●   ●

The 911 call came through to the Miami Police Communication Center at
7:32 A.M.

A complaint clerk responded. "Nine-one-one Emergency, may I help
you?" Simultaneously the caller's phone number and a name, T. DAVANAL,
appeared on an ID box above the clerk's computer.

A woman's breathless voice. "Send the police to 2001 Brickell Avenue, just
east of Viscaya. My husband has been shot."

As the caller spoke, the complaint clerk typed the information, then
pressed a computer "F" function key, sending the data to a woman dispatcher
in another section of the spacious room.

The dispatcher reacted promptly, knowing that the address given was in
Zone 74. Her own computer already displayed a list of patrol cars available,
with their numbers and locales. Making a selection, she called by radio,
"One-seven-four."

When Unit 174 responded, the dispatcher sent a loud "beep," prefacing an urgent message. Then by voice, "Take a three-thirty at 2801 Brickell Avenue, east of Viscaya." The "three" was for "emergency with lights and siren," the "thirty" notified a reported firearm discharge.

"QSL. I am at Alice Wainwright Park, close by."

While the dispatcher was speaking, she signaled Harry Clemente, the Communications sergeant in charge of dispatch and radio traffic, who left his central desk and joined her. She pointed to the address on her screen. "That's familiar. Is it who I think it is?"

Clemente leaned forward, then said, "If you mean the Davanals, you're goddam right!"

"It's a three-thirty."

"Holy shit!" The sergeant read the other information. "They got trouble. Thanks, I'll stay close."

The original complaints clerk was still speaking with the 911 caller. "A police unit is on the way to you. Please let me verify your last name. Is the spelling D-a-v-a-n-a-l?"

Impatiently: "Yes, yes. It's my father's name. Mine is Maddox-Davanal."

The clerk was tempted to ask, *Are you* the *famous Davanal family?* Instead she requested, "Ma'am, please stay on the phone until the police unit arrives."

"I can't. I have other things to do." A click as the caller's phone connection ended.

At 7:39 A.M. the dispatcher received a radio call from Unit 174. "We have a shooting here. Request a Homicide unit to Tac One."

"QRX"—shorthand for "stand by."

Malcolm Ainslie was at his desk in Homicide, with his portable radio switched on, when he heard Unit 174's message. Still sorting papers, he motioned to Jorge. "You take it."

"Okay, Sarge." Reaching for his own radio, Rodriguez told the dispatcher, "Thirteen-eleven going to Tac One for Unit one-seven-four." Then, selecting the Tac One channel—exclusive to Homicide: "One-seven-four, this is thirteen-eleven. QSK?"

"Thirteen-eleven, we have a DOA at 2801 Brickell Avenue. A possible thirty-one."

On hearing the address, followed by 31 for "homicide," Ainslie looked up sharply. Abandoning files and papers, he pushed his chair back from the desk and stood. He nodded to Jorge, who transmitted, "One-seven-four, we're en route to you. Secure the scene. Call for more help if needed." Pocketing the radio, he asked, "Is that the home of that rich family?"

"Damn right. The Davanals. I know the address; everyone does." In Miami there was no escaping the family name and its fame. Davanal's department stores were a huge Florida-wide chain. There was also a Davanal-owned TV station which Felicia Maddox-Davanal managed personally. But more than that, the family—originally mid-European but American-Floridian since World War I—was prestigious and powerful, both politically and financially. The Davanals were constantly in the news, sometimes referred to as "Miami's royalty." A less kindly commentator once added, "And they behave that way."

A telephone rang. Rodriguez answered, then passed the phone to Ainslie. "It's Sergeant Clemente in Communications."

"We're on to it, Harry," Ainslie said. "The uniforms called. We're leaving now."

"The DOA is Byron Maddox-Davanal, the son-in-law. His wife made the nine-one-one. You know about the name?"

"Remind me."

"He was plain Maddox when he married Felicia. Family insisted on his name change. Couldn't bear the thought of the Davanal name someday disappearing."

"Thanks. Every bit of info helps."

As he replaced the phone, Ainslie told Rodriguez, "A lot of power people will be watching this one, Jorge, so we can't screw up a thing. You go ahead, get a car and wait downstairs. I'll tell the lieutenant."

Newbold, who had just arrived in his office, looked up as Ainslie strode in. "What's up?"

"A possible thirty-one on Byron Maddox-Davanal at the family home. I'm just leaving."

Newbold looked startled. "Jesus! Isn't he the one who married Felicia?"

"He is. Or was."

"And she's old man Davanal's granddaughter, right?"

"You got it. She made the nine-one-one. Thought you'd want to know." As Ainslie left hurriedly, the lieutenant reached for his phone.

·   ·   ·

"It looks like some feudal castle," Jorge observed as they approached the imposing Davanal residence in an unmarked car.

The turreted, multi-roofed house and its grounds sprawled over three and a half acres. Surrounded by a high, fortress-like wall of quarried stone with buttressed corners, the entire place had a medieval flavor.

"I wonder why they didn't include a moat and drawbridge," Ainslie said.

Beyond the whole complex was Biscayne Bay and, farther out, the Atlantic Ocean.

The massive, rambling house, only partly seen from outside, was accessible through a pair of handsome wrought-iron gates bearing decorative heraldry. At the moment the gates were closed, but on the far side of them a long winding driveway was visible.

"Oh, goddam, not already!" Ainslie exclaimed. He saw a mobile TV van immediately ahead and realized that the Miami media people, monitoring police radio, must have recognized the Davanal address. The van bore the insignia of WBEQ, the Davanal-owned TV station. Perhaps someone inside had tipped them off to be here first, he thought.

Three police blue-and-whites were near the entrance gates, roof lights flashing. Either Unit 174 had asked for help or more units had responded anyway—probably the latter. Nothing like a nosy cop, Ainslie reflected. An argument appeared to be taking place at the gate between two uniforms and the TV crew, among them an attractive black reporter, Ursula Felix, whom Ainslie knew. Already, yellow POLICE LINE DO NOT CROSS tape was in place across the entranceway, though a uniform officer, recognizing Ainslie and Rodriguez, opened a gap, leaving room for their car to pass.

Jorge slowed, but the reporter rushed forward, blocking them. Ainslie lowered his window. "Hey, Malcolm," she pleaded, "talk some sense into these guys! The boss lady, Mrs. Davanal, wants us inside; she phoned to say so. WBEQ is the Davanals' station, and whatever's going on, we want to catch the morning news." As she spoke, Ursula Felix pressed herself against the side of the car. Her ample breasts, made more prominent by a tight silk blouse, were so close that Ainslie could have touched them. Her jet black hair was tightly braided, and a heady perfume wafted into the car.

So there *had* been a call from inside, Ainslie thought—and not from just anyone. Felicia Maddox-Davanal had made the call, a woman who had reportedly become a widow only minutes before.

"Look, Ursula," he said, "right now this is a crime scene, and you know the rules. We'll have a PIO here soon, and he'll let you know whatever we can release."

A cameraman behind the reporter cut in, "Mrs. Davanal doesn't recognize rules when there's Davanal property involved, and it's theirs both sides of the gate." He gestured to the TV van and the house.

"And the lady runs a tight ship," Ursula added. "If we don't get through, we could be out on our asses."

"I'll keep that in mind." Ainslie motioned to Jorge to drive forward through the heavy gates.

"You'll be lead detective," he told Jorge, "though I'll work closely with you."

"Yes, Sergeant."

Gravel crunched beneath their tires as they negotiated the driveway, passing high palms and fruit trees, then a parked white Bentley near the house. They stopped at an impressive main entrance where one of a pair of ponderous double doors was ajar. As Ainslie and Jorge alighted, the door opened fully and a tall, dignified, middle-aged man appeared, impeccably groomed and clearly a butler. He glanced at both detectives' ID badges, then spoke with a British accent.

"Good morning, Officers. Please come inside." In the spacious, grandly furnished hallway he turned. "Mrs. Maddox-Davanal is telephoning. She asked that you wait for her here."

"No," Ainslie said. "There's been a report of a shooting. We'll go to the scene immediately." A wide carpeted corridor branched off to the right; near the end was a uniformed officer who called out, "The body's this way."

As Ainslie moved, the butler insisted, "Mrs. Maddox-Davanal particularly asked—"

Ainslie paused. "What is your name?"

"I'm Mr. Holdsworth."

Jorge, already making notes, added, "First name?"

"Humphrey. But please realize that this house is—"

"No, Holdsworth," Ainslie said. "*You* realize. This house is now a crime scene, and the police are in charge. A lot of our people will be coming and going. Do not get in their way, but don't leave; we'll need to question you. Also, do not disturb anything in the house from the way it is now. Is that clear?"

"I suppose so," Holdsworth said grudgingly.

"And tell Mrs. Maddox-Davanal we would like to see her soon."

Ainslie walked the length of the corridor, Jorge following. The waiting uniform, whose name tag read NAVARRO, announced, "In here, Sergeant," and led the way through an open door into what appeared to be a combined exercise room and study. Ainslie and Jorge, both with notebooks in hand, stood in the doorway, taking in the scene before them.

The room was large and sunny, with early-morning sunlight coming through open French doors. Beyond the doors was an ornate patio providing a spectacular view of the surrounding bay and distant ocean. Within the room and nearest the detectives, a half-dozen black-and-chrome exercise machines were lined up like spartan sentries. An elaborate weightlifting machine dominated, then a rowing simulator, a program treadmill, a climbing device, and two machines of unclear purpose. Easily thirty thousand dollars' worth, Ainslie guessed.

In the same room, facing the exercise area, was the study—elegant and luxurious, with lounge chairs, several tables and cabinets, oak bookshelves filled with leather-bound volumes, and a handsome modern desk with a reclining chair pushed back some distance from the desk.

On the floor between desk and chair was a dead white male. The body was lying on its right side, with the top left side of the head missing, and around the head and shoulders was a mélange of blood, bone splinters, and brains. The bloody mess, beginning to coagulate, extended beyond the body and onto the floor at front and sides. The dead man was dressed in tan slacks and a white shirt, now drenched with blood.

Though no weapon was visible, all signs pointed to death by gunshot.

"Since you arrived," Rodriguez asked Navarro, "has anything been touched or changed?"

The young officer shook his head. "Nothing. I know the drill." A thought struck him. "The dead man's wife was in the room when I got here. She could have moved something. You'll have to ask her."

"We will," Jorge said. "But let me ask you this for the record. There's no weapon in sight. Have you seen one here or anywhere else?"

"I've been looking since I got here, but haven't seen one yet."

Ainslie asked, "When you found Mrs. Maddox-Davanal here, how did she seem?"

Navarro hesitated, then gestured to the body. "Considering the way everything was, and this being her husband and all, she seemed pretty calm; you could even say poised. I wondered about it. The other thing . . ."

Ainslie prompted, "Go ahead."

"She told me there was a TV crew coming from WBEQ. That's the—"

"Yes, the Davanals' station. What about it?"

"She wanted me—pretty much ordered me—to make sure they were let in. I told her she'd have to wait for Homicide. She didn't like that." The young policeman hesitated again.

"If there's something else on your mind, let's hear it," Jorge said.

"Well, it's only an impression, but I think the lady's used to being in control—of everything and everybody—and she doesn't like things any other way."

Ainslie asked, "And all that was happening while her husband was lying there"—he pointed to the body—"like that?"

"Just like that." Navarro shrugged. "I guess the rest is for you guys to figure out."

"We'll try," Jorge said, scribbling notes. "Always helps, though, when we draw an observant cop."

Jorge then made the routine calls on his portable radio, summoning an ID crew, a medical examiner, and a state attorney. Soon this room and other parts of the house would be crowded and busy.

"I'll take a look around," Ainslie said. Stepping carefully, he approached the open French doors. He had already noticed that one door seemed to be out of line with the other; inspecting closely, he observed what looked like fresh pry marks on the outside of both doors, around the knobs and lock. Outside he saw several brown footprints on the patio, as if someone had stepped in loose dirt or mud. Beyond the footprints he saw a flower bed fronting a four-foot wall, with more prints in the soil, as if the same person had come over the wall, then approached the house. The prints appeared to be from some kind of athletic shoes.

Within the past few minutes the earlier sunshine had given way to darkening clouds, and now rain seemed likely. Ainslie hurried back inside and instructed Officer Navarro to cordon off the rear of the house and have another uniform officer guard the area.

"As soon as the ID crew gets here," he told Jorge, "have them photograph those footprints before the rain washes them out, and get plaster casts of the ones in the soil. Looks as if someone broke in," Ainslie continued. "In which case it would be before the victim came to this room."

Jorge considered. "Even so, Maddox-Davanal would have seen an intruder—remember, he has a contact wound, so they'd be close. Judging by those exercise gizmos, the guy must have been fit, so you'd expect him to put up a fight, but there's no sign of one."

"He could have been taken by surprise. Whoever fired the shot could have hidden, then come up behind him."

"Hidden where?"

Together they looked around the spacious room. It was Jorge who pointed to a pair of green velvet curtains on either side of the French doors. The curtain on the right was held back by a looped sash, but on the left side the sash was hanging downward and the curtain was loose. Ainslie crossed to the left curtain, drew it toward him carefully, and looked behind it. On the rug were traces of mud.

"I'll get ID onto that, too," Jorge said. "What we need now are some times. Of death, of discovery of the body . . ."

The butler, Holdsworth, appeared and addressed Ainslie. "Mrs. Maddox-Davanal will see you now. Please follow me."

Ainslie hesitated. In a Homicide inquiry it was the investigating detective who sent for those to be questioned, not the other way around. Yet it was not unreasonable, he thought, that a wife would prefer to stay away from the room where her husband's dead body still lay. Ainslie had the right, if he chose, to take anyone, including Davanal family members and staff, to Police Headquarters for questioning, but what, at this point, would that gain?

"All right, lead on," he told Holdsworth, and to Jorge: "I'll come back with some answers about times."

• • •

The drawing room to which Malcolm Ainslie was escorted matched the rest of the house in spaciousness, style, and signs of obvious wealth. Felicia Maddox-Davanal sat on a large wing chair, upholstered in a handsome silk brocade. She was a beautiful woman of about forty, with a classic aristocratic face, straight nose, high cheekbones, smooth brow and jaw—the last hinting at an early face-lift. Her light brown hair, thick and shining, with blond highlights, fell loosely to her shoulders. She wore a short cream-colored skirt that showed her well-shaped legs, and a matching silk blouse with a wide, gold-trimmed belt. She was perfectly groomed in every way—face, hair, nails, and clothes—and knew it, Ainslie thought.

Without speaking, she motioned him to an armless French antique chair facing her—a somewhat rickety gem and decidedly uncomfortable, he noted with amusement. If it was an attempt to make him feel servile, it wouldn't happen.

As he usually did in circumstances of bereavement, Ainslie began, "I'd like to say I'm sorry about your husband's death—"

"That is not required." Davanal's voice was firmly composed. "I will deal myself with personal matters. Let us confine ourselves to official business. You are a sergeant, I believe."

"Detective-Sergeant Ainslie." He was on the point of adding "ma'am" but didn't. Two could play the dominance game.

"Well, before anything else, I wish to know why a crew from my own television station—entirely Davanal-owned—has been prevented from coming to this house, which is also Davanal property."

"Mrs. Maddox-Davanal," Ainslie said quietly but firmly, "as a courtesy I will answer that question, even though I think you already know the answer. But when I have finished I will take over this interview." He was conscious, as he spoke, of the woman's cool gray eyes focused unwaveringly on him. He met her gaze with equal aplomb.

"About the TV crew," he said. "A so-far unexplained death has occurred here, and for the time being, no matter who owns this house, the police are in charge. And not allowing the media—*any* media person—into a homicide investigation is standard and lawful police procedure. Now, having dealt with that, I would like to hear, please, all that you know about your husband's death."

"Just a moment!" An elegant forefinger was pointed toward him. "Who is your superior officer?"

"Detective-Lieutenant Leo Newbold."

"*Only* a lieutenant? In light of your attitude, Sergeant, and before going any further, I shall speak to the chief of police."

Unexpectedly and out of nowhere, Ainslie realized, a confrontation had occurred. Still, it was not unprecedented; sudden stress, especially a violent death, sometimes had that effect on people. Then he remembered Officer Navarro's comment: *The lady's used to being in control . . . she doesn't like things any other way.*

"Madam," Ainslie said, "I will accompany you to a telephone right now, where you may, by all means, call Chief Ketledge." He let his voice become steely. "But while you are talking, inform him that when your conversation is over, I am taking you *into custody*—and that means *restrained in handcuffs*—to Homicide headquarters because of your refusal to cooperate in the investigation of your husband's shooting death."

They faced each other, Davanal breathing heavily, her lips tightly set, her eyes reflecting hatred. At length she looked away, then, turning back, said in a lowered voice, "Ask your questions."

Ainslie took no pleasure in his dialectical victory, and in a normal tone he asked, "When and how did you first learn of your husband's death?"

"Shortly before seven-thirty this morning. I went to my husband's bedroom, which is on the same floor as mine, wanting to ask him a question. When I saw he wasn't there, I went to his study on this floor—he often gets up early and goes there. I found his body as you saw it. Immediately I called the police."

"What was the question you wanted to ask your husband?"

"What?" Davanal appeared startled by Ainslie's unexpected query, and he repeated it.

"It was . . ." She seemed at a loss for words. "I really don't remember."

"Is there a connecting door between your bedroom and your husband's?"

"Well . . . no." An awkward pause. "These are strange questions."

Not so strange, Ainslie thought. First, there was no ready explanation for Davanal going to her husband. Second, the absence of a connecting bedroom door said something about the pair's relationship. "Your husband appears to have received a gunshot wound. Did you hear a shot being fired, or any other noise that could have been a shot?"

"No, I did not."

"Then it's possible your husband could have been killed quite some time before you found him?"

"I suppose so."

"Did your husband have any great problems or enemies? Can you think of anyone who might have wanted to kill him?"

"No." Mrs. Maddox-Davanal had recovered her composure, and went on, "You will learn this sooner or later, so I may as well say it now. In certain ways my husband and I were not close; he had his interests, I have mine, they did not overlap."

"Had this arrangement been going on a long time?"

"For about six years; we were married for nine."

"Did you argue a lot?"

"No." She corrected herself. "Well, we quarreled occasionally about trivial things, but in important ways, hardly at all."

"Were either of you considering a divorce?"

"No. The arrangement we had suited us both. For me there were certain advantages in being married; in a way, it provided a kind of freedom. As for Byron, the plain fact is, he was on to a pretty good thing."

"Will you explain that?"

"When we were married, Byron was a very attractive and popular man, but he didn't have much money and no great job prospects. After our marriage, both of those things were taken care of."

"Could you be specific?"

"He was given two important management posts—first in Davanal's department stores, then at WBEQ."

"Was he still doing either of those jobs?" Ainslie asked.

"No." Felicia hesitated, then went on, "The truth is, Byron didn't measure up. He was lazy and lacked ability. In the end we had to remove him from our business scene entirely."

"And after that?"

"The family simply gave Byron an allowance. That's why I said he was on to a pretty good thing."

"Would you be willing to say how much the allowance was?"

"Is that essential?"

"Probably not. Though I think before this inquiry's over it will come out anyway."

There were several seconds of silence, then Felicia said, "It was two hundred and fifty thousand dollars a year. Byron lived here for free as well, and all that exercise equipment he loved so much was paid for."

A quarter of a million dollars annually, Ainslie reflected, and for doing nothing. The Davanal family, by not having to pay that anymore, would benefit from Byron Maddox-Davanal's death.

"If you're thinking what I think you are," Mrs. Maddox-Davanal said, "forget it!" Then, as Ainslie made no answer, she went on, "Look, I won't waste time or words—for this family, that kind of money's petty cash." She paused. "The real point is that while I didn't love Byron, hadn't for a long time, I still liked having him around. You might even say I'll miss him."

The last observation was made thoughtfully, as if in confidence. Somehow, since their exchange began, her antagonism had evaporated; it was almost, Ainslie thought, as if having been defeated in a showdown, she had surrendered and become a friendly ally. He did not believe, though, everything Felicia Maddox-Davanal had told him—particularly about discovering her husband's body. At the same time his instincts suggested she had not killed her husband, though she possibly knew or guessed who had. In any event, she was hiding something.

"I'm a bit confused," Ainslie said. "You've told me you still liked your husband despite your separate lives. Yet, just after discovering his death, his body even in the same room, you were more concerned about getting your TV crew in. It seems—"

Davanal cut in. "All right, all right! I know what you're suggesting—that I'm cold-blooded; well, maybe I am in part. But what's more important, I'm pragmatic." She stopped.

Ainslie told her, "I'm still listening."

"Well, I realized immediately that Byron was dead, and I had no idea who killed him. It was a fact; nothing I could do would change it. But what I *could* do was make sure that WBEQ—my TV station, which I run personally—broke the news ahead of every competitor, and that's what I did. I sent for one of my crews, then when they weren't allowed in, I got on the phone and gave our newsroom everything I knew. By now it's all over Florida, probably much wider, but we were first, which, in a competitive market, *matters*."

"With all your experience," Ainslie said, "you really did know that your TV people wouldn't be allowed in, didn't you?"

Davanal grimaced. "Oh sure. But I was . . . What's that macho phrase about pushing?"

"Pushing the envelope?"

"Yeah. Been doing it all my life. It's second nature."

"Nothing wrong with that, normally. Not a good idea, though, in a homicide investigation."

They faced each other, then she said, "You're an unusual kind of policeman. There's something about you, I'm not sure what, that makes you differ-

ent . . . and makes me curious." The closing words were accompanied by her
first smile and a hint of sensuality.

"If you don't mind," he responded matter-of-factly, "I still have more questions."

She sighed. "If you must, all right."

"At seven-thirty this morning—the time you said you found your husband's body—and during last night, who else was in this house?"

"Let me think." As she answered and they continued, more facts emerged.

Felicia's parents, Theodore and Eugenia Davanal, lived in the house but
were currently in Italy. Theodore was, in effect, the reigning Davanal, though
he delegated much responsibility to Felicia. A valet and lady's maid worked
for Felicia's parents and lived in, but they, too, were in Italy.

The oldest living Davanal was Wilhelm. Aged ninety-seven and the family
patriarch, he had a suite of rooms high up in the house, where a manservant
and his wife, a nurse, took care of him. "Grandfather is in this house now, and
so are Mr. and Mrs. Vazquez," Felicia explained, "though we see very little of
any of them."

According to Felicia, Wilhelm Davanal was senile, with moments of lucid-
ity, "though they are becoming fewer."

The butler, Humphrey Holdsworth, lived in with his wife, who was a cook.
Two gardeners and a chauffeur, all with families, lived in separate accommo-
dations on the grounds outside.

All of those people, Ainslie knew, must be questioned about any activity
they might have seen or heard the previous night.

"Coming back to the discovery of your husband's body," he said to Felicia.
"I believe that when the police—Officer Navarro—arrived, you were in the
study."

"Yes." She hesitated. "Well, after I first found Byron, I ran out and called
nine-one-one from a phone in the hallway. Then . . . I can't really explain
this . . . but I was drawn back. I suppose I was partly in shock. It was all so
sudden and horrible."

"That's understandable." Ainslie was sympathetic. "My question is, during
those two occasions when you were alone with your husband's body, did you
touch anything, or change or move anything, anywhere in that room?"

"Absolutely not." Felicia shook her head. "I suppose my instincts were that
I shouldn't. But I couldn't, simply couldn't, bear to go even close to Byron or
that desk . . ." Her voice trailed off.

"Thank you," Ainslie said. "For now, I have no more questions."

Felicia Maddox-Davanal stood as their session together ended, her composure once more regained.

"I regret we got off to a bad start," she said. "Perhaps we'll learn to like each other better as time goes by." Unexpectedly, she reached out and touched Ainslie's right hand lightly, letting the tips of her fingers linger for a second or two. Then she turned and a moment later was gone.

• • •

While still alone in the drawing room, Ainslie made two calls on his police radio. Then he returned to Byron Maddox-Davanal's exercise room and study, now bustling with activity. The ID crew had arrived and was working, and the ME, Sandra Sanchez, was closely studying the corpse. The assistant state attorney, Curzon Knowles, who had worked on the Elroy Doil serial killings, was observing, questioning, and making notes.

Outside it was raining, Ainslie saw, but Rodriguez assured him, "We got pictures of those prints in time, good plaster casts, too." Now photos were being taken of the muddy earth behind the curtain with the unfastened sash, after which the mud would be removed and a sample preserved. Elsewhere, fingerprints were being sought.

"Let's talk," Ainslie said. Taking Jorge aside, he described his interview with Felicia Maddox-Davanal, then dictated the names of all others to be questioned. "I've called in Pop Garcia," he told Jorge. "He'll work with you, help out with interviews and anything else you need. I'm leaving now."

"Already?" Jorge regarded him curiously.

"There's someone I want to see," Ainslie said. "A person who knows a lot about old families, including this one. Who maybe can advise me."

8

HER NAME WAS LEGENDARY. In her time she had been considered the most outstanding crime reporter in the country, her reputation far wider than her Florida readership and regular newsbeat of Miami. Her knowledge about events and people was encyclopedic—not only people in crime, but in politics, business, and the social milieu, remembering that crime and those other groups often overlapped. She was now semi-retired, meaning that when she felt like it she wrote a book, which publishers eagerly printed and readers grabbed, though recently she had felt less like writing and more like sitting with her memories and dogs—she owned three Pekingese named Able, Baker, and Charlie. Her intellect and memory, though, were sharp as ever.

Her name was Beth Embry, and while she kept her age a secret, even in *Who's Who in America*, she was believed to be well past seventy. She lived in the Oakmont Tower Apartments in Miami Beach, with an ocean view, and Malcolm Ainslie was one of her many friends.

The second phone call Ainslie had made from the Davanal house was to Beth, asking if he could pay her a visit. Now she greeted him at her apartment doorway. "I know why you're here; I saw you on the morning news, arriving at the Davanals'. As usual, you were shafting a reporter."

He protested, "I never shafted you."

"That's because you were scared of me."

"Damn right," he told her. "Still am." They laughed, then he kissed her on the cheek while Able, Baker, and Charlie bounded and barked around them.

Although Beth Embry had never been conventionally beautiful, she had a bright vitality that was evident in every body movement and facial expression. She was tall and lean, still athletic despite her age, and invariably wore jeans and colorful cotton shirts—today's was a yellow and white check.

The two of them had met ten years ago when, as a newspaper reporter, Beth began showing up early at the homicides Ainslie was investigating and asking for him personally. At first he was wary, then discovered he often got as much from her in background and ideas as he gave out in information. As time went by, a mutual trust grew, prompting Ainslie to direct a few "scoops" Beth's way, knowing she would conceal their source. Then, once in a while, Ainslie would go to Beth for information and advice, as he was doing now.

"Wait a second," she told him. Gathering the three barking Pekingese into her arms, she took them to a back room and closed the door.

Returning, Beth said, "I read that you went to Elroy Doil's execution. Were you making sure he got his just deserts?"

Ainslie shook his head. "Wasn't my choice. Doil wanted to talk to me."

She raised her eyebrows. "A pre-death confession? Do I smell a story?"

"Maybe someday. But not yet."

"I'm still writing occasionally. Do I get a promise?"

Ainslie considered, then said, "Okay, if I'm involved, I promise you'll be the first to know any outcome. But deep throat."

"Of course. Have I ever let you down?"

"No." Though, as always with Beth Embry, there were maneuvers and trade-offs.

The mention of Doil reminded him that by now Ruby Bowe would have begun her inquiry. Ainslie hoped he could quickly resolve this new case. Meanwhile he asked Beth, "Are we off the record now, about the Davanals?"

She answered, "Non-attributable, okay? Like I said, I'm not writing much—the kids on the crime beat are pretty good—but once in a while I get antsy, and I especially might about the Davanals."

"You know a lot about them? And okay, non-attrib."

"The Davanals are part of our history. And Byron Maddox-Davanal, as they made him call himself, was a sad sack. Doesn't surprise me he's been killed; wouldn't have surprised me if he'd killed himself. Do you have a suspect?"

"Not yet. Superficially it looks like an outside job. Why was Byron a sad sack?"

"Because he found out the hard way that 'Man doth not live by bread alone,' even when it's thickly buttered." Beth chuckled. "Any of that familiar to you?"

"Sure. Except you've a couple of different sources in there—started out with Deuteronomy, then finished with Matthew and Luke."

"Hey, I'm impressed! That seminary put its brand on you for life. Any chance you'll flip again and be reborn?" Beth, a churchgoer, rarely failed to needle Ainslie about his past.

"For you," he told her, "I'm turning the other cheek. That's from Matthew and Luke, too. Now tell me about Byron."

"Okay. At first he was the family's great white hope for a new generation of Davanals; that's why they made him change his name when he married Felicia. She's an only child, and unless she conceives, which isn't likely now, the Davanal dynasty will die with her. Well, there was never a shortage of Byron's sperm around town, and presumably he put some in Felicia, but it didn't take."

"I hear he wasn't successful in the family businesses, either."

"He was a disaster. I suppose Felicia told you that, and about his allowance for not working."

"Yes."

"She tells everybody. She had such contempt for him, which made his life even emptier than it was."

"Do you think Felicia might have killed her husband?"

"Do you?"

"At the moment, no."

Beth shook her head decisively. "She wouldn't kill him. First, Felicia's too smart to do anything so stupid. Second, Byron was useful to her."

Ainslie remembered Felicia's words: *The arrangement we had suited us both . . . it provided a kind of freedom.*

It was not hard to guess what her "freedom" meant.

Beth was looking at him shrewdly. "You've figured it out? With Byron in her life, she never had to worry about one of her many men coming on too strong and wanting to marry her."

"Many men?"

Beth put her head back and laughed. "You couldn't count them! Felicia *eats* men. But she tires quickly, then discards them. If any got serious, all she had to say was 'I'm already married.' "

Again, Beth looked searchingly at Ainslie. "Did Felicia come on to you? . . . *She did!* My God, Malcolm, you're blushing!"

He shook his head. "It was momentary, and probably my imagination."

"It wasn't, my friend, and if she fancies the taste of you, she'll try again. Be warned, though—Felicia's honey may be sweet, but she's a queen bee with a sting."

"You mentioned the Davanal dynasty. How far back does it go?"

Beth considered. "To the end of the last century—1898, I'm pretty sure. There was a book written; I remember a lot of it. Silas Davanal and his wife, Maria, came here as immigrants from Upper Silesia; that's between Germany and Poland. He had a little money, not much, and opened a general store. By the end of his life it was Davanal's Department Store, and had made the first fortune. Silas and Maria had a son—Wilhelm."

"Who's just barely alive, right?"

"That sounds like Felicia again. Wilhelm's wife died many years ago, but he's still sharp, even at ninety-seven. I've heard there isn't much that goes on in that old house that he misses. You should talk to him."

Senile, Felicia had told him. "Yes, I will."

"Anyway," Beth continued, "with each Davanal generation the family got richer and more powerful, and that includes Theodore and Eugenia—both of them tyrants."

"Frankly, they all sound like tyrants."

"Not necessarily. It's just that they're all driven by intense pride."

"Pride about what?"

"Everything. They've always cared hugely about appearances. Their public persona must be impeccable, making them superior, even perfect, people. And any dirty little secrets are buried so deep that even you, Detective-Sergeant, might have trouble finding them."

"From what you've told me," Ainslie said, "Felicia isn't always impeccable."

"That's because she's more tuned in to her times. All the same, she's pretty intense about pride and in any case has to conform because Theodore and Eugenia still control the family fortunes. She had trouble with her parents over Byron. They never wanted outsiders to know the marriage failed; that's why Byron got his allowance—to keep it all quiet. And again, they don't much care what kind of life Felicia leads, as long as it's well concealed."

"Is it really concealed?"

"Not as much as Theodore and Eugenia would like. The way I heard, there was a big family row and an ultimatum: If Felicia brought disgrace in any way on the family name, she'd be cut off from running that TV station she loves so much."

They talked on, Ainslie relating in return some additional details of the Maddox Davanal case. At the end, as they both rose, he said, "Thank you, Beth. As always, you've given me a lot to think about."

Able, Baker, and Charlie, released from their confinement, leaped and barked excitedly as he left.

•   •   •

As Malcolm Ainslie returned to the Davanal house, the remains of Byron Maddox-Davanal were being removed in a body bag—destination the Dade County morgue, for autopsy. Sandra Sanchez had already left, leaving behind an opinion that the victim's death occurred somewhere between 5:00 and 6:00 A.M., roughly two hours before Felicia Maddox-Davanal's reported discovery.

In the study and exercise room, the earlier activity had tapered off, though the lead technician, Julio Verona, was still recording evidence. He told Ainslie, "There's something I'd like to show you, when you have a minute."

"Okay, Julio." But first Ainslie went to Detectives Jorge Rodriguez and José Garcia and asked, "What's new?"

Jorge grinned and motioned to Garcia. "He thinks the butler did it."

Garcia said sourly, "*Very* funny!" Then, to Ainslie, "I don't believe that Holdsworth guy, is all. I questioned him, and all my instincts say he's lying."

"About what?"

"Everything—not hearing a shot or any disturbance, when he lives on this floor, and not being on the scene until he was called by the dead man's wife, *after* she'd called nine-one-one. He knows more than he's telling; I'd stake my life on it."

"Have you checked his background?" Ainslie asked.

"Sure have. He's still a British citizen; has been in the States fifteen years on a green card, and never in trouble. I called U.S. Immigration in Miami; they have a file on Holdsworth."

"Anything helpful?"

"Well, this is funny in a way, but Holdsworth does have a criminal record in England and was smart enough to declare it when he made his green card application. Would have been discovered if he hadn't, but it's peanuts."

"Let's hear."

"When he was eighteen—thirty-three years ago—he snatched a pair of binoculars from the backseat of a parked car. A cop saw, and arrested him; he pleaded guilty, got two years' probation, no record since. The Immigration guy I talked to says that when someone applies for a green, they don't take something minor and that long ago seriously, as long as the applicant's declared it. Guess I wasted my time."

Ainslie shook his head. "It's never wasted. Save your notes, Pop. Did anything come from other interviews?"

"Not much," Jorge answered. "Two people—the chauffeur's wife and a gardener—now believe they heard the shot, but thought it was traffic. They have no idea about time, except it was still very dark."

"Has anyone talked to the old man—Wilhelm Davanal?"

"No."

"I'll do that," Ainslie finished.

He, Jorge, and Garcia then joined Julio Verona across the room.

"Take a look at this," Verona said. From a plastic bag, using rubber gloves, the ID chief produced a small gold clock, which he placed on the desk formerly used by Byron Maddox-Davanal. He explained, "Where I just put the clock is exactly where ID found it. Here's a photo confirming that." Verona produced a Polaroid print.

"Look on the back of the clock," Verona continued, "and you'll see there's blood—quite a lot for such a small surface. *But*"—he paused for emphasis— "assuming it's the victim's blood, and remembering the distance from the body, there is no way blood could have got on the *back* of that clock where it is now."

"So what's your theory?" Ainslie asked.

"During the killing, or immediately after, the clock got knocked off the desk into some blood on the floor. Later, some person—maybe the killer— saw the clock, picked it up, and put it back on the desk, where it sat until our crew took this photo."

"Any fingerprints?"

"Sure are—a good set. What's more, two of the prints were bloody, and there were no other prints at all."

"So if you find a match," José Garcia said excitedly, "we'll have the killer."

Verona shrugged. "That'll be for you guys to decide, though I'd say who-ever matches those prints will face tough questions. Anyway, they're being checked against records, and we'll have an ID, if any, tomorrow. Matching the blood with the victim's will take another day. And there's something else. Over here."

The ID chief led the way, stopping at a polished oak cabinet in the exer-cise area. "This was locked; we found some keys in a desk drawer." Opening the cabinet, he revealed an interior lined with red felt and containing firearms. A Browning automatic shotgun, a Winchester semiautomatic deer rifle, and a Grossman .22 automatic rifle were all upright and held in place by metal clips. Alongside, resting on several metal hooks, was a Glock 9mm automatic pistol. Beyond it were a few more empty hooks, shaped to contain another handgun.

The cabinet had several interior drawers. Verona opened two and announced, "It's obvious that Maddox-Davanal liked to shoot, and there's plenty of ammunition here for the shotgun, both rifles, and the Glock hand-gun, which also has a fully loaded clip. As well, there's a box of .357 Magnum hollow-points."

"Bullets for which there's no handgun," Ainslie said.

"Right. Obviously a handgun's missing, and it could have been a .357 Mag-num pistol."

Ainslie considered. "Chances are Maddox-Davanal had permits for his guns. Has anyone checked?"

"Not yet," Verona said.

"Let's do it." Using his police radio, Ainslie placed a phone call to the Homicide offices. Sergeant Pablo Greene answered.

"Pablo, will you do me a favor and go to a computer?" Ainslie asked. "I need a check of Dade County Firearms Registration." A few minutes' pause, then, "The name's Maddox-Davanal, first name Byron . . . Yeah, we're still at the house . . . We'd like to see if anything's registered to him."

While waiting, Ainslie asked Verona, "Were any bullets found here at the scene?"

The ID chief nodded. "Yes, one. It was against the baseboard behind the desk, and must have gone through the victim's head, hit the wall, then fell. It was pretty distorted and we won't be sure until the lab's examined it, but it might have come from a .357 round."

Ainslie spoke into his radio. "Okay, Pablo, go ahead." He listened while making notes. "Got it! . . . Yeah . . . It fits . . . We have that one, too . . . And that . . . Ah! Give me that again . . . Yes, I have it now . . . And that's everything, right? . . . Thanks, Pablo."

Putting away the radio, he told the others, "All these guns are registered to Maddox-Davanal. He also registered a Smith & Wesson .357 Magnum revolver, which isn't here."

The four men stood thoughtfully, silent, weighing the implications.

"Are you guys having the same feeling I am," Garcia said, "that if the missing gun was the murder weapon, this is starting to look like an inside job?"

"It's possible," Jorge agreed. "Except whoever made those footprints outside, then forced open the French doors, could have got the gun before hiding."

"But how'd they know the gun was there, and where the keys were kept?" Garcia asked.

"Maddox-Davanal could have had friends who knew all that," Ainslie said. "Gun owners are big talkers, and they like to show their guns off. Another thing—Julio says the Glock pistol has a loaded clip, so the Smith & Wesson .357 was probably loaded, too."

"And ready to shoot," Garcia added.

"I'm wondering about 'inside,' too, José," Ainslie said, "though let's not lock our minds up yet."

"There's one thing we need," Julio Verona told the others. "We've got a fair number of fingerprints from this room, and we should get voluntary prints from any of the house people who normally come here."

"I'll arrange that," Jorge Rodriguez said.

"Be sure you include Holdsworth," Ainslie told him. "And I guess Mrs. Davanal."

•　　•　　•

That night and the next morning, the "Super-Rich Davanals' Bloody Murder," as one newspaper headline described it, was the dominant story carried by local TV, press, and radio, and there was national coverage, too. Most reports quoted an interview with Felicia Maddox-Davanal on the Davanals' own WBEQ-TV, where she referred to "the savage murder of my husband." Asked if she knew whether police had any suspect in mind, she had answered, "I'm not sure they have anything in their minds. They seem totally lost." She promised that a reward would be posted by the family for information leading to the arrest and conviction of Byron Maddox-Davanal's killer, after—as she put it—"my father returns from Italy, where he is still confined to his hotel in a state of shock."

An AP reporter in Milan, however, who had tried unsuccessfully to interview Theodore Davanal the day after his son-in-law's death, reported that Theodore and Eugenia were observed lunching at the exclusive Ristorante L'Albereta di Gualtiero Marchesi and, in the presence of friends, were laughing uproariously.

Meanwhile, at the Brickell Avenue house, Miami Homicide continued its investigation. During the second day, Malcolm Ainslie, Jorge Rodriguez, and José Garcia met at midmorning in the exercise room and study.

Jorge reported that two housemaids and a male houseman had agreed to voluntary fingerprinting. "But when I asked Mrs. Davanal, she said absolutely no; she wasn't going to be fingerprinted in her own home." The butler, Holdsworth, had also refused.

"That's their privilege," Ainslie mused. "Though I wanted Holdsworth's prints."

"I can try for them without his knowing," Jorge suggested. Police detectives often obtained fingerprints surreptitiously, though officially the practice was frowned on.

"Too risky in this house." Then Ainslie asked Garcia, "That old British police record of Holdsworth's—did you say he was convicted?"

"Pleaded guilty, got probation."

"Then they'll have his prints on record."

Garcia said doubtfully, "After thirty-three years?"

"The Brits are thorough; they'll have them. So call your U.S. Immigration contact again and have them get those old prints sent here—by computer, fast."

"I'll do it now." Garcia nodded eagerly and went to a corner of the room and used his police radio.

Julio Verona, who had arrived a few minutes earlier, said, "Let's hope you find something. Those prints from the clock were a dead end. Nothing comparable either in our records or the FBI's. Oh, and by the way, Dr. Sanchez would like to talk to one of you two at the morgue."

Jorge glanced at Ainslie, who said, "We'll go together."

•   •   •

"There's something funny about this Maddox-Davanal death, something that doesn't fit." Sandra Sanchez sat behind a desk in her second-floor office at the Dade County morgue on Northwest Tenth Avenue. Files and papers were spread around. The ME was holding some handwritten notes.

"Doesn't fit in what way, Doctor?" Jorge asked.

Sanchez hesitated, then said, "The murder scenario I heard all of you discussing. Not my business, really. All I'm supposed to do is give you the cause of death . . ."

"You do a lot more than that, and we all know it," Ainslie assured her.

"Well, it's the bullet trajectory, Malcolm—difficult to follow exactly because so much of the head was blown away. But from what remains, and after X-rays, the bullet appears to have entered the dead man's right cheek, gone upward through his right eye into the brain, then out through the top of the head."

"Sounds enough to kill him," Jorge said, "so what's wrong?"

"What's wrong is that for someone to dispatch him that way, it had to be at extremely close range, with the gun held practically under his nose, then fired."

Jorge asked, "Couldn't the whole thing have been so fast and unexpected that the victim never knew what was happening?"

"Yes, it could, though that's hard to buy. And it leaves two questions: First, why would a shooter take a chance he didn't have to by getting that close to an athletic guy like Davanal? Second, fast or not, the victim would have resisted instinctively, even put up a fight, and there's no evidence of it."

Ainslie reminded Jorge, "When we first viewed the body, you pointed out there was no sign of resistance." He asked Sanchez, "So what else is on your mind? I know there's something."

"Yes, and it's a simple question. Have you considered the possibility of suicide?"

Ainslie was silent, then said slowly, "No, we haven't."

"With plenty of reason," Jorge broke in. "There's strong evidence of forced entry. A patio door was jimmied, there were shoe prints outside, and no gun, which there'd have to have been for suicide . . ."

"Detective," Sanchez shot back, "there is nothing wrong with my hearing, and I was at the death scene for an hour, listening—as I said at the beginning."

Jorge flushed. "Sorry, Doctor; I'll think about your question. There's one thing, though—with a self-inflicted gunshot wound there's always a powder burn on the victim's hand. Was one discovered?"

"The answer's no," Sanchez replied, "even though both hands were checked before autopsy. But anyone who knows about guns can wash a powder burn off. Which brings up another question for you to consider, Malcolm: Is it possible that all that other evidence could be faked?"

"Yes, it *is* possible," Ainslie answered, "and in view of what you've told us, we'll take a fresh look."

"Good." Sanchez nodded her approval. "Meanwhile I'm labeling the death 'unclassified.' "

9

AMONG SEVERAL MESSAGES awaiting Malcolm Ainslie on his return to Homicide was one from Beth Embry. She hadn't left a name, but he recognized the number and called at once.

"I've been canvassing some of my old connections," she announced without preamble. "And I've learned two things about Byron Maddox-Davanal that may interest you."

"You're a love, Beth. What have you got?"

"The guy was in deep money trouble, and I do mean deep. Also, he'd got a young girl pregnant and her lawyer was coming after Byron for support and, failing him, the Davanal family."

Informational shocks, Ainslie thought, were arriving like beach-pounding waves. "Deep trouble sounds right," he answered. "And there's something you said the last time we talked—that it wouldn't surprise you if Byron had killed himself."

"Do things look that way?" Beth sounded startled.

"It's a possibility, though no more at the moment. Tell me about the money trouble."

"Gambling debts. Byron owed the Miami mob. Big. More than two million dollars. They were threatening his life, also threatened to go to Theodore Davanal."

"Who wouldn't pay them a cent."

"Don't be so sure. Anyone who's clambered to the stratosphere like the Davanals have things to hide, and the mob could know about them. But if Theodore had paid them off, it would have meant the end of Byron's cushy freeloading."

Ainslie thanked Beth again, promising to keep her informed.

Jorge had returned to his desk next to Ainslie's. "How about the suicide notion? Are you taking it seriously?"

"I take Sandra Sanchez seriously. And the notion just got more plausible." Ainslie described his conversation with Beth Embry.

Jorge whistled softly. "If it *is* true, it means the Davanal woman lied. I saw her on TV—she talked about 'the savage murder of my husband.' So what's she hiding?"

Ainslie already had a possible answer. It hinged on something Beth Embry had said the first time around, and consisted of one word: *pride*. And Beth had said of the family, *Their public persona must be impeccable, making them superior, even perfect, people.*

"Do we question Mrs. Davanal again?" Jorge asked.

"Yes, but not yet. Let's turn a few more stones over first."

That same day, Wednesday, the Dade County Coroner's Department released the body of Byron Maddox-Davanal to his wife, Felicia, who announced that a funeral service and burial of her late husband would take place on Friday.

• • •

Through most of Thursday the Davanal household was occupied with funeral arrangements and, considerately, the Homicide detectives made themselves inconspicuous. Malcolm Ainslie, however, did ride an elevator in the mansion, two floors up, to meet the Vazquezes—husband and wife— who looked after the patriarch Wilhelm Davanal. He found the couple in their third-floor apartment. They were friendly and helpful and clearly caring of their charge. Yes, they had learned early about the murder of Byron, and were shocked. And yes, "Mr. Wilhelm" knew of it, too, though he would not attend the funeral, owing to the strain involved. Nor would it be possible for Ainslie to meet Mr. Wilhelm during this visit, since he was asleep.

Karina Vazquez, a registered nurse and a responsible, maternal figure in her mid-fifties, explained, "The old gentleman doesn't have much energy and sleeps a lot, especially during the day. But when he's awake—contrary to what you may hear from his family—he's as sharp as a tack."

Her husband, Francesco, added, "Sometimes I think of Mr. Wilhelm as a fine old watch. It will eventually stop, but until it does, its movement works as well as ever."

"I can only hope," Ainslie said, "that someone will speak that way about me someday." He continued, "Do you think the old gentleman can tell me anything about the death?"

"I wouldn't be surprised," Karina Vazquez answered. "He's very tuned in to family affairs, but keeps a lot to himself, and Francesco and I don't ask questions. I know Mr. Wilhelm often wakes up in the night, so maybe he heard something. But we haven't discussed it, so you'll have to ask him yourself."

Ainslie thanked them and agreed to return.

• • •

Though there hadn't been much time, Felicia did her best to arrange a grand funeral for her late husband. The chosen church, a large one, was St. Paul's Episcopal in Coral Gables. News releases were rushed to the media and announcements made on WBEQ. The Davanal stores in the Miami area were closed for three hours so that employees could attend, word being passed that anyone using the time for some other purpose would have his or her name recorded. A Requiem Eucharist was arranged, with full choir, and a bishop, dean, and canon to officiate. Pallbearers included the city's mayor, two state senators, and a U.S. congressman, all drawn by a Davanal summons like iron filings to a magnet. The church was filled, though conspicuously absent were Theodore and Eugenia Davanal, still in Milan.

Malcolm Ainslie, Jorge Rodriguez, and José Garcia were at the funeral, not as mourners but as observers, their eyes scanning the congregation. Despite newly kindled suspicions about suicide, the possibility that Byron Maddox-Davanal had been murdered had not been eliminated, and experience showed that some murderers were morbidly drawn to a victim's funeral.

As well as the detectives, three members of a police ID crew, using concealed cameras, discreetly shot photos of attendees and their car license plates.

•   •   •

During the late afternoon of that day, while the detectives were back at their desks in Homicide, a uniformed U.S. Immigration officer was escorted in, then taken to Garcia.

The two, who knew each other, shook hands. "Thought I'd bring this over," the Immigration man said. He handed the detective an envelope. "It's those fingerprints you wanted. They just came in by e-mail from London."

"Hey, thanks a lot!" Garcia, enthusiastic as usual, beamed. They chatted briefly, then the detective saw the visitor out.

Back at his desk, Garcia waited briefly for Ainslie to finish a phone call, then gave up and headed for the neighboring ID Department to see Julio Verona.

Ten minutes later Garcia was back. Approaching Ainslie, he called out, "Hey, Sergeant, we got a break—a hot one!"

Ainslie swung his chair around.

"It's that son of a bitch butler, Holdsworth; I told you he was lying. Those were *his* prints on that little clock—bloodstained prints—a perfect match. And ID has the blood report back. The blood on the clock is the same type as the victim's."

"Nice going, Pop . . ." Ainslie was interrupted by a shout from another desk: "Call on line seven for Sergeant Ainslie."

Motioning the others to wait, Ainslie picked up his phone and identified himself. A voice responded, "It's Karina Vazquez, Sergeant. Mr. Wilhelm is awake and says he'll be glad to see you. I think he knows something. But please come quickly. He could fall asleep anytime."

Replacing the phone, Ainslie sighed. "Great news, José; gives us a lot to chew on. But there's something I have to take care of first."

•   •   •

On the fourth floor of the Davanal mansion, Mrs. Vazquez escorted Ainslie to a spacious bedroom with handsome light-oak paneling and wide windows overlooking Biscayne Bay. Facing the windows was a large four-poster bed with a slight, gaunt figure in it, propped up by pillows—Wilhelm Davanal.

"This is Mr. Ainslie," Mrs. Vazquez announced. "He's the policeman you agreed to see, Mr. Wilhelm." While speaking, she moved a chair beside the bed.

The figure in the bed nodded and, motioning to the chair, said softly, "Sit down."

"Thank you, sir." As Ainslie did so, Vazquez murmured from behind, "Do you mind if I stay?"

"No. I'd like you to." If anything significant emerged, a witness would be useful.

Ainslie regarded the old man facing him.

Despite age and frailty, Wilhelm Davanal remained a patrician figure, with hawklike features. His hair, totally white, was thin but neatly combed. He held his head straight and upright. Only pockets of loose skin around his cheeks and neck, watery eyes, and a tremor in his hand betrayed his body's near century of wear and tear.

"Pity about Byron." The old man spoke in a weak voice, which Ainslie strained to hear. "Didn't have much backbone, no damn good in our business, but I liked him. Came to see me often; not many others do, too busy. Byron sometimes read to me. Do you know who killed him?"

Ainslie decided to be direct. "We're not sure anyone did, sir. We're looking into the possibility of suicide."

The old man's expression did not change. He seemed to be considering, then said, "Not surprised. Once told me his life was empty."

While Ainslie made quick notes, Vazquez whispered from behind, "Don't waste time, Detective. If you've got questions, ask them quickly."

Ainslie nodded. "Mr. Davanal, last Monday night, or early Tuesday morning, did you hear any noise that might have been a shot?"

This time the voice was stronger. "I heard the shot. Loud. Knew exactly what it was. Know the time, too."

"What time was that, sir?"

"Few minutes after half past five. Have a luminous clock there." With a shaking hand the old man gestured to a small table on his left.

Ainslie remembered that Sandra Sanchez had estimated Byron Maddox-Davanal's death as having occurred between 5:00 and 6:00 A.M.

"After the shot, Mr. Davanal, did you hear anything else?"

"Yes, I had my windows open. Few minutes later, lot of commotion down below. Some on the patio. Voices."

"Did you recognize anyone's voice?"

"Holdsworth. He's our . . ."

The old man's voice was drifting. Ainslie prompted, "Yes, I know he's the butler. Did you recognize any others?"

"I think . . . I think it was . . ." The words trailed off and he said weakly, "Some water." Vazquez brought it, and held him while he sipped. Then Wilhelm's eyes closed sleepily and his head fell back. The nurse lowered him to the pillow, then turned to Ainslie.

"That's all for now, Detective. Mr. Wilhelm will probably sleep for seven or eight hours. I did warn you." She reached over, shifting the old man in the bed to make him comfortable, and a moment later, "I'll see you out."

Outside the bedroom, Ainslie paused. "Mrs. Vazquez, I know the way and can let myself out. Right now there's something more important I need you to do."

She looked at him curiously. "What's that?"

"Later I may want to take a sworn statement from you about the questions and answers you just heard. So I'd appreciate it if you'd go somewhere quiet and write down everything you remember Mr. Davanal and me saying."

"Of course, I'll do it," Karina Vazquez said. "Just let me know when you need me."

As Ainslie drove back to Homicide, he wondered if the name that Wilhelm Davanal had almost spoken was Felicia.

•　　•　　•

"I want an arrest warrant for Humphrey Holdsworth on a charge of murdering Byron Maddox-Davanal," Malcolm Ainslie told Lieutenant Newbold.

Ainslie, Jorge Rodriguez, and José Garcia faced the lieutenant in his office. A few minutes earlier, Ainslie, reading from his notes, had described the evidence against Holdsworth.

"His fingerprints were the only ones on the desk clock that had the victim's blood on it. Therefore, in view of the distance between the clock and the body, it must have been picked up by Holdsworth and placed back on the desk. There was also blood on two of Holdsworth's fingerprints, though we haven't identified it yet.

"Holdsworth lied in a statement to Detective Garcia when he claimed to have known nothing about Byron Maddox-Davanal's murder until Felicia Maddox-Davanal told him *after* she'd called nine-one-one, which we know was at seven-thirty-two A.M.

"Contradicting Holdsworth's statement, Wilhelm Davanal states that at approximately five-thirty A.M. on the day of the murder he heard a loud gunshot, then, a few minutes later, Holdsworth's voice. He knows the butler well, is certain it was him. The sound came from below Mr. Davanal's open bedroom window, on the patio directly outside the murder scene."

Newbold asked, "Do you all think Holdsworth did the killing?"

Ainslie responded. "Within these four walls, sir, no. But we have enough to bring him in, scare him stiff, and make him talk. He knows everything that went on at that scene; all three of us are agreed on that." He glanced at the other two.

"Sergeant's right, sir," Garcia offered. "And it's the only way we're gonna squeeze the truth out of him. Lady Macbeth over there sure as hell won't open her lily lips."

Rodriguez nodded agreement.

"If I approve this," Newbold said, "what's your plan, Malcolm?"

"To get the warrant drawn tonight, then find a judge to sign it. Early tomorrow morning we'll have a squad car join us to pick up Holdsworth. Being handcuffed in a caged car will give him something to think about; also, the faster we get him away from the Davanal house, the better."

"Looks like the best bet we have," Newbold said. "So do it."

•   •   •

It was early evening when Ainslie reached the state attorney's offices on Northwest Twelfth Avenue. He had telephoned Curzon Knowles and knew he'd be waiting.

Seated in the attorney's office, Ainslie described the evidence against Holdsworth. Knowles was familiar with the background.

"Sounds like enough for a warrant," he acknowledged. "We'd need more to convict, though I suppose you're counting on a confession." He regarded Ainslie shrewdly. "Or maybe some finger pointing elsewhere."

Before becoming a lawyer, Knowles had been a New York City police detective and knew from experience the sometimes devious routes to solving a tangled crime. Ethically, though, Ainslie knew they should not discuss the possible misuse of an arrest warrant and he answered warily, "There are always other possibilities, counselor, but at this moment Holdsworth is our strongest suspect."

The attorney smiled. "Funny thing is, when I saw that scene, and knowing Byron slightly, the first thing I thought of was suicide. But Davanals don't kill themselves, do they?"

Though Knowles eyed him cagily, Ainslie said nothing.

The attorney stood. "My secretary's gone home. Let's see how good I am at the computer."

They moved to an outer office, where Knowles, using two fingers at the keyboard but otherwise adept, prepared an affidavit that he printed and Ainslie formally swore and signed. An arrest warrant followed.

"Now," Knowles said, the paperwork complete, "let's see which judges are on call." Back at his desk, he produced a list showing three judges available for extracurricular needs, along with phone numbers and home addresses. "Any preference?" He passed the list over.

"I'll try Detmann." Ainslie had appeared before Ishmael Detmann as a witness several times, and it helped if a judge knew the officer seeking the warrant.

"I'll phone him for you."

Moments later Knowles reported, "The judge's wife says they're having dinner, but her husband will be free by the time you get there."

•   •   •

Judge Detmann, who lived in a small house in Miami Shores, opened the front door himself. Portly, dignified, and graying, he took Ainslie to a study, where Mrs. Detmann brought them both coffee. Seated in facing chairs, the judge looked up from the papers Ainslie had presented him. "You've found a villain pretty quickly. Is your case strong?"

"We think so, Your Honor; so does a state attorney." Again, Ainslie was cautious, knowing that whatever ensued during the day ahead would become public knowledge fast.

The judge glanced down. "Knowles—yes, he's appeared before me many times. Well, his imprint is good enough for me." The judge reached for a pen and signed.

•   •   •

At home, Ainslie set his bedside alarm for 5:00 A.M.

At 5:50, still in darkness, he and Jorge Rodriguez entered the Davanal estate in an unmarked car, followed by a Miami Police blue-and-white. The second car contained two uniform officers, one of them a sergeant.

At the house main entrance, all four police exited the cars and, by prearrangement, Rodriguez took the lead. Facing the massive double doors, he pressed a bell push and held it down for several seconds. After a pause, he pressed it again, then several times insistently. This time there were sounds from inside and a male voice calling, "All right, all right, whoever it is! I'm coming!"

There followed sounds of a bolt being withdrawn, and one of the double doors opened a few inches, restrained by a security chain. The gap revealed the face of the butler, Holdsworth.

Rodriguez announced, "Police officers. Take the chain off, please."

Metallic sounds followed, then the door opened fully, revealing that Holdsworth had dressed hurriedly; his shirt was partially open, and he was pulling on a jacket. When he saw the group outside he protested, "For goodness' sake! What's so urgent?"

Jorge moved closer. Speaking clearly, he declared, "Humphrey Holdsworth, I have a warrant for your arrest on a charge of murdering Byron Maddox-Davanal. I caution you that you have the right to remain silent . . . You need not talk to me or answer any questions . . ."

Holdsworth's jaw dropped, his face displaying shock and disbelief. "Please! Wait!" he implored breathlessly. "This has to be a mistake! It can't be me . . ."

Unheeding, Jorge continued, "You have the right to an attorney . . . If you cannot afford an attorney, one will be supplied . . ."

"No! No! No!" Holdsworth shouted, reaching out for the document Rodriguez was holding. But Ainslie was faster. Moving forward, he seized Holdsworth's arm and ordered, "Be quiet and listen! There's no mistake."

As Rodriguez concluded, he told Holdsworth, "Put your hands behind you."

Before Holdsworth realized what was happening, he was handcuffed. Ainslie signaled the uniform officers. "You can take him now."

"Oh, *do* listen!" Holdsworth pleaded. "This is not fair, not right! Besides, I must tell Mrs. Davanal! She'll know what "

But the uniform officers were propelling him toward their patrol car. Opening the rear door, they thrust Holdsworth inside, pushing down his head to clear the doorway. Then, with the prisoner in the rear cage, struggling and shouting, the blue-and-white moved out.

• • •

The uniform officers delivered Holdsworth to Homicide headquarters, where he was placed in an interrogation room and handcuffed to a chair. Ainslie and Rodriguez, who arrived soon after, left him alone for half an hour, then entered the interrogation room together. They sat down, facing the prisoner over a large metal table.

Holdsworth glared at them, but when he spoke he was calmer than he had been at the house. "I want a lawyer immediately, and I demand that you tell me—"

"Stop!" Ainslie raised a hand. "You want a lawyer and you'll have one. But until your lawyer gets here, we can't question you or answer your questions. First, though, there's some minor paperwork." Ainslie motioned to Rodriguez, who opened a folder, producing a notepad and a form.

Rodriguez asked, "Your full name, please."

"You know it perfectly well," Holdsworth snapped.

Ainslie leaned forward and said calmly, "If you cooperate, this will go much faster."

A pause. Then: "Humphrey Howard Holdsworth."

"Date of birth?"

When the routine information was complete, Rodriguez handed him the form. "Please sign this. It says you've been informed of your rights and have chosen not to answer questions until your lawyer is present."

"How *can* I sign it?" With his left hand Holdsworth gestured to his right, still handcuffed to his chair.

Rodriguez removed the handcuffs.

While Holdsworth rubbed his right wrist and peered mistrustingly at the printed form in front of him, Ainslie rose from his seat. "I'll just be a minute," he told Jorge, and crossed to the door. Opening it, he put his head outside and shouted to no one, "Hey, don't bother bringing those old fingerprints from England yet. We're waiting for a lawyer, so I'll have them later."

Holdsworth turned his head sharply. "What's that about fingerprints from England?"

"Sorry." Returning, Ainslie shook his head. "We can't talk until your lawyer's here."

"Wait a second," Holdsworth said impatiently. "How long will that take?"

Rodriguez shrugged. "It's your lawyer."

Holdsworth was indignant. "I want to know about the fingerprints *now!*"

Rodriguez inquired, "Do you mean you want to talk, and *not* wait for a lawyer?"

"Yes, yes!"

"Then don't sign that form I gave you. Here's another, which says you've been advised of your rights and have chosen—"

"Never mind!" Holdsworth picked up a ballpoint pen and scribbled a signature. He turned to Ainslie. "Now tell me."

"The fingerprints are yours. They were taken thirty-six years ago." Ainslie's voice was quiet and unhurried. "We had them sent from England, and they match those on a desk clock found at the murder scene. It had the victim's blood on it."

A silence followed, lasting several seconds. Then Holdsworth said gloomily, "Yes, I remember picking up that damn clock and putting it on the desk. I wasn't thinking."

Ainslie asked, "Why did you kill Byron Maddox-Davanal, Mr. Holdsworth?"

The butler's face twisted with emotion, then he blurted out, "I didn't kill him! There *was* no murder! It was suicide—that idiot killed himself!"

With the words, Holdsworth's composure broke. Holding his head in his hands, he moved it dejectedly from side to side and spoke haltingly. "I told Mrs. Davanal it wouldn't work, that the police are clever and it would all come out. But no!—she wouldn't listen to me, she knew best, knew it all! But she was wrong. And now *this!*" When Holdsworth looked up his eyes were brimming with tears.

"That old business in England," he said. "The reason for the fingerprints. I declared it—"

"We know about that," Rodriguez told him. "It's trivia, doesn't count."

"I've lived in America fifteen years." Holdsworth was sobbing now. "I've never been in any trouble, and now a murder charge . . ."

"If all you've told us checks out, the murder charge will probably be dropped," Ainslie said. "You're still in serious trouble, though, and what we want from you is complete cooperation—answers to all our questions, nothing held back."

"Ask what you want." Holdsworth straightened, and lifted his head. "I'll tell you everything."

●   ●   ●

The facts, as they emerged, were simple.

Four days earlier, at 5:30 A.M., both Holdsworth and Felicia Maddox-Davanal were awakened by the loud sound of a shot. Still in their night-clothes, they met in the main floor corridor and entered Byron's study-cum-exercise room to find him dead, his head blown partially away. A gun was in his right hand.

"I just felt sick; I didn't know what to do," Holdsworth told Ainslie and Rodriguez. "But Mrs. Davanal was calm. She's always been strong. She took over and began giving orders, both of us believing we were the only ones in the house awake."

According to Holdsworth, Felicia declared, "No one must know my husband killed himself." She went on to say it would mean a terrible disgrace for the family, and Mr. Theodore would never forgive her if she let it become public, so it had to be made to look like murder.

Holdsworth said, "I tried to tell her it wouldn't work. That's when I warned her about the police being smart, and that it would all come out, but she wouldn't listen. She said she'd been with TV reporters at crime scenes and knew just what to do to make things look the way she wanted. She also demanded my loyalty, said I owed a lot to the Davanals, which was true, but now I wish—"

"Let's stay with the facts," Ainslie interrupted. "What happened to the gun?"

"Mrs. Davanal took it out of Mr. Byron's hand. It was one of those he kept in his cabinet."

Ainslie recalled Felicia's reply when asked if she had touched or moved anything while alone in the room with her husband's body: *I couldn't, simply couldn't, bear to go close to Byron or that desk.*

"Where is the gun now?"

Holdsworth hesitated. "I don't know."

Rodriguez looked up from notes he had been making. "Yes, you do. Or you have a pretty fair idea."

"What happened is that Mrs. Davanal asked me how to get rid of the gun so it would never be found. I advised her to throw it down a storm drain; there's one a block away."

"And did she do that?"

"I don't know. I didn't want to know. And that's the truth."

Rodriguez pressed on. "And that business outside—the forced French door, footprints. Who did that?"

"I'm afraid I did. I used a big screwdriver on the door and, for the footprints, wore a pair of my own Nike shoes."

"Was that Mrs. Davanal's idea?"

Holdsworth looked shamefaced. "No, it was mine."

"Where are the screwdriver and shoes now?"

"That same morning, before the police arrived, I walked down the street and threw them in a Dumpster. It was cleared the next day. I checked."

"Is that everything?" Ainslie asked.

"I think so . . . Oh, there was one other thing. Mrs. Davanal got some soap and warm water and washed Mr. Byron's hand, the one that held the gun. She said it was to get rid of a powder burn—she'd learned about that with the TV people, too."

"Have *you* learned anything from all this?" Rodriguez asked.

For the first time, Holdsworth smiled. "Only that I was right about the police being smart."

Suppressing a smile himself, Ainslie said, "Don't get too confident; you've still got things to answer for. You've impeded a police investigation with lies, you helped conceal evidence, and planted false evidence. So for the time being we're going to hold you here."

Soon after, a uniform officer escorted Holdsworth to a holding cell.

When they were alone, Jorge asked Ainslie, "So what comes next?"

"Time to pay our respects to Felicia Davanal."

10

FELICIA DAVANAL WAS NOT AT home. It was 7:50 A.M. No one knew where she had gone.

Karina Vazquez, standing in the front hall with the two detectives, explained, "All I know is that Mrs. Davanal went out of here in a tremendous rush and seemed to be upset. Then I heard her go tearing down the driveway in her car." In the absence of a butler, Wilhelm Davanal's nurse appeared to have taken charge of the lower portion of the house. She added, "It may have had to do with Mr. Holdsworth." Mrs. Vazquez looked from one detective to the other. "You've taken him away, haven't you? Arrested him? His wife is frantic. She's on the phone, trying to get a lawyer."

"A lot of things are happening," Ainslie said noncommittally. "There's been perjury and deceit around here, as you probably know."

"I figured as much," Vazquez conceded. Then a sudden thought: "Maybe Mrs. Davanal went looking for you."

"It's possible," Rodriguez acknowledged. He called Homicide headquarters by radio, then told Ainslie, "No, she hasn't been there."

From behind, they heard hurried footsteps as Francesco Vazquez appeared. He announced breathlessly, "Mrs. Davanal's in the TV studios—WBEQ! They just announced she'll go on the air at eight o'clock to talk about her husband's death."

"That's in three minutes," Ainslie said. "Where can we watch?"

"Follow me," Mrs. Vazquez instructed, and the others fell in behind as she led the way along a corridor and into a home theater, elaborately equipped. A giant television screen covered most of one wall. Francesco Vazquez moved to a control panel, which he manipulated, and a picture appeared—the conclusion of a commercial—accompanied by striking surround sound. A graphic followed—WBEQ—The Morning News—then a woman news reader at a desk, who announced, "Exclusive to WBEQ—an important revelation about the death, believed to have been murder, of Byron Maddox-Davanal. Here is Mrs. Felicia Maddox-Davanal, managing director of this station."

A fast cut revealed a close-up of Felicia's face. It was strikingly beautiful. Ainslie guessed a makeup artist had helped. Her expression was serious.

In the home theater, Mrs. Vazquez gestured to two rows of armchairs. "You can sit down."

"No, thanks," Ainslie said. He and Rodriguez remained standing, the Vazquezes with them.

In a clear and level voice, looking directly into the camera, Felicia began, "I am here, in humility and with remorse, to make a public confession and apology. The confession is that my husband, Byron Maddox-Davanal, was not murdered, as I—and others, at my urging—claimed. Byron died by his own hand; he committed suicide. He is dead, and neither guilt nor blame can any longer be attached to him.

"Yet both of those things—guilt and blame—can and must attach to me. Until this moment of truth I have lied about the manner of my husband's death, have deceived friends and family, made untrue statements to the media and police, concealed evidence, and created false evidence. I do not know what penalty I will pay for this. Whatever it is, I shall accept it.

"My friends, fellow citizens of Miami, the police, and TV viewers—I apologize to you all. And now, having made this confession and apology, I will tell you why—misguidedly—I acted as I did."

Ainslie breathed to Rodriguez, "The bitch has outflanked us again."

"She knew Holdsworth would break," Rodriguez murmured, "so she did this before we could get to her."

Ainslie grimaced. "She'll come out of this smelling like spring flowers."

Karina Vazquez said, "You'd have to get up extra early to outsmart Mrs. Davanal."

Felicia was continuing, her voice more subdued, but clear. "From my earliest youth, sharing the views of others in my family, I have regarded suicide as something shameful—an act of cowardice to escape accountability, leaving others to clean up the mess left behind. The exception, of course, is when someone wants to end the terrible pain of terminal illness. But that was not the case in the death of my husband, Byron Maddox-Davanal.

"Our marriage—and I must continue to be honest—was not, in all its parts, fulfilling. To my great sadness I have no children . . ."

Watching and listening, Ainslie wondered how much advance preparation Felicia had done. Though her words sounded spontaneous, he doubted that they were. She might even be using a TelePrompTer; there had been time for any script to be copied, and she did, after all, control the TV station.

"Something I must make clear," Felicia was now saying, "is that no blame whatever attaches to anyone other than me. A member of my household staff even urged me not to do what I did. Unwisely, I ignored his advice, and I want him especially not to be blamed in any way . . ."

"She's letting Holdsworth off the hook," Rodriguez murmured.

"I do not know," Felicia continued, "what problems—real or imagined— caused my husband to end his life . . ."

"She knows damn well," Rodriguez added.

Ainslie turned away. "We're wasting time here," he said. "Let's go."

Behind them, as they walked away, they could hear Felicia's voice.

●   ●   ●

From his desk at Homicide, Ainslie phoned Curzon Knowles.

"Yes, I watched the lady," the lawyer said in response to Ainslie's question. "If there was an Emmy category for 'Real-Life Hypocrisy,' she'd be a shoo-in."

"You think others will agree?"

"Nope. Apart from cynical prosecutors and cops, everyone else will believe she's fine and noble—a Davanal royal at work."

"What about any charges?"

"You're joking, of course."

"I am?"

"Malcolm, the only thing you've got on this woman is that she gave false information to a police officer and impeded an investigation—both misdemeanors. But as for taking her to court, especially with her being a Davanal and having the best lawyers money can suborn, no prosecutor here would touch it. And in case you're wondering, I went upstairs and talked with Adele Montesino. She agrees."

"So we let Holdsworth go, then?"

"Of course. Let no one suggest American law isn't a level playing field for the rich and the not-quite-so-rich. I'll cancel the arrest warrant."

"You sound skeptical about our systems, counselor."

"It's an ongoing disease I've developed, Malcolm. If you hear of a cure, let me know."

Which appeared to end the Maddox-Davanal case, except for two postscripts. One was a phone message for Ainslie, asking him to call Beth Embry.

As promised, he had kept Beth informed of developments, with the understanding that her source would not be revealed, though so far nothing with her by-line had appeared in print. In returning her call, he asked why.

"Because I've become an old softy instead of what I used to be—a let-the-shit-fall-where-it-may reporter," she told him. "If I wrote about why Byron killed himself, I'd have to describe his gambling debt to the mob, which wouldn't matter, but also the name of the girl he got pregnant, and she's a nice kid who doesn't need it. Incidentally, I want you to meet her."

"You know that Felicia lied when she said she didn't know why Byron killed himself."

"Felicia's definition of truth is what portion of it suits her at the moment," Beth acknowledged. "Now, about the girl. She has a lawyer, and I think you know her—Lisa Kane."

"Yes, I do." Ainslie liked Kane. She was young and intelligent, and often served as a public defender. The difference with Kane was that despite the small fee public defenders received, she would go the extra mile and work to the limit for her clients.

"Could you meet her tomorrow?"

Ainslie agreed he would.

•   •   •

Lisa Kane was thirty-three, looked ten years younger, and some days as if she were still in high school. She had short red hair, a cherubic face with no makeup, and was dressed, when she met Ainslie, in jeans and a cotton T-shirt.

Their rendezvous was a small, dilapidated apartment block, three stories high, in Miami's crime-notorious Liberty City. Ainslie had come alone in an unmarked police car, Lisa in a vintage Volkswagen bug.

"I'm not sure why I'm here," he said. In fact, curiosity had brought him.

"My client and I need some advice, Sergeant," Lisa answered. "Beth said you'd be able to give it." She moved to a stairway and they climbed to the third floor, avoiding garbage and animal droppings, and emerged on a balcony with crumbling cement and rusty railings. Lisa stopped at a door halfway along and knocked. It was opened by a young woman, probably in her early twenties. Taking in her two visitors, she said, "Please come in."

Inside, Lisa announced, "This is Serafine . . . Sergeant Ainslie."

"Thank you for coming." The girl put out her hand, which Ainslie took, at the same time looking around him.

In contrast to the squalid exterior, the small apartment was spotless and gleaming. The furniture was a mixture. Several pieces—a bookcase, twin side tables, a reclining chair—looked expensive; the rest was of poorer quality, but all well cared for. A glimpse into another room revealed the same.

And then there was Serafine—attractive, poised, dressed in a flowered T-shirt and blue leggings, her brown eyes regarding Ainslie gravely. She was black and, it was evident, several months pregnant.

"I'm sorry about the way things are outside," she said, her voice deep and soft. "Byron wanted me to . . ." Abruptly, shaking her head, she stopped.

Lisa Kane took over. "Byron wanted to find a better place for Serafine, but other things got in the way." Then, gesturing, "Let's sit down."

When they were seated, Serafine spoke again, looking directly at Ainslie. "I'm carrying Byron's children. You probably know that."

"Children?"

"My doctor told me yesterday. It's twins." She smiled.

"There's some background," Lisa said. "Byron Maddox-Davanal and Serafine met because she was supplying him with drugs. She and I met when I got her off a drug-trafficking charge with probation. She's clean now, the probation's over, and Byron was off drugs months before he died; he was never a heavy user."

"I'm ashamed, though," Serafine said. She glanced toward Ainslie, then turned her eyes away. "When it happened, I was desperate . . ."

"Serafine has a four-year-old son, Dana," Lisa continued. "She was an unmarried mother, without support, couldn't find a job, and around here there aren't many ways to get money for food . . ."

"I see it all the time." Ainslie's tone was understanding. "So how does Maddox-Davanal fit in?"

"Well, I guess you could say that he and Serafine responded to each other; somehow they filled each other's needs. Anyway, Byron started coming here to get away from his other life, and Serafine weaned him off drugs; she never did any herself. Maybe it wasn't love, but whatever it was worked. Byron had some money, apparently not much, but enough to help. He bought some things"—Lisa motioned around her—"gave Serafine money for food and rent, and she quit selling drugs."

Sure, Byron had money, Ainslie thought. *You can't imagine how much.*

"And of course they had sex," Lisa added.

Serafine broke in. "I didn't plan to get pregnant, but something went wrong. When I told Byron, he didn't seem to mind, said he'd take care of things. He was worried about something else, though, really worried, and one time he talked about being caught in a rat trap. It was right after that he stopped coming."

"We're talking about a month ago, and the money stopped, too," Lisa said. "That's when Serafine called me for help. I tried phoning the Davanal house, but couldn't get Byron and he didn't return my calls. I thought okay, so I went to see Haversham and . . . you know, 'We the People.' "

Ainslie did know. The prestigious Haversham law firm had so many important partners that its full title on a letterhead occupied two lines. It was also well known that the firm represented most of the Davanal interests. "Did you get some result?" he asked.

"Yes," Lisa answered, "and it's why we need your advice."

•   •   •

The Haversham law firm, it emerged from Lisa's recounting, was smart enough to take an unknown young lawyer seriously, treating her with respect. She met with a partner named Jaffrus, who listened to her story, then promised to investigate her client's complaint. A few days later, Jaffrus called Lisa and arranged another meeting, which, as it turned out, took place about a week before Byron Maddox-Davanal's suicide.

"They didn't futz around," Lisa now told Ainslie. "It was obviously confirmed that Byron was responsible, so Haversham's agreed to financial support for Serafine, but under one condition: the Davanal name must never, ever, be used in connection with her child, and there'd be a means to guarantee that."

"What kind of means? What guarantee?" Ainslie asked.

Serafine, Lisa explained, would have to certify under oath, in a legal document, that her pregnancy resulted from fertilization in a sperm bank, with an anonymous donor. Documentation would then be obtained from a genuine sperm bank to confirm the arrangement.

"Probably after a big donation," Ainslie said. "And how much money would there be for Serafine?"

"Fifty thousand a year. But that's before we knew about her twins."

"Even for one child, it isn't enough."

"That's what I thought. It's why I need your advice. Beth said you'd been around the family and you'd know where we should aim."

Serafine had been listening intently. Ainslie asked her, "How do you feel about the sperm-bank thing?"

She shrugged. "All I care is that my children get to live someplace better than this and have the best education. If I have to sign a piece of paper to do it, even if it's not true, okay. And I don't care about the Davanal name. Mine's just as good—maybe better."

"What *is* your last name?"

"Evers. You know it?"

"Yes, I do." Ainslie remembered Medgar Evers, the civil rights activist of the 1960s, a World War II U.S. Army veteran who was shot and killed by a renegade white segregationist, now serving a life sentence for his crime.

"Are you related?" he asked.

"Distantly, I think. Anyway, if one of my children is a boy, I've decided to call him Medgar."

"And if there's a girl, you could call her Myrlie." Ainslie had once met the former wife of Evers, now—as Myrlie Evers-Williams—chairperson of the NAACP board of directors.

"I hadn't thought of that." Serafine smiled again. "Maybe I will."

Ainslie thought back to his conversation with Felicia Davanal, in which she had revealed that Byron received a quarter of a million dollars annually, plus a luxurious life, for, in effect, doing nothing. And then her impatient words: *For this family, that kind of money's petty cash.*

He told Lisa, "Here's my advice. Ask for two hundred thousand dollars a year until the twins are twenty, half to be paid to Serafine for living expenses, the rest to be in trust for the children's education, and her present son . . ."

"Dana."

"There should be room for Dana's education in there, too. Stay with that figure, and if Haversham's—which really means the Davanals—refuses or tries to bargain, tell them to forget the oath and the sperm bank, and you'll take the case to court, Davanal name and all."

"I like the way your mind works," Lisa said. Then, doubtfully, "Though it's a long way from what was offered."

"Do it," Ainslie said. "Oh, and if you want, try to convey to Mrs. Davanal that the settlement idea came from me. It might help."

Lisa regarded him steadily, but merely nodded and said, "Thank you."

•   •   •

Forty-eight hours later, Ainslie was at home when Lisa Kane telephoned. Her voice was breathless. "I can hardly believe it! I'm with Serafine, and I've just had word from Haversham's. They've accepted everything: no changes, no argument, just the way I—no! . . . just the way *you* proposed."

"I'm sure the way you handled it—"

Lisa wasn't listening. "Serafine told me to say she thinks you're wonderful. So do I!"

"Do you know, by chance, if Mrs. Davanal—"

"Mike Jaffrus at Haversham's phoned her with your message, and she sent one back. She wants to see you. Said you should call her house to fix a meeting." Lisa's voice changed, her curiosity too much to contain. "Is there something going on between you two?"

Ainslie laughed. "Beyond a little cat-and-mouse game—nothing."

•   •   •

"One thing I've learned from this experience," Felicia Davanal said, "is not to be indiscreet when talking with a savvy detective, especially if he was once a priest. It can really cost you."

She was with Malcolm Ainslie in the same drawing room where they had met originally. This time, though, he was in a comfortable armchair that matched the one in which Felicia sat, only a few feet away. She was as lovely as before, though more relaxed, obviously because Byron's death was no longer a mystery with unanswered questions hanging between them.

"It sounds as if you've done some digging," Ainslie said.

"My TV station has an efficient research department."

"Well, I hope they made sure there's enough petty cash to handle the settlement."

"Touché!" She leaned back and laughed. "Malcolm—if I may call you that—I'm getting to like you more and more." She paused, then went on, "The report I read about you was highly complimentary. It made me wonder."

"Wonder what, Mrs. Davanal?"

"Felicia—please!"

He inclined his head in acknowledgment. Instinct told him where this conversation was going, and he was uncertain how to handle it.

"I wonder why you're still a policeman when you're so clearly qualified to be something more."

"I like being a cop." Then, after a moment's hesitation, "Felicia."

"That's absurd! You're highly educated, a scholar with a doctorate. You wrote a book on comparative religions that is still a standard reference . . ."

"I was coauthor, and it's a long time ago."

Felicia waved a hand dismissively and continued, "Everything shows you're a *thinking* person. Anyway, I have a suggestion. Why don't you join the Davanal organization?"

He was startled. "In what capacity?"

"Oh, I don't know exactly; I haven't consulted anyone yet. But we always have a need for outstanding people, and if you chose to join us, something matching your abilities could be found." A soft smile accompanied the words, then Felicia reached forward, putting her fingertips on Ainslie's hands. As she moved them slightly, her touch was like gossamer, subtly conveying a promise. "I'm sure that whatever was worked out, it would bring you and me closer." She moistened her lips with her tongue. "If that would interest you."

Yes, it interested him; he was human, Ainslie thought. He felt a mental and physical stirring as temptation beckoned. Then pragmatism prodded. He recalled Beth Embry's words: *Felicia eats men . . . If she fancies the taste of you, she'll try again . . . a queen bee with a sting.*

Sting or not, it would be exciting to be devoured by Felicia, and drown in

her honey—perhaps worth whatever outcome followed. Ainslie had had one
affair that he did not regret even now, despite the penalties of Cynthia's mal-
ice. Where passion was involved, conventional morality often took second
place; his hours of listening in the confessional had demonstrated that. In his
own case, though, he reasoned, the episode with Cynthia had been enough.
With Karen now pregnant with their second child, this was no time to start
dancing to Felicia's wild tune.

He reached out, touching her hand, as she had his. "Thank you, and I may
regret this. But I'll let things stay the way they are."

Felicia had style. She stood, still smiling, and put out her hand formally.
"Who knows?" she said. "Some other time our paths may cross."

●   ●   ●

Driving back to Homicide, Ainslie reminded himself that the *affaire-
Davanal*, apart from postscripts, had lasted only seven days. It seemed much
longer. He was impatient now to hear Ruby Bowe's report.

11

IT TOOK BOWE EXACTLY ELEVEN days to determine whether or not Elroy Doil had been telling the truth during his "confession" to Malcolm Ainslie. Until that eleventh day, the crucial questions remained: Had Doil murdered the Esperanzas in the way he claimed? And had he murdered the Ikeis?

Even if the answers to both questions were yes, there would, of course, still persist the most critical question: If everything Doil had said about the Esperanzas and Ikeis was true, had he also been truthful in his vehement assertion that he did *not* murder Miami City Commissioner Gustav Ernst and his wife, Eleanor? And if Doil was eventually believed about *that*, was there another murderer—a copycat killer—still at large?

• • •

Bowe had begun her search at the Metro-Dade Police Department—Miami's neighboring force—in their imposing building on Northwest 25th Street. She asked if the investigator who had handled the Esperanza double murder case seventeen years earlier was still available.

"Before my time here," a lieutenant in Homicide told her. He reached behind his desk to a shelf of indexed volumes. "Let's see what we have." Then, after turning pages, "Yep, here it is. Esperanza, Clarence and Florentina, case unsolved, still officially open. Are you guys going to close it for us, Detective?"

"Looks like we might, sir. But first I'd like to talk with whoever was in charge."

The lieutenant referred to the page in front of him. "Was Archie Lewis, retired six years ago, lives in Georgia somewhere. It's a Cold Case Squad affair now—you people have one of those, right?"

"Yes, we do."

The Cold Case Squad dealt with old, unsolved serious crimes, especially homicides, which nowadays were being reinvestigated with the aid of new technologies used to review bygone records and evidence. Police departments with such squads were surprisingly successful in solving crimes that their perpetrators hoped had been forgotten long ago.

"We rotate those cold cases around the squad members," the lieutenant said. "Right now the Esperanzas belong to Vic Crowley."

Detective Crowley, who appeared soon after, was balding and amiable. "I went through that old file," he told Ruby. "Figured there was nothing we could work on. Dead as the Esperanzas."

"It may still be." Bowe explained how Elroy Doil had confessed to the Esperanza killings before his execution, though the truth was still in doubt. "I'd like to look at the reports in your file and see if there's anything to support Doil's story."

"Then what? You gonna disinter the guy and charge him? Oh well, I guess you got reasons. Let's do some digging ourselves."

Crowley led the way to a storeroom where the Esperanza file, faded with age and bulging, was in the second cabinet he tried. Returning to his desk, the detective spread out the file's contents and after a few minutes announced, "Here's what you want, I think." He passed over an official Offense-Incident Report form, which Bowe studied, turning pages.

On the third page she found it—a property department receipt for evidence collected at the double-homicide scene, which included "Money clip, gold color, initials HB." An investigator's report on a subsequent page recorded that the clip had probably been dropped by the murderer, since the initials did not match those of either victim, and the next of kin—a nephew— told police he had not seen the money clip before.

"That has to be the one," she informed Crowley. "Doil told Sergeant Ainslie that he got it in another robbery, then missed it after he ran from the Esperanzas'."

"You wanna see the real thing? I guess it's still in Property."

"I guess I'd better. If I don't, somebody's sure to ask why I didn't."

"Don't they always?"

Crowley made a copy of the property report for Ruby, then led the way out of doors to a large separate building—the Property Department, where a crowded series of vaults and secure rooms contained the detritus of countless crimes.

With surprising speed, two dusty boxes of evidence in the seventeen-year-old murder case were located, and when the first box was unsealed, a gleaming money clip was visible inside a plastic bag. Examining it more closely, Ruby saw the engraved monogram *HB*. "Hasn't tarnished, so hasta be real gold," Crowley said. "Wonder who the 'HB' guy was."

"That," Ruby said, "is what I need to find out next."

• • •

Metro-Dade Criminal Records was in another section of the main police building. Here crime reports from Dade County's twenty-seven municipalities, ranging over the past twenty years, were stored. Recent records were computerized, older ones were on microfilm. Like the rest of Metro-Dade's headquarters, the offices were clean, well-lit, and modern.

Ruby Bowe had brought with her a note of Elroy Doil's tape-recorded confession, in which, referring to the money clip, he said, "Got it in a robbery, coupla months before I knocked off them slants."

She decided to begin her search of robbery records three months before the Esperanzas' murders, which occurred on July 12, 1980.

"Do you have any idea what you're taking on?" a records clerk asked when Ruby told her. "You could be here for weeks." She held up a single microfilm cassette. "In there, from 1980, are one day's Offense-Incident Reports for Dade—about fifteen hundred pages on film, including robbery, burglary, auto theft, rape, battery, alarms—you name it! So for three months of reports you'd be looking at about thirty thousand pages."

"Can't the robberies be separated?"

"Nowadays, by computer, they can. The ancient stuff on microfilm— no way."

Ruby sighed. "However long it takes, there's a robbery case I have to find."

"Good luck," the woman wished her. "Dade County has an average of seventeen thousand robberies a year."

•   •   •

As the hours passed, Ruby's eyes grew weary. She was seated in the Criminal Records main office, facing a state-of-the-art Canon Microprinter, which both read microfilm and made printed copies if needed. The microfilmed pages were copies of standard police forms—Offense-Incident Reports. The standardization made scanning faster because at the top of each form was "Type of Incident," and only when this showed "Robbery" did Ruby pause to view the whole page quickly. Slightly lower was "Nature of Offense," and when this read "Armed Robbery" she paid extra attention, believing Elroy Doil was more likely to have committed that type of crime. A further item was "Property Taken," and if no money clip was listed—as had been true in every case so far—Ruby moved on.

The remainder of the first day produced nothing, and in late afternoon Ruby quit after arranging to resume her search the following morning.

The next day produced nothing, either, although by this time Ruby was moving at high speed through the microfilm reels, having learned to keep the non-robbery reports sliding by. By the end of that day she had reviewed and discarded five microfilm cassettes.

The next morning, while threading film from a new cassette through the reader-printer's setup reels, she wondered doubtfully, *Did this robbery ever happen as Elroy Doil claimed? And if it did, was it ever recorded?* The nagging questions stayed with her through the next two hours as she realized how much more searching lay ahead.

Suddenly Ruby's attention was riveted on an armed robbery case, number 27422-F, dated April 18, 1980. At 12:15 A.M. that day a robbery occurred outside the Carousel Nite Club on Gratigny Drive, Miami Lakes. She zoomed in to magnify the details. These showed that the robber, wielding a knife, approached his male victim, Harold Baird, and demanded all of Baird's money and jewelry. Four hundred dollars in cash was taken, as well as two rings worth a hundred dollars each, and a gold money clip worth two hundred. The clip bore the victim's initials, HB. The report described the perpetrator as "a very large white male, identity unknown."

With a sigh of relief, Ruby pressed the machine's printout button and reached for the emerging copy of Report 27422-F. Then she leaned back and relaxed, knowing she had found proof that at least part of what Doil had told Sergeant Ainslie was true.

Now on to Tampa.

•   •   •

Back at her Miami Homicide desk, Ruby telephoned the Tampa Police Department, was transferred to the Detective Bureau, and then to its Homicide Squad, where a Detective Shirley Jasmund took Ruby's call.

"We have some information here," Ruby announced, "about what we think is an old case of yours—a husband and wife named Ikei, murdered in 1980."

"Sorry, I was still in school that year—fifth grade." Detective Jasmund giggled, but added, "Somewhere, though, I've heard that name. How'd you spell it?"

When Ruby told her, Jasmund responded, "It may take a while to look up, so give me a number and I'll call back."

Three hours later Ruby's phone rang and Jasmund's voice announced, "We found that file, looks interesting. An old couple—Japanese, both in their seventies—stabbed to death in a summer home they had here. Bodies shipped back to Japan for burial. No serious suspects, it says here."

"Are there details about the crime scene?" Ruby asked.

"Sure are!" Ruby heard the sound of pages turning. "Officers' reports say it was *very* messy. Bodies brutalized, bound and gagged, facing each other . . . money taken, and . . . wait, here's something odd . . ."

"What?"

"Hold on, I'm reading here . . . Well, there was an envelope found beside the bodies. It had blobs of sealing wax on the back, seven in a circle it says, and inside was a printed sheet—a page from the Bible."

"Does it say what part of the Bible?"

"No . . . Yes! Here it is. Revelation."

"That's it! The case I want." Ruby's voice was excited. "Look, we have a lot of information to exchange, so I'm going to fly up to you. Would tomorrow be okay?"

"Let me ask my sergeant."

The sound of muffled voices followed, then Jasmund's again. "Tomorrow's fine. You've got us all curious, including our division captain, who's been listening. He said to tell you that the Ikeis' relatives in Japan still phone each year with the same question: Is there any news? That's where I heard the name."

"Tell the captain that when he gets his next call from Japan, I think he'll have answers."

"Will do. And when you know what time you'll get in, call and we'll have a squad car meet you at the airport."

• • •

An early Gulfstream Airlines flight from Miami to Tampa took sixty-five minutes, and Ruby Bowe was at the City of Tampa Police Department by 8:30 A.M. Detective Shirley Jasmund came to the front desk to escort her to the Detective Bureau, and the two women—black and white—liked each other immediately. "Word's gone around about you," Jasmund said. "Even the chief has been told about that old case with the Japanese. When we're all through, he wants a report."

Jasmund, in her mid-twenties, was outgoing and lively, with shining brown eyes, dark hair, high cheekbones, and a slim figure that Ruby envied, having recently put on a few pounds herself. *You'll have to lay off the junk food soon, honey,* she told herself for the umpteenth time.

"We have a meeting set up," Jasmund told her. "With Sergeant Clemson, Detective Yanis, and me."

• • •

"The reason that Japanese family keeps calling us year after year," Detective Sandy Yanis of Homicide told Ruby, "is that they care so much about their ancestors. It's why they had the bodies flown back for burial, but apparently they won't rest well until whoever killed them is found and punished."

"They can rest soon," Ruby said. "It's ninety-eight percent certain that the man who did the killing was Elroy Doil, executed three weeks ago at Raiford for another crime."

"I'll be damned. I remember reading about that."

Yanis, clearly an old hand, with a lanky, rugged physique, appeared to be in his late fifties. His face was seamed, the lines intersected by a long scar on his cheek that looked like an old knife wound. What remained of his graying hair was brushed back untidily. Half-moon glasses perched on the end of his nose; mostly he looked over them with a penetrating gaze.

The four were crowded into Sergeant Clemson's tiny office. In Miami's Metro-Dade headquarters, which she'd visited yesterday, broom closets would be larger, Ruby thought. Shirley Jasmund had already explained that the Tampa police headquarters, built in the early sixties, was inadequate and outmoded. "The politicians keep promising a new one but can never seem to find the money, so we struggle on."

Yanis quizzed Ruby. "You said you were ninety-eight percent certain about your guy Doil. How about the other two percent?"

"There's supposedly a knife hidden in a graveyard here in Tampa. If we find it, that ninety-eight becomes a hundred."

"Let's not play games," Sergeant Clemson said. "Be specific." He was younger then Sandy Yanis; though senior in rank, he seemed to defer to the older detective.

"All right." Once more Ruby described Elroy Doil's pre-execution confession to fourteen murders, including the Ikeis in Tampa—a case that no one in Miami Homicide had heard of—then Doil's emphatic denial of the Ernst double murder attributed to him, though he had not been formally charged.

"He was a pathological liar, and at first no one believed him," Ruby continued. "But now there are some doubts, and I have the job of checking everything he said."

Jasmund asked, "Have you caught him out in anything?"

"So far, not one thing."

"So, if whatever he said about Tampa checks out," Yanis prompted, "you might have another unsolved murder on your hands."

Ruby nodded. "A copycat."

"So what about the knife and a graveyard?" Clemson put in.

Reading from a notebook, Ruby quoted Doil's own words. " 'There's a cem'tery near where the Ikeis lived. Had ta get rid o' the knife I used, hid it in a grave. Know what was on the marker? Same last name as mine. Saw it, knew I'd remember if I wanted the fuckin' knife back, but I never got it.'

"Question: 'You buried the knife in a grave? Was it deep?'

"Answer: 'No, not deep.' "

Clemson opened a file on his desk. "The address where the Ikeis lived is 2710 North Mantanzas. Is there a cemetery near there?"

"Sure is," Yanis said. "Mantanzas runs into St. John, and there's a grave-yard right behind called Marti Cemetery. It's small, old, and owned by the city."

"In case you hadn't realized it," Clemson told Ruby, "Sandy is our resident oracle. He's been around forever, forgets nothing, and knows every arcane corner of Tampa. Which is why he does pretty much what he likes and we put up with his peculiar ways."

"About memory," Yanis said, "I do have trouble remembering birthdays. Haven't a clue how many I've had."

"The bean counters know," Clemson rejoined. "When it's time they'll be around here with your pension check."

Ruby felt she was hearing an exchange that had taken place many times before.

More seriously, Yanis told her, "Most of the guys who work in Homicide get promoted out or move on to something else after six or seven years. The stress is too great. Me, I'm hooked on it all. I'll be here till they carry me out, and I remember old cases like the Ikeis, and love to see 'em closed. So let's get on—start digging in that cemetery. Won't be the first time I've done that."

·   ·   ·

Sergeant Clemson used a speakerphone to call an assistant state attorney so the others could hear their conversation. After having the problem described to him, the attorney was uncompromising.

"Yes, Sergeant, I do realize we're not talking exhumation. But the reality is, no matter how near the surface the knife might be, you can't go disturbing *any* human grave without a judge's order."

"Any objection to us checking first, to find if there *is* such a grave?"

"I guess not, as part of an official investigation. But be careful. People are touchy about graves; it's like invading someone's privacy, or worse."

Afterward Clemson told Yanis, "Sandy, find out if there's a grave in that cemetery for someone named Doil. If there is, you can swear an affidavit, then ask a judge to sign an order letting us dig there." He added for Ruby, "This is going to take a couple of days, maybe more, but we'll move as fast as we can."

·   ·   ·

Ruby accompanied Yanis to City Hall and the Real Estate Division to meet an assistant property manager, Ralph Medina, whose responsibilities included Marti Cemetery. Medina, a small, middle-aged civil servant with a friendly attitude, explained, "Marti doesn't need much managing, takes maybe four, five percent of my working time. One good thing—once our tenants are inside, they never complain." He smiled at his own joke. "But if I can help, I will."

It was Ruby who described the purpose of their visit, Elroy Doil's pre-execution statement, and what they were seeking. She then inquired how many people were buried in the cemetery who had had that same last name.

"How do you spell that?"

"D-o-i-l."

Medina produced a file, ran a finger down several lists, then shook his head. "There's no such name. No one with that name's ever been buried at Marti."

"What about similar names?" Yanis asked.

"There are some spelled D-o-y-l-e."

"How many of those?"

Medina checked his lists again. "Three."

Yanis turned to Ruby. "What do you think?"

"I'm not sure. Doil's words were 'same last name as mine,' and the idea of disturbing three graves without real reason . . ." She shook her head.

"Yeah, know what you mean. Mr. Medina, when were the people in those Doyle graves buried?"

The answers took several minutes to find. At length: "One was in 1903, another in 1971, the last in 1986."

"Forget the third; that's six years after the Ikei murders. About the other two—are you still in touch with the families?"

Again, more searching through registers, files, and yellowed pages, then the pronouncement, "The answer's no. The 1903 burial shows no contact at all; it was so long ago. After the 1971, there was an exchange of letters, then nothing."

"So you couldn't contact relatives of those dead people, even if you wanted?" Yanis queried.

"No, probably not."

"And if we obtained a judge's order to search those two graves just a foot or so below the surface, you'd cooperate?"

"With a judge's order, of course."

●   ●   ●

As Ruby and Yanis left City Hall together, she said, "So you decided to go ahead anyway."

"We have to," he answered tersely, adding, "It's a long shot with those different names, and maybe we'll waste our time. But it's a bigger risk to pass up a chance of finding the truth about how those old people died."

She regarded him curiously. "You really care about the answer, don't you? Even though it's all those years ago."

"For me," he told her, "those old cases never go away, no matter how many years you wait. So you tried to solve a case ten, fifteen years ago, but couldn't. Then something new comes up—like now—and you try again, every bit as hard as before."

"Not everyone does," Ruby said. "It's good that you care."

As if he had not heard, Yanis tapped his forehead, then continued, "I have a list in there that won't go away. Right up top is a little girl named Juanita Montalvo. She was ten years old; fifteen years ago, here in Tampa, she disappeared. A lot of us worked hard on that case. We got nowhere, but somehow, someday, before I finish, I want to know what happened to Juanita, and where she is, even if it's buried in the woods and we have to dig to find her."

"Did you know her?"

"Not before she disappeared. But afterward I learned so much about her—she was a nice kid, everybody said so—I have a feeling I really did." Yanis glanced at Ruby. "You think I'm spooked, don't you? That maybe I've been in Homicide too long?"

"Absolutely not," she told him. "Though I think you're hard on yourself."

"Maybe so. But I'll still go to the limit, along with you, to learn what happened to the Ikeis."

•   •   •

The preliminary arrangements took two full days.

The assistant state attorney prepared an affidavit and a judicial order allowing the police to open two graves, which Detective Yanis and Ruby Bowe took for a judge to sign.

Initially the judge, who clearly knew Yanis well, demurred at the notion of disturbing two graves, asking, "Why don't I authorize just one, Sandy? Then, if you don't find what you want there, I'll consider a second order."

The veteran detective pleaded persuasively, "I promise, Judge, that if we find what we're looking for at the first grave, we won't go near the second. But if we do have to search the second, having your okay in advance will save the city a lot of money—not to mention your own valuable time."

"Your bullshit, I see, is as deep as ever," the judge commented. He turned from Yanis to Ruby. "Pardon my language, Detective, but what's your thinking on this?"

"Sometimes, Your Honor, I think bullshit makes sense."

"I'm an old fox who's outfoxed," the judge remarked as he scribbled a signature.

•　•　•

The workforce that assembled at 7:00 A.M. the next day at Marti Cemetery comprised four detectives—Yanis, Jasmund, Bowe, and an Andy Vosko, borrowed from Robbery—and three uniform officers from the ID Department. The City Real Estate Division's Ralph Medina also arrived—"Just to keep an eye on my turf," he commented—and a police photographer was taking pictures of the two designated graves.

Ample equipment had been stockpiled, too. There were wooden boards, an assortment of spades and hand trowels, coils of light rope, two sifting screens, and the ID crew had brought technical gear in boxes and leather cases. Also lined up were a dozen gallon-size bottles of drinking water. "By the end of this day we'll have finished those," Yanis declared. "It's gonna be a hot one." Although it was still officially winter, the sky was clear, the sun already climbing, the humidity high.

As instructed, everyone had dressed in old clothes, mainly jumpsuits and rubber boots, and had brought gloves. Ruby had borrowed baggy jeans from Shirley Jasmund, though they were pinching Ruby at her waistline and crotch.

The first grave to be opened was the older of the two, the burial place of a Eustace Maldon Doyle, who, according to a crumbling but still readable gravestone, died in 1903. "Hey, that's the year the Wright brothers flew the first airplane," someone said.

"It's the oldest part of the cemetery," Yanis acknowledged. "And closest to the house where the Ikeis were killed."

The first procedure, supervised by the ID sergeant, was to nail four boards together, forming a rectangular enclosure six feet by four. This was lowered over the grave and marked the limit of the dig. Next, several lengths of light rope were secured on top of the wooden frame by the ID crew, creating a grid—a total of twenty-four twelve-inch squares. The purpose was to explore one square at a time, and also to keep a record of exactly where anything was found.

But *would* anything be found, Ruby Bowe wondered. Despite the activity, since arriving here today her doubts had grown. The name on this grave, she was reminded, was not what Elroy Doil had claimed it to be. In any case he was a notorious liar, so was Doil ever here at all? Her thoughts were interrupted by the ID sergeant's voice.

"Your turn now, Sandy," he told Yanis. "We're the gurus here. You guys are the chain gang."

"At your service, bossman." Taking a spade himself, Yanis instructed the other detectives, "Okay, let's play tic-tac-toe," and began digging carefully in one of the twelve-inch squares. The other three Tampa detectives, along with Ruby, followed suit, choosing squares some distance from Yanis and each other.

"We'll go down six inches to begin," Yanis ordered. "Then, if we need to, another six."

The ground was hard, and only small amounts of earth could be lifted at one time. Gradually and carefully the dirt was transferred to a bucket, then as each bucket was filled, its contents were shaken into sifting screens.

The process was painstaking and tedious, and after a while they were all perspiring. At the end of an hour only twelve squares had been excavated to a six-inch depth, and, following a brief water break, work continued on the remaining twelve. At the end of two hours only three objects had been found—an old leather dog collar, a five-cent coin dated 1921, and an empty bottle. The dog collar and bottle were discarded. The nickel, Yanis announced amid mild amusement, would go to the city treasury. Then they all began to dig another six inches down.

Finally, at the end of four hours and no results, Yanis declared, "That's it, everyone. Take a break and a drink, then we'll work on the other grave."

A chorus of weary sighs arose from the crew as they contemplated another four hours of back-straining labor.

Work started on the second grave at 11:40 A.M., with the temperature at eighty-five degrees Fahrenheit. It continued for an hour and a half, then Shirley Jasmund said quietly, "I think I have something."

They all stopped and looked up.

With her spade, Detective Jasmund gently probed downward in the square she was working on and said, "It's quite small. Solid, though. Maybe a stone."

Ruby's heart sank. Whether a stone or something else, it was clearly not a knife.

"May we take over?" the ID sergeant asked.

Jasmund shrugged as she handed him her spade. "I do the work, you get the glory."

"Them's the breaks, kid!" The sergeant passed the spade clear of the grave, then, kneeling, loosened the object in the ground with his fingers.

It was not a stone. Even with some earth still clinging to it, the object was revealed as a gold and enamel brooch—clearly valuable.

The ID sergeant dropped the discovery into a plastic bag. "We'll look at it more closely in the lab."

"Okay, gang," Yanis echoed. "Let's keep digging."

Another hour and ten minutes passed and, along with the time, Ruby's spirits drooped. She had decided that this portion of her quest was close to ending in failure when Robbery's Andy Vosko spoke up.

"Got something here," he said, then added, "This time it's bigger."

Again everyone stopped work to watch, and again the ID sergeant moved in and took charge. Using a hand trowel, he carefully loosened the largish object and, as earth fell away, the vague shape became clear—it was a knife. Producing tongs, the sergeant used them to hold the knife while one of the ID crew women brushed the remaining earth away.

"It's a bowie knife," Ruby said breathlessly, viewing the sturdy wooden handle and long single-edged blade—straight, then curving concavely to a single sharp cutting point. "It's what Doil used in his killings." Her mood turned upbeat and she felt gratitude to Sandy Yanis for his persistence despite Ruby's own doubts.

The knife was now in another plastic bag. "We'll look at this in the lab, too," the ID sergeant said. "Nice going, Sandy!"

"I suppose it isn't likely," Ruby queried, "that you'll find fingerprints or blood after all these years."

"Highly *un*likely," the sergeant answered. "But . . ." He glanced toward Yanis.

"Yesterday," Yanis said, "I went to look at the Ikeis' clothing—nightclothes they were wearing when they were killed; we still have it all in Property. What it showed was that they were stabbed *through* their clothing, which means there may be threads from the clothing still on that knife. If the threads and the clothing match . . ." He raised his hands, leaving the sentence unfinished.

Ruby said admiringly, "You just taught me something I didn't know."

"He does that to all of us," Jasmund echoed. "All the time."

"So we found what you were looking for," Andy Vosko said. "Do we quit or go on?"

"We go on," Yanis answered, and so they did for another hour, but nothing more was found.

• • •

Ruby Bowe booked a late-evening flight back to Miami. Shirley Jasmund drove Ruby to the airport; Sandy Yanis came along. As they parted at the terminal entrance and Ruby said good-bye, she reached out impulsively and hugged them both.

12

SO WHAT'S THE VERDICT?" Malcolm Ainslie asked.

"The verdict," Ruby Bowe responded, "is that when Elroy Doil told you he murdered the Esperanzas and the Ikeis, he was telling the truth. Oh sure, a few details were different, and he left out one item entirely, but none of it changes the basic facts." She paused. "Shall I go back to the beginning?"

"Do that." It was the morning following Ruby's return from Tampa, and both were at Ainslie's desk in Homicide.

Ainslie listened while Ruby described what she had learned, first at Metro-Dade, then Tampa. At the end she added, "I had a phone call at home early this morning. The lab people in Tampa have identified threads on the bowie knife that match the Ikeis' clothing, so for sure it's the knife that killed them, just as Doil said. And the brooch we found in the grave . . ." Ruby consulted her notes. "It's been identified as cloisonné—very old, very valuable, and Japanese. Sandy Yanis figures the old lady had the brooch somewhere close to her when she was killed, and Elroy Doil fancied it."

"Then got scared of having it found on him, and left it in the grave, too," Ainslie finished.

"Exactly. So Doil didn't tell the complete truth after all."

"But what he did tell me has checked out, and you've proved it to be true."

"Oh, there's something else." From among the papers Ruby had brought back, she produced copies of the envelope that, according to Shirley Jasmund, was found beside the Ikeis' bodies—the envelope with seven seals in a circle on the rear and, inside, a page from Revelation. Ainslie studied both.

"It's chapter five," he said, looking at the torn page. "Three verses are marked." He read them aloud:

" 'And I saw in the right hand of him that sat on the throne a book written within and on the backside, sealed with seven seals.

" 'And I saw a strong angel proclaiming with a loud voice, Who is worthy to open the book, and to loose the seals thereof?

" 'And one of the elders saith unto me, Weep not: behold, the Lion of the tribe of Juda, the Root of David, hath prevailed to open the book, and to loose the seven seals . . . '

"It's Doil's handiwork." Ainslie remembered his conversation with Father Kevin O'Brien of Gesu Church, who had described Doil's obsession at age twelve with—as the priest expressed it—"God's wrath, pursuit, revenge, and killing."

Ainslie added, "It matches everything he did much later."

"Why that page beside the bodies?" Ruby asked.

"Only Doil knew that. My guess is he saw himself as the Lion of Judah, which led him to the serial killings." Ainslie shook his head ruefully, then, touching the envelope and the page, said, "If we'd had this sooner, and known about the Ikeis, we'd have nailed Doil long before we did."

There was a silence which Ruby broke. "You just said 'serial killings.' How does the Ernst case stand now?"

"It stands alone." In his mind Ainslie could hear Elroy Doil's desperate, frantic words: *I done them others, but I don't wanna die blamed for what I never done.*

"There were doubts that Doil was telling the truth," Ainslie said. "But now it looks very much as if he was, so I guess the Ernst case will be reopened."

•　•　•

"The Ernst case *is* reopened, as of now," Leo Newbold said. "And it's looking very much as if you were right all along, Malcolm."

Ainslie shook his head. "That doesn't matter. The question is, where do you suggest we start?" The two were in Newbold's office, with the outer door closed.

"We'll start by keeping everything very quiet, and for as long as possible." Newbold hesitated before adding, "That means even in Homicide, and tell Ruby not to discuss this with anyone else."

"I already have." Ainslie regarded his superior curiously as he asked, "What are you thinking?"

The lieutenant shook his head uncertainly. "I'm not sure. Except, if the Ernst murder was a copycat killing—the way it now looks—then whoever did it set it up deliberately to look like another serial. And that same person knew a helluva lot about Doil's other murders—stuff that was never in the newspapers or on TV."

Ainslie chose his words carefully. "You're suggesting someone had inside information, or there were deliberate leaks to the outside?"

"Goddam, I don't know what I'm suggesting! All I know is, I'm nervous as hell—wondering if someone in the PD, even in this department, knows something about the Ernst case that you and I don't." Newbold rose from his chair, paced his office, and returned. "Don't tell me you're not thinking the same thing, because I know damn well you are."

"Yes, I have been." After a pause Ainslie said, "What I thought I might do to begin is study all the files on every case, sort out what facts were made public and what we kept under wraps. Then we can see how it all compares with what happened at the Ernsts'."

Newbold nodded. "A good idea, but don't do it in the office. If anyone sees those files spread around, they could guess what's happening. Take them home and stay there for a couple of days. I'll cover for you."

Ainslie was startled. He had intended to be cautious, but not to the extent of mistrusting his colleagues. Yet he supposed Newbold was right. Also, lots of people, including outsiders, came and went from Homicide, and there was always curiosity about what was going on.

That evening, therefore, having discreetly transferred five bulging files to his car—one each for the double murders of the Frosts, Larsens, Hennenfelds, Urbinas, and Ernsts—Ainslie drove home, prepared for an intensive, probing study.

*   *   *

"I don't know why you're working at home," Karen said the next day, "but just having you here with all that stuff spread out is great. Is there any way I can help?"

Malcolm looked up gratefully. "Could you print some of my notes on your computer?"

Jason, returning from school, was equally pleased. Joining his father at the dining room table, he shoved some Homicide files aside to clear space for his homework, and the two worked side by side, interrupted only when Jason had questions like, "Dad, did you know that when you multiply by ten, all you have to do is add a zero? Isn't that neat?" . . . "Dad, did you know the moon is only two hundred and forty thousand miles away? Do you think I'll ever go there?" . . . And finally, "Dad, why don't we do this all the time?"

*   *   *

It took Ainslie two full days to pore over the files he had brought home, extract details, make notes, and finally create a crime-by-crime chart, but at the end he had drawn some important conclusions.

He began by reviewing the crime-scene details that were kept from the media—withheld in hopes that a suspect might incriminate himself by volunteering such knowledge. Included in those facts were the series of bizarre objects left beside the victims, beginning with the four dead cats. Something else not disclosed was the radio that police found playing loudly at all the crime scenes. Yet another detail was that each couple, while bound and gagged, was positioned facing each other. The fact that all of the victims' money had been taken *was* disclosed, but there was never any mention that valuable jewelry, which could have been removed, had consistently been left.

Some reporters, however, had private sources of information within the Police Department, and whatever they learned unofficially was broadcast or printed, restricted or otherwise. Which left two questions: First, had the news media managed to publicize *everything* about the four double killings preceding the Ernsts'? Almost certainly not, Ainslie thought. And, second, was there a possibility—as Leo Newbold had implied—of a leak within the Police Department, either accidental or deliberate? In Ainslie's opinion, that answer was yes.

Ainslie considered next: Were there any differences between the murders of Gustav Ernst and his wife and the other Doil killings? Yes, he discovered, there were several.

One concerned the radios left playing at every murder scene. At the Frost murders at the Royal Colonial Hotel, the radio had been tuned to HOT 105 and was playing hard rock, that station's staple fare. The Clearwater murders of Hal and Mabel Larsen were next and, because no radio was referred to in the report, Ainslie phoned Detective Nelson Abreu, the senior investigator. "No," Abreu reported, "as far as I know, no radio was on, but I'll check and call you." He did so an hour later.

"I just talked to the uniform who was first on the scene, and yes, there *was* a radio on, he tells me now, says he remembers it was loud rock and roll, and the idiot turned it off and didn't report it. He was a new kid, and I've reamed him out good. Was it important?"

"I'm not sure," Ainslie said, "but I appreciate your checking."

Abreu was curious about the query's background. "The Larsens' next of kin have asked whether Doil definitely did those killings here. Do you have anything on that?"

"Not at this moment, but I'll tell my lieutenant you'd like to know if any-thing breaks."

Abreu chuckled. "I get it. You know something but can't tell me."

"You're in this business," Ainslie said. "You know the way things are."

He knew that Doil's Raiford confession had not been circulated so far, and for the time being he hoped it would not be. Eventually, though, for the peace of mind of the victims' survivors, the full story would undoubtedly be released.

After the Larsens came the Fort Lauderdale slayings of Irving and Rachel Hennenfeld. During a liaison visit to Miami, Sheriff-Detective Benito Montes reported that when the bodies were found, a radio was "playing hot rock, so goddam loud you couldn't hear yourself speak."

Then there were Lazaro and Luisa Urbina, killed in Miami. A neighbor turned off a loud-playing radio while he called 911, but left the dial setting unchanged—at HOT 105.

A radio was also playing loudly when the bodies of Gustav and Eleanor Ernst were discovered by Theo Palacio, their majordomo. Palacio, too, turned off the radio, but remembered it was FM 93.1, WTMI, "a favorite station of Mrs. Ernst," he'd said, because it played classical music and show tunes. WTMI *never* played hard rock.

Was the type of music at the murder scenes significant? Ainslie thought it might be, especially when combined with another difference at the Ernsts'— the presence of the dead rabbit, which, from the beginning, Ainslie was convinced was not a symbol from Revelation.

So, he asked himself, was it possible that whoever had committed the Ernst murders had heard of the Frosts' four cats and mistakenly believed another animal would fit the bill? Again the answer seemed a likely yes.

Also significant was that Ainslie's Revelation theorem had become known to a small group of senior investigators the day *after* the Ernst murders, and *before* that time the meaning of the murder-scene symbols was anybody's guess.

Another time factor raised questions, too.

After each of the preceding killings—Frosts, Larsens, Hennenfelds, and Urbinas—the elapsed time before the next double killing was never less than two months and averaged two months, ten days. Yet between the Urbinas' and the Ernsts' murders, the gap was only three days.

It was as if, Ainslie thought, wheels had been set in motion for the Ernsts' deaths, which *would* have occurred after the normal time gap if the Urbina killings had not abruptly intervened. And while news of the Urbina killings spread quickly, was it, perhaps, too late to stop the wheels rolling on the Ernst murders?

A fleeting thought occurred to Ainslie, but he dismissed it instantly.

●   ●   ●

As to Elroy Doil's final killing, that of Kingsley and Nellie Tempone, while the crime lacked some of Doil's previous hallmarks—probably because he was interrupted and tried to flee—the timing came close to fitting what had gone before, and Ainslie had a theory about that.

It was Ainslie's belief that, notwithstanding the court ruling about sanity, Doil *was* insane. If so, it was possible he had a compulsion to commit murder on a regular schedule and, tragically for the Tempones, Doil's killing time had come.

But the validity of that theory, Ainslie knew, would never be known.

Immediately following his two-day research, Ainslie went on an expedition to the Miami Police Property Unit.

•   •   •

Property, a pivotal, bustling organization, was located on a lower ground floor of the main Police Department building. Its commander, Captain Wade Iacone, a heavyset, graying, twenty-nine-year police veteran, greeted Ainslie in his office.

"Just the man I needed to see! How are you, Malcolm?"

"Fine, sir. Thanks."

Iacone waved a hand. "Forget the formality. I was about to send you a tickler, Malcolm—about those Doil serials. Now that the guy is dead and the case is wound up, there's a mountain of stuff we'd like to clear. We desperately need the space."

Ainslie grimaced. "Forget the tickler, Wade. One of the cases has been reopened."

"Tickler" was jargon for a periodic memo sent to police officers who had brought in crime evidence—for storage, perhaps, while awaiting trial, or in the hope of making an arrest eventually. In effect the tickler said, "Hey! We've held this for you a long time and it's taking up space we urgently need. Please consider whether you need it any longer, and if not, let's get it out of here." More often than not, removing the evidence involved getting a court order.

Another code word, "stuff," referred to vast quantities of items stored in the Property Unit, including narcotics—cocaine and marijuana in case-numbered plastic bags, worth several million dollars on the street; hundreds of firearms, including guns, rifles, machine pistols, ammunition, "enough to start an insurrection," as Captain Iacone once declaimed; blood and body fluids from homicides or sexual assaults and preserved in refrigerators; then more prosaic stolen TV sets, stereos, and microwaves, plus hundreds of sealed and stacked-high cardboard boxes containing the bric-a-brac of other crimes, including homicide.

As for space, there was never enough. "We're loaded full from floor to rafters, and then some," was Iacone's constant complaint, though somehow new objects and boxes were unfailingly squeezed in.

"So what's going on?" Iacone asked Ainslie.

"One of those serial killings may not be solved, so the evidence will have to stay. But you said 'mountain.' Is there really that much?"

"There wasn't a huge amount until Commissioner Ernst and his wife were killed," Iacone answered. "That's when the big bundle came. All sealed boxes. They told me there was so much because the case was so important."

"May I see them?"

"Sure."

The Property commander led the way through offices and storerooms where a staff of twenty worked—five police officers, the remainder civilians— producing remarkable order from the packed miscellany around them. Anything stored—no matter how old, and twenty years of storage was not unique—could be located in minutes via computer, using a case number, name, or storage date.

Iacone demonstrated the procedure, stopping unhesitatingly at a pile of more than a dozen large boxes, each sealed with tape bearing the words CRIME SCENE EVIDENCE. "These were brought in right after the Ernst killings," he said. "I believe your guys collected a lot of stuff from the house, mainly papers, and were going to go through it all, but I don't believe anyone did."

It was easy to guess what had happened, Ainslie realized. Immediately after the Ernst murders, Homicide's special task force began its surveillance of suspects, using every available detective and drawing on other departments, too. As a result, the Ernsts' papers and effects, while needing to be safeguarded, would have become a secondary concern. Then, with the Tempone killings and the arrest and conviction of Doil, the Ernst case was assumed closed, and the many boxes, it now appeared, had never been carefully examined.

Ainslie told Iacone, "Sorry I can't take the Doil stuff off your hands, but what we will do is take a few of those boxes at a time, study the contents, then bring them back."

Iacone shrugged. "That's your privilege, Malcolm."

"Thanks," Ainslie answered. "It could be important."

13

WHAT I WANT YOU TO DO," Ainslie told Ruby, "is go through every one of those boxes stored in Property and see what you can find."

"Are we looking for anything special?"

"Yes, something that will lead us to whoever killed the Ernsts."

"But you've nothing more specific?"

Ainslie shook his head. A sense of foreboding he could not explain warned him that uncharted seas lay ahead. Who *had* murdered Gustav and Eleanor Ernst, and why? Whatever answer emerged would not be simple, he was sure. A line from the Bible's Book of Job occurred to him: *The land of darkness and the shadow of death.* He had an instinct he had entered it, and found himself wishing someone else was handling this case.

Ruby was watching him. "Is something wrong?"

"I don't know." He forced a smile. "Let's just find out what's in those boxes."

The two of them were in a small room on the far side of the main police building, away from Homicide. Ainslie had arranged temporary use of the space because of Leo Newbold's wish to keep the revived investigation as quiet as possible. The room was little more than a cupboard with a table, two chairs, and a phone, but it would do.

"We'll go down to Property," he told her, "and I'll authorize you to remove the Ernst boxes as you're ready for them. The whole thing shouldn't take more than a few days."

A prediction that, as it turned out, was wholly wrong.

• • •

At the end of two weeks, with some impatience, Ainslie went to visit Ruby for the third time in her temporary quarters. As on the two previous visits, he found her surrounded by piles of paper, much of it spread around the floor.

On the last occasion she had told him, "I don't believe either of the Ernsts could bear to throw away any piece of paper. They squirreled *everything—*

letters, bills, handwritten reminder notes, news clippings, canceled checks, invitations—you name it—and most of it's here."

Ainslie had said then, "I've talked with Hank Brewmaster, who had the case at the beginning. The problem was, there was an enormous quantity of papers in the house—box after box, stored in almost every room. Well, because we were so swamped at the time, no one could be spared to go through everything, though it had to be preserved in case there was important evidence. So what happened is all that stuff was scooped up from the Ernsts' house, then afterward no one got around to going through it."

Today, Ruby had a tattered exercise book open in front of her and was making notes on a pad alongside it.

Gesturing to an open cardboard carton, he asked, "Is it more of the same?"

"No," Ruby said, "I may have found something interesting."

"Tell me."

"Mrs. Ernst was the one who accumulated the most paper, and a lot is in her handwriting—spidery and hard to read. All innocuous, I thought, until two days ago, when I found what's turned out to be a diary. She wrote it in exercise books—lots of them, going back years."

"How many?"

"Could be twenty, thirty, maybe more." Ruby motioned to the cardboard carton. "This was full of them. My guess is, there'll be more in others."

"What do they say?"

"Well, that's a problem. Apart from the difficult handwriting, it's in a kind of code—a personal shorthand, you could call it—for privacy I suppose, especially from her husband; she must have concealed her diary from him over all those years. If anyone's patient enough, though, they can learn to read it."

Ruby pointed to the tattered pages in front of her. "For example, instead of using names, she uses numbers. After a while I realized '5' stood for herself and '7' for her husband. Then I caught on—'E,' for 'Eleanor,' is the fifth letter of the alphabet; 'G,' for 'Gustav,' the seventh. A simple code. Two numbers with a hyphen between is two names. I figured that '4-18-23' meant 'Dr. W.'—whoever he is, or was. And she compresses words, skips the vowels mostly. I'm getting the hang of it, but wading through all these will take time."

He must make a judgment, Ainslie knew. Was it worth keeping Ruby on this tedious search, which could drag on much longer and most likely produce nothing? Other matters in Homicide were, as usual, pressing. He asked, "Is there anything at *all* you can tell me? Anything important?"

Ruby considered. "Okay, maybe there is, and I guess I was holding back, wanting to have more." Her voice took on an edge. "Try this for size. What the diaries show already is that our late, high and mighty City Commissioner Gustav Ernst was a wife-beater of the worst kind. He beat his wife from the beginning of their marriage, sending her to the hospital at least once. She kept quiet because she was ashamed and scared, and thought no one would believe her, which is what her bastard of a husband told her. In the end all she could do was transfer the pain and torment—in her lonely private code— to these miserable pages. It's all in here!"

Abruptly, Ruby flushed. "Oh fuck! I hate this shit." Impulsively she seized one of the exercise books and flung it wildly across the tiny room.

After a pause, Ainslie retrieved the book and returned it to the table. "She was probably right; she might not have been believed, especially all those years ago, when no one ever talked about battered wives; people didn't *want* to know. Do *you* believe it all?"

"Absolutely." Ruby was calm again. "There's too much detail to have invented it, and every bit rings true. Maybe you should read some."

"I will later," Ainslie said, confident of Ruby's judgment.

She looked over at the exercise-book diary and added thoughtfully, "I think Mrs. Ernst knew, perhaps even hoped, that what she was writing would be read someday."

"Have you come across any reference to—" Ainslie stopped, realizing the question was unneeded. If the answer was yes, Ruby would have told him.

"You're wondering about Cynthia, aren't you?"

He nodded without speaking.

"I'm wondering, too, but there hasn't been anything yet. The books I've had are from the Ernsts' early marriage years; so far, Cynthia isn't born. When she is, she'll be in there as '3.' "

Their eyes met directly.

"Keep going," Ainslie said. "Take whatever time you need, and call me when there's something I should see." He tried to dismiss that gnawing apprehension, but did not succeed.

It was almost two more weeks before Ruby Bowe telephoned again. "Can you come down? I have some things to show you."

•   •   •

"What I've found," Ruby said, "changes a lot of things, though I'm not sure how."

Once more they were in the tiny, windowless room, still crammed with papers. Ruby sat at her small table.

"Let's get on with it," he said, aware of having waited long enough.

"Cynthia *has* come on the scene, and within a week of her being born, Mrs. Ernst found her husband playing with the baby—sexually. Here's what she wrote." Ruby pushed an open exercise book across the table and pointed partially down a page. Peering closely, Ainslie saw:

Fnd 7 tdy tchng 3, cd only b sxl. He had rmvd hr diapr & ws peerng at hr. Thn nt knwng I hd sn hm, he bnt dwn & dd smthng unspkbl. Ws so dsgstd & fraid for 3. Is ths prvt, hr fthr, wht sh mst fce thru chldhd? Tld hm ddnt cre whtvr he dz to me, bt mst nvr do tht agn to 3, & if he dd wd cll chld prtctn ppl nd he wd go to jl. He ddnt sm shmd bt prmsd nt to do it ny mre. Nt sre if blv hm, knw hs dpravd. Cn I prtct 3? Agn nt sre.

"Read it to me," he said. "I get the idea, but you'll be faster."

Ruby read aloud:

" 'Found Gustav today touching Cynthia, it could only be sexually. He had removed her diaper and was peering at her. Then, not knowing I had seen him, he bent down and did something unspeakable. Was so disgusted and afraid for Cynthia. Is this pervert, her father, what she must face through childhood? Told him I didn't care whatever he does to me, but he must never do that again to Cynthia, and if he did would call child protection people and he would go to jail. He didn't seem ashamed but promised not to do it any more. Not sure if believe him, know he's depraved. Can I protect Cynthia? Again not sure.' "

Without waiting for a reaction, Ruby said. "There are bits and pieces like that over the next two years, and despite Mrs. Ernst's threat, it's clear she did nothing. Then after a year and a half, there's this." Reaching for another exercise book, she pointed to a passage:

Hv wrnd 7 so mny tms bt stll he gs on, smtms hrtng 3 so sh crs out. Whn I trd to rgu wth hm he sd, "Its nthng. Jst a lttl fectshn frm hr dad." Tld him . . .

With a gesture, Ainslie indicated that Ruby should read it. She did so.

" 'Have warned Gustav so many times but still he goes on, sometimes hurting Cynthia so she cries out. When I tried to argue with him he said, "It's nothing. Just a little affection from her dad." Told him, "No, it's sick. She hates it and she hates you. She's afraid." Now every time Gustav comes near Cynthia she cries and curls up defensively, shrinking away. I keep threatening to call someone, child welfare people or police or even our own Dr. W., and

Gustav laughs, knowing when it comes right down to it I can't, and that's the truth. The shame and disgrace would be too awful. How could I face people afterward? Can't even *speak* of this to anyone, not even for Cynthia's sake. I have had to bear this burden alone and so will Cynthia.' "

"Does this shock you?" Ruby asked.

"After nine years in Homicide nothing shocks me, but I'm worried about what's to come. There *is* more—right?"

"Lots. Too much to cover now, so I'll skip ahead and we can come back to the other stuff later." She consulted notes. "Cruelty came next. When Cynthia was three, Gustav began beating her—'slapping her hard for trivial reasons or sometimes for no reason at all,' the diary says. He hated her crying, and once, as 'punishment,' put her legs in steaming hot water. Mrs. Ernst took Cynthia to a hospital, reporting the burn as an accident. She says in her notes that she knows she was not believed, but nothing happened.

"Then, when Cynthia was eight, Gustav had sex with her for the first of many times. After that, Cynthia shrank from anyone who tried to touch her, including her mother, showing terror at the idea of being touched." Ruby's voice faltered. She drank water from a glass and pointed to a pile of exercise books. "It's all in there."

Ainslie asked, "Do you want a break?"

"I think so, yes." Ruby went to the door, murmuring as she left, "I'll be back soon."

Left alone, Ainslie found his thoughts were in tumult. He had not erased from memory the fervent excitement of his affair with Cynthia, nor ever would. Despite her bitterness at his decision to end it, and afterward her deliberate sabotage of his own career, he still cared about Cynthia and would never wish to harm her in return. But now, with this new knowledge, his thoughts and pity went out to her in waves. How *could* supposedly civilized parents abuse and violate their own child—the father with degraded lust, the mother so spineless that she took no action whatever to aid her daughter?

The door opened quietly and Ruby slipped in. He asked, "Do you feel like going on?"

"Yes, I want to finish, then maybe I'll go and get drunk tonight and put this out of mind."

But she wouldn't, he knew. Ruby, because of her father's tragic shooting death by a fifteen-year-old junkie, strictly abstained from all drugs and alcohol. This experience would not change that.

"The inevitable happened when Cynthia was twelve," she continued, returning to her notes. "She got pregnant by her father. Let me read you what Mrs. Ernst wrote."

This time Ruby did not show the diary version in code, but read directly from her transcribed notes.

" 'In this terrible, shameful situation, arrangements have been made. With the help of Gustav's lawyer, L.M., Cynthia was spirited out of town to Pensacola under another name and to a discreet hospital where L.M. has connections. Medical advice is she must have the child, pregnancy too far advanced for anything else. She will stay in Pensacola until it happens. L.M. also arranging to have baby immediately adopted; I told him we don't care how, where, or to whom, as long as all is kept quiet and never traceable. Cynthia will not see the child or hear of it again, and neither will we. Thank goodness!

" 'Something good may even come out of this. Before L.M. agreed to handle the case, he gave the biggest dressing-down to Gustav I ever heard. He said Gustav sickened him and used words I won't repeat. Also he gave an ultimatum: Unless Gustav gives up for all time his abuse of Cynthia, L.M. will inform the authorities of his actions and Gustav will go to prison for a long time. L.M. said he really meant it and, if he had to do it, "the hell with client privilege." Gustav was truly frightened.'

"Some time after that there's a reference to Cynthia's baby being born," Ruby said. "No other information, not even the child's sex. Then Cynthia came home and, soon after, there was this in the diary:

" 'Despite all our precautions, somehow something must have leaked. A child welfare person came to see me. From her questions I could tell she didn't know everything, but did have information that Cynthia had a child at age twelve. Was no point in denying that, so I said yes she had, but about the rest I lied. I said we had no idea who the father was, though Gustav and I had been concerned for some time about Cynthia mixing with undesirable boys. From now on we would be more strict. Am not sure she believed me altogether, but there's nothing she can do to disprove what I said. Those people are such busybodies!

" 'Just as the woman left, I discovered Cynthia had been listening. We didn't say anything to each other, but Cynthia had a fierce look. I think she hates me.' "

Ainslie said nothing, his thoughts too complex to express. His disgust was overwhelming, particularly that neither Gustav nor Eleanor Ernst had given the slightest thought to the welfare of the newborn child—*her* grandson or granddaughter, *his* son or daughter; apparently neither had cared which.

"I skipped ahead," Ruby continued, "reading just parts of the diary in the years when Cynthia was growing up. There's been no time to read it all; maybe no one ever will. But the picture is that Gustav Ernst stopped molest-

ing Cynthia and began trying to help her, hoping—according to the diary—
she'd 'forgive and forget.' He gave her lots of money—and he had plenty. It
was all still happening when he was a city commissioner and Cynthia joined
the Miami Police. He used his influence to put pressure on the PD, first to
get her into Homicide, then to have her promoted fast."

"Cynthia was good at her job," Ainslie said. "She'd probably have gone
ahead anyway."

Ruby shrugged. "Mrs. Ernst thought it helped, though she didn't believe
Cynthia would ever be grateful for anything she and Gustav did. Here's
something Mrs. Ernst wrote four years ago:

" 'Gustav is living in a fool's world. He thinks that all is well between the
two of us and Cynthia, that the past has been put behind and left there, and
that Cynthia cares about us now. What nonsense! Cynthia doesn't love us.
Why should she? We never gave her reason to. Now, looking back, I wish I
had done some things differently. But it's too late. All too late.'

"I have one more diary piece to read, and maybe it's the most important,"
Ruby said. "This is Mrs. Ernst four months before she and Gustav were
killed:

" 'I've caught Cynthia looking at us sometimes. I believe a fierce hatred for
us both is there. It's part of Cynthia's nature that she never forgives. Never!
She doesn't forgive anyone for even the smallest offense against her. She gets
back at them somehow, makes them pay. I'm sure we made her that way.
Sometimes I think she's planning something for us, some kind of revenge,
and I'm afraid. Cynthia is very clever, more clever than us both.' "

Ruby put her notepad down. "I've done what you asked me to. There's just
one thing left." She saw Ainslie's troubled face, and her expression softened.
"This must have been hard for you, Sergeant."

He said uncertainly, "What do you mean?"

"Malcolm, we all know why you were never made lieutenant. By now you
should probably be a captain."

He sighed. "So you know about Cynthia and me . . ." He let his words
tail off.

"Of course. We all knew it while it was happening. We're detectives,
aren't we?"

In other circumstances Ainslie might have laughed. But something dark
and unspoken was hanging in the air. "So what's left?" he asked. "You said
there was one thing. What?"

"There's a sealed box in Property that was brought in with the others from
the Ernst crime scene, but has Cynthia's name on it. It looks as if she stored
it in her parents' house and it got caught up with all the rest."

"Did you check who signed the box in?"

"Sergeant Brewmaster."

"Then it's official evidence, and we have the right to open it."

"I'll get it," Ruby said.

• • •

The cardboard carton that Ruby brought was similar to the others, with the same CRIME SCENE EVIDENCE tape around it. But when that tape was removed there was more tape beneath, colored blue, bearing the initials "C.E.," and secured by sealing wax at several points.

"Take that off carefully and save it," Ainslie instructed.

A few minutes later Ruby had opened the carton flaps and folded them back. Both peered inside, where several plastic bags were visible, each containing an object. One, near the top, was a gun that looked like a Smith & Wesson .38 revolver. In another bag was an athletic shoe, with another shoe beneath. Both shoes bore stains. A fourth bag contained what appeared to be a T-shirt with a similar stain. There were other plastic bags below; in one, a portion of a recording tape was visible. Each bag had a label attached, with handwriting that Ainslie recognized as Cynthia's.

He could hardly believe what he was seeing.

Ruby was puzzled. "Why is this here?"

"It was never intended to be. It was concealed in the Ernst house and, just as you said, brought here by mistake." Ainslie added, "Don't touch anything, but see if you can read what's written about the gun."

She leaned closer. "It says, 'The weapon which P.J. used to shoot his ex-wife Naomi with her friend Kilburn Holmes.' There's a date. 'August twenty-first'—six years ago."

"Oh Jesus!" Ainslie said in a whisper.

Ruby straightened, facing him. "I don't understand any of this. What is it?"

He answered grimly, "The artifacts of an unsolved homicide. Unsolved until now."

Although the Jensen-Holmes case was not handled by Ainslie's Homicide team, he remembered it well because of Cynthia's long association with the novelist Patrick Jensen. He recalled again that Jensen had been a strong suspect following the murders of his ex-wife and her young male friend, killed by .38-caliber bullets from the same gun. Jensen was known to have purchased a Smith & Wesson .38-caliber revolver two weeks earlier, but claimed to have lost the gun, and no murder weapon was found. In the absence of specific evidence, no charges were laid.

An obvious question: Was the gun in the box just unsealed the missing weapon? Another: If the evidence was real, why had Cynthia labeled it, then concealed it for six years? Such labeling was routine for a trained Homicide detective, which Cynthia was. Concealing evidence was not.

Ruby broke in. "Does this 'unsolved homicide' fit in somehow with the Ernst murders?"

It was one more question Ainslie was already asking himself. The questions were endless. Was Patrick Jensen involved in the Ernst murders? If so, was Cynthia protecting him from that, as well as from an earlier crime?

Weighing it all, Ainslie felt a mood of deep depression sweep over him. "Right now I'm not sure of anything," he told Ruby. "What we do need is an ID crew to go through this box."

He lifted the tiny office's single phone.

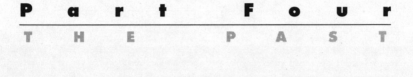

Part Four
THE PAST

1

CYNTHIA ERNST COULD REMEMBER the precise moment when she decided that someday she would kill her parents. She was twelve years old, and two weeks earlier she had given birth to her father's child.

A plainly dressed, middle-aged woman had arrived unannounced at the family's mansion in the exclusive, security-protected Bay Point community on Biscayne Bay. Producing credentials that described her as a child welfare worker, she had asked the housekeeper for Mrs. Ernst.

When Cynthia heard the stranger's voice she moved quietly into the corridor outside the main-floor drawing room, where her mother had taken the woman and closed the door behind them. Equally quietly, Cynthia opened the door just enough to peer through and listen.

"Mrs. Ernst, I'm here officially to talk about your daughter's baby," the woman was saying. She looked about her, seemingly impressed by her surroundings. "I have to say that in matters like this, there's usually poverty and family neglect. Clearly that isn't the case here."

"There has been no neglect, I assure you. Quite the contrary." Eleanor Ernst spoke quietly and carefully. "My husband and I have cared for our daughter devotedly ever since she was born, and dearly love her. As to what has happened, we are as distressed as any couple can be, though we tell ourselves that somehow we've failed miserably as parents."

"Perhaps it will help if we talk about the background. How, for example, did your daughter . . ." The visitor consulted a notebook. "Your daughter Cynthia . . . what were the circumstances under which she became pregnant? And what about the father? What do you know of him—especially his age?"

Cynthia moved even closer to the doorway, not wanting to miss a word.

"The truth is, we know nothing at all about the child's father, and Cynthia has refused to tell us." Eleanor's voice was little more than a whisper. She dabbed at her eyes with a small handkerchief, then continued, "Unfortunately, young as she is, our daughter has had many boyfriends. I am sorry to say this, but I am afraid she is shamefully promiscuous. My husband and I have been worried about her for some time."

"In that case, Mrs. Ernst"—the welfare woman's voice had sharpened—

"wouldn't it have been logical to seek professional advice? You and your husband are informed people and must know such facilities exist."

"In retrospect, perhaps we should have. But the fact is we didn't." Eleanor added pointedly, "It's always easy for others to have hindsight."

"Do you plan to have counseling now? And to include your daughter?"

"Gustav and I may well consider that. Until now the preparations we've had to make have preoccupied us. After the awful event, the child was put up for adoption—we'd made prearrangements." Eleanor paused. "Do I really have to answer these questions? My husband and I have been hoping for total privacy."

The visitor had been making entries in her notebook. "The welfare of a child overrides privacy, Mrs. Ernst. But if you doubt our agency's right of inquiry, you can always ask your lawyer."

"That won't be necessary." Eleanor had become placating. "I will tell you that my husband and I, and also Cynthia, have learned a great deal from what has occurred. In a way it has drawn the three of us closer. We have had long talks, and Cynthia has given her solemn word that from now on she will mend her ways."

"Perhaps I should talk with your daughter."

"I'd much prefer you didn't. In fact, I beg of you not to. Something like that would almost certainly undo all the progress we have made."

"Are you really sure?"

"I truly am."

Nowadays, as an adult, Cynthia sometimes wondered why she hadn't barged in at that moment and blurted out the truth. Then she realized that while such an action would have embarrassed her parents and prompted questions, in the long run she most likely would not have been believed. She had read of notorious child-abuse cases in which adults who denied such charges were believed, and children weren't. The accused adults could hire fee-hungry practitioners who skillfully demolished children's statements, while the children—even if they understood—had no such recourse.

In any case, Cynthia—perhaps with instinctive insight—did not burst in, and the two women's voices faded as, having heard enough, she moved away.

Ten minutes later her mother and the welfare worker emerged, Eleanor accompanying the visitor to the front door and closing it after her. As she turned, Cynthia stepped into view and faced her mother.

Eleanor paled. "Cynthia! My God! How long have you been there?"

Cynthia glared back, silently, her gaze fierce and accusing. In most respects she still looked like a twelve-year-old girl, with short brown bangs and freckles, but her eyes, intensely green and filled with resolve, belonged to a much older woman.

Eleanor Ernst's hands were clasped nervously together, her eyes shifting. She was elegantly dressed, with coiffed hair and high heels. "Cynthia," she said, "I insist you tell me how long you've been there. Have you been listening?"

Still no words.

"Stop looking at me like that!" As Eleanor took a few steps forward, Cynthia stepped back.

After several moments her mother drew her hands to her face and quietly wept. "You heard, didn't you? Oh, darling, I had no choice; surely you see that. You know I love you. Please give Mommy a hug. You know I'd never hurt you . . . Please let me hold you."

Cynthia watched with an expression of utter detachment, then slowly turned and walked away.

The lying, hypocritical words she had heard her mother speak were seared forever in her mind. She already hated her father for his physical abuse from the earliest moments she remembered. In some ways she despised her mother even more. Even at twelve, Cynthia knew that her mother could have, and should have, sought outside help, and her failure to do so could never be forgiven.

But Cynthia, clever and shrewd even at twelve, swallowed her rage for the sake of her future. To realize all her burgeoning plans, she needed her parents—especially their contacts and resources. Therefore, as time went on, in public she maintained a veneer of politeness and occasional affection. In private she rarely spoke to them.

Her father, she knew, accepted the deception, grateful for the image it conveyed to outsiders. Her mother behaved as though not a thing in the world was wrong.

And if either parent ever disagreed with her wishes, Cynthia would cross her arms and look at them with a cold, steady glare, as if to say, *I know what you did to me, and you know, too. Wouldn't it be better if no one else knew? Take your choice.*

This unspoken threat, an appeal to their shame, guilt, and cowardice, worked unfailingly. After a few tense, awkward moments, Gustav Ernst would invariably yield under the fierceness of his daughter's gaze and mumble, "I simply don't know what to do with you."

Eleanor, as usual, would shrug helplessly.

A disagreement between both sides emerged a couple of years later when Cynthia's schooling became an issue.

She had attended elementary and middle schools in Miami, and her report cards rated her an outstanding student. What Gustav and Eleanor planned next, at age fourteen, was a highly regarded private day school in

Coral Gables, called Ransom-Everglades. But Cynthia, at fourteen, had other ideas. At the last moment, when the Ransom-Everglades arrangements were virtually complete, she announced that she would go to Pine Crest, a boarding school in Fort Lauderdale, some twenty-five miles north of Miami. She had applied to the school herself and agreed to attend when they accepted her.

Gustav was totally opposed. "You deliberately went against our wishes," he said over dinner that night. "If we had selected Pine Crest, you would have wanted Ransom-Everglades."

Eleanor watched helplessly, knowing that Cynthia would eventually have her way.

And so she did, employing her usual technique. Sitting at the dinner table, she did not touch her food. Instead she stared resolutely at her father, a glint of absolute power in her eyes, until he finally put down his fork and huffed, "Oh, for heaven's sake, do whatever you want."

Cynthia nodded, rose from the table, and went to her room.

Four years later it all happened again, when Cynthia was poised to enter college. Now she was eighteen and possessed the cunning and beauty of a full-grown woman. Cynthia knew her mother desperately wanted her to attend Smith College in Northampton, Massachusetts, Eleanor's prestigious alma mater, and for four years had let Eleanor believe she would.

Cynthia looked to be a strong candidate; she had a four-point grade average at Pine Crest and was inducted into the National Honor Society. Also, Eleanor was a substantial financial donor to Smith, which supposedly didn't count, though possibly did.

The letter of acceptance was sent to the Ernsts' home and Eleanor opened it. She immediately called Cynthia at school to relay the news.

"Yes, I expected they'd take me," Cynthia said coolly.

"Darling, I can't tell you how thrilled I am. I want to have a celebration. How about dinner on Saturday? Are you free?"

"Sure, sounds fine."

Already Cynthia was enjoying the symmetry of events, and the following Saturday evening the three of them sat at the same long oak dining table, her parents at each end, Cynthia in the middle. The table was set with their best Herend china and English linen. Candles were lit. Cynthia had even put on a formal dress. Her parents, she could see, were glowing with happiness.

Then, after pouring the wine, her father raised his glass and said, "To another generation of Smith graduates!"

"Hear, hear!" Eleanor echoed. "Oh, Cynthia, I'm so proud of you. After graduating from Smith, the world will be waiting for you."

Toying with her own wineglass, Cynthia said, "That might be true, Mother, if I were going to Smith." Amused, she watched her mother's happiness fall away. They had been through this drill so many times that every nuance was predictable.

"Whatever do you mean?" her father asked.

"I applied to Florida State at Tallahassee," Cynthia answered brightly. "They accepted me last week, and I've told them I'm coming." She raised her wineglass. "So how about that toast? To Tallahassee!"

Eleanor was too aghast to speak.

Her husband's brow was suddenly beaded with perspiration. "You will *not* go to that pathetic state school instead of Smith. I forbid it!"

At the other end of the table, Eleanor stood up. "Do you have any idea what a *privilege* it is to be accepted at Smith? The tuition there is more than twenty thousand dollars a year. Doesn't that tell you how exclusive—"

"At Tallahassee it's *three* thousand," Cynthia interrupted. "Think of the money you'll save." She regarded her parents placidly.

"Do you think we *care* . . . Oh!" Eleanor buried her face in her hands.

Gustav pounded the table. "That will not work this time, young lady!"

Now Cynthia stood, too, and glared at both parents in turn. The unspoken words were deafening.

Gustav tried to return her stare, but, as had happened before, he looked away and sighed. Finally, shrugging in defeat, he left. Seconds later, Eleanor followed.

Cynthia sat down and finished her dinner.

Three years later, having completed four years' worth of courses, Cynthia graduated from Florida State University with highest honors and membership in Phi Beta Kappa.

•　　•　　•

Cynthia had many male friends in high school and college, and to her surprise, she found she enjoyed sex, despite childhood memories. As she saw it, however, sex was all about power. She would *never, ever, again* be a docile partner. In every sexual relationship she sought to dominate, no matter what kind of sex was involved, or with whom. A further surprise was that men enjoyed her dominance. Most became more aroused because of it. One partner, a linebacker, said after an intense night of lovemaking, "Jesus, Cyn, you're sexy as hell, but *cruel*."

Still, for all her involvements, Cynthia never fell in love, never allowed herself to. She simply was not prepared to relinquish that much independence.

Much later the same game plan was partially true of her affair with Malcolm Ainslie. Like most of the men who preceded him, he enjoyed her "sexual calisthenics," as he once labeled them, and responded in kind. But Cynthia never quite possessed Malcolm, or dominated him totally as she had others; there was a strength within him she could never overcome. During their affair she had tried to break up Malcolm's marriage—with mischief, a close cousin of power, as her sole objective. She had not the slightest intention of marrying him herself—or anyone else, for that matter. To Cynthia, marriage represented little more than surrendering control, something she vowed she would never do.

In direct contrast to Malcolm was the novelist Patrick Jensen, whom Cynthia dominated from the moment they first met. Initially their relationship was about sex, though eventually it became more complex. Her alliances with both men began about the same time, though Cynthia kept the two apart, running—as she thought of it—on parallel tracks.

Patrick had been going through a difficult time when his liaison with Cynthia began, mainly because of the breakup of his marriage. His wife, Naomi, had divorced him and, after a bitter contest, won a handsome settlement. According to friends, during the seven years the Jensen marriage lasted, it was filled with Patrick's tempestuous rages, prompting Naomi to make three complaints of physical abuse to police. Each time, they were withdrawn after Patrick promised to reform. He never did. Even following the divorce, Patrick publicly exhibited his jealousy of Naomi when she was with another man, and once had to be restrained.

For Patrick, Cynthia Ernst was a haven in every way. He conceded that she was far stronger than he was, and willingly became a compliant cohort, relying on her guidance more and more. For her part, Cynthia believed she had found someone she could both control and use in advancing her long-term personal plans.

That belief was confirmed late one night when Patrick arrived at Cynthia's apartment.

From her bed she heard an insistent pounding on her outer door. Peering through a peephole, she could see Patrick glancing up and down the hall and running his fingers through his hair.

When she opened the door he rushed in and said, "Jesus, Cynthia, I've done something terrible! I've got to get away. Can I take your car?" He hurried to a window and looked both ways—up and down the street below. "I've got to get out of here . . . got to go somewhere! Cyn, I need your help." He looked at her imploringly, his fingers still rifling his hair.

"My God, Patrick, you're dripping with sweat." Cynthia told him firmly, "You have to calm down. Sit down and I'll get you a Scotch."

She joined him on a couch with the drink, then massaged his neck. He started to talk, subsided, then suddenly blurted out, "Oh God, Cyn, I killed Naomi! Shot her." His voice choked.

Cynthia inched away. As a police officer—a Homicide detective, especially—her duty was clear. She should arrest Patrick, give him a Miranda warning, and take him into custody. Thinking fast, weighing possibilities and opportunities, she did none of those things. Instead she went to her bedroom, took a tape recorder from a bedside drawer, inserted a new tape and, as she reentered the living room, pressed RECORD. Patrick was crying, his head in his hands. Cynthia put the machine on a table near him, shielded from view by a plant.

Then she said, "Patrick, if you want me to help you, you have to tell me exactly what happened."

He looked up, nodded, then began, his voice still breaking. "I didn't plan it, didn't intend . . . but always hated the thought of Naomi with someone else . . . When I saw those two together, her and that creep, I was blinded, angry . . . I'd been carrying a gun. I pulled it out, without even thinking, fired . . . Suddenly it was over . . . Then I saw what I'd done. Oh God, I'd killed them both!"

Cynthia was aghast. "You killed *two people?* Who was the other?"

"Kilburn Holmes." He said abjectly, "He'd been seeing Naomi, was with her all the time. People told me."

"You stupid fucking idiot!" For the first time, Cynthia felt cold fear. It was a double murder in which Patrick was certain to be a suspect, and what she was doing—assuming she continued—could cost her own career and freedom.

"Did anyone see you?" she asked. "Was there any witness?"

Patrick shook his head. "No one, I'm sure of that. It was dark and late. Even the shots didn't draw attention."

"Did you leave anything, *anything whatever,* at the scene?"

"I'm sure I didn't."

"As you were leaving, did you hear noise? Was there an alarm, voices?"

"No."

"Where is the gun?"

"Here." From a pocket he produced a Smith & Wesson .38.

"Put it on that table," she told him.

Cynthia paused, calculating the risks she might be taking, weighing them against the leverage they would give her over Patrick. She saw her duty clearly, but she also saw him as a useful tool.

Making a decision, she went to her kitchenette and returned with a plastic bag and kitchen tongs. Without touching the gun, which would have Patrick's fingerprints on it, she placed it in the plastic bag and sealed it. Then she pointed to a T-shirt he was wearing. "Take that off; it's got blood on it. And those sneakers, too."

Again, touching nothing except the plastic bags, she put the T-shirt and shoes in other bags. "Now give me your house keys and take off the rest of your clothes."

When Patrick hesitated, Cynthia snapped, "Do *exactly* what I say! Now, where was it that you killed them?"

"In the driveway of Naomi's house." He shook his head and sighed.

With her back to Patrick and blocking his view, Cynthia turned off the tape recorder. In any case, she realized, he was still too dazed to notice.

Patrick had now shed all his clothes and was naked. He stood nervously, his shoulders slouched, eyes to the floor. Again Cynthia went to the kitchenette, and brought back a large brown bag, into which she stuffed the clothes.

"I'm going to your house," she said. "I'll dump these somewhere and bring you back fresh clothes. While I'm gone, take a *very* hot shower and scrub yourself—use a nail brush—all over, and especially your hand that held the gun. Where did you get the gun?"

"I bought it two months ago." He added gloomily, "My name's on record."

"If the gun isn't found and there's no other evidence, you're safe. So you lost it a week after you bought it. Remember that, and don't change that story."

"I won't," Patrick mumbled.

As Cynthia left, he was entering her bathroom.

•   •   •

On the way to Patrick's house, taking a roundabout route, Cynthia disposed of his clothes in several different garbage cans and a Dumpster. At the house, she quickly put together fresh clothes for him to wear.

At 5:30 A.M., Cynthia returned to her apartment and upon opening the door saw Patrick sitting on the couch, hunched over the glass coffee table with a rolled-up dollar bill in his nose.

"How dare you do that here!" she screamed.

His head shot up, revealing four lines of cocaine on the tabletop, which he had not yet inhaled.

Patrick wiped his nose and sniffed. "Jesus, Cynthia, no big deal. I just thought it would help me through this."

"Flush it down the toilet—and any more you have. *Now!*"

Patrick started to object, then headed for the bathroom, muttering, "It's not like I'm an addict."

Cynthia silently acknowledged that Patrick was not, in fact, an addict. Like others whom she knew, he used the drug intermittently. She herself never used drugs, or anything else that might diminish her control.

Patrick returned from the bathroom blustering about the two hundred bucks he had flushed away. Ignoring him, Cynthia began to label and describe the items she had placed in plastic bags, including the gun and bloodstained clothing, making sure that Patrick was watching. Afterward, she put everything in a cardboard carton, intending to add the tape recording later.

Patrick, pacing the room restlessly, asked, "Why are you doing all that?"

"Just to make everything tidy." Cynthia knew it was an unsatisfactory answer, but it didn't matter. Patrick was high now, hyper and inattentive. Dismissing the query, as she expected, he launched into a description of how he kept his writer's notes in a similarly organized way.

Later, after Cynthia had hidden the box of damning evidence, she would answer Patrick's question more precisely—and in a way he would like less.

· · ·

The following evening, alone, Cynthia played back the tape. The quality was good. She had brought home another recorder and an extra tape to accomplish the next step.

First, on the original recorded tape where Patrick described the double killing, Cynthia performed what tape technicians with a sense of history termed a "Nixon-Woods-Watergate"—erasing a previously recorded portion by running the tape and holding down the RECORD button with no microphone connected. Using a stopwatch and notes, she wiped out all traces of her own voice. Afterward, just as on President Nixon's crucial Watergate tape, there were long gaps, but no matter—Patrick's performance was clear and damning, as he would realize when Cynthia played it back to him. Meanwhile she made an extra copy of the edited tape for that purpose, putting the original in the carton with the other evidence.

She sealed the carton carefully with blue plastic tape bearing her initials, then drove with it to her parents' Bay Point house. There Cynthia had a private room on the top floor, where she stayed occasionally and stored some personal effects. Unlocking the room, she placed the carton on a high shelf in a cupboard, out of sight behind other boxes. She planned to reopen the carton and remove the labels that bore her handwriting; also, while wearing gloves, she would replace the plastics bags, which had her fingerprints, with new ones that did not. Somehow, though, as time went by and other pressures mounted, it never happened.

From the beginning, Cynthia did not intend to have anyone view the carton's contents. She simply wanted Patrick to see her assemble and catalog the items, giving her a permanent hold over him. Then eventually, she supposed, she would put the evidence in a metal strongbox and throw it into the Atlantic Ocean, miles offshore.

●   ●   ●

Almost at once after the discovery of the bodies of Naomi Jensen and Kilburn Holmes, Patrick Jensen became Miami Homicide's prime suspect and was questioned intensively. To Cynthia's relief, there were no adequate grounds on which to arrest and charge him. It was true that Jensen had opportunity and no alibi. But, beyond that, there was a total lack of evidence. She had also cautioned Patrick to say as little as possible while being questioned, and not to volunteer anything. "Remember, *you* do not have to prove your innocence," she had emphasized. "It's the cops who must prove your guilt."

Two minor pieces of evidence were found by an ID crew at the murder scene, but neither was conclusive. A handkerchief found near the bodies matched others Jensen owned. But nothing on the handkerchief proved that it was his.

Similarly, a fragment of paper clutched in Kilburn Holmes's hand matched another fragment found in Jensen's garbage. Again, it proved nothing. The bullets in both bodies were identified as .38 caliber, and records showed that Jensen had bought a Smith & Wesson .38 two months before. But he claimed to have lost the gun a week after buying it, a search of his house did not reveal it, and, without the murder weapon, nothing could be done.

Cynthia was also glad that Ainslie's team was not involved with the case, which was handled by Sergeant Pablo Greene, with Detective Charlie Thurston as lead investigator. Since Cynthia was known to have socialized with Jensen, Thurston did ask her, almost diffidently, "Do you know anything at all about this guy that might help us?"

She had answered, pleasantly enough, "No, I don't."

"Do you believe Jensen would have been capable of killing those two?"

"I'm sorry to say this, Charlie," Cynthia replied. "But yes, I do."

Thurston nodded. "So do I."

And that had been the end of it. It clearly did not occur to Sergeant Greene, Detective Thurston, or anyone else in Homicide that Detective

Cynthia Ernst, while having been acquainted in the past with someone who was now a murder suspect, could even remotely be involved.

The reason, of course, was that the face Cynthia presented to her colleagues, superiors, and most others she met was cooperative and friendly. Only criminals with whom she dealt saw her cold and ruthless side.

Patrick Jensen encountered that side when Cynthia next saw him, after cautiously avoiding him for several months.

2

FOR CYNTHIA'S NEXT MEETING with Jensen she chose the Cayman Islands, the ultimate discreet destination where total privacy is possible if that is what you want. Cynthia did.

They traveled separately and stayed at different hotels. Cynthia's reservation at Grand Cayman's Hyatt Regency was in the name of Hilda Shaw. To avoid using an identifying credit card, she sent a cash deposit via Western Union and added more cash on arrival. At the check-in desk, no one raised an eyebrow.

Jensen, obeying phoned instructions from Cynthia, made his own separate reservation at the nearby, more modest Sleep Inn. But for most of the three days and nights in Grand Cayman, he stayed in Cynthia's room, which overlooked sculptured gardens.

When they first met there, having been apart for three months, they seized each other, hurriedly tore off their clothes, and made violent love—so violent that when Cynthia climaxed she pounded both clenched fists on Jensen's shoulders.

He protested, "Jesus Christ, that hurts!"

When they were lying calmly amid the rumpled sheets, Patrick said, "So much happened that last night we were together, I never got around to thanking you for what you did for me. So I thank you now."

"Thanks aren't important." Cynthia's voice was deliberately offhand. "I simply paid a purchase price."

Patrick laughed. "What does that mean?"

"It means I own you."

There was a silence. Patrick said slowly, "I suppose you're talking about that box of tricks? You've got it hidden away somewhere."

She nodded. "Naturally."

"And you think that if I disobey you somehow, or offend you, you can open it up and say, 'Hey, guys!—look at all this evidence. Now you can nail that bastard Jensen.' "

"You write good dialogue." Cynthia gave a small, tight smile. "I couldn't have said it better."

Patrick's face had the ghost of a smile, too. "But there's a detail or two you've overlooked. Even you. Like your handwriting on those labels. And some fingerprints . . ."

"All of that's gone," she lied, reminding herself that it was a detail she must attend to soon. "I labeled the bags so you'd remember what I was doing. Now only *your* fingerprints are on everything. And, oh yes, there's an audiotape."

Cynthia described how everything Jensen had said in her apartment that night—his admission of having killed Naomi and her friend Kilburn Holmes—had been recorded. "I brought a copy of the tape with me. Want to hear it?"

He gestured dismissively. "Never mind; I believe you. But I could still rope you in by explaining how you helped me hide the evidence. So if they found me guilty, you'd be fucked—an accessory at least."

Cynthia shook her head. "No one would believe you. I'd deny everything and *would* be believed. And something else." Her voice hardened. "The evidence would be found in some place where *you* could have hidden it. Unfortunately, you wouldn't know where that was until an anonymous tip-off caused the police to find it."

They faced each other fully then, each calculating. Paradoxically, Jensen leaned back and laughed. With apparent good nature he lifted both hands in a signal of surrender. "Darling Cynthia, you're really a skewed genius. Well, you said you own me. I now admit you do."

"You don't seem to mind."

"This may be some kind of perversion, but the funny thing is, I rather like it." He added thoughtfully, "It would make a great story."

"Which you will never write."

"Then what *will* I do—since I'm to be some kind of pet you're holding on a leash?"

The moment had come. Cynthia's eyes riveted him. "You will help me kill my parents."

•   •   •

"Listen to me," Cynthia ordered. "Listen very carefully."

Moments earlier, when Jensen had tried to talk—to reason with her, as he saw it, after her shattering statement—she'd silenced him. He sat quietly waiting.

Now, taking her time, drawing on earliest childhood memories plus details she had coaxed from her mother, Cynthia laid before him, graphically and persuasively, the whole story, sparing him—and herself—nothing.

•   •   •

As a newborn . . . Gustav's sick sexual obsession with Cynthia . . . his obscene probing . . . her own innocent terror, growing each day until, at the age of three, even the sight of her father approaching made her hide under the covers, sobbing, shrinking away . . .

Eleanor did nothing, thinking of herself only—of her own potential shame and disgrace if Gustav's perversion was revealed . . .

Meanwhile, Cynthia's young mind was developing, even while Gustav persisted in abusing her . . . Her memories, now crystallizing, would be carried with her down the years, along with fear and rage . . .

The memories were monstrous—of Gustav's ever-increasing sexual interest in his daughter, stimulated now by beatings . . . hard, stinging slaps and blows for trivial "offenses," their nature neither explained nor understood . . . And more, still more "punishment"—for what? . . . The bruises, the burned legs . . . the endless lies her mother told . . .

When Cynthia was six, her father first rubbed himself against her . . . And later, as her body grew—the ultimate perversion and humiliation—he began raping her, an act so disgusting and painful that she screamed . . . Gustav, obsessed with his own satisfaction, took no notice, perhaps even enjoying his daughter's despair . . . Still Eleanor did nothing . . .

Thus, with the stage set—finally, inevitably Cynthia's pregnancy happened at age twelve . . . The horror for a child—now hidden away, shielded from outsiders' view, knowing she was ungainly, her body expanding amid strange sensations and movement inside her . . . Aware, too, she was in deep disgrace, made to feel guilty, yet helpless to help herself, and with no one to talk with, to lean on, or to trust . . . And at the degrading, secret, painful birthing, the baby she never saw whisked away . . .

The sole consolation: The sexual assaults by Gustav, which had continued through her pregnancy, somehow ceased, for reasons she never knew—until much later, when her mother reluctantly revealed their lawyer's threat to expose Gustav if he didn't stop . . .

Then, like some evil postscript, Eleanor and her statement to the welfare woman—that official person who accepted the glib lies and never insisted on hearing Cynthia's story . . .

Eventually, and despite everything, Cynthia's coldly pragmatic calculation . . . her decision to bide her time, to use her parents until her independence was assured, and then to exercise her long-festering hatred and to kill them—as they had killed so much in her . . .

That retribution time was nearer now, as she began to plan . . . And she had her instrument . . .

• • •

Throughout the entire recital, Patrick Jensen scarcely moved. But his face was a mirror of successive emotions—incredulity at first, then disgust, anger, horror, and concern. At one point his eyes even brimmed with tears. At another he reached out as if to take Cynthia's hand, but she withdrew it.

At the end he shook his head in anguish. "Unbelievable." His voice was barely audible. "I can hardly believe—"

"Goddam! You'd *better* believe it," Cynthia cut in sharply, combatively.

"I didn't mean that . . . Give me a minute." After a pause, "I do believe you. Every single thing. But it's so—"

Impatiently, "So what?"

"So hard to find words to fit. In my life *I've* done bad things, but this kind of sick—"

"Oh, Patrick, get off it. You murdered two people."

"Yeah, I know." He grimaced. "I'm a shit, okay. Yes, I did kill—out of passion, or impulse, or whatever. But what I'm saying is that your parents, over a long period, with lots of time to *think* about what they were doing . . . well, the way I see it, your parents are the stinking scum of the earth."

Cynthia said, "Good. So maybe you understand why I want to kill them."

After the briefest hesitation, Jensen nodded. "Yes, I do."

"So you will help me."

•   •   •

For two hours Cynthia and Patrick Jensen talked—sometimes heatedly, occasionally calmly, at moments persuasively, but never lightly. Their thoughts, arguments, doubts, discussions, denials, threats, persuasions, were all arranged, discarded, and rearranged, like jumbled dominoes.

At one point Patrick tried: "And suppose I *don't* say yes to your insane proposition, if I tell you the hell with it, go screw yourself. Then would you really open up that box of snakes that could put me in the chair? If you did that, you'd accomplish nothing."

"Yes, I'd do it," Cynthia answered. "I wouldn't make the threat if I didn't mean it. Besides, you deserve to be punished, if not by me, then for Naomi."

"Then what would *you* do, Lady Noble Avenger?" Jensen's voice was contemptuous. "Without me, how would you plow the killing fields?"

"I'd find someone else."

And he knew she would.

Much later, Jensen argued, "I told you that what I did was a crime of passion; I admitted that, and wish I could undo it. But I *couldn't*—simply *know* I couldn't—do a cold-blooded, premeditated murder." He threw up his hands. "Like it or not, that's the way it is."

"I know all that," Cynthia said. "I've known it all along."

Jensen sputtered, "Then for God's sake, why in hell—"

"I want you to arrange for someone else to do it," she said calmly. "And pay them."

Jensen inhaled a deep breath, held it, then let it out. Both his body and his brain felt an overwhelming sense of relief. Then, a moment later, he wondered: *Why?*

He already knew the answer. Cynthia, adroitly and with cynical psychology, had maneuvered him to a point where what she now proposed was the better of two choices: Go to prison for life, or perhaps pay the ultimate penalty of death for the murders of Naomi and her friend, or take a chance in arranging for someone else to do another killing for which he, Patrick, had no stomach. He might not even have to be present when it happened. There would be a chance of discovery and exposure, of course, with a penalty for that, too. But that had been the case since the night he killed Naomi.

Cynthia was smiling slightly as she watched him. "You've figured it out, haven't you?"

"You're a witch *and* a bitch!"

"But you'll do it. You don't really have a choice."

Strangely, in his storyteller's mind, Jensen was already thinking of it as a game. He supposed it was perverse, undoubtedly despicable. Just the same, it was a game that he could play and win.

"I know you've been hanging out with a pretty scummy crowd lately," Cynthia prompted. "All you have to do is find the right guy."

In fact, Jensen had been slowly immersing himself in the criminal underworld, beginning more than two years earlier when he decided to write a novel about drug trafficking. In the course of researching the story he had sought out some small-time drug dealers—not difficult because of his own occasional cocaine use—who, in turn, had referred him to bigger sharks.

Two or three of those bigger operators, while agreeing to meet him out of curiosity, were slow to relax, but finally decided that a real, live author, "a smart guy with his name on books," could be trusted. The inherent vanity of most career criminals and the compulsion to be noticed also opened doors for Jensen. In bars and nightclubs, with drinks and confidences flowing, a question he often encountered was "You gonna put me in a book?" His stock answer was "Maybe." Thus, in time, Jensen's criminal acquaintanceships widened, beyond what he needed for research, and he began doing some occasional drug deals and drug transporting himself, surprised to find how easy it was, and how pleasantly profitable.

The profit was helpful because his crime novel did not do well, nor did another that followed, and it appeared that Patrick's high-flying best-seller days might be over. At the same time he had made some bad investments, based on poor advice, and his accumulated money was diminishing alarmingly.

The combined factors made Cynthia's bizarre objective at least more feasible, not entirely unthinkable, perhaps even interesting.

"You know we'll have to pay someone a lot for this job," he said to Cynthia. "And I don't have that kind of money."

"I know," she said. "But I have plenty." And she did.

Gustav Ernst, as part of his attempts to make peace with his daughter after the long years of abuse, had given Cynthia a generous monthly allowance, which supplemented her salary and enabled her to live well. For her part, she accepted it as her due.

In addition, Gustav also arranged for substantial sums of money to be placed in a Cayman Islands bank account in Cynthia's name. But Cynthia had not acknowledged the Caymans money or used any of it, though the accumulated amount, she knew, was now in excess of five million dollars.

For many years Gustav Ernst had been a successful financial entrepreneur; his specialty was buying major interests in small, innovative companies in need of venture capital. His instincts were uncanny. Most companies he chose would burgeon in a short time, their stock soaring, at which point Gustav sold out. His net worth reputedly was sixty million dollars.

Gustav's younger brother, Zachary, had shed his United States citizenship as increasing numbers of wealthy Americans were doing to avoid punitive taxation. Now Zachary divided his residency between the Caymans and the Bahamas, both congenial, sunny tax havens. It was Zachary who opened Cynthia's Cayman account and put money in it periodically, always as a tax-free "gift." On each occasion Cynthia received a confirming letter along the following lines:

> *My dear Cynthia:*
> *I do hope you will accept the latest gift I have placed in your*
> *account. These days I seem to have more money than I need, and since*
> *I have no wife, children, or other relatives, it gives me pleasure to pass*
> *these sums along to you. I trust you are able to make use of them.*
>
>

From your affectionate
Uncle Zack

Cynthia knew the money was, in fact, from Gustav, who had his own arrangements with Zachary involving tax avoidance—or was it evasion? Cynthia neither knew nor cared, except for being aware that avoidance was legal, evasion illegal.

She did care, however, about her own legal position and, while not acknowledging the letters, saved them and sought a tax consultant's advice.

He reported back, "The letters are fine. Keep them in case you ever need to prove the deposits were gifts and nontaxable. About your Cayman account and your receiving gifts there, all of that is perfectly in order. But each year on your U.S. tax return you must report having that account, and declare any interest earned as income. Then you'll be in the clear."

Subsequently one of Cynthia's tax returns was audited and approved, with the consultant's advice confirmed, so she never had to worry about breaking the law. Even so, she kept her Cayman wealth a secret from everyone except the consultant and the U.S. Internal Revenue Service. She had no intention of telling Jensen, either.

For a few minutes he had been silent, thinking.

"Plenty of money will be a help," he resumed. "To do what you have in mind, making sure the killings stay unsolved and no one talks . . . the price will be steep—maybe two hundred thousand dollars."

"I can pay that," Cynthia said.

"How?"

"Cash."

"Okay. So what's our time frame?"

"There isn't one—not yet. You can take however long you need to find the right person—someone who's clever, tough, brutal, discreet, and totally reliable."

"It won't be easy."

"That's why you'll have plenty of time." She would savor the waiting, Cynthia thought, knowing that eventually her revenge, which she had planned so long ago, would be fulfilled.

"While you're at it," Patrick said, "figure on a lot of money for me, too."

"You'll get it, and part will be for protecting me. You are not to mention my name to whoever you hire. Don't even hint of my involvement at *any time*, to *anyone*. Also, the fewer details I know, the better—except I *must* be told a date at least two weeks ahead."

"So you can have an alibi?"

Cynthia nodded. "So I can be three thousand miles away."

3

TAKE HOWEVER LONG YOU NEED," Cynthia had told Patrick Jensen. But it was almost four years—certainly longer than Cynthia had intended—before the irrevocable steps were taken.

The intervening time passed quickly, however—particularly for Cynthia, who was climbing the promotion ladder at the Miami Police Department with exceptional speed. Yet neither Cynthia's successes nor the passage of time tempered the hatred she felt toward her parents. Nor did it diminish her need for revenge. From time to time she reminded Jensen of his commitment to her, which he acknowledged, insisting that he was still looking for the right guy—someone resourceful, ruthless, brutal, and dependable. He had not, so far, appeared.

At times, in Jensen's mind, the whole concept seemed eerie and unreal. As a novelist he had often written about criminals, but all of it was abstract—no more than words on a computer screen. The true darkness of crime, as he saw it then, was in a world that belonged to others—a whole different brand of people. Yet now he had become one of them. Through a single crazy act he had committed a capital crime and, in that instant, his formerly law-abiding life was gone. Did others enter the underworld in that same headlong, unplanned way? He supposed many did.

As time passed, he sometimes asked himself, *What have you become, Patrick Jensen?* And answered objectively, *Whatever it is, you've gone too far; there can be no turning back . . . Virtue's a luxury you can't afford anymore . . . There was once a time for conscience, but that time has gone . . . If someone ever discovers and discloses what you've done, nothing—nothing at all—will be forgotten or forgiven . . . So survival is all that matters—survival at any cost . . . even at the cost of other lives . . .*

All the same, Jensen was still haunted by that sense of unreality.

In contrast, he was sure, Cynthia had no such illusions. She possessed an inflexibility that never abandoned a target. He had seen that trait at work, knew that because of it he would not escape his mission as Cynthia Ernst's surrogate executioner, and that if he failed her, she would keep her promise and destroy him.

In essence, Jensen came to realize, he was no longer the same person he had once been. Instead he had become a self-protective, ruthless stranger.

●   ●   ●

Despite the delay in her primary objective, Cynthia had taken care of a secondary one by using her senior rank, plus some biased research and use of old records, to thwart Malcolm Ainslie's promotion to lieutenant. Her motives were clear enough, even to Cynthia. After a childhood of what amounted to complete and utter rejection, she was determined that no one—*no one*—would ever reject her again. But Malcolm had, and for that, she would never forget, never forgive.

Eventually, after the long delay in her final reckoning with Gustav and Eleanor Ernst, Cynthia decided she had waited long enough. She conveyed her impatience to Patrick during a weekend in Nassau, Bahamas, where again they were registered at separate hotels, Cynthia at the luxurious Paradise Island Ocean Club.

After a long and satisfying morning of sex, Cynthia suddenly sat up in her bed. "You've had more than enough time. I want some action, or *I'll* take some." She leaned over and kissed his forehead. "And trust me, sweetheart, you won't like the kind of action I have in mind."

"I know." Jensen had been expecting this kind of ultimatum for some time and asked, "How long do I have?"

"Three months."

"Make it six."

"Four, beginning tomorrow."

He sighed, knowing that she meant it, aware also that for reasons of his own the time had come.

●   ●   ●

Jensen had produced one more book, which, like the two preceding it, was a failure compared with his earlier best-sellers. As a result, the publishers' advances Patrick received for all three books, which he had spent long ago, were not earned out and no more royalty payments were forthcoming. The next step was predictable. His American publishing house, which during his successful years paid him handsome advances against books not yet written, declined to do so anymore, insisting instead that he submit a finished manuscript before any contract was signed and money changed hands.

This left Jensen in a desperate situation. During the preceding few years he had not moderated his expensive living habits, and not only were his current assets nil, but he was deeply in debt. Thus the possibility of receiving two hundred thousand dollars to hire a killer—of which Jensen intended to keep half, plus a similar sum he envisaged for his own services—was now urgent and attractive.

Through a series of coincidences, he moved closer to finding his man. These coincidences, initially unconnected to Patrick, involved the police, a group of disabled veterans from Vietnam and the Gulf War, and drugs. The vets, who had suffered wartime wounds that confined them to wheelchairs, were once mired in a postwar life of drugs, but had kicked the habit and were now anti-drug crusaders. In the uneasy, mixed-race area where they lived—between Grand Avenue and Bird Road in Coconut Grove—they had declared a private war on those who sold drugs and helped ruin the lives of so many, especially young people. The group's members were aware that others in their community were trying to fight drugs and traffickers, but mostly not succeeding. However, the vets in wheelchairs *were* succeeding and, in their special way, had become vigilantes and undercover police informers.

Paradoxically, their leader and inspirer was neither a military veteran nor a reformed drug user, but a former athlete and scholar. Stewart Rice, age twenty-three, sometimes known as Stewie, had suffered a fall four years earlier while climbing a sheer mountain face, leaving him permanently paralyzed below the waist and confined to a wheelchair. He, too, felt strongly about young people and drugs, and his alliance with the vets resulted from shared opinions and the camaraderie that people in wheelchairs feel instinctively for each other.

As Rice expressed it to newcomers to the group, which had begun with three Vietnam vets and expanded to a dozen, "Young people, kids, with whole bodies and active lives, are being destroyed by the drug scum who should be in jail. And we're helping put them there."

The wheelchair group's modus operandi was to collect information about who was dealing, where, when, how often, and when new supplies were expected, then pass all that information anonymously to the Police Department's anti-drug task force.

Rice again, speaking with a trusted friend. "Those of us in chairs can move around where the drug action is, and hardly anyone takes notice. If they think about us at all, they figure we're panhandling, like all those guys on Bird Road. They believe that because our legs are paralyzed or our arms don't work, we're that way, too, in our heads—especially the druggies and dealers who've destroyed the few brain cells they once had."

At the police end, anti-drug task force members were skeptical when the informational phone calls began—calls Rice always made himself, using a cellular phone to avoid tracing. Immediately after a tip-off, whoever answered would demand the caller's identification, but "Stewie" was the only name Rice gave before hanging up quickly. But soon, after discovering the information was usable and dependable, a call beginning, "This is Stewie," was greeted by, "Hi, buddy! What you got for us?" No tracing was attempted. Why spoil a good thing?

As a result, gang drug trafficking was increasingly disrupted by police. Arrests and convictions mounted. Parts of Coconut Grove were becoming cleaner. Then the pattern broke.

Major drug traffickers, aware that some kind of espionage must be occurring, began asking questions. At first there were no answers. Then an arrested dealer overheard one drug cop say to another, "Stewie sure came through this time."

Within hours a question was buzzing through the Grove: "Who the fuck is Stewie?"

The answer came quickly. Along with it, through neighborhood gossip, the wheelchair group's tactics were exposed.

Stewart Rice had to die, and in such a way as to warn others like him.

The contract killing was ordered for the next day, which was the point at which—through coincidence—Patrick Jensen became involved.

•   •   •

Jensen had become a regular at the Brass Doubloon, a noisy, smoky bar and lounge well known as a hangout for drug dealers, and that night when he walked in, a voice from a table called across, "Hey, Pat! You writin' somethin' new, man? Come tell us!" The voice belonged to a narrow-faced, pockmarked ex-con with a long rap sheet, named Arlie. He was with several others, also part of the scene that Jensen had come to know during his search for a crime story. One in the group whom Jensen had not seen before was a huge, hard-featured man with wide shoulders, powerful arms, close-cropped hair, and a mulatto's complexion. The stranger, dwarfing the others, was scowling. He growled a question, which another at the table answered.

"Pat's okay, Virgilio. He writes books, see. You tell him shit, he makes a story. Just a story—nothing real, don't do us no harm."

Someone else added, "Yeah, Pat keeps his mouth shut. He knows he'd better. Right, Pat?"

Jensen nodded. "Absolutely."

A space was opened for him and a chair pulled in. Facing the huge newcomer, he said easily, "No need to tell me anything, Virgilio, and I just forgot your name. I'll ask one question, though." Everyone stared. "Can I buy you a drink?"

The huge man, still scowling, looked at Jensen steadily. Then he said, in a heavily accented voice, "I buy drinks."

"Fine." Jensen did not look away, either. "A double Black Label."

A barman behind them called, "Coming up!"

Virgilio stood. Looming even larger on his feet, he announced tersely, "First I piss." He turned away.

When he had gone, the second man who had spoken, whose name was Dutch, told Patrick, "He's sizin' you up. Better hope he likes you."

"Why should I care?"

"Because nobody messes with Virgilio. He's Colombian; comes and goes here. On his home turf, four finks double-crossed their boss, talked to Colombian cops. Virgilio got the job of showin' 'em they did bad. Know what he did?"

Jensen shook his head.

"He found them, tied 'em to trees, their arms stretched out. Then he used a chain saw on every one—cut off their right arms."

Jensen took a hasty sip of Scotch.

Arlie whispered, "Do you some good to know Virgilio. Be some action tonight. You interested?"

"Yes." Even as he spoke, a new thought occurred to Jensen.

"When he gets back," Dutch said, "wait for a bit, then go to the can and take your time. We'll ask Virgilio if it's okay to let you in."

Jensen did as he was told. Soon afterward, a nod.

·   ·   ·

"Keep on following the jeep," Dutch instructed Jensen. "And when they stop and turn off their lights, do the same."

It was almost 3:00 A.M. They were in Jensen's Volvo, having driven thirty-five miles south on Florida's Turnpike, led by a Jeep Cherokee ahead, with Arlie driving and Virgilio his passenger. Then, just past Florida City, an entrance to the Everglades, they turned onto Card Sound Road, a desolate byway leading to Key Largo. By the light of a half moon, Jensen could make out the tidewater and broken-down houseboats nestled along mudbanks on either side. There were no homes or villages to provide ambient light, nor was there any sign of other cars. Motorists shunned this route at night, preferring the more traveled and safer U.S. 1 Highway.

"I sure as hell couldn't live in one of those shitheaps," Dutch said. "Could you?" Their headlights had revealed a pile of debris that was once a boat, with a crude sign reading, *Blue Crabbs for Sale.* Jensen, wondering by now why he was here at all, didn't answer.

At that moment the jeep in front swung off the road onto a gravelly area, stopped, and its lights went out. Jensen followed, turned off the Volvo's lights, and got out. The two from the jeep stood waiting. Nothing was said.

The big Colombian walked to the water's edge, peering out into the darkness.

Suddenly, headlights appeared. A tradesman's van, with a "Plumber's Pal" logo on its side panel, pulled off the road and stopped next to Virgilio and Arlie's jeep. Immediately two male figures left the van; Patrick noticed they were wearing gloves. The newcomers went to the van's rear doors, where the others joined them. Jensen hung back.

Inside the van, a shape was visible. As the object was pulled to the rear, Patrick saw it was a mechanical-type wheelchair that had been transported on its back. A figure was in the chair and, though secured by ropes, appeared to be struggling. Virgilio moved forward; he, too, had slipped on gloves. Then, as if the heavy chair were weightless, Virgilio lifted it out and stood it upright. Patrick, who now faced the chair, could see that the seated figure was a young male, gagged and bound. He could see the captive's eyes moving desperately from side to side, and the mouth working, too, trying to eject the gag. Somehow, for a moment, the man in the chair succeeded and spat part of the gag loose. Looking at Jensen, who was separate from the others, he blurted, "I've been kidnapped! My name's Stewie Rice. These people will kill me! Please help—"

The words had barely finished when Virgilio smashed an enormous hand against Stewie's face. A spurt of blood emerged from his mouth along with a sharp cry, stifled as Dutch reached out and readjusted the gag. Still the captive's eyes roved, frantically pleading. Jensen had to look away.

"We move quick," Virgilio pronounced, propelling the wheelchair toward the water, again lifting it easily when it stuck. The pair who had arrived in the van followed, one carrying a chain, the other a cement block. Dutch joined them and beckoned Jensen to follow. Reluctantly, he did so. Arlie remained on shore.

Now they were in the water, whose course had been dredged out years before as a canal. Although shallow at the edge, farther out it plunged down to eight or ten feet. The two who had brought the wheelchair waded forward, maneuvering around a tangle of mangroves.

Ahead through the blackness was a mangrove islet, one of several, surrounded by shallow water and sea grass. The two from the van, who appeared to know the locale, had stopped where they felt the water deepen. One said, "Here'll do."

Virgilio, propelling the chair and its panicked occupant on his own, pushed it forward until the captive was more than half immersed. Now the other two used the chain to secure the chair, passing it in turn through each wheel, now underwater, then at one end fastening it to a plant stump on the islet, and at the other end to the cement block they had brought.

"Sure as hell won't float," Dutch said. "Tide's rising now, be over his head in a coupla hours." He laughed. "Give the bastard some time to think."

The figure in the wheelchair, who had clearly overheard, moaned and struggled harder, but the only effect was to shift the wheelchair deeper in the water.

In the darkness Jensen shuddered. Since facing the captive, he had known he was part of a murder, as an accessory at least. But he knew, too, that if he had tried to leave, he could become a victim also. Virgilio would not hesitate to make that happen.

Deep within, a small voice from the past asked, *What am I? When did I stop caring?* . . . And Jensen was reminded of his earlier thought: *The person I once was no longer exists.*

"We go," Virgilio pronounced.

As they moved toward shore, leaving the wheelchair and its occupant, Jensen tried not to imagine what Stewie Rice's dying would be like. Inevitably he did. He envisioned the tide rising gradually while Rice watched helplessly until salt water—a little at a time—began to lap at his face . . . Soon he would hold his head as high as possible, inhaling when he could, preserving each breath against the inexorable rise of the water . . . Survival until the absolute last moment would be instinctive . . . Perhaps he would succeed in breathing intermittently, though knowing he would shortly fail . . . Then, as the water rose still more, in desperation he would choke and splutter . . . and finally, as his mouth and nose were covered and his lungs filled, mercifully he would drown . . .

Jensen pulled his thoughts away.

On shore, Virgilio approached. He put his face near Patrick Jensen's. "You keep this big secret. Or I fuckin' kill you."

"I have to keep it that way, don't I? I'm in it, too." Jensen kept his face close to the other's and his voice level. He had decided the only way to deal with Virgilio was not to be intimidated.

"Yeah," the big man conceded. "You in it, too."

"I want to talk to you privately sometime," Jensen said quietly. "Just the two of us."

Virgilio seemed surprised. His mind clearly working, he raised a questioning eyebrow.

"Yes," Jensen said, knowing a message had passed between them and was understood.

"I go Colombia," Virgilio said. "When I back, I find you."

Jensen knew he would. He also knew he had found his killer.

● ● ●

A couple of Harley-Davidson riders, passing by in the early morning, were the first to see the wheelchair partly submerged. From Alabama Jack's, a popular bikers' bar a short distance ahead, they called 911, and Metro-Dade police responded. Two uniform officers and paramedics waded out from shore; the senior paramedic declared the man dead. Stewart Rice was readily identified from credit cards and papers on him. By this time the local news people, having heard police radio calls, arrived in full flood.

Dramatic pictures of the wheelchair being brought ashore, with the slumped figure still secured by ropes, appeared widely in newspapers and on TV. Unwittingly, this attention fulfilled the criminal objective—providing a warning to others, especially the wheelchair vets. In the face of wide knowledge about their group and its methods, the drug vigilance ceased, as did tip-offs to the police anti-drug task force.

"Too bad about Stewie," one task force member said to another soon after. "Somebody must have talked too much. Always happens."

● ● ●

Several days after the event, Jensen phoned Cynthia at her apartment to ask for a meeting. Before leaving the Bahamas, she had warned him they should not be seen together until their objective was accomplished, and for some time beyond. Therefore Jensen was not to come to the apartment, but should telephone her there and nowhere else, and they would arrange any absolutely necessary rendezvous at a place where neither was likely to be recognized. During the phone call, Cynthia instructed him to meet her the following Sunday in Boca Raton, a manageable drive, but well clear of Miami. She named Pete's Restaurant on Glades Road, where they were unlikely to encounter anyone who knew them.

Jensen arrived early and remained in his car until Cynthia appeared and parked nearby. He joined her and they entered the pleasant restaurant together, choosing an indoor verandah table, facing a lake and fountain, where they could talk privately. Cynthia ordered a Greek salad, Jensen the catch of the day without knowing what it was; the name somehow seemed appropriate.

When their waiter had gone, he came directly to the point.

"I've found the man we need." He described Virgilio, and what had been revealed about the burly Colombian by his cronies at the Brass Doubloon.

"How do you know he —" Cynthia began, but Jensen waved her down.

"There's more. I watched him operate." Lowering his voice, he began describing the events of a few days earlier, beginning with Card Sound Road. He had reached the point when the tradesman's van arrived, then the appearance of the wheelchair, when Cynthia, glaring, snapped across the table, "Shut up, goddam you!" Jensen paused and she added, "Don't tell me that. I don't want to know."

Patrick shrugged. "Well, you know now. The point is, Virgilio did the wheelchair murder. You must have heard about it."

"Of course I heard." Cynthia, angry and flushed, was breathing heavily. "You stupid idiot! You didn't have to tell me, and now *forget you did*. Wipe those last few minutes out."

"Okay, if you say so, but let me tell you this." Jensen paused as their food arrived. When the waiter had gone, he leaned forward, lowering his voice still more. "The point is, this guy Virgilio *enjoys* killing; I watched him that night. He's smart and not the slightest bit afraid."

Cynthia waited, still visibly disturbed, before asking, "Are you sure he'll contact you again?"

"Yeah, I'm sure. He's clearly gone to Colombia while things cool down, but he'll be back; that's when I'll talk to him about doing your parents. I know he'll do it. In the meantime we have to take care of some things. Cash, for one."

"I have it ready."

"Two hundred thousand?"

"That's the amount you said."

"And then the same for me."

Cynthia hesitated, then: "All right, but afterward."

"Fair enough."

More calmly now, she announced, "I have had an idea about the killings."

"Tell me."

"There have been two murders recently, one in Coconut Grove, another in Fort Lauderdale; both look as if they were done by the same person, with some odd features. Homicide thinks there may be more."

"What features?"

"At Coconut Grove—it was at the Royal Colonial Hotel—there were dead animals left at the scene."

"I read about the Royal Colonial, though nothing about dead animals."

"It was held back from the press."

"And Fort Lauderdale?"

"I don't remember exactly, but something similar." Cynthia reflected.

"What I was thinking was that if my parents' killings could be made to look like those two . . ."

"I'm with you," Jensen said. "It would divert any suspicion, make it look like one more by the same person. Can you get more details?"

She nodded.

"Good. Then let's meet again two weeks from now."

They left the restaurant soon after, Cynthia settling their bill with cash.

•   •   •

Jensen's Volvo was behind Cynthia's BMW convertible as both turned onto I-95 for the return journey south to Miami. Cynthia drove faster and Jensen let her car disappear from sight, then took the next freeway exit and drove to a shopping area, where he parked.

Without leaving the car, he groped under his jacket and shirt. He removed a small tape recorder. He rewound the tape and, using a tiny earphone, listened. Despite their guardedly low voices, the recording was excellent. Every part was clear, including Cynthia's reaction when she learned the name of the wheelchair murderer, followed by their agreement on Virgilio as the man to kill her parents.

Jensen smiled. *Cynthia,* he mused, *you are not the only one who can record incriminating conversations.* He hoped never to have to use today's recording, but one thing was now certain. If something went wrong, if he was exposed and went down, he sure as hell would take Cynthia Ernst with him.

4

"REMEMBER THOSE TWO HOMICIDES I talked about last time?" Cynthia asked. "The one at Coconut Grove and—"

Jensen said edgily, "Of course I do. You were going to find out more."

"Well, I have."

It was the third week of June, two weeks after their liaison at Boca Raton. They had needed to get together again, though Cynthia's work schedule made a meeting in the Caymans or Bahamas impractical. Instead she chose Homestead, a small-town gateway to the Everglades, thirty-five miles south of Miami. They drove there separately, then met at Potlikkers restaurant.

The drive had left Jensen feeling tired; he had not slept well the night before, or for a succession of nights before that, either. And there had been nightmares—the details vague, except they left him drenched with sweat, and in the hazy no-man's-land before waking, he recalled a wheelchair half-immersed and Virgilio's menacing face inches from his own.

Potlikkers' decor was rustic, and Jensen and Cynthia were seated on benches at a knotty pine table away from other diners. She had brought a small leather attaché case and now set it beside her. She looked across at him. "Something wrong?"

"For Christ's sake! Is anything *right?*" He almost laughed, and considered saying, *No, nothing's wrong. We're just meeting here to plot two murders for which we both have motives, in case you hadn't noticed, and some of the best brains in the detective business will be trying to solve them . . . They may even do it, and who knows? Maybe we'll be electrocuted side by side . . . But, no! . . . Apart from that, there's nothing wrong at all.*

"Keep your voice down," Cynthia said. "And don't lose your nerve. There's no need, because everything is going to work—remember, I'm in a position to judge that. Have you heard from your man, the guy you talked about? And don't use a name."

Jensen nodded. "Three days ago."

The long-distance call had come fifteen days after the wheelchair murder.

There was no indication of where the call was coming from, and Patrick hadn't asked, but guessed it was Colombia.

"You know who I am, but do not say." The voice was clearly Virgilio's.

"Yes, I know."

"I come soon. You still want?"

"Yes." Obviously, Virgilio was using the fewest words possible. Jensen did the same.

"One week, maybe two. Okay?"

"Okay."

And that was the total exchange. After Jensen had described it, Cynthia asked, "You're sure your instinct's right? He understands what we want?"

"I'm sure. You don't arrange to meet his kind for lightweight jobs, and he knows it. So tell me about those other murders. The odd features—isn't that what you called them?"

"Yes." A pause. "At Coconut Grove, four dead cats were left beside the victims."

"Four cats?" Jensen's voice was unbelieving.

"Don't ask me why because I don't know, nor does anyone else. In Homicide they're still guessing."

"You said there was a similar case in Fort Lauderdale. What about that?"

"It's more complicated. The man's feet were burned, and no one knows why, except for a belief that both things were symbols in some killer's crazy mind."

"So what are you suggesting?"

"Copy the first one. Tell your man to take a dead animal and leave it."

"Not four cats, I hope."

Cynthia shook her head. "It should be the same but different, and one will do—maybe a rabbit. It's just another symbol. Besides, there are other things."

"Such as?"

She described how, in both the Frost and Hennenfeld cases, the victims were found gagged and bound and facing each other. "And the murder weapon both times was a bowie knife. You know what that is?"

Jensen nodded. "I used it once in a story. Not hard to get. Next."

"Again at both murders a radio was playing loud. Hard rock."

"No sweat." Jensen was concentrating, memorizing; he would write none of this down, either now or later.

"Every bit of money that's there should be taken," Cynthia said. "My father always carries plenty and leaves it beside his bed. But my mother's jewelry must *not* be touched. That's how it was with those other scenes. Make that very clear."

"Shouldn't be difficult. Jewelry's identifiable and can be traced; I guess the other guy knew it, too."

"Now about the house," Cynthia said. "You may need this."

She passed a folded real-estate brochure across the table. It featured the Bay Point community, and as Jensen opened it, he saw a page displaying the layout of streets and lots. On one of them a house site was marked with an X.

"This is the . . . ?"

"Yes," Cynthia said, "and something else you should know is that there's a staff of three—a butler and his wife, the Palacios; she also works and they both live in. A day maid comes in early and leaves at about four in the afternoon."

"So at night there are four people in the house?"

"Except on Thursdays. That's when the Palacios always go to West Palm Beach to visit Mrs. Palacio's sister. They leave by late afternoon and are never back before midnight, sometimes later."

Jensen's memory was loaded. "I might forget that. Let me get it right." He reached for the brochure and fumbled in his pocket for a pencil.

Cynthia clucked impatiently. "Give that to me." On the brochure she wrote:

>   D.maid—in early, leaves 4p.
>   P's—Thurs out late afternoon, back midnite

Pocketing the brochure, Jensen asked, "Anything else I should know about those other killings?"

"Yeah, they were messy." Cynthia grimaced as she described the knife slashes and body mutilations accompanying the Frost and Hennenfeld killings—information she had obtained from Miami Homicide's files.

•   •   •

A few days earlier, during a weekday evening, Cynthia had walked from her own department to the Homicide offices. Senior officers from other departments often dropped into Homicide to chat and pick up stories about important cases; also, the coffee there was always good. Cynthia, as a former Homicide detective, frequently came and went, sometimes on Community Relations business.

She had chosen a time when the offices were quiet. Only two detectives were at their desks, along with Sergeant Pablo Greene, the senior officer present. After friendly greetings she told him, "I'd like to look at a file."

"Be my guest, Major." Greene waved airily to the file room. "You know where everything is, but call if you need help."

"I will," Cynthia said.

Alone inside the file room, she worked swiftly. Knowing where to look, she located the files for the Frost and Hennenfeld murders and took them to a table. The first file was large, but Cynthia quickly extracted two sets of notes, one by Bernard Quinn, who had been lead investigator, the other by Malcolm Ainslie as supervisor. Skimming both, she paused at usable information and transferred it to her own small notebook. Within minutes she closed the Frosts' file and opened the other. This was slim because it was not a Miami case, but had resulted from the visit of Sheriff-Detective Benito Montes of Fort Lauderdale. He had, however, supplied a copy of the original Offense-Incident Report and supplementary notes that gave details.

After replacing both files, she returned to the main office and bid a friendly good night to Sergeant Greene and the other two detectives. Checking her watch, she saw she had been in Homicide barely twelve minutes, and no one knew which files she had reviewed.

Back in her own office, she studied and memorized the notes she had made, then tore out the notebook pages and flushed them down a toilet.

•   •   •

In the Homestead restaurant, while hearing of the brutality of the two double murders at Coconut Grove and Fort Lauderdale, Jensen decided that Virgilio would have no difficulty fulfilling that demand. The same applied to binding and gagging the victims and leaving them facing each other, which Cynthia specified as essential.

Weighing it all, Jensen mentally endorsed Cynthia's idea of imitating those two earlier crimes; in a perverted way, he thought, the concept was brilliant. Then he checked himself. In the way of life to which he had become committed, it was not perverted at all, but brilliant . . . period!

"You're doing a lot of thinking," Cynthia said from across the table.

He shook his head and lied. "Just memorizing all those ground rules."

"Add this to the list, then: no fingerprints."

"That won't be a problem." Jensen remembered Virgilio slipping on gloves before helping lift the wheelchair from the tradesman's van.

"There's one other thing," Cynthia said, "and this really is the last."

Jensen waited.

"Between the Coconut Grove murders and Fort Lauderdale's, there was a time gap of four months and twelve days; I worked it out."

"So?"

"Serial killers often strike pretty much at regular intervals, which means whoever did those two could pull off another, either during the last few days of September or the first week of October. I worked that out, too."

Jensen was puzzled. "How would that affect us?"

"We'll beat the bastard to it by setting our date in mid-August. Then, if there's another of the same type of killing on one of those other dates, sure, there'll be an interval, but no one will think twice about it because the gaps won't seem a factor."

Cynthia stopped. "What's wrong? Why the long face?"

Jensen, who had looked increasingly doubtful, took a deep breath. "You want to know what I think?"

"I'm not sure I care, but go ahead if you want."

"Cyn, I think we're trying to be too clever."

"Which means?"

"The more we talk, the more I get the feeling that something can go wrong, terribly wrong."

"So what are you suggesting?" Cynthia's tone was icy.

Jensen hesitated. Then, with conflicting emotions, knowing the significance of his own words, he answered, "That we quit, call the whole thing off. Here and now."

After a sip of a diet soda beside her, Cynthia asked softly, "Aren't you forgetting something?"

"I suppose you mean the money." Jensen passed his tongue across his lips as she nodded.

"I brought it with me to give to you." Cynthia touched the leather attaché case on the seat beside her. "But never mind, I'll take it back." Picking up the case, she rose to leave, then paused, looking down at Jensen.

"I'll pay our bill on the way out. After all, you're going to need every last cent you have for a defense lawyer, and tomorrow I suggest you look for one. Or if you really can't afford it, you may have to take a public defender, though they're not very good, I'm afraid."

"Don't go!" He reached out to grasp her arm and said wearily, "Oh, for Christ's sake, sit down."

Cynthia returned to the bench but said nothing.

Jensen's voice was resigned. "Okay, if you want me to spell it out, I surrender . . . *re*-surrender. I *know* you hold all the aces, and I *know* you'd use them and never have a moment's regret. So let's go back to where we were."

Cynthia asked, "You're sure of that?"

He nodded submissively. "Sure."

"Then remember that the date for it all to happen must be as close as pos-

sible to mid-August." She was all business once more, as if the past few minutes had not occurred. "We won't meet again, not for a long time. You can
phone me at the apartment, but keep it short and be careful what you say.
And when you tell me the date, add five days to the real one and I'll subtract
five. Is that clear?"

"It's clear."

"Now, is anything else on your mind?"

"One thing," Jensen answered. "All this conspiracy stuff has given me a
raging hard-on. How about it?"

She smiled. "I can hardly wait. Let's get the hell out of here and find a
motel."

As they left the restaurant together she said, "Oh, by the way, take good
care of this." And passed him the leather case.

●   ●   ●

Despite Jensen's commitment to Cynthia and his acceptance of her money,
doubts still plagued him. Also, the mention of seeking a lawyer kindled
an idea.

Every Tuesday, Jensen played racquetball at Miami's Downtown Athletic
Club along with another regular named Stephen Cruz. The two had met
there and after many months shared an easy camaraderie on the court.
Jensen had learned from other club members and media reports that Cruz
was a successful criminal defense lawyer. One afternoon, while he and Cruz
were showering after a tough, satisfying game, Jensen said on impulse,
"Stephen, if a day ever came that I was in legal trouble and needed help,
could I call on you?"

Cruz was startled. "Hey, I hope you haven't been doing anything . . ."

Jensen shook his head. "Nothing at all. It was only a passing thought."

"Well, of course, the answer's yes."

They left it there.

5

TWO HUNDRED THOUSAND DOLLARS in cash—exactly. Jensen had counted it in the bedroom of his apartment, not note by note, which would have taken too long, but by riffling through the various bundles and keeping a penciled tally as he progressed. The notes were all used, he was relieved to see, with denominations mixed. Hundred-dollar bills were in the majority, and all were the new counterfeit-proof hundreds introduced in 1996—another advantage, Jensen reasoned, aware that despite U.S. government propaganda claiming the old-type hundreds were mainly okay, many people and businesses declined to accept them since countless quantities worldwide were fake, and those who got stuck with them lost out.

Fifties were the next largest in number; no problem there, even though a new fifty-dollar bill was due soon. And there were many bundles of twenties, though those took more space, but nothing smaller.

Jensen suspected that Cynthia had specified precisely the types of bills— the assortment was typical of her thoroughness—and had brought them from the Cayman Islands, probably spread over several journeys there and back. Bringing more than ten thousand dollars into the United States without making a customs declaration was technically illegal, but Cynthia had once told him that U.S. Customs in Miami seldom bothered Miami police officers, especially senior officers, if they discreetly showed an identification badge.

Cynthia, of course, had no idea that Jensen knew about her Caymans wealth. Four years ago, however, when they had been together in her Grand Cayman hotel room, Cynthia, complaining of an upset stomach, had excused herself and gone to the bathroom. Jensen had seized the opportunity to open a briefcase she had left in view. Searching quickly through the papers inside, he had come across a Cayman bank statement showing a credit in Cynthia's name of more than five million dollars, at which he whistled softly. There was also a letter from someone called Uncle Zack certifying that a recent deposit was a gift, and some other papers clipped together indicated that Cynthia had informed the IRS about the account and had paid taxes on the interest. *Pretty smart*, Jensen thought.

Without knowing what use he could make of the information, or if it would ever have *any* use, he pulled out a notebook and swiftly wrote down basics; he would have liked to make copies, but there wasn't time. What he had, though, were essentials—the name of the Cayman bank, an account number, and the latest balance; Cynthia's tax consultant's name, with a Fort Lauderdale address; an IRS letter with date and reference, and who had signed it; and, for what it was worth, the name "Uncle Zack." Later Jensen removed the page from his notebook, dated and signed it, and preserved it carefully.

Jensen had another thought about Cynthia's Cayman bounty—an instinct, really—which came to him in stages: she didn't think of it as real money and would probably never use it for herself; therefore she would not be overly concerned about how much went out and who received it. He was sure, for instance, that she suspected Jensen had lied to her about the amount needed to pay Virgilio, and that he intended to keep some of that money himself in addition to the large sum afterward that Cynthia had agreed to pay him personally.

Jensen *was* cheating, of course, and had no intention of offering Virgilio more than eighty thousand dollars to do the Ernst killings, though he might go to a hundred thousand if he had to. As he thought about it all while putting the bills back in the attaché case, Jensen smiled. And his upbeat feeling continued, effectively banishing the doubts and fears he had felt at the Homestead restaurant.

•   •   •

Five days later, shortly after 7:00 P.M., a buzzer sounded in Jensen's third-floor apartment on Brickell Avenue. The buzzer was actuated from a push-button panel outside the main entrance below. Using an intercom system, he responded, "Yes, who is it?" There was no answer, and he repeated the question. After a second silence, he shrugged and turned away.

A few minutes later the same process was repeated. Jensen was irritated but thought nothing of it; sometimes neighborhood kids played with the buzzer system. A third time, though, it occurred to him that someone was sending a message, so it was with slight unease that he left the apartment and went downstairs. But apart from a fellow tenant who was entering the main door, no one was in sight.

Jensen had parked his Volvo on the street outside, and on impulse he left the building and walked toward it. As he did so, he was startled to see a figure filling the front passenger seat; moments later he realized it was Virgilio. Jensen had locked the car before leaving it, and now, using a key to open the driver-side door, he was about to ask, "How the hell did you get in?" then changed his mind. Virgilio had already demonstrated he was a person of apt talents.

Motioning with an enormous hand, the Colombian instructed, "Drive."

Behind the wheel, and with the motor running, Jensen asked, "Anywhere special?"

"Someplace quiet."

For about ten minutes Jensen drove aimlessly, then turned into the parking area of a closed hardware store, turned off the engine and lights, and waited.

"You talk," Virgilio ordered. "You have job for me?"

"Yes." Patrick saw no reason not to come directly to the point. "I have friends who want two people killed."

"Who your friends?"

"You will not know. That way, it is safer for everyone."

"Okay." Virgilio nodded. "The ones to die—important people?"

"Yes. One is a city commissioner."

"Then cost much money."

"I will pay you eighty thousand dollars," Jensen said.

"No good." The Colombian shook his head vigorously. "Much more. One hunnert fifty."

"I don't have that much. I could maybe get one hundred thousand, but no more."

"Then no deal." Virgilio put his hand on the car door as if to leave, then stopped. "One hunnert twenty. Half now, half when job done."

The haggling had gone far enough, Jensen thought, regretting that he hadn't started at a lower figure, like fifty thousand. Still, even a hundred and twenty left eighty thousand for himself, plus the subsequent payment Cynthia had promised, and he knew she would keep her word.

"I'll have the sixty thousand ready in two days," he said. "You can call me the same way you did tonight."

The big man grunted his agreement, then gestured to the car's steering wheel. "Where those people live? You show me."

Why not? Jensen reasoned. Starting the engine again, he drove to Biscayne Boulevard and Bay Point, stopping short of the exclusive community's security checkpoint.

"The house is inside that fenced area," he reported. "You can be sure the fence has an alarm system, and there are security guards."

"I find way in. You have map showing house?"

Jensen opened the car's glove compartment, where he had placed a copy of the real-estate brochure Cynthia had given him five days earlier. The original he had kept himself, storing it in a safe location. He pointed to the page that showed the Bay Point streets, the lot marked X, and bearing Cynthia's handwritten note:

D.maid—in early, leaves 4p.
P's—Thurs out late afternoon, back midnite

"That's important," Jensen said, and explained the maid's working hours and the once-a-week absences of the butler and his wife.

"Good!" Virgilio pocketed the brochure. He had screwed up his face while listening, clearly concentrating to memorize everything, and twice had asked for information to be repeated, nodding his understanding when it was. Jensen reminded himself that whatever else Virgilio might be, he was intelligent.

Now Jensen went on to discuss the needed similarity to two other recent murder scenes and explained why. "It's to your advantage also," he pointed out, and Virgilio nodded agreement. Jensen described the required features: a dead animal must be left, perhaps a rabbit; a radio had to be playing loud hard rock—the local station HOT 105 . . . "Know it," Virgilio interjected . . . Positively no fingerprints . . . Virgilio nodded forcefully . . . All money on or near the victims to be taken, but jewelry not touched . . . There, too, a gesture of agreement . . . A knife to do the killing. "A *bowie* knife, do you understand? Can you get one?" . . . Virgilio: "Ya." . . . Jensen repeated Cynthia's report of the earlier murder scenes—the victims bound, gagged, facing each other, and the ugly brutality . . . While he could not be certain in the car's semidarkness, at that point Jensen believed Virgilio smiled.

"That's a lot to remember. Do you have it all?"

The Colombian touched his forehead with a finger. "Okay, is all here."

Next they discussed a date, Jensen remembering Cynthia's insistence that it should be as close as possible to mid-August.

"I go away, then come," Virgilio said, and Jensen suspected he would take his sixty thousand dollars' down payment to deposit in Colombia.

Finally they agreed on August 17.

Later, as they neared Jensen's apartment, Virgilio repeated the substance of his warning the night of the wheelchair murder. "Hey. You double-cross me, I fuckin' kill you."

"Virgilio, I would never, *ever*, double-cross you," Jensen said, and meant it. At the same time he resolved to stay well clear of Virgilio after the Ernst murders. He was capable of killing anyone, including Jensen, if he thought it necessary to cover his own tracks.

•   •   •

That same evening, Jensen phoned Cynthia and, without identifying himself, said only, "The date is August twenty-second."

Mentally she subtracted five, then answered, "I understand fully," and hung up.

6

CYNTHIA HAD BEEN IN LOS ANGELES for eight days when she learned of her parents' violent deaths. During that time she felt as if she were living two lives, one as she waited tensely, suspended in time, the other routine, normal, even prosaic.

Ostensibly she had come to L.A. to give a series of lectures to a segment of the L.A. Police Department about Miami's experience with police community relations—something she had done successfully for other forces. She also planned to spend a few vacation days with an old friend from her Pine Crest School years, Paige Burdelon, now a Universal Pictures vice-president, living in Brentwood.

On June 27, after Cynthia had received the message from Patrick Jensen that the long-awaited date was August 17, she made arrangements to fly from Florida to California on August 10. Her trip and the planned lectures were reported by the *Miami Herald* in Joan Fleischman's widely read "Talk of Our Town" column—the result of a friendly phone call from Cynthia the day before she left. Similarly, the *Los Angeles Times* made the same mention—the result of a suggestion by Cynthia to her West Coast counterpart, Commander Winslow McGowan. "It's not that I want publicity," she assured him, "but the more the public realizes that their police are concerned about the community, the better you and I can do our jobs." The commander had agreed; thus her absence east, and presence west, were very much on record.

Paige Burdelon was delighted to learn of Cynthia's plans. "You have to stay with me," she enthused over the phone. "Since Biffy and I split, I rattle around this big condo like a stranger in my own home. Come on, Cyn, we'll have a blast, I promise."

Cynthia accepted happily, and went directly to Paige's from LAX airport.

•　•　•

The police department lecture series, six hour-long sessions scheduled over two weeks, began the day after Cynthia's arrival. Her audience, gathered in a large conference room at the LAPD headquarters, comprised eighty selected officers from the department's eighteen divisions, all of varying ranks and ethnicity, with about two thirds in uniform, the remainder in plain clothes. Currently the LAPD was attempting to convert a single area-wide force, for many years directed despotically from the top, into a group of localized forces with friendly community liaisons. At the same time the department hoped to put behind it a painful era symbolized by a bellicose ex-chief, Darryl Gates, the Rodney King travesty, and the Simpson debacle. Miami's comparable transformation, which began much earlier and with considerable success, was respected nationwide as a prototype worth copying.

As Cynthia expressed it to her audience in an opening statement, "Just as in medicine, where the emphasis nowadays is on prevention, so should it be in police work. That's why the job of community relations has become so important. On the face of it, our job is simple: we must teach people to take precautions that decrease their chances of becoming victims of crime; at the same time we have to keep our citizens, especially kids, from being drawn into crime. We haven't always done that, which is why critics believe that our bulging prison populations are not a sign of our success, but a symptom of our failure."

The audience stirred; some even groaned at the last remark. Cynthia added crisply, "I am not here to placate you, but to make you think."

She was also thinking herself—somehow with her mind divided . . . *the interminable wait . . . lying awake nights, imagining that man entering Bay Point . . . finding her parents . . .*

She pushed those thoughts away, going on to describe Miami's Community Relations programs, ranging from the CATE (Crimes Against The Elderly) Detail, through the Gang Detail—helping kids, so they didn't join one; neighborhood crime watches; a Missing Persons/Juvenile Detail—among the busiest functions; a Crime Prevention Detail, and a dozen more.

"Of course," Cynthia added, "while community relations is a current hot button in police work, we also let the public know that for those who do insist on committing burglary, rape, arson, homicide, we're still in the business of solving crimes—with sharper investigative tools and tougher penalties."

The remark drew laughter and approving nods.

Despite the initial skepticism, Cynthia's speech was applauded loudly at the end, followed by many questions—so many that her first lecture ran half an hour overtime.

As the group was filing out, one of the older officers, a heavily built uniformed commander with a lined face and graying hair, stopped beside her. "You're a determined lady," he said in a gravelly voice. "I'm one of the old guard, soon to be out to pasture. Not saying I agree with your stuff; some I don't. But like you said, I'll go home and think."

Cynthia smiled; her own rank as major equaled an LAPD commander. "Thank you for that. Who could ask more?"

Winslow McGowan, a tall, reedy man about Cynthia's age, joined her and said, "Congratulations, it went well." He waited until they were alone, then added hesitantly, "Listen, Cynthia, it's none of my business, but ever since you arrived, you've seemed a bit distracted. Is everything okay, or have I messed up somehow with the arrangements?"

Cynthia was startled; until this moment she was convinced she had kept all private thoughts to herself. But McGowan was clearly a perceptive man.

"All the arrangements are fine," she assured him. "Absolutely no problems." But, she decided, she must be more careful.

●   ●   ●

Cynthia's concern with what was soon to occur three thousand miles away was eased by the whirlwind of activity Paige had organized. On their first morning together, Cynthia drove with Paige to work in her black Saab convertible, heading to one of the Universal sound stages, where a police thriller was being shot. They were cruising north on Interstate 405, the wind blowing through their hair.

"Just like *Thelma and Louise*," Paige laughed. She was tall and slim, with shoulder-length blond hair and blue eyes. "A generic L.A. girl" was the way she described herself.

"What's the movie we're going to see being filmed?" Cynthia asked.

"*Dark Justice*. It's a great story! A seven-year-old girl is murdered one night in an alley near the police station. The investigating detective is a good cop—intelligent, a family man—but the more that's uncovered, the more the evidence points to him."

"The detective killed the kid?"

"That's how it was written. The guy has acute schizophrenia, so he doesn't know he did it."

Cynthia laughed. "You have to be kidding."

"No, really; it's fascinating. We have a psychiatrist on call to make sure our kooky bits are right."

"So what happens?"

"Tell you the truth, I don't know. The writers were told to change the ending after we landed Max Cormick for the role. His agent said it would ruin his career to play the murderer of a little kid. So I think we're going to make his partner the killer now."

"His partner? That's a bit predictable."

"You think so?" Paige sounded concerned.

"Oh, for sure. What about the detective's wife?"

"The wife! Of course. Wait a second." Excitedly, Paige picked up the car phone and hammered out a number. "Michael, listen. I'm here with an old friend who's a Miami cop. She thinks Suzanne should be the murderer."

A pause. "Hold on . . . Cyn, why would his wife be the murderer?"

Cynthia shrugged. "Maybe she's in love with someone else and wants her husband trashed. So instead of doing it herself, she sets him up so he'll be jailed for life or die in the gas chamber."

"Michael, did you hear that? . . . Okay, think about it."

Paige hung up the phone and smiled. "Now I can take you to the best restaurants in town—courtesy of the studio."

"What for?"

"You're a story consultant."

•   •   •

Paige drove into the back lot of Universal Studios, stopping outside one of the large white sound stages. Inside, the cavernous space buzzed with activity. Cynthia looked around in amazement. It was as if a genuine detective office had been dropped into the middle of the building, then surrounded with lights, scaffolding, cameras, and a regiment of people.

She leaned into Paige's shoulders and whispered, "Do I get to meet Max Cormick?"

"Come." Paige led the way to a group of chairs, where the celebrated star was waiting for his next take. He was tall and confident, about forty, with slightly gray hair and hazel eyes.

"Max, good morning," Paige said. "I'd like you to meet Major Cynthia Ernst. She's from the Miami Police Department."

He looked confused. "We have a cop from Miami in this?"

"No, no." Cynthia smiled. "I'm not an actress."

"Oh, sorry. It's just that . . . well, you look more like an actress than a cop."

"From all I hear, I'd make more money if I were."

The actor nodded with some embarrassment. "Yeah. Stupid, isn't it?"

"Well, maybe not. I tried acting once in school and found it tough. I was so busy trying to understand the role that it never seemed real."

Max Cormick took her arm and led her toward a table of food. "Major, as an actor you don't *think* about acting—*ever*. If you do, it shows. An actor only thinks about being himself—the new self he's just become in a world that's now his. New life, family, job—everything!"

Cynthia nodded, apparently with polite interest. In fact, she had memorized every word.

•   •   •

August 18. Six days later.

The door chime in Paige's condominium sounded at 6:50 A.M. After a few seconds it sounded again.

Cynthia, still in bed, though awake, heard the first chime, then, after the second, Paige's muffled voice protesting, "Who the hell . . . at this hour . . ." followed by the sound of her adjoining bedroom door opening. Before she could reach the outer door, the chime sounded a third time.

"All right, all right! I'm coming!" Paige called out with irritation.

By now Cynthia could feel her pulse quickening, but she lay back calmly, letting what was about to happen take whatever form it would.

At the main doorway, Paige peered through a peephole and saw a police uniform. She released two locks and a chain on the door, then opened it.

"I'm Winslow McGowan, ma'am." The voice was quiet and cultured. "I've been working with Major Ernst, who I believe is staying with you."

"Yes, she is. Is something wrong?"

"I'm sorry to disturb you so early, but I need to see her."

"Come in, sir."

Paige called out, "Cyn, are you up? You have a visitor."

Taking her time, Cynthia pulled on a robe and went out. Smiling brightly, she greeted McGowan. "Hello, Winslow. What brings you here so early?"

Instead of answering, he asked Paige, "Is there somewhere Cynthia and I can talk quietly?"

"Sure." Paige gestured behind her. "Use the den. When you're finished, call me. I'll have coffee ready."

As she and McGowan sat down, Cynthia said, "You sound serious, Win. Is something wrong?" Behind the casual question her mind was working, replaying Max Cormick's words at Universal Studios. *You don't* think *about acting*—ever. *If you do, it shows . . .*

"Yes," McGowan said, answering her question. "I have some bad news, *very* bad news. Cynthia, you've got to prepare yourself."

"I *am* prepared. Just tell me!" Her voice was anxious. Then, as if she had a sudden thought, "Is it my parents?"

McGowan nodded slowly. "It *is* your parents . . . the worst possible . . ."

"Oh, no! Are they . . ." Cynthia stopped, as if unwilling to complete the sentence.

"Yes, my dear. I wish there were some other way to tell you this, but . . . I'm afraid they are both dead."

Cynthia put her hands to her face and shrieked. Then she cried out, "Paige! Paige!"

When Paige appeared, running, Cynthia screamed, "Paige, it's my mom and dad . . ." As her friend's arms enfolded her, she turned her face toward McGowan. "Is it . . . was it . . . an accident?"

He shook his head. "No accident." Then he said, "Cynthia, let's take this slowly. There's just so much a human being can handle. Right now I think you've had enough."

Paige nodded agreement, her arms tightly around Cynthia, "Sweetie, I beg you! Take it easy. Take your time."

It was another fifteen minutes before Cynthia—*as her new self in a new scenario*—absorbed the few details known so far about her parents' murders.

•   •   •

From that point on, she merely let things happen. Winslow McGowan and Paige were presuming Cynthia to be in a state of shock, an assumption she supported by her dazed, obedient behavior. McGowan, who had been joined by two more uniform officers who were making phone calls, told her quietly, "We're arranging to get you home. I've canceled your remaining lectures, and you're booked on a nonstop Miami flight early this afternoon. A department car will take you to the airport."

Paige chimed in, "And I'm traveling with you, Cyn. Wouldn't dream of letting you go alone. I'll go pack your bags. Is that okay?"

Cynthia nodded compliantly, murmuring, "Thank you." It would be useful to have a companion for the journey, though she wouldn't want Paige around for long in Miami, she decided.

Lying full length on a couch to which she had been steered, Cynthia closed her eyes, separating herself from the activity around her.

At last, she reflected, her parents were dead, and after long years of waiting, the objective she had planned so carefully was accomplished. So why didn't she feel the euphoria she had anticipated, but only, instead, a curious flatness? Perhaps, she thought, it was because no one other than she and Patrick Jensen would ever know the truth—the reason for the murders or her ingenious planning behind it.

Still, she did not for a moment regret her decision. Such an ending was necessary, a need that *had* to be fulfilled to redress the wrong done to her. It was a suitable retribution for the loathsome, despicable way in which Gustav and Eleanor Ernst had treated her as a child, making Cynthia in so many ways the person she had become. A person whom she acknowledged that at times she didn't like.

Ah! There was a vital question: Would she have been different, *could* she have been, if it were not for the rage and hatred instilled in her by her father's perverted abuse and her mother's hypocritical inaction . . . those all-consuming hatreds that had never gone away? *Of course! . . . Yes! . . .* She *would* have been a different person . . . less strong, perhaps . . . kinder, maybe. Who knew? But in any case, the question was irrelevant—half a lifetime too late! The mold that shaped Cynthia was broken long ago. She was what she was now, and would not—*could* not—change . . .

Her eyes were still closed when Paige's soft voice filtered through her ruminations. "Cyn, everything's taken care of. We leave for the airport in a few hours. Maybe for a while you should go back to bed and sleep."

Gratefully she did. Later, the eastward journey—thanks to Paige—passed uneventfully.

•   •   •

Before arriving in Miami, Cynthia discreetly rubbed a few grains of salt into her eyes. It was a subterfuge she had learned years ago during the same school dramatics she had spoken of to Max Cormick, and the effect was to produce tears and red-rimmed eyes. During the days that followed Cynthia shed no genuine tears, but more salt and residual red eyes helped.

Apart from that pretense of grief, from her moment of arrival onward, Cynthia let it be known that her strength and composure had returned, and set out to learn whatever was known about her parents' murders. Her own police status, providing immediate access to all units of the Police Department, made that simple.

On her second day back, Cynthia visited her parents' mansion in Bay Point, now encircled by yellow police tape. Inside a main-floor drawing room she talked with Sergeant Brewmaster, in charge of the Homicide investigation.

His first words on seeing her were, "Major, I want to say how terrible we all feel . . ." but she stopped him with a gesture.

"Hank, I appreciate that, and I'm grateful. But if I hear too much of it, especially from an old friend like you, I might break down. Please understand."

Brewmaster said, "Yes, I do, ma'am. And I promise we'll do every last thing we can to nail the bastard who . . ." His own voice, choking too, trailed off.

"I want to hear everything you know," Cynthia told him. "From what I've heard already, I gather you see my parents' deaths as some kind of serial killings."

Brewmaster nodded. "It does look that way, a definite pattern, though there are slight differences." *That jackass Patrick,* she thought. "First, though, have you heard about the Homicide conference two days ago—just *before* your parents' deaths—when Malcolm Ainslie linked four earlier double murders with the Bible and the book of Revelation?"

She shook her head, a slight anxiety stirring.

"When we started looking at those four cases," Brewmaster continued, "laying the details out, there were what you'd call symbols left at each scene. It was Malcolm—because he knows about that stuff from being a priest—who recognized what they meant."

Cynthia looked confused. "You keep saying four double murders. I thought there were only two previous ones that seemed to match."

"Well, there was another one—the Urbinas in Pine Terrace—also like those others, and only three days before your parents' deaths. And even before that, there turned out to be one more we hadn't heard about." Brewmaster described Ruby Bowe's revelation, at the Homicide conference, of the overlooked BOLO from Clearwater and the similar slayings there of Hal and Mabel Larsen. "Those Clearwater killings happened about midway between the Frost and Hennenfeld cases."

Alarm bells rang in Cynthia's head. Clearly, in the short time she had been away a great deal had changed—changes unforeseen. Her mind was in turmoil. She had to update quickly.

"You said there were differences about my parents' murders. What did you mean?"

"First thing, whoever the perp was, he left a dead rabbit behind. Malcolm thinks it doesn't fit, though I'm not sure I agree."

Cynthia waited.

Brewmaster continued, "At those other crime scenes, everything fitted in with Revelation and the theory that the killer is some kind of religious freak. But according to Malcolm, the rabbit isn't specific, the way the other symbols were. But as I said, I'm not so sure."

Leaving a rabbit, Cynthia thought bleakly, had been her own idea. At the time no one, even in Homicide, had the slightest notion what any of those earlier symbols meant, and it was still that way when she left for Los Angeles.

"Something else really different is the time frame," Brewmaster went on. "Between each of the other serial killings there was a gap of about two months—never less than two. But between the Urbinas and the Ernsts—sorry, your folks—just three days." He shrugged. "Of course, it may mean nothing. Serial killers don't operate on logic."

No, Cynthia thought, but even serial killers had to plan, and as little as three days from one double killing to the next was not convincing . . . Goddam! Of all the wrong timing and bad luck! Her careful calculations had been totally thrown off by the extra Clearwater case. She remembered Patrick's words at Homestead: *Cyn, I think we're trying to be too clever.*

"Those fourth killings," she asked Brewmaster. "What did you say the names were?"

"Urbinas."

"Did the case get much attention?"

"The usual. Front pages of the newspapers, plenty on TV." It was Brewmaster's turn to be curious. "What makes you ask?"

"Oh, I didn't hear anything in L.A. Guess I was too busy." It was a weak response, Cynthia knew, and realized she must be wary when dealing with super-sharp Homicide detectives. Brewmaster's answer, though, suggested Patrick must have known about the Urbina murders; therefore, somehow, he ought to have postponed the Ernst killings. But most likely Patrick had no way to get in touch with the Colombian, and the die was cast . . .

Brewmaster broke in on her thoughts. "There *were* other things right in line with the serial killings, ma'am." His tone was respectful, as if half apologizing for his query moments ago. "All of your father's cash was taken, but your mother's jewelry was untouched; I checked that carefully. And something else, though I don't like mentioning this . . ."

"Go on," Cynthia said. "I think I know what's coming."

"Well, the wounds inflicted were pretty much like the ones in the earlier cases . . . are you sure you want to hear this?"

"I have to know sometime. It might as well be now."

"The wounds were real bad; the MO says a bowie knife was used again. And the victims . . ." Again Brewmaster hesitated. "They were bound and gagged and facing each other."

Cynthia turned away and applied a handkerchief to her eyes. On it were still a few grains of salt from a previous application; she used them before turning back, coughing slightly.

"One more thing that was like those other cases," Brewmaster added, "is that a radio was left on—loud."

Cynthia nodded. "I remember that. At those two first scenes, wasn't it rock?"

"Yes." Brewmaster consulted a notebook. "This time it was WTMI— classical and show-biz music. The butler said it was your mother's favorite station."

"Yes, it was." Silently, Cynthia cursed. Despite her precise instructions to Patrick, his Colombian killer had turned the radio on, but failed to change the station to rock music. Maybe he didn't get the full instructions; either way, it was too late. At this moment, Brewmaster didn't seem to think the difference was important, though others in Homicide might when making a thorough study; Cynthia knew how the system worked.

Goddam! Suddenly, unexpectedly, she felt a shiver of fear run through her.

CYNTHIA DID NOT SLEEP WELL during her third night back in Miami, still nervous after learning of developments—unexpected yet significant—during her brief absence. Now, she wondered, what else could go wrong?

Also on her mind was the fact that she needed to meet with Malcolm Ainslie—especially since Ainslie was head of a special task force set up to deal with the current series of serial murders, in which her parents' deaths were included. Thus, while Hank Brewmaster remained in immediate charge of the Ernst investigation, the overall responsibility was Ainslie's.

Though uneasy about a meeting with Ainslie at this point, she knew it had to happen. Otherwise it might appear as if she was avoiding him, leaving her motives open to question, particularly by Ainslie himself.

What it came down to, Cynthia realized in a moment of private honesty, was that Ainslie was the Homicide investigator she feared the most. Despite her bitter anger when he broke off their affair, and her determination to keep the promise she had made—*You'll regret this, Malcolm, for the rest of your miserable life*—she had never for one moment changed her view that, of all the detectives she had known, Ainslie was the best.

She was never sure exactly why. Somehow, though, Malcolm had an ability to look beyond the immediate aspects of any investigation and put his own mind inside the minds of both the victims and suspects. The result was—and Cynthia had seen it happen—he often reached the right conclusions about Homicide cases, either alone or ahead of everyone else.

The other detectives in Homicide, particularly the younger ones, had sometimes looked on Malcolm as an oracle and sought his advice, not only about crimes but about their own personal lives. Detective Bernard Quinn, now retired, had made a collection of what he called "Ainslie Aphorisms" and tacked them up on a notice board. Cynthia remembered a few. One or two seemed appropriate now:

We catch people because no one is ever as clever as he or she thinks.

Mostly, small mistakes don't matter. But with murder, it only takes a tiny mistake to leave a hole for someone to peer through and learn the truth.

Educated people think they have an edge in cleverness, but sometimes that extra education makes them overreach and get caught.

All of us do foolish things—sometimes the most obvious—and we wonder later how we could have been so stupid.

The most skillful liars sometimes say too much.

Criminals seldom remember Murphy's Law: If something can go wrong, it will. Which is a big help to detectives.

Ainslie's background, Cynthia supposed—the priesthood and his erudition—contributed to all that, and clearly, from what Hank Brewmaster had described, that same facility solved the linkage between those bizarre objects left at the serial crime scenes.

Cynthia pushed the memories away. Until the present she had never thought of Malcolm's intellect as affecting her personally. Now she did.

She decided not to delay a meeting, but to stage it immediately, on her own terms. Early in the morning after her restless night, Cynthia arrived at Homicide, where she commandeered Lieutenant Newbold's office and left word that Sergeant Ainslie should report to her as soon as possible. He arrived soon after, having stopped at the Ernst house on his way.

Having made clear the difference in authority between them—a major was three ranks higher than a sergeant—and that no shred of a personal relationship remained, Cynthia had posed sharp questions about her parents' murders.

Even while probing and listening to answers, she was aware of Malcolm's appraisal and welcomed it. From the way he looked at her, she knew he had noticed her especially red-rimmed eyes. His facial expression reflected sympathy. Good! So her grief at her parents' deaths was evident, and Malcolm did not doubt it; therefore objective number one had been achieved.

A second objective was to make her official authority so strong and demanding, with insistence on a speedy solution to her parents' killings, that it would simply not occur to Ainslie that she could be involved in any culpable way. As the interview progressed, Cynthia knew she had succeeded.

Toward the end she was conscious of a wariness on Malcolm's part when she questioned him about the symbols he had linked to Revelation. She also suspected that he did not intend to keep her as fully informed about all special task force developments as she demanded. But she decided not to press too far, having handled what could have been an uneasy confrontation with so much advantage to herself.

Finally, as the door closed behind Ainslie, Cynthia reflected that perhaps she had overestimated his talents after all.

• • •

The elaborately formal funeral for Gustav and Eleanor Ernst, with all the trappings of officialdom, was preceded by a wake the day before, lasting eight hours and attended by an estimated nine hundred people. The entire two-day observance was something Cynthia knew she had to go through, though she longed for it all to be over. Her role was to behave as a bereaved daughter, yet maintain a composure and dignity befitting her senior police rank. From overheard remarks, and condolences addressed to her, she knew at the end she had succeeded rather well.

One conversation occurring during the wake would, she hoped, have an ongoing effect. It was with two people whom she knew well: Miami's Mayor Lance Karlsson and City Commissioner Orestes Quintero, one of the two remaining commissioners. She had met both frequently before. The mayor, a retired industrialist, normally jovial, spoke sadly of Cynthia's father, adding, "We shall miss Gustav greatly." Quintero, younger and heir to a liquor fortune, nodded agreement. "It will be difficult to replace him. He understood the city's workings so well."

"I know," Cynthia replied. "I only wish there were some way I could pick up where he left off."

She saw the two men glance at each other. A thought clearly struck both; the mayor gave the slightest of nods.

"I should talk to some other people; please excuse me," Cynthia said. As she moved away, she knew she had effectively planted a seed.

At both the wake and the funeral she saw Ainslie several times. He was second-in-command of the police honor guard and looked smart in dress uniform, something she had not seen him in before. Gold aiguillettes and white gloves heightened the ceremonial impact. She learned from another honor guard officer that at every free moment, in a rear room, Ainslie was on the radio, communicating with his special task force surveillance teams, now maintaining a twenty-four-hour watch on six possible suspects in the serial killings.

After their earlier meeting, Cynthia was unsure how to treat Ainslie, and simply ignored him.

• • •

A day after the funeral, Cynthia was at her desk in Community Relations when she received a phone call that the caller described as confidential. She listened for a few moments, then answered, "Thank you. My answer is yes."

Twenty-four hours later the Miami City Commission, headed by Mayor Karlsson, announced that, as permitted by city charter, Cynthia Ernst had been named to complete the remaining two years in her father's elected term as a commissioner.

The next day Cynthia announced her resignation from the Miami police force.

●   ●   ●

As more days passed, and Cynthia assumed her new responsibilities, she felt increasingly secure. Then, two and a half months later, one of the suspects who had been under special task force surveillance, Elroy Doil, was arrested and charged with murder. The arrest was at the murder scene of Kingsley and Nellie Tempone, with "Animal" Doil's guilt conclusive, and from additional evidence it was believed by police, the media, and the public that he was guilty of all the preceding serial killings.

Only one factor clouded the successful end to the task force's operation. That was a decision by State Attorney Adele Montesino that Doil would be tried for only one double murder—the Tempones'—where, in Montesino's words, "we'll have a cast-iron prosecution" and an "airtight certain case." In the remaining cases, she pointed out, the evidence, while strong, was less conclusive.

The decision had provoked protests from the families of other serial killing victims, in which Commissioner Cynthia Ernst joined, wanting Doil to be convicted of her parents' murders, too. But in the end it made no difference. Doil denied doing any of the murders, including the Tempones', despite his presence at the murder scene. A jury found him guilty and he was sentenced to die in the electric chair—a process speeded up by Doil's own decision not to exercise his rights of appeal.

●   ●   ●

During the seven months between Animal Doil's sentencing and his scheduled execution, something happened to provide an unnerving shock to Cynthia Ernst.

Amid the increasing activity of her new life as a city commissioner, a thought occurred to her one day—out of nowhere, it seemed—that a task she had intended to complete a long time ago had never been done. Incredibly, she had forgotten the box of evidence, put together the same night that

Patrick admitted having shot and killed Naomi and Kilburn Holmes. What she needed to do, Cynthia now realized—in fact, ought to have done long ago—was dispose of that box and its contents, completely and forever.

She knew exactly where the box was stored. After carefully taping and sealing it at her own apartment, she had taken it to her parents' house and her private room.

Although, since her parents' deaths, the Ernst house had been mostly unoccupied, Cynthia had left it pretty much as it was, waiting until Gustav's and Eleanor's wills were finally probated before deciding whether to sell it or even, perhaps, move into Bay Point herself. In the end she alone would decide because she was the major beneficiary under both her parents' wills. Occasionally, Cynthia used the house for entertaining and continued to employ the butler, Theo Palacio, and his wife, Maria, as caretakers.

Cynthia chose the following Wednesday to take the action so long overdue. She told her secretary, Ofelia, to reschedule her appointments for that day and not to make any others. At first she considered moving the box to a public incinerator, then learned that many had closed for environmental reasons, and at the few remaining it was no longer possible for an individual to throw an object in a furnace personally. Unwilling to trust anyone else, she returned to her original idea of deep sixing the box.

She knew a charter boat owner who had done jobs for her father in the past—a closemouthed, surly ex–U.S. Marine with the reputation of operating on the borders of legitimacy, but who was reliable. Cynthia phoned him, learned he was available on the chosen date, then instructed, "I shall want your boat all day and will be coming with a friend, but there's to be no crew except you." After grumbling about having to do everything himself, the boat owner agreed.

The statement about a friend was a lie. Cynthia had no intention of bringing anyone, and she would only retain the boat for as long as it took to reach deep water, throw the box overboard—by then inside a metal trunk—and return to shore. She would pay for a full-day cruise, however, which would keep the owner quiet. She also knew of an out-of-the-way store where she could buy a suitable trunk, paying with cash the day before.

Having made her decisions, Cynthia drove to Bay Point and went to her room. Remembering exactly where she had left the box, she moved other items to get to it. To her surprise, it wasn't there. Obviously her memory was faulty, she decided. She continued to move everything, finally emptying the entire cupboard, but—no question about it—the sealed box was gone. Her concern, which she had deliberately suppressed, suddenly escalated.

Don't panic! It's somewhere in the house . . . has to be . . . it's natural not to find it immediately after all this time . . . so stop, think, consider where else to look . . . But after searching through other rooms and cupboards, including what had been her parents' rooms, she was no further ahead.

Eventually she used an intercom and summoned Theo Palacio to the top floor. He appeared quickly.

When she described the missing box, Palacio responded at once. "I remember seeing it, Miss Ernst. The police took it, along with a lot of other things. It was the day after . . ." He stopped and shook his head sadly. "I think it was the second day the police were here."

She said, "You didn't tell me!"

The butler spread his hands helplessly. "So much was happening. And it being the police, I thought you'd know."

•   •   •

The facts emerged piecemeal.

As Theo Palacio explained, "The police had a search warrant. One of the detectives showed it to me, said they wanted to go through the house, look at everything."

Cynthia nodded. It was normal procedure, but something else she had not foreseen despite her careful planning.

"Well," Palacio continued, "among what they found were boxes and boxes of papers—a lot of it your mother's—and from what I understood, the detectives couldn't look at it all here, so they took the whole lot away to go through somewhere else. They went around the house, piling up the boxes and sealing them, and one of the boxes was yours. It was already sealed; I think that's why they took it."

"Didn't you tell anyone the box belonged to me?"

"To tell the truth, Miss Ernst, I didn't think of it. As I said, a lot was going on; Maria and I were so upset. If I did wrong, I'm—"

Cynthia cut him off. "Leave it!" Her mind was calculating swiftly.

A year and two months had passed since her parents' deaths; therefore the crucial box had been removed for that long. So whatever had happened to it, one thing was certain: it had not been opened, or she would have heard. Cynthia was also pretty sure that she knew where the box was.

•   •   •

Back in her City Commission office, after canceling arrangements for the boat, she willed herself to be objective. There were occasions when ultra-calm was needed, and this was one. For a moment at the Bay Point house she had almost given way to despair—provoked by horror at the incredibly foolish thing she had done, or rather had failed to do. One of Ainslie's Aphorisms came back to her: *All of us do foolish things—sometimes the most obvious— and we wonder later how we could have been so stupid.*

First things first.

Her discovery had raised two vital questions, the first already answered: the box had *not* been opened. The second: Was it likely to remain unopened? Of course, she could sit back and *hope* the answer would be yes. But sitting back was not Cynthia's style.

She consulted a phone list and dialed the number of the Miami Police Property Department. An operator answered.

"This is Commissioner Ernst. Captain Iacone, please."

"Yes, ma'am."

A moment later, "Good afternoon, Commissioner. It's Wade Iacone; what can I do for you?"

"I'd like to come to see you, Wade." Each knew the other well from Cynthia's time in Homicide. "When would be convenient?"

"For you, any time."

She arranged to be at Property in an hour.

•   •   •

The Property Department, within the main Police building, was, as always, bustling, noisy, with active staff—sworn and civilian—all cataloging, arranging, and safeguarding a jam-packed depository of countless miscellaneous items, ranging from huge to minuscule and, in value, from precious to worthless. The only common denominator was the fact that everything was connected with a crime and might be required as evidence. Within the department a series of large storerooms seemingly were filled to capacity, yet a relentless stream of new objects was somehow squeezed in each day.

Captain Iacone met Cynthia and escorted her to his tiny office. Space in Property was at a premium, even for its commander.

When they were seated, Cynthia began, "When my parents were killed . . ." then paused as Iacone, a longtime veteran, shook his head sadly.

"I could hardly believe it at the time. I was so sorry."

"It's still hard to come to terms with." Cynthia sighed. "But with the case closed now, and Doil being executed soon . . . Well, there are some things I have to do, and one of them is recover a lot of my parents' papers that were taken from our house over a year ago, and some may be stored here."

"There *was* something. I don't remember exactly, but I'll check." Iacone swung around, facing a computer terminal on his desk, and typed a name and instruction. Instantly a column of figures appeared on the monitor.

The Property chief nodded. "Yes, we do have some things from your parents—quite a lot. It's coming back to me now."

"I know how much flows through here. I'm surprised you remember at all."

"Well, it was an important case; we were all concerned about it. It was all boxes, and the detectives said they'd take them out when they could and search through them." Iacone glanced back at the computer. "I guess they never did."

Curiosity made Cynthia ask, "Any idea why?"

"The way I heard, there were a lot of pressures at the time. A twenty-four-hour surveillance was on for the serial killer; there was a shortage of working bodies, so no one had time to search through boxes. Then the serial guy was caught."

"Yes."

"Which meant the case was wound up, and no one bothered with the boxes."

Cynthia smiled warmly. "Does it mean I can have them back? There were some personal papers of my parents'."

"I should think so. In fact I'd like to clear the space." Iacone glanced at the numbers on the computer, then rose. "Let's go take a look."

●   ●   ●

"If anyone gets lost in here," Iacone said, grinning, "we send out search parties."

They were in one of the warehouse areas, where boxes and packages were piled from the floor to a ceiling high above. Aisles between piles were narrow and meandered like a maze. But everything in sight was numbered. "Whatever we're looking for," Iacone explained, "we can find it in minutes." He stopped and pointed. "Here are the boxes from your parents."

There were two piles, Cynthia saw, a dozen or more stout containers, all sealed with tape bearing the printed words CRIME SCENE EVIDENCE. Then, near the top of the second pile, she caught a glimpse of a box with some blue sealing tape protruding from beneath the official layer. *Found it!* she thought, recognizing the tape.

Now, how to get that box out.

"So, can I take all this away?" She motioned to the pile. "I'll sign whatever's needed."

"Sorry!" Iacone shook his head. "I'm afraid it isn't that simple, though not so difficult, either. What I need, to let you have everything, is a signed release from whoever brought the evidence in."

"Who was that?"

"On the computer it showed Sergeant Brewmaster. But Malcolm Ainslie could sign; he was in charge of the task force. Or Lieutenant Newbold. You know all three, so any one of them."

Cynthia considered carefully; she had hoped her own authority as a commissioner would suffice. As for asking any of the trio named, she would have to think about it.

On the way out, as if chatting casually, she asked, "Does most of this stuff here stay around a long time?"

"Too damn long," Iacone complained. "That's my biggest problem."

"What's the oldest evidence stored?"

"I honestly don't know. But plenty has been around for twenty years, some of it for more."

Even as Iacone was speaking, Cynthia made her decision about asking for a signed release. She wouldn't. Brewmaster would have been the easiest to approach, but still might ask questions. Newbold would almost certainly check with the other two. As for Ainslie . . . he was the creative thinker; he could see through veneers.

On the other hand, if she did nothing the boxes might stay here undisturbed for twenty years or more. So, for the time being, she would leave everything, including the critical evidence box, well enough alone and take her chances.

For the longer future—though not all that distant when she thought about it—Cynthia had something else in mind.

She planned to become Miami's next mayor.

The incumbent mayor, Karlsson, had let it be known that when his present term expired in two more years he would not seek reelection. When she heard this, Cynthia made her decision to succeed him. One, possibly two, of the other commissioners might be mayoral candidates, but she believed she could take on anyone and win. The time was right for women to be elected to almost anything; nowadays even men were dissatisfied with other men in public office. Looking at males in the highest places, including the United States Oval Office, the question was increasingly being asked: *Is that really the best the system can produce?*

As mayor, Cynthia would have exceptional influence in the Police Department. Among other major matters, the mayor could sway decisions about who would be the next chief of police, and who else would move up in the topmost ranks. The role created automatic deference, and with that kind of authority she foresaw a time when she could get those packages—including *the* one—out of Property without the slightest difficulty.

So let it ride for now.

"Thanks for everything, Wade," she told Iacone as he escorted her out.

• • •

During the three and a half months between that time and the scheduled execution of Elroy Doil, Cynthia felt herself grow increasingly more anxious. The fact was, she realized as the weeks and days moved by with excruciating slowness, that only with Doil's death in the electric chair would there be assurance that the twelve serial killings attributed to him would become permanently closed cases. It was true that Doil had been tried and convicted only for the Tempones' murder, but it seemed certain that no one who mattered doubted he was guilty also of all the others, including the slayings of Gustav and Eleanor Ernst.

So, who *did* know that Doil did not commit one pair of murders?

Cynthia asked herself that question while alone in her apartment late one night. The answer: she herself, Patrick Jensen, and the Colombian. That was all; just three.

Well . . . strictly speaking, four, if you included Doil himself, she reasoned. Though it made no difference, really, because whatever he said, no one would believe him. At Doil's trial he'd denied absolutely everything—small things that didn't matter, and even his well-established presence at the Tempones' house, where he was actually caught and apprehended.

And something else: As far as Doil's execution was concerned, she was not allowing an innocent man to go to his death by keeping quiet and doing nothing. Doil was as guilty as hell of all those other murders and deserved the electric chair. It was simply that since he was chair-destined anyway, he might just as well do Cynthia and Patrick a favor by carrying their load, too. Too bad they couldn't say thank you!

"*But there's many a slip . . .*" Impatiently, Cynthia kept reminding herself of the cliché, wanting to get the execution over and move forward to a new time.

For some while now Cynthia had been meeting Patrick Jensen at intervals again, socially and for sex, and in these final weeks she had been seeing him even more frequently. Instinct told her that it wasn't entirely wise, but there were times when she felt the need of company, and there was no one else with whom she could relax so completely. They were two of a kind, she knew, both being aware that the survival of each depended on the other.

It was that kind of thinking that made Cynthia decide she wanted Patrick with her at Florida State Prison for the execution, which she had arranged to attend with approval from the prison governor. There were two reasons for her presence: she was the closest relative of two of Doil's presumed victims, and her status as a Miami city commissioner gave her preference. When she broached the idea to Patrick, he immediately agreed. "We have a vested interest in seeing the guy snuffed out. Besides, I can use the scene in a book."

So she had called the governor a second time, and despite the difficulty of witnessing an execution—there was a three-year waiting list—because of Cynthia's influence, Jensen was included.

There were moments when Cynthia worried about Patrick's deepening depression. Over the years she had known him, he had always been a thinker, which went with being a writer, she supposed, but nowadays he brooded more than ever. Once when they were talking he quoted Robert Frost gloomily:

> *Two roads diverged in a wood, and I—*
> *I took the one less traveled by,*
> *And that has made all the difference.*

"Frost was right about a difference," Patrick pronounced. "Except for him it meant the right road. Me, I took the wrong one, and from that road you don't ever get back."

Cynthia asked, "You're not getting religion, are you?"

For a change, Patrick laughed. "Not likely! Anyway, that's a last resort after getting caught."

"Don't talk about getting caught!" she snapped. "You won't be, especially after . . ." Though she stopped, they both knew she was referring to Doil's execution, now only days away.

●   ●   ●

It was a paradox, Cynthia thought, to feel relief on entering the grimness of a prison, but she did, knowing that the moment she had waited for was approaching fast, and at 6:12 A.M.—she checked her watch—less than an hour away. Earlier the twenty execution witnesses, mostly well-dressed strangers, had assembled at the nearby town of Starke and been driven by bus to the State Prison. On the way, there had been little conversation, and now the group was filing through heavy steel gates and past a fortress-like control room. Patrick was beside her when Cynthia saw two figures off to one side; they had halted to allow the line of witnesses to pass.

One of the figures was a prison officer, the other . . . *Malcolm!*

The shock was like a sudden, ice-cold shower.

Questions raced through Cynthia's mind. *What is he doing here?* There could be only one answer: He had come to see Doil before he died! *Why?*

She caught Patrick's eye; he had seen Ainslie, too, and she guessed he had reached the same conclusion. But there was no time to talk; escorts were hurrying the witness group on.

Cynthia was sure that Malcolm had seen her as well, but their eyes had not met. She continued onward with the others, her thoughts tumultuous. *Assuming there was a deathwatch meeting between Malcolm Ainslie and Doil, what would be its substance? Could Ainslie still have doubts about Doil committing the Ernst murders? Was that why he was here—to find out in these final minutes of Doil's life whatever else he could? He definitely had that kind of mind and persistence. Or were her racing thoughts just hysteria, and Ainslie's purpose—whatever it was—quite different? He might be in the prison for something unrelated to Doil. But she didn't believe it.*

The witnesses had entered their glass-fronted booth, which faced the execution chamber, and a prison guard who was checking a list directed them to metal chairs. Cynthia and Patrick's seats were central in the front row. As everyone settled down, one seat was empty on Cynthia's right.

An additional shock: Just as activity in the execution chamber was beginning, the same guard brought Malcolm Ainslie to the seat beside her. As he looked sideways, she sensed he was inclined to speak, but she averted her gaze and continued looking forward. Patrick, though, glanced across at Ainslie and gave a small smile. Cynthia didn't think it was returned.

As the execution proceeded, only part of her mind was on it, the other part still dazed and racing with nervous thoughts. But as Doil's body convulsed while successive cycles of two thousand volts surged through him, she felt slightly sick. Patrick seemed fascinated by it all. Then, almost before she realized, everything was over. Doil's corpse was in a body bag, and all the witnesses were standing, prepared to leave. At that point Malcolm turned toward her and said quietly, "Commissioner, I feel I should tell you that shortly before his execution, I talked to Doil about your parents. He claimed—"

The shock at having the news she had dreaded so suddenly confirmed was too much. Barely aware of her words, Cynthia shot back, "Please, there is nothing I want to hear." Then, remembering Doil was supposedly guilty of her parents' deaths, "I came to watch him suffer. I hope he did."

"He did." Ainslie's voice was still quiet.

She groped for some authority. "Then I'm satisfied, Sergeant."

"I hear you, Commissioner." His tone was noncommittal.

They moved outside the witness enclosure, and it was then that Patrick made a clumsy effort to introduce himself, which Ainslie acknowledged coolly, clearly knowing who Patrick was and implying that he did not care to know him better.

The exchange ended when Ainslie's prison officer escort appeared and showed him out.

On the bus conveying the witnesses back to Starke, Cynthia sat beside Patrick but did not speak. She found herself wishing she had not interrupted when Malcolm began, *I spoke to Doil about your parents. He claimed . . .*

What was it Doil had claimed? Most probably his innocence. And if so, did Ainslie believe him? Would he probe still more?

A new and sudden thought occurred to her. When, long ago, she used her superior rank to abort Malcolm Ainslie's promotion to lieutenant, had she made the gravest error of her life? The irony was glaring: If she had not done so, Ainslie would probably not be a Homicide detective now.

The procedure following promotion from sergeant to lieutenant was automatic—the person promoted was moved to some other department in the force. If it had occurred that way, Ainslie would have been busy elsewhere and not involved with the serial murders. Therefore others in Homicide—lacking his specialized knowledge—were unlikely to have perceived the link between the killings and the Book of Revelation, and thus so many other things would not have happened as they had. Even more specifically, Ainslie would not be prolonging the investigation of the Ernst murders as he might be doing now.

Involuntarily, Cynthia shuddered. Was it possible that Malcolm Ainslie who had remained in Homicide because of what now seemed her long-ago misjudgment—would, at some unknown time ahead, become her nemesis?

Whether that was possible, or even likely, she wasn't sure. But because it just might happen, and for what he had done to her and hadn't . . . and for everything he was and represented . . . and for so much else—logical or not—she knew now that she *hated, hated, hated* him!

Part Five

1

SINCE MALCOLM AINSLIE'S DECISION to summon an ID crew to the small temporary room in Police Headquarters, momentous discoveries had transpired. It was, as a state attorney would describe it later, "like honest daylight lighting up black evil."

The objects in the box unsealed by Ruby Bowe appeared to show convincingly that six and a half years earlier Patrick Jensen had killed his ex-wife, Naomi, and her friend Kilburn Holmes. It was a crime for which Jensen had been a strong suspect, though detectives were unable to prove his guilt.

It was also apparent from the box that Cynthia Ernst, who at that time was a Homicide detective, had conspired to conceal the evidence of Jensen's crime. Ainslie, though stunned and depressed by what he saw, brushed aside his personal feelings and waited impatiently for ID assistance to arrive.

The ID chief, Julio Verona, who responded personally to Ainslie's call, made a fast inspection of the box and contents, then declared, "We won't touch any of this here. Everything must go to our labs."

Lieutenant Newbold, who had also been called and briefed by Ainslie, told Verona, "Okay, but do everything as fast as you can, and tell your people this is ultra-secret; there must be no leaks."

"No leaks. I guarantee it."

Two days later, at 9:00 A.M. on a Thursday, Verona returned to the same small room with the box of evidence and his report. Ainslie was waiting for him along with Newbold, Bowe, and Assistant State Attorney Curzon Knowles, chief of the state attorney's Homicide division.

Newbold had offered to move the proceedings to Knowles's office in another building, several miles away—state attorneys were notorious for insisting that the police come to them, rather than the other way around—but Knowles, a former New York cop himself, always liked coming to what he called "the heat." Thus the five were standing in the small, crowded space.

"I'll report on the plastic bags first," Verona told the others. "Four of them bear fingerprints matching Cynthia Ernst's." As they all knew, police officers had their prints recorded, and they were not removed from the files when someone left the force.

The ID chief continued, "Then there's the handwriting on the labels. We have a couple of handwritten memos in our files from when Commissioner Ernst was a major, and our handwriting expert says it's a perfect match." He shook his head. "To be so careless . . . she must have been crazy."

"She never intended any of this to be found," Knowles said.

"Keep going," Newbold told Verona. "There was a gun."

"Yes, a Smith & Wesson .38."

One by one, the ID supervisor listed the checked items and results:

The revolver bore the fingerprints of Patrick Jensen. Several years previously his house had been broken into, and he had let himself be fingerprinted to compare his prints with others left by the thief. Routinely, Jensen had received his fingerprint card back, but what he and other non-suspects were not told was that copies often were retained on file.

The gun, sent to the firearms lab, was loaded and fired into a tank of water. Immediately after, the bullet was placed in a double microscope along with one of the two original bullets removed from the dead victims. The distinctive markings on both bullets, put there by the rifling of the gun barrel, were identical. The same was true of the second crime-scene bullet. "There's no doubt whatever," Verona declared, pointing to the box. "This is the gun that was used to kill both those people."

Bloodstains on a T-shirt and sneakers found in the box showed the presence of both Naomi Jensen's and Kilburn Holmes's DNA.

"Then here's the clincher," Verona announced, producing an audiotape cassette. "This is a copy; the original is resealed and back in the box. Apparently it's a statement by Jensen of how he did the killing. But there are gaps. It looks as if someone else's voice was originally on the tape, but has been wiped out."

He produced a portable player-recorder, inserted the tape, and pressed PLAY. As the tape ran, there were several seconds of silence, then sounds like objects being moved, followed by a faltering male voice, at moments choking with emotion, though the words were clear.

"I didn't plan it, didn't intend . . . but always hated the thought of Naomi with someone else . . . When I saw those two together, her and that creep, I was blinded, angry . . . I'd been carrying a gun. I pulled it out, without even thinking, fired . . . Suddenly it was over . . . Then I saw what I'd done. Oh God, I'd killed them both!"

A silence followed. "Here's where someone wiped the tape," Verona said. Then, again, the same voice from the player.

" . . . Kilburn Holmes . . . He'd been seeing Naomi, was with her all the time . . . People told me."

Verona stopped the tape. "I'll leave you to listen to the rest. It's bits and pieces, obviously answers to questions that were erased, and all the same voice. Of course, I can't say for sure it's Jensen speaking; I've never met him. But we can run a voice test later."

"Make your test," Ainslie said. "But I can tell you right now, that was Jensen." He was remembering their encounter at Elroy Doil's execution.

*   *   *

When Julio Verona had left, there was a silence, which Leo Newbold broke. "So, anyone have any doubts?"

One by one the others shook their heads, their expressions somber.

The lieutenant's voice was distressed. "*Why?* In God's name, *why* would Cynthia do it?"

Ainslie, his expression anguished, raised his hands helplessly.

"I could make some guesses," Curzon Knowles said. "But we'll know better when we've talked with Jensen. You'd better bring him in."

"How do you want us to handle that, counselor?" Ainslie asked.

Knowles considered, then said, "Arrest him." He gestured to the box that Verona had left. "All the evidence we need to convict is here. I'll prepare an affidavit; one of you can take it quietly to a judge."

"It was Charlie Thurston's case," Newbold pointed out. "He should make the arrest."

"All right," Knowles agreed. "But let's have as few people involved as possible, and warn Thurston not to talk to *anyone*. For now, we must continue keeping a lid on this, screwed down tight."

Newbold asked, "So what do we do about Cynthia?"

"Nothing yet; that's why we need a tight lid. First I have to talk to Montesino. Before we arrest a city commissioner, she'll probably want to go before a grand jury, so Ernst mustn't even hear a whisper."

"We'll do our best," Newbold acknowledged. "But this stuff is red hot. If we don't move fast, word will fly."

*   *   *

By early afternoon, Detective Charlie Thurston had been called in and given the arrest warrant for Patrick Jensen. Ruby Bowe would accompany him as backup. Newbold told the balding veteran, Thurston, "We don't want anyone else knowing about this. No one!"

"Fine by me," Thurston acknowledged, then added, "For a long time I've wanted to collar that prick Jensen."

From Police Headquarters it was only a short distance to Jensen's apart-

ment. Ruby, at the wheel of an unmarked car, said to Thurston on the way,
"You got a problem with Jensen, Charlie? You sounded pretty intense back
there."

Thurston grimaced. "I guess bad memories got to me. When the case was
running, I saw a lot of him, and from the beginning we were positive Jensen
killed those two people. But he was arrogant as hell, all the time acting as if
he knew we'd never nail him. One day I went to ask a few more questions and
he laughed, told me to beat it."

"Do you think he'll be violent?"

"Unfortunately, no." Thurston chuckled. "So we'll have to take him in
unmarked. Looks like we're here."

As Ruby stopped the car a few yards from a six-story brick building on
Brickell Avenue, Thurston surveyed it. "Guy's come down in the world a bit;
had a fancy house when I last knew him." He checked the warrant. "Says
here apartment 308. Let's do it."

Moments later, at a push-button panel by the main glass doorway, the
third-floor number was confirmed, though neither detective had any intention of alerting Jensen from below. "Someone'll come soon," Thurston said.

Almost at once a slight, elderly woman wearing a tam, tweeds, and high
boots appeared in the hallway inside with a small dog on a leash. As she
released the door, Thurston held it open and showed his identification badge.
"We're police officers, ma'am, on official business."

As Ruby produced her badge, the woman peered at both. "Oh dear, and
just as I'm leaving! Is this going to be exciting, Officers?"

Thurston responded, " 'Fraid not. We're just delivering a parking ticket."

The woman shook her head, smiling. "I read your badges. Detectives don't
do that." She tugged at the dog's leash. "Come, Felix; it's plain we're not
wanted here."

•   •   •

Thurston rapped twice on the door of apartment 308. They heard movement
inside, then a voice. "Who is it?"

"Police officers. Open up, please!"

In the door a small circle of light appeared as a peephole was used, followed a moment later by the sound of a latch, and the door opened. As it did,
Thurston pushed it wide open and strode in. Patrick Jensen, wearing an open
sport shirt and slacks, stepped two paces back. Ruby, entering behind
Thurston, closed the door.

Thurston, arrest warrant in hand, spoke crisply. "Patrick Jensen, I have a
warrant for your arrest on a charge of murdering Naomi Mary Jensen and

Kilburn Owen Holmes . . . I caution you that you have the right to remain silent. You need not talk or answer questions . . . You have the right to an attorney . . ." As the Miranda words rolled on, Thurston watched the other man's face, which seemed strangely unperturbed. It was almost, the detective thought, as if this moment had been expected.

At the end, Jensen said quietly, "May I phone him from here?"

"Yes, but I have to check you for a weapon first." While Jensen held up his hands, Thurston patted him down, then announced, "Okay, sir, you can go ahead and use the phone. One call."

Jensen went to it and tapped out what was plainly a familiar number. After a moment he said, "Stephen Cruz, please." A pause, then, "Stephen, it's Patrick. Remember I said a day might come when I'd need your help? That day is here. I've been arrested." Another pause, then, "Murder."

Jensen listened with the phone to his ear; obviously Cruz was giving him instructions. He replied, "I haven't said anything, and I won't." Addressing the detectives: "My lawyer wants to know where I'm being taken."

Thurston replied, "Police Headquarters—Homicide."

Jensen repeated the information, said, "Yeah, see you soon," and hung up.

"We'll have to handcuff you, sir," Ruby Bowe said. "Would you like to put on a jacket first?"

"Actually, I would." Jensen sounded surprised. Going to a bedroom, he buttoned his shirt and slipped on a jacket, after which Ruby swiftly secured his hands behind him. "You guys are being pretty polite about this," he said. "Thank you."

"Doesn't cost us anything," Thurston acknowledged. "We can go the rough route when we need. We prefer not to."

Jensen looked at him intently. "Haven't we met before?"

"Yes, sir. We have."

"I remember now. I was pretty obnoxious at the time."

The detective shrugged. "It was a long time ago."

"Not too long for an apology—if you'll accept it."

"Sure." Thurston's voice became coolly matter-of-fact. "But I think you've got a lot more than that to worry about right now. Let's get moving."

Ruby Bowe was speaking on her radiophone.

·   ·   ·

"They got Jensen and they're on the way," Ainslie told Leo Newbold and Curzon Knowles. Since their earlier session Knowles had been away, consulting with his superior, State Attorney Adele Montesino, and had just returned.

"Jensen's already called his lawyer," Ainslie added. "Stephen Cruz. He's on his way, too."

Knowles nodded. "Good choice. Cruz is tough, though he can be reasoned with."

"I know him," Newbold said. "But however good he is, nothing can argue with the new evidence we have."

"I have an idea about that box of evidence," Knowles continued. "Before Jensen gets here, why don't we take that box to an interview room, open it, and spread everything out on the table? The moment Jensen sees it all, he'll know he's cooked, and maybe start talking."

"Great idea." Newbold glanced at Ainslie. "Malcolm, will you set it up?"

•   •   •

At Police HQ, Jensen was in the course of being processed—fingerprinted, photographed, his pockets emptied, their contents stored and recorded, other paperwork proceeding. He was, he knew, enmeshed in the cogs of an impersonal machine. Who knew when he would be free from it, if ever? While concerned, at this moment he found himself not worrying all that much.

Ever since the detectives' arrival at his apartment, his thoughts had been in a curious limbo. He had long feared what had so recently occurred; at moments in the past it had been a haunting nightmare. But now that it was reality the immediate fear was gone—perhaps, he thought, because of the inescapability of whatever lay ahead. In a foolish moment of passion and emotion he had committed a capital crime, and now, according to the law and in whatever way the judicial system chose, some punishment was likely. Being human, he would use every possible means to escape or diminish that punishment, though only later would he know how good those chances were.

Of course, at this point he still did not know what had changed to prompt his arrest so suddenly, but he knew enough of the system to realize it was something important and compelling. If it were not, he would have been brought in for questioning before a warrant was procured.

After the routine processing, Jensen, still handcuffed, was taken in an elevator up several floors to Homicide. There he was escorted to an interrogation room—nowadays, in official "soft-speak," referred to as an interview room.

Jensen was hardly through the doorway when he saw on a table ahead the opened box bearing Cynthia Ernst's personal blue sealing tape. And, beyond the box, its contents—laid out one by one in a neat, highly visible, condemning row.

Involuntarily Patrick stopped, all movement frozen, as enlightenment, despair, and a sudden hatred of Cynthia exploded in his mind.

Moments later, having been pushed forward by his uniformed police escort, he was directed to a chair, handcuffed to it, and left alone.

●   ●   ●

It was a half hour later. Malcolm Ainslie, Ruby Bowe, Curzon Knowles, Stephen Cruz, and Patrick Jensen were all, by now, gathered in the interview room. Leaving Jensen alone for the intervening time had been deliberate on the detectives' part.

"I'm quite sure you recognize all of this," Ainslie said to Jensen, gesturing to the assortment on the table. Everyone was seated except Ainslie, who circled the table as he spoke. "Especially the gun that killed your former wife, Naomi, and her friend Holmes. Incidentally, the gun has your fingerprints all over it, and it fired the bullets that killed them both—all of that has been certified by experts who'll testify in court. And, oh yes, there's a tape recording, unmistakably your voice, in which you describe exactly how you killed them both. Would you like me to play that?"

"Don't answer that question," Stephen Cruz advised. "If the sergeant wishes to play a tape, let it be his decision. Also, you do not need to respond to those other things he said."

Cruz, a small-boned figure in his late thirties, with a sharp, decisive voice, had arrived soon after Jensen was delivered in custody. While waiting, he had chatted amiably with Knowles and Newbold, then was brought to the interview room.

Jensen, visibly distressed, looked directly at Cruz. "I need to talk with you alone. Can we do that?"

"Sure." Cruz nodded. "That's your privilege anytime. It'll mean transferring you to—"

"No need for that," Knowles interjected. "The rest of us will go, and leave you here. Okay with you, Sergeant?"

Ainslie answered, "Of course." He collected all of the evidence and followed Knowles and Ruby Bowe out.

Jensen shifted uncomfortably in his seat; earlier his handcuffs had been removed. "How do we know they're not listening?" he asked.

"Two reasons," Cruz informed him. "One, there's something called lawyer-client privilege. Two, if they listened and got caught, they'd face disciplinary action." He paused, surveying his racquetball partner and new client. "You wanted to talk, so go ahead."

Jensen took a deep breath and released it, hoping his muddled thoughts would clear. He was weary of concealment, and here and now at least he wanted to disclose the truth. Also, in whatever way the police had obtained the damned box, he decided, the blame was Cynthia's. Long ago she'd led him to believe she would destroy it all. Instead, despite all he had done and risked to protect and aid her, she had kept it, and it had betrayed him. In return, he knew that he would hold true to a promise of his own.

Jensen looked up at Cruz and began, "You heard what they said just now. Well, Steve, those *are* my fingerprints on the gun, I guess those bullets really match, and on the tape you didn't hear, it *is* my voice. So what do you think?"

"My strong impression," Cruz answered, "is that you are in deep shit."

"Actually," Jensen said, "it's deeper than you think."

2

'M GOING TO TELL YOU EVERYTHING," Jensen said, still sitting in the Homicide interview room with Stephen Cruz.

As Jensen poured out his story, Cruz listened, his face trying to mask shock, incredulity, and finally resignation, yet not succeeding. At the end, after a long and thoughtful pause, he said, "Patrick, are you sure you're not making all this up, that it isn't just another novel you're about to write? You're not bouncing the plot off me to find out what I think?"

"There was a time when I might have done just that," Jensen replied dolefully. "Unfortunately, every word is true."

Jensen felt some relief that at least in this limited sense everything was out in the open. Even *sharing* seemed to ease the load he had carried alone for so long. Common sense, though, warned him that the feeling was an illusion. Cruz's next words confirmed it.

"I'd say that your first need isn't so much a lawyer, but a priest, or someone of that ilk to say a prayer."

"That may come later if I get so desperate," Jensen said. "Right now I have a lawyer, and what I want from you is the bottom line: Where do I stand? What should I aim for? What are my chances?"

"All right." Cruz had risen from his chair and began to pace the length of the small room, glancing at Jensen as he talked. "According to what you've told me, you are heavily involved in the murders of five people. There's your ex-wife and her man; and the guy in the wheelchair, Rice. Then there are Gustav and Eleanor Ernst, who were important people, and don't think that doesn't make a difference; also, that Ernst case is clearly murder one. Certainly for the Ernsts, and maybe also those first two people, you could face the death penalty. How's that for a bottom line?"

Jensen started to speak, but Cruz silenced him with a gesture. "If you'd killed *only* your ex-wife and the man, I could have claimed it was a crime of passion and have you plead manslaughter, which, in cases where a firearm's used, carries a maximum sentence of thirty years. Since you'd have had a clean record, I'd have argued for less and maybe got fifteen, even ten. But with those other two killings in the wings . . ." Cruz shook his head. "Those change everything."

He looked out the window. "There's one thing you should come to terms with, Patrick. Even if you avoid the death penalty, there's no way you can escape prison time—probably a lot of time. It's unlikely, I think, that you and I will ever play racquetball again."

Jensen grimaced. "Now that you know the kind of person I am, I doubt you'd want to."

Cruz waved the remark away. "I leave judgments like that to the judges and juries. But while I'm your attorney—and by the way, sometime soon you and I have to talk money, and I warn you I'm not cheap—anyway, as an attorney, whether I like or dislike my clients—and I've had some of each—they all get the utmost I can give, and the fact is I'm *good!*"

"I accept all that," Jensen said. "But I have another question."

Cruz resumed his seat. "Ask it."

"What is Cynthia's legal position? First, because of failing to report what she knew about Naomi's and Holmes's killing, and then concealing the evidence—the gun, clothing, audiotape, all the rest?"

"She'll almost certainly be charged with obstruction of justice, which is a felony, and in a homicide case extremely serious; also conspiracy after the fact, and for all of that there'd likely be a prison term of five years, even ten. On the other hand, if she had a top-notch lawyer she might get away with two years, or even—though not too likely—probation. Either way, her civic career is over."

"What you're saying is, she'd make out much better than me."

"Of course. You admitted you did that killing. She didn't know about it in advance, and whatever she did was after the fact."

"But in the case of the Ernsts—Cynthia's parents—she knew in advance. She planned it all."

"So you say. And I'm inclined to believe you. But in my opinion Cynthia Ernst will deny it all, and how could you prove otherwise? Tell me—did she meet this Virgilio, who you say did the actual killing?"

"No."

"Did she put anything in writing to you, ever?"

"No." He stopped. "But, say . . . there *is* something. It's not much, but . . ." Jensen described the real-estate brochure with the layout of streets in Bay Point, on which Cynthia had marked the Ernst house with an X, then in Jensen's presence had written words showing the maid's working hours and the nighttime absence every Thursday of the butler Palacio and his wife.

"How many words?"

"Probably a dozen; some abbreviations. But it's Cynthia's handwriting."

"As you said, it isn't much. Anything else?" As they talked, Cruz was making notes.

"Well, we were in the Cayman Islands together, for three days at Grand Cayman. That's when Cynthia first told me about wanting to kill her parents."

"Without a witness, I presume?"

"Okay, so I couldn't prove it. But wait." Cruz listened while Jensen described the separate travel and hotel arrangements. "I flew Cayman Airways; saved my ticket, still have it. She was on American Airlines and used the name Hilda Shaw; I saw her ticket."

"Would you know the American flight number?"

"It was the morning flight; there's only one. Shaw would be on the manifest."

"Which still proves nothing."

"It shows a connection because later on Cynthia must have drawn that four-hundred-thousand-dollar payment from her account at a Cayman bank."

Cruz threw up his hands. "Have you any idea how impossible it would be to get a Cayman bank to testify about a client's account?"

"Of course. But suppose the whole thing—details of the Cayman account—was on record with the IRS?"

"Why would it be?"

"Because it damn well is." Jensen described how, during the time in the Caymans, he had looked covertly into Cynthia's briefcase and, after discovering the account's existence, had made quick notes of important points. "I have the bank's name, account number, the balance then, and the guy who put money there as a gift—an 'Uncle Zack.' I checked later; Gustav Ernst had a brother, Zachary, who lives in the Caymans."

"I can see how you wrote books," Cruz said. "So how'd the IRS get in?"

"Cynthia did it. Seems she didn't want to break U.S. laws, so she got a tax adviser—in fact, I have his name and a Lauderdale address—who told her it was all okay providing she declared the interest and paid tax, which she did. There was a letter from the IRS."

"Of which you have details, no doubt."

"Yes."

"Remind me," Cruz said, "never to put my briefcase down when you're around." His face twitched with a half-smile. "There isn't much that's funny in all this, except Cynthia Ernst was such a smartass about being legal, she created evidence that could work against her. On the other hand, having all that money doesn't prove a goddam thing, unless . . ."

"Unless what?"

"Unless that smirk on your face—which I don't much like—means there's something else you haven't told me. So if there is, let's hear."

"Okay," Jensen said. "There's a tape recording I have, *another* tape. It's in a safe-deposit box to which I have the only key, and on that tape is proof of everything I've told you. And, oh yes, those other papers—the one with Cynthia's handwriting about the Palacios, my notes from the Caymans, and the airline ticket—they're in the box, too."

"Cut the smart talk." Cruz moved within inches of Jensen's face and whispered menacingly, "This is not some fucking game, Jensen. You could be on your way to the electric chair, so if you've an important tape recording, you'd damn well better tell me everything about it—*now.*"

Jensen nodded compliantly, then went on to describe the recording he had made secretly a year and nine months earlier, during a lunch in Boca Raton. It was the tape on which Cynthia had approved hiring Virgilio to murder her parents; agreed she would pay two hundred thousand dollars each to Virgilio and Jensen; explained her own plan to make the murders look like other serial killings; and was told by Jensen that Virgilio had committed the wheelchair murder, knowledge she had subsequently kept to herself.

"Jesus Christ!" Cruz paused, considering. "Add that all up and it could change everything . . . Well, not everything. But quite a lot."

●   ●   ●

"My client is willing to cooperate in return for certain considerations," Stephen Cruz informed Knowles when the session in the Homicide interview room resumed.

"Cooperate in what way?" Curzon Knowles asked. "Because we certainly have all the evidence we need to convict Mr. Jensen for the murders of Naomi Jensen and Kilburn Holmes. Also, by the way things look, we can probably get the death penalty."

Jensen paled. Involuntarily, he reached out and touched Cruz's arm. "Go on, tell him."

Cruz swung toward Jensen and glared.

With a slight smile, Knowles asked, "Tell me what?"

Cruz recovered his composure. "Looking at it all from here, it appears you have a good deal less evidence with which to confront Commissioner Cynthia Ernst."

"I don't see why that concerns you, Steve, but since you mention it, there is enough. At the time she was a sworn police officer, and criminally delinquent by aiding, abetting, and concealing a crime. We would probably ask for twenty years in prison."

"And probably find a judge who'll give her five, or maybe two. She might even walk."

"Walking's impossible, though I still don't see—"

"You will in a moment," Cruz assured him. "Please listen to this: With the state's cooperation, he can give you a much bigger prize—Cynthia Ernst on a platter as the hidden-hand murderer of her parents, Gustav and Eleanor Ernst." In the interview room there was a sudden stillness and the sound of indrawn breath. All eyes were on Cruz. "Whatever penalty you sought in that event, Curzon, would be yours and Adele's decision—but obviously *there* you could go the limit."

Part of an attorney's training was never to show surprise, and Knowles did not. Just the same, he hesitated perceptibly before asking, "And by what piece of wizardry could your client do that?"

"He has, safely hidden away where even a search warrant won't reach, two documents that incriminate Ms. Ernst, but also—more important—a tape recording. Unedited. On that recording is every bit of evidence you'd need to convict, spoken in Cynthia Ernst's own voice and words."

Cruz went on to describe, from notes made earlier, a broad outline of what the tape contained concerning Cynthia, though he omitted any direct reference to Patrick Jensen or to the wheelchair murder. Instead, Cruz said, "There is also on the tape, and I suppose you could consider it a bonus, the name of another individual who is guilty of another, entirely different murder, so far unsolved."

"Is your client involved in both of those additional crimes?"

Cruz smiled. "That is information which, in my client's interest, I must withhold for the time being."

"Have you listened to this alleged tape recording yourself, counselor? Or seen the documents, whatever they are?"

"No, I haven't." Cruz had anticipated the question. "But I have confidence in the accuracy of what has been described to me, and I remind you that my client is well versed in words and language. Furthermore, if you and I reached an agreement and the evidence fell short of what was promised, anything we had arranged would be renegotiable."

"It would be null and void," Knowles said.

Cruz shrugged. "I suppose so."

"But if everything did work out the way you say, what would you want in return?"

"For my client? Taking everything into account—allowing him to plead manslaughter."

Knowles threw back his head and laughed. "Steve, I really have to hand it to you! You have the most incredible balls. How you can ask for a slap on the wrist in these circumstances, and do it with a straight face, I really don't know."

Cruz shrugged. "Sounded reasonable to me. But if you don't like the idea, what's your counteroffer?"

"I don't have one, because at this point you and I have gone as far as we can," Knowles told him. "Any decisions from here on must be Adele Montesino's, and she may want to see us together, probably today." The attorney turned to Ainslie. "Malcolm, let's break this up. I need to use a phone."

●   ●   ●

Knowles had left for the state attorney's headquarters, while Stephen Cruz returned to his downtown office, agreeing to be available when needed.

Meanwhile, Newbold, aware that the Police Department's role was becoming more complex, had advised his superior, Major Manolo Yanes, commander of the Crimes Against Persons Unit, of the broad issues pending. Yanes, in turn, had spoken with Major Mark Figueras, who, as head of Criminal Investigations, summoned an immediate conference in his office.

Newbold arrived, along with Ainslie and Ruby Bowe, to find Figueras and Yanes waiting. Seated around a rectangular conference table with Figueras at the head, he began vigorously, "Let's go over everything that's known. Everything."

Normally, while general Homicide activity was reported to superiors, specific case details seldom were—on the principle that the fewer people who knew the secrets of investigations, the more likely they would stay secret. But now, at Newbold's prompting, Ainslie described his early doubts about the Ernst case, followed by Elroy Doil's confession to fourteen killings but his vehement denial of having killed the Ernsts. "Of course we knew Doil was a congenital liar, but with the lieutenant's approval, I did more digging." Ainslie explained his search through records, the inconsistencies with the Ernst murders, and Bowe's research at Metro-Dade and Tampa.

He motioned to Ruby, who took over, Figueras and Yanes following her report closely. Ainslie then summarized: "The test was—had Doil told me the truth about everything else, *apart* from the Ernsts? As it turned out, he had, which was when I really did believe he *hadn't* killed the Ernsts."

"It's not proof, of course," Figueras mused, "but a fair assumption, Sergeant, which I'd share."

It was apparent that the two senior officers were looking to Ainslie as the principal figure in the discussion, clearly regarding him with respect and, strangely it seemed, at moments with a certain deference.

Next, Ainslie had Bowe describe her examination of the boxes from the Ernst house, the revelations about Cynthia's childhood, and, finally, the discovery of the evidence proving Patrick Jensen a murderer, evidence that Cynthia had concealed—all of that detail so new that it had not, until today, progressed beyond Homicide's domain.

Following it all was the arrest of Jensen earlier that day, prompting Jensen's accusations against Cynthia Ernst, and the promise of documents and a tape recording.

Figueras and Yanes, though accustomed to a daily diet of crime, were clearly startled. "Do we have *any* evidence," Yanes asked, "anything at all, linking Cynthia Ernst to the murders of her parents?"

Ainslie answered, "At this moment, sir, no. Which is why Jensen's documents and tape—if they're as incriminating as his lawyer claims—are so important. The state attorney should have everything tomorrow."

"Right now," Figueras said, his glance including Newbold, "I'll have to report this to the top. And if there *is* an arrest—of a city commissioner—it must be handled *very, very* carefully. This is beyond hot." He removed his glasses, rubbed his eyes, and muttered, "My father wanted me to be a doctor."

• • •

"Let's not waste time playing games," Florida's state attorney, Adele Montesino, said sternly to Stephen Cruz. "Curzon told me about your fantasy that your client plead guilty to manslaughter, so okay, you've had your little joke. Now we'll deal with reality. This is my offer: Assuming the documents and the tape recording offered by your client are as good as he claims, and he is willing to testify confirming what is there, for him we will not seek the death penalty."

"Whoa!" Raising his voice, Cruz faced her squarely.

It was late afternoon, and they were in her impressive office, with its mahogany-paneled walls and bookcases laden with heavy legal volumes. A large window looked down on a courtyard with a fountain; beyond were office towers and a seascape in the distance. The desk at which Montesino sat, if used as a dining table, would have seated twelve. Behind the desk, in an outsized padded chair capable of tilting and swiveling in all directions, was the state attorney—short and heavyset, and fulfilling once more her professional reputation as a pit bull.

Stephen Cruz sat facing Montesino, Curzon Knowles on his right.

"Whoa!" Cruz repeated. "That's no concession, none at all when what my client is being held for is a crime of passion . . . you remember passion, Adele—love and haste." A sudden smile accompanied the words.

"Thank you for that reminder, Steve." Montesino, whom few presumed to address by her first name, was noted for her sense of humor and a love of bandying words. "But here's a reminder for *you*: the possibility, which you and your client raised voluntarily, that he may be involved in another crime—the Ernst murders, a case which is clearly murder one. In that event my offer not to seek death is generous."

"An interpretation of generosity would depend on the alternative," Cruz countered.

"You know it perfectly well. Life in prison."

"I presume there would be a rider—a recommendation at sentencing that after ten years, clemency might be recommended to the governor."

"No way!" Montesino said. "All of that went out the window when we abolished the Parole Commission."

As all three knew, Cruz was indulging in rhetoric. Since 1995 a Florida life sentence had meant exactly that—life. True, after serving ten years a prisoner could petition the state governor for clemency, but for most—especially if the conviction had been for first-degree murder—any hope would be slim.

If Cruz was dismayed, he didn't show it. "Aren't you overlooking something? That, given those harsh alternatives, my client may decide *not* to produce the tape and documents we've spoken of, and take his chances on a jury trial?"

Montesino gestured to Knowles. "We've discussed that possibility," Knowles said, "and in our opinion your client has a personal vendetta against Ms. Ernst, who has also been named in this whole matter. And to pursue that vendetta he will produce the tape and whatever else, anyway."

"What we *will* do," Adele Montesino added, "is take a fresh look at possible plea bargains when all the evidence is in and when we know what your client actually did. But no other *guarantees* than the one I've already offered. So no more argument, no more discussion. Good afternoon, counselor."

Knowles escorted Cruz out. "If you want to deal, get back to us fast, and by fast I mean today."

●   ●   ●

"*Oh Jesus! God!* The *whole* of the rest of my life in jail. It's impossible, inconceivable!" Jensen's voice rose to a wail.

"It may be inconceivable," Stephen Cruz said. "But in your case it is *not* impossible. It's the best deal I could get you, and unless you prefer the electric chair—which, in view of all you've told me, is a clear possibility—I advise you to take it." In presenting hard facts to a client, as Cruz had learned long ago, there came a time when plain, blunt words were the only ones to use.

They were in an interview room at Dade County Jail. Jensen had been brought here, in restraints, from the cell to which he had been moved from Police Headquarters, a block away. Outside it was dark.

Cruz had had to get special clearance for the late interview, but a phone call from the state attorney's office had cleared the way.

"There is one other possibility, and as your legal counsel I'll point this out. That is, you do *not* produce the tape, and go to trial solely for the killings of Naomi and her man. In that event, though, you'd always have hanging over you the possibility that proof implicating you and Cynthia in the Ernsts' murders could come out later."

"It *will* come out," Jensen said glumly. "Now that I've told them, the cops—especially Ainslie—won't stop digging until they *can* prove it. Ainslie talked to Doil just before his execution, and afterward started to tell Cynthia something Doil had said about her parents, but she cut him off. I know Cynthia was scared stiff, wondering how much Ainslie had discovered."

"You know that Ainslie was once a priest?"

"Yeah. Maybe that gives him some special insights." Making a decision, Jensen shook his head. "I won't hold the tape and papers back. I want it all to come out now, partly because I've had enough of deceit and lies, and partly because whatever happens to me, I want Cynthia to get hers, too."

"In which case we're back to the plea bargain you've been offered," Cruz said. "I've promised to give an answer—yes or no—tonight."

It took another half hour, but in the end Jensen conceded tearfully, "I don't want to die in the chair, and if that's the only way not to, I suppose I'll take it." He gave a long, deep sigh. "A few years ago, when I was riding high, with everything I'd ever wanted coming true, I never dreamed that one day I'd be in this position."

"Unfortunately," Cruz acknowledged, "I meet others who say exactly the same thing."

As Cruz left the room, escorted by a guard, he called back, "Early tomorrow I'll make arrangements to get that tape and papers."

● ● ●

The next morning, at the First Union Bank at Ponce De Leon and Alcazar in Coral Gables, Malcolm Ainslie entered first. The bank had just opened, and he went directly to the manager's office; a secretary seemed ready to stop him, but he flashed his police badge and walked in.

The manager, fortyish and well dressed, saw Ainslie's credentials and smiled. "Well, I guess I *was* driving a little fast coming in this morning."

"We'll overlook it," Ainslie said, "if you'll help with a small problem."

He explained that a customer of the bank, now a prisoner, was waiting in an unmarked police car outside. He would be escorted to his safe-deposit box, which he would open, and the police would remove whatever the box contained. "This is entirely voluntary on your customer's part—you may ask him if you wish—so no warrant is needed, but we'd like to do the whole thing quickly and quietly."

"So would I," the manager said. "Do you have . . ."

"Yes, sir." Ainslie handed over a paper on which Jensen had written his name and the safe-deposit box number.

As he saw the name, the manager raised his eyebrows. "This is like a scene from one of Mr. Jensen's books."

"I suppose so," Ainslie said. "Except this isn't fiction."

Earlier that morning, Friday, Ainslie had gone to where Jensen's personal effects, taken from him immediately after his arrest, were stored at Police Headquarters. Among the effects was a key ring from which Ainslie removed what was obviously a safe-deposit box key.

The process in the bank's safe-deposit vault was brief. Jensen, whose hands were free, though handcuffs secured his left hand to Ruby Bowe's right, went through the usual formality of signing, then opened his box with the key.

With the box removed from its housing, a woman technician from ID staff stepped forward. Wearing rubber gloves, she opened the box lid and took out four items: an apparently old, folded real-estate brochure, a small notebook page filled with handwriting, an airline ticket stub, and a tiny Olympus XB60 audiotape. The technician inserted everything in a plastic container, which she sealed.

The technician would rush the items to ID, where they would be checked for fingerprints, then two copies made of everything, including the tape, regarded as the most important. Ainslie would deliver the original items and one set of copies to the state attorney's office. The second set was for Homicide.

"Okay, that's it. Let's go," Ainslie said.

Only the manager, hovering in the background, had a question. "Mr. Jensen, I notice the box is now empty. Will you be wanting it anymore?"

"Highly unlikely," Jensen told him.

"In that case, may I have the key?"

"Sorry, sir." Ainslie shook his head. "It's evidence; we'll have to retain it."

"But who will pay the box rent?" the manager asked as the visitors filed out.

•   •   •

The rest of Friday was a patchwork of sharing information. Ainslie delivered the original documents and tape, along with a set of copies, to Curzon Knowles at the attorney general's office. Ainslie returned to Homicide and, in the privacy of Leo Newbold's office, he, Newbold, and Bowe listened to their copy of the tape.

The sound quality was excellent, with every word from both Jensen and Cynthia Ernst audible and clear. Part way through, Bowe breathed excitedly, "It's exactly what Jensen promised. *Everything* is there!"

"You can tell he's steering the conversation," Newbold pointed out. "Cagily, but making sure he gets everything that matters on the tape."

"It's like Cynthia walked into her own mousetrap," Bowe observed.

Malcolm Ainslie, his thoughts in turmoil, said nothing.

•   •   •

A phone call from the state attorney's office, requesting Ainslie's presence, came in late afternoon. He was shown into Adele Montesino's office. Curzon Knowles was with her.

"We've listened to the tape," Montesino said. "I presume you have as well."

"Yes, ma'am."

She nodded.

"I thought I should tell you this personally, Sergeant Ainslie," Montesino said. "The grand jury has been summoned for next Tuesday morning. We will be seeking three indictments of Commissioner Cynthia Ernst, the most important being for murder in the first degree—and we'll require you as a witness."

Knowles added, "That gives us the weekend and Monday for preparation, Malcolm, and we'll need all of it—arranging witnesses and evidence, including a statement from you about what Jensen has revealed, and a good deal more. If you don't mind, we'll go right from here to my office and begin."

"Of course," Ainslie murmured automatically.

"Before you go," Montesino said, "let me say this to you, Sergeant. I have learned that while everyone else accepted the Ernst murders as part of the other serial killings, you were the one—the only one—who didn't believe it and set out, with patience and great diligence, to prove the contrary, which you finally have. I want to thank and congratulate you for that, and in due course I'll convey those thoughts to others." She smiled. "Have a good night's rest. We have four tough days ahead."

•   •   •

Two hours later, driving home, Ainslie supposed he should feel a sense of triumph. Instead he felt nothing but overwhelming sadness.

WE'VE WORKED LIKE HELL TO put everything together," Curzon Knowles told Ainslie. "Everyone's cooperated, we think the case is strong but, Christ, this heat sure doesn't help!" It was nearly nine o'clock on Tuesday morning, and Knowles and Ainslie were on the fifth floor of the Dade County Courthouse in Miami, in a small office reserved for prosecutors. Close by was the grand jury chamber where today's business would be done.

Both men were in shirtsleeves, having shed their jackets because the building's air conditioning had failed overnight and a repair crew was reportedly working somewhere below—so far without effect.

"Montesino will be putting you on as the first witness," Knowles said. "Try not to melt in the meantime."

Voices in the corridor outside signaled that the grand jury members were filing in. There were eighteen, with an equal number of men and women and a mix of Hispanic, black, and white.

•   •   •

The primary purpose of any grand jury is simple: to decide whether sufficient evidence exists to initiate criminal charges against a person. Some grand juries have a secondary function—to stage inquiries where local civic systems are corrupt or malfunctioning—but the direct criminal focus is more significant and historic.

Unlike a regular court trial, grand jury proceedings are surprisingly informal. In the Dade County facility a circuit judge was available but rarely present. His duties were impaneling and swearing in the jury—usually for a six-month term—and appointing a foreperson, a vice-foreperson, and a clerk. The judge would give legal rulings if required and, at the end of any proceeding, accept the grand jurors' decisions.

Within the grand jury chamber, jurors sat around four long tables. Along one end of the tables was another table at which the foreperson, the vice-foreperson, and the clerk sat facing their colleagues. At the opposite end was the prosecutor, usually an assistant state attorney, who described the evidence available and examined witnesses. Today the state attorney herself would do both.

A court stenographer was present when witnesses were examined.

Grand jurors could, and did, interrupt proceedings with questions. Everything that transpired, however, was secret—all those involved in the process took an oath to that effect, and unauthorized disclosure was an indictable offense.

At the outset, standing at the multi-table complex, Adele Montesino began casually, "I apologize for the excessive heat. We've been promised that air conditioning will be restored soon; meanwhile anyone who wants to shed some clothing may do so within reason, though of course that's easiest for the men—if less interesting."

Amid mild laughter, several men removed their jackets.

"I am here today to seek three indictments against the same person," Montesino continued. "The first is for murder in the first degree, and the accused is Cynthia Mildred Ernst."

Until this moment the jurors had seemed relaxed; now, abruptly, their tranquillity disappeared. Startled, sitting upright in their chairs, some gasped audibly. The foreperson, leaning forward, asked, "Is that name a coincidence?"

Montesino responded, "No coincidence, Mr. Foreman." Then, facing all the jurors, "Yes, ladies and gentlemen, I *am* speaking of Miami City Commissioner Cynthia Ernst. The two people she is charged with feloniously killing are her late parents, Gustav and Eleanor Ernst."

Mouths were agape. "I don't *believe* it!" an elderly black woman declared.

"At the beginning I scarcely believed it, either," Montesino acknowledged, "but now I do, and I predict that before I'm finished, and you have heard witnesses and listened to an incredible recording, you will believe it, too—or at least sufficiently to order a regular jury trial."

She shuffled papers on the table in front of her. "The second indictment I am seeking, also against Cynthia Ernst, is for aiding, abetting, and concealing a crime while serving as a police officer. That crime was the murders of two *other* people, and I shall bring you evidence in support of that charge also. The third indictment is for obstruction of justice by possessing knowledge of a crime, namely the perpetrator of a murder, and failing to report it."

Again the grand jurors seemed stunned, glancing at each other as if asking, *Can this be true?* There was a low buzz of spoken exchanges.

Adele Montesino waited patiently for silence, then called her first witness for the murder-one indictment—Ainslie, who was escorted in by a bailiff and directed to the prosecutor's table. Before entering, Ainslie had replaced his jacket.

The state attorney began, "Mr. Foreman, ladies and gentlemen of the grand jury, this is Sergeant Malcolm Ainslie of the Miami Police Department, a Homicide detective. Is that correct, sir?"

"Yes, ma'am."

"A personal question, Sergeant Ainslie: Since *you* are not being charged with anything, why are you sweating?"

The room erupted with laughter.

"Would you like the bailiff to take your jacket?"

"Please." In a pocket of his mind, Ainslie reasoned that Montesino was smart to keep the jury happy; later they were more likely to give her what she wanted. He wished he were happy himself.

"Sergeant Ainslie," Montesino began, "will you tell us, please, how you were first involved with inquiries into the deaths of Gustav and Eleanor Ernst."

Ainslie, tired and strained, breathed deeply, summoning strength for this personal ordeal.

•   •   •

Since last week, after learning conclusively—first of Cynthia Ernst's concealment of Patrick Jensen's guilt of a double murder, then that Cynthia had arranged her own parents' murders—Malcolm Ainslie had accomplished what was required of him in the way of duty, though at times he moved more like a robot. Certain things, he realized, he had to do himself; today's testimony was one, so were other initiatives and responsibilities. But for the first time in years he wished desperately that he could walk away and have someone else take over.

Through the few preceding days—so packed with action and disclosures—his mind had been in turmoil. Last Friday night, when all the substance of the investigation came together, sadness had overwhelmed him. And on that occasion and so many others, central in his thoughts was Cynthia—Cynthia, whose passion he had once welcomed and shared; whose competence he had so often admired; whose integrity he used to believe in. Then, more recently, there was the Cynthia he had desperately pitied after learning of her childhood abuse, and of her child having been snatched away before she even saw it.

True, there had been forewarnings. Malcolm recalled the sense of foreboding that had touched him a month ago in the temporary office where he instructed Ruby Bowe to search through the boxes retrieved from the Ernst house after the murders. By then they knew for sure that Doil had not killed Gustav and Eleanor Ernst, and that was when Cynthia's possible involvement had fleetingly crossed his mind. He had kept the thought to himself, scarcely believing it possible, then dismissed it. Now it was back, and it was real.

What must he do now? Of course, he had no choice. Despite all of his pity for Cynthia, his compassion for her suffering, and even understanding the hatred she had felt toward her parents, he could never, *ever*, condone their murder; and what he had to do—as at this moment—he would do, though with pain and sorrow.

There was one thing, though—amid all the conflicts and emotions—that he knew for sure.

A year and a half ago, at a time of great personal distress that Malcolm's work in Homicide had caused him, Karen had asked him, "Oh, sweetheart, how much more can you take?" And he had answered, "Not too many like tonight."

That answer had been an equivocation, and both knew it. Now he had another, different answer, and he would tell Karen before the ending of this day. It was, *Dearest, I've had enough. This will be the last.*

But for the moment Ainslie focused on answering Adele Montesino's question: *Will you tell us, please, how you were first involved . . .*

·   ·   ·

"I was in charge of a task force investigating a series of apparent serial killings."

"And did the Ernsts appear to be victims of the same serial killer?"

"Initially, yes."

"And later?"

"Serious doubts arose."

"Will you explain those doubts?"

"Those of us investigating the case began to think that whoever killed the Ernsts had tried to make their deaths appear to be one more killing in the series we were investigating, though in the end it didn't work."

"A moment ago, Sergeant, you referred to 'those of us investigating the case.' Isn't it true that you, initially, were the *only* detective who believed the Ernst murders were not serial killings?"

"Yes, ma'am."

"I didn't want you to get away with too much modesty." Montesino smiled, and some of the jurors with her.

"Is it also true, Sergeant Ainslie, that a pre-execution interview you had with Elroy Doil, an admitted serial killer, suggested that the Ernst murders were not serial killings, and that afterward you followed an investigative trail that caused you to decide Cynthia Ernst had planned them and retained a paid killer?"

Ainslie was shocked. "Well, that's passing over an awful lot of—"

"Sergeant!" Montesino cut him off. "Please answer my question with a simple yes or no. I think you heard it, but if you wish, the stenographer can read it back."

He shook his head. "I heard it."

"And the answer?"

Ainslie said uncomfortably, "Yes."

He knew the question was flagrantly leading; it skirted facts, and was unfair to the accused. At a regular trial, defense counsel would have leapt up with an objection, which any judge would have sustained. But at a grand jury hearing there could be no objections because no defense counsel was allowed, or a defendant, either. In fact, so far as anyone knew, the accused— Cynthia Ernst—was entirely unaware of what was taking place.

Something else: In front of grand juries, prosecutors presented as much or as little evidence as they chose, usually disclosing the least amount they had to. They also used devices—as Montesino was clearly doing—to speed things along when they were confident of getting an indictment anyway.

Ainslie, who had testified before other grand juries, increasingly disliked the experience and knew that many more police officers felt the same way, believing the grand jury system was one-sided and contrary to evenhanded justice.

•   •   •

As a scholar with wide interests, Ainslie knew the system's history—that grand juries originated in medieval England around the year 1200, when such juries accused those suspected of crimes and then tried them. During succeeding years the two functions were separated, and grand juries became "inquisitorial and accusatorial" only. Britain, after more than seven centuries, abolished grand juries in 1933, believing them incongruous in modern law. The United States retained them, though criticisms made it likely that eventually—perhaps in the century soon to come—the British example would be followed.

A problem with American grand juries was their secrecy, which permitted inconsistencies and barred even local supervision to a point where one legal critic described a grand jury as "a body of semi-informed laymen exempt from technical rules."

Some states had largely eliminated grand juries—Pennsylvania and Oklahoma were examples; a few states nowadays allowed defendants and defense attorneys to be present. Only thirteen states required a grand jury indictment for *all* felony prosecutions; thirty-five did not. Several states advised jurors against accepting hearsay evidence; two examples were New York and Mississippi. Others allowed it, including Florida, which permitted hearsay evidence if given by an investigator. The list of inconsistencies—and inevitable injustices—was complex and long.

Some United States lawyers felt that grand jury procedures were still disconcertingly close to the Salem witch trials of 1692—though usually not prosecutors.

●   ●   ●

Even with Adele Montesino's shortcuts, a succession of witnesses and questioning continued for two hours. Malcolm Ainslie, after nearly an hour on the stand, had been dismissed and sent from the room, though instructed to stand by because his testimony would be needed again. He was not allowed to hear other witnesses; no one other than jurors or court officials ever attended a full grand jury performance.

For the principal murder-one accusation, the subject of motive—Cynthia's lifelong hatred of her parents—was addressed by Detective Ruby Bowe, who, smartly attired in a beige suit, was responsive to questions, and articulate.

Bowe described her discovery of Eleanor Ernst's secret diaries, though Adele Montesino's questioning stopped before reaching Cynthia's pregnancy. Instead, at the prompting of Montesino, who had clearly familiarized herself with the diaries' clarified version, Bowe jumped ahead, reading aloud the diary entry that began, *I've caught Cynthia looking at us sometimes. I believe a fierce hatred for us both is there,* and concluded, *Sometimes I think she's planning something for us, some kind of revenge, and I'm afraid. Cynthia is very clever, more clever than us both.*

Bowe had expected the questioning would return to Cynthia's pregnancy and childbearing, but Montesino concluded, "Thank you, Detective. That is all."

Afterward, when Ruby Bowe discussed the omission with Ainslie, he said wryly, "Bringing out the pregnancy by her father might have created too much sympathy for Cynthia. If you're a prosecutor you can't let that happen."

Setting the stage for the tape recording, the state attorney called as a witness Julio Verona, the Police Department's ID chief. After establishing his qualifications, Montesino proceeded. "I believe that the recording this grand jury is about to hear was subjected to tests to establish that the voices on it are indeed those of Cynthia Ernst and Patrick Jensen. Is that correct?"

"Yes, it is."

"Please describe the tests and your conclusion."

"In our own police records we already had recordings of Commissioner Ernst when she was a police officer, and of Mr. Jensen, who was once questioned in connection with another case. Those were compared with the recording you have just referred to." Verona described the technical tests on specialized acoustic equipment, then concluded, "The two voices are identical on both recordings."

"And now we'll play the recording that is part of the evidence in this case," Montesino told the grand jury. "Please listen carefully, though if there's anything you miss and want to hear again, we can play it as many times as you wish."

Julio Verona stayed to operate the tape, using high-quality sound equipment. As the voices of Patrick Jensen and Cynthia Ernst were heard—at first ordering their meal, then in lowered tones discussing the Colombian, Virgilio—every grand juror was visibly concentrating, anxious not to miss a word. When Cynthia was heard protesting after Jensen told her Virgilio was the wheelchair murderer—*Shut up! Don't tell me that! I don't want to know*—a male Hispanic juror proclaimed, *"Pues ya lo sabe."* To which a young, blond Caucasian woman added, "But the bitch kept it to herself!"

Other jurors shushed the pair, and another voice asked, "May we hear that over again, please?"

"Certainly." The state attorney nodded to Verona, who stopped the tape, rewound it slightly, and recommenced playing.

Then, as the recorded voices continued—two payments of two hundred thousand dollars, one for the Colombian, the same for Patrick; Cynthia suggesting "odd features" to make the deaths appear to be serial killings—murmurs, then exclamations of disgust, anger, and resolve surfaced among the jurors, one man declaring as the recording stopped, "Guilty as hell, an' I don't need to hear no more!"

"I understand what you're saying, sir, and I respect your feelings," Adele Montesino responded. "But there are two more indictments being sought here, and I must ask your patience for a little longer. By the way, I don't know if anyone's noticed, but we seem to have some air conditioning again."

There was scattered applause and some sighs, this time of relief.

Fairly quickly, a few gaps were filled. An IRS inspector produced Cynthia Ernst's subpoenaed tax records, showing she had declared and paid taxes on interest earned in a Cayman Islands bank account, the interest having resulted from deposits—stated to be a series of gifts and therefore not taxable—exceeding five million dollars. "I point out to you," the inspector said at the end, removing his bifocals, "that Ms. Ernst's taxes are entirely in order."

"But the existence of the account," Montesino advised the grand jury, "supports the statement you heard on tape about Ms. Ernst's intention to pay four hundred thousand dollars for the murders of her parents." Montesino did not mention the irony that Cynthia's compliance with U.S. tax laws had created evidence that otherwise would have remained concealed in the Caymans and been off limits to any U.S. court.

Malcolm Ainslie was recalled. He described the opening of Jensen's safe-deposit box, which included the tape recording the grand jury had heard, as well as other items. One of those was an airline ticket counterfoil showing a round-trip Miami–Grand Cayman journey, by Jensen, aboard Cayman Airways.

"What is the significance of that flight?" Montesino asked.

"Two days ago, in the presence of his attorney," Ainslie replied, "Mr. Jensen told me that he and Cynthia Ernst spent three days together in the Caymans, during which they planned the Ernst murders; also that they traveled there separately—Miss Ernst on American Airlines from Miami, using the name Hilda Shaw."

"And did you verify that second statement?"

"Yes. I went to American Airlines headquarters in Miami, and, using their computer records, they confirmed there was a passenger with the name Hilda Shaw on their flight 1029 to Grand Cayman that same day."

It was all hearsay evidence, Ainslie realized, which would have been thrown out of a regular court, but was usable in this sometimes zany proceeding.

Related to the second indictment—Cynthia's concealment of the two murders by Jensen—Ainslie produced the box of damning evidence against Jensen, put together and hidden by Cynthia Ernst. Then, prompted by Montesino, he showed and described the contents one by one.

Julio Verona was recalled next. He testified that fingerprints found on plastic bags in the evidence box were those of Cynthia Ernst, and that handwriting on several labels had been examined and certified as hers also.

"Concerning the third indictment," Montesino told the grand jury, "I will not call any witness to confirm that Cynthia Ernst learned the name of the guilty party in what has become known as the Wheelchair Murder, and subsequently failed to report that information to police, as required by law. That is because you—the grand jurors—are, in effect, witnesses yourselves, having heard exactly what happened during the recording that was played."

Again, murmurs and nods acknowledged her words.

·   ·   ·

Montesino was brief with her finale.

"This has been a long and painful session, and I will not prolong it, except with this reminder. Your task now is *not* to decide the innocence or guilt of Cynthia Ernst. That will be a trial jury's responsibility—*if* you decide that the evidence presented is sufficient to take these matters onward through the courts. I do believe, most strongly, that it is *far more* than sufficient, and that justice will be served by your issuance of three true bills—indictments. Thank you."

Moments later, after the state attorney and other staff departed, the grand jurors were left alone.

But not for long. Barely fifteen minutes later the judge and the state attorney were summoned, after which the judge received the grand jurors' decisions and read them aloud. In each case an indictment called for the arrest of Cynthia Ernst.

4

YOU GUYS WILL HAVE TO MOVE fast," Curzon Knowles warned
Ainslie as he handed him a plastic cover containing two signed
copies of the three indictments. "Once those jurors get out of here,
secrecy oath or not, someone will talk, and word about Commissioner Ernst
will spread like a brush fire and surely get to her."

They were in a hallway outside the courtroom. As Knowles walked with
him toward an elevator, Ainslie asked, "Can you keep everyone here for a
while? You have more cases with this jury?"

"One. We planned it that way, but don't count on more than an hour. After
that, you take your chances."

Knowles continued, "They already know about the indictments at the
Police Department; Montesino called the chief. And, oh yes, I've been told
to tell you that as soon as you arrive, you should go directly to the office of
Assistant Chief Serrano." He glanced at Ainslie curiously. "Pretty unusual for
the brass to be directly involved in a homicide."

"Not when it's a city commissioner. The mayor and commissioners are a
special breed, and treated very warily."

As a state officer dealing with many towns and cities statewide, Curzon
Knowles was not tuned in to local politics as, in Miami, even a detective-
sergeant was.

Ostensibly, Ainslie knew, the Police Department was independent of city
politics, but in reality it was not. The city commission controlled the Police
Department budget through the city manager, who also appointed the chief
of police and had the power to remove one; there was an occasion when he
had done so. Commission members possessed inside knowledge about senior
police officers who were in line for promotion. And some commissioners had
friends on the force, so quiet influence on their behalf could be, and sometimes was, applied.

Occasionally, Ainslie knew, too, there had been difficulties between the
city commission and the Police Department—the commission highly protective of its authority, and touchy when it was infringed. All of which was why,

five days ago, Lieutenant Newbold had brought the startling developments to the attention of his superiors, Majors Figueras and Yanes. They, in turn, had passed the information higher, and those at top command, once concerned, had stayed involved.

As the elevator doors closed, Knowles mouthed from outside, "Good luck."

Good luck with what? Ainslie wondered as the elevator descended. His concept of luck right now would be to have his role in this drama end when he delivered the indictments to the assistant chief. But he suspected it would not.

His own deep depression of the previous Friday had continued over the weekend and through yesterday, as the net of retribution tightened around Cynthia.

In his own personal domain there had been some change. Late Friday night he had told Karen of his decision to quit Homicide when this present duty was done, and perhaps the Police Department completely, though he wasn't sure about that. At the news, Karen had put her arms around him and, close to tears, assured him, "Darling, I'm so relieved. I've seen what these awful things do to you. You can't take any more, and you should get out altogether. Don't worry about the future; we'll manage! *You're* more important than anything else—to me, to Jason, and"—she touched her rounded stomach, now showing four months of pregnancy—"and whoever."

That night with Karen he had spoken of Cynthia; he'd cited her childhood tragedies, described the woman filled with hate that those tragedies created, then told of Cynthia's crimes—a fierce transfer of her hatred, with an impost under law now coming due.

Karen had listened, then reacted with some of her plain reasoning, which, through their nine years of marriage, he had come to know and value. "Of course I'm sorry for her; anyone would be, especially another woman. But the fact is, there's nothing either done *to* her or *by* her that can be undone now; it's all too late. So whatever happens, other people—you and I especially—don't have to share Cynthia's despair or guilt, and have our lives wrecked, too. So yes, Malcolm, do what you have to this very last time, and then—*get out!*"

As Karen spoke Cynthia's name, Ainslie wondered, as he had before, if she was aware of his and Cynthia's long-past affair.

But apart from all else, the objective was to get this present mission—definitely his last—over as fast as possible.

The elevator door opened at the courthouse main floor.

• • •

Exercising police privilege, Ainslie had left his unmarked car parked outside, and the journey to Police Headquarters—three blocks north and two west—was brief.

When he entered the office suite of Assistant Chief Otero Serrano, head of all police investigations, a secretary said, "Good afternoon, Sergeant Ainslie. They're waiting for you." She rose and opened a door to an interior office.

Inside, a conversation was in progress among Serrano, Mark Figueras, Manolo Yanes, and Leo Newbold. As Ainslie entered, voices quieted, heads turned toward him.

"Are those the indictments, Sergeant?" Chief Serrano, tall and athletically built, was behind his desk. A former detective, he had a distinguished record.

"Yes, sir." Ainslie handed over the plastic cover he was carrying, and Serrano removed the two copies of each indictment, passing the extra set to the other three.

While all four were reading, Ruby Bowe was ushered in quietly. She moved close to Ainslie and whispered, "We have to talk. I've found her child."

"Cynthia's?" Startled, he glanced around. "Do we . . ."

She whispered back, "I don't think so. Not yet."

As those in the room continued reading, low groans were audible, then Figueras breathed, "Christ! It couldn't be worse."

"Things happen," Serrano said resignedly, "that you think never would."

A door from outside opened, and Chief of Police Farrell Ketledge came in. A hush fell over the room as everyone straightened up. The chief said quietly, "Carry on." Moving to a window, standing alone, he told Serrano, "This is your show, Otero."

The reading resumed.

"Cynthia screwed us well and truly," said Figueras. "Got herself promoted *after* she hid that killing of Jensen's wife and friend."

"Goddam media will have a field day," Manolo Yanes predicted.

Despite the more significant murder-one indictment, Ainslie realized, it was the second and third indictments—Cynthia's participation in murders while a Homicide detective, and her concealing knowledge of another—that hurt them most.

"If this goes to trial, it could take years," Leo Newbold said. "We'll be under the gun the whole time."

The others nodded gloomily.

"That's all, then," Serrano intervened. "I wanted to share what's happening because we'll all be involved. But we must move."

"Might not be so bad if Ernst did hear before we got to her." It was

Manolo Yanes's voice. "Then she could do the decent thing and swallow a bullet. Save everyone a potful of trouble."

Ainslie expected Yanes's words to produce a sharp rebuke. To his surprise, there was none; only a silence followed, during which not even the chief spoke. *Was a subtle message being conveyed?* As he dismissed the thought as unworthy, Serrano turned toward him.

"You may not like this, Sergeant Ainslie, but you're the one we've chosen to make the arrest." He paused, his tone becoming considerate. "Does this give you any kind of problem?"

So he knew. Ainslie supposed they all knew about him and Cynthia. He recalled Ruby's words: *We're detectives, aren't we?*

"I won't enjoy it, sir. Who would? But I'll do what's necessary." In a peculiar way, he felt he owed it to Cynthia to see this through.

Serrano nodded approvingly. "Because it's a city commissioner, everything from this moment on will be under the closest public scrutiny. You have an outstanding reputation, and I'm confident there'll be no fumbling, no mistakes."

Ainslie was conscious of all eyes on him, and, just as during the session with Figueras and Yanes five days earlier, a note of respect seemed evident that transcended rank.

Serrano consulted a paper brought in by his secretary moments earlier. "We've kept tabs on Ernst since early this morning. Half an hour ago she went to her City Hall office. She's there now." He looked up at Ainslie. "You must have a woman officer with you. It will be Detective Bowe."

Ainslie nodded. Nowadays a woman suspect was almost never arrested by a male officer alone; it made sexual harassment claims too easy.

Serrano continued, "I've ordered a uniform backup. They're already below, waiting for your orders. And you'll need this." He passed over an arrest warrant, prepared in anticipation of the indictments. "Go do it!"

• • •

Ruby glanced at Ainslie in the crowded elevator. He murmured, "Save it. Tell me on the way." Then, as they left the elevator, "You get us a car. I'll talk to our backup."

Two uniform officers, Sergeant Ben Braynen, whom Ainslie knew well, and his partner, were beside a Miami Police blue-and-white at the building's staff-restricted exit. "We're your strong right arm," Braynen said, greeting him. "Orders came from the top. You must be mighty important."

"If I am, it's temporary," Ainslie told him. "And I'll get the usual check on payday."

"So what's the mission?"

"We go to City Hall in the Grove, the commissioners' offices. I'm doing an arrest with Bowe, and you're our backup." He produced the arrest warrant, pointing to the principal name.

"Holy shit!" Braynen said incredulously. "This for real?"

Ruby Bowe, in an unmarked police car, pulled ahead of the blue-and-white and stopped.

"As real as sin," Ainslie said, "so follow us. We may not need you, but it'll be good to know you're there."

When Ruby and Ainslie were clear of the police compound, he said, "Okay, let's hear."

"What's important," Ruby said, "is that Cynthia may be expecting us. Because of what I discovered late last night."

"We don't have much time. Better talk fast."

•   •   •

As Ruby told it . . .

Ever since learning from Eleanor Ernst's diaries that Cynthia had given birth to her father's child, Ruby had tried to find out what had happened to the baby—a child whom no one cared about, except to dispose of, its sex not even mentioned in Eleanor's notes.

"It was a girl," Ruby said. "I found that out early, at the adoption center." But the center had not been helpful beyond that, denying access to old records, claiming that confidentiality barred the way. Ruby had not persisted, she explained, because the information was not crucial. The child's existence was already known, and finding out more would not aid the investigation into the Ernsts' deaths.

"I wanted to know, though," Ruby said. "A couple of times I dropped in at the center, and there was an older social worker who I thought might bend the rules and help, but she was scared. Two days ago she phoned. She's retiring in a week. I went to her home last night and she gave me a paper."

The paper, as described by Ruby, showed that the adoption of Cynthia's child had lasted less than two years. The adoptive parents were convicted of abuse and neglect, and the child was taken away. There followed a long series of foster homes until the girl was thirteen, when the record stopped. "It's a sad story of indifference and cruelty," Ruby said, adding, "I was going to check with the last home listed, then didn't need to, when I saw the name the baby was given. And still uses."

"Which is?"

"Maggie Thorne."

It was familiar, Ainslie thought. He just couldn't place it.

Ruby prompted, "It was Jorge Rodriguez's case—the German tourist, Niehaus, shot and killed. I think you were . . ."

"Yes . . . I was."

It sprang back in memory: the wanton, needless killing . . . an international furor and the hapless guilty pair—a young black male, Kermit Kaprum; a white female, Maggie Thorne . . . tests showed shots were fired by both accused, two fatal shots by Thorne . . . under questioning, both confessed.

At the time, Ainslie recalled, there had been something familiar about the young woman's face. He had tried using flash recognition, but it hadn't worked. Now he knew why. It wasn't the accused girl whom he had seen before, but her mother, Cynthia. Even now, in memory, Thorne's resemblance to her was uncanny.

"There's something else," Ruby said as she turned the car onto Bayshore Drive. "The woman from the adoption center who gave me the report tried to cover herself. If they break confidentiality for any reason, they're supposed to notify the child's original parent, and my woman did. She sent a form letter addressed to Cynthia about her daughter, Maggie Thorne—Cynthia probably never knew that name before—saying the police had asked for the information and been given it. The letter was mailed on Friday and went to the Ernsts' old home address in Bay Point. Cynthia may have it now."

"The Niehaus case." Ainslie's mind was swirling, his voice barely under control. "In the end, what happened?" There were so many cases. He half remembered, but wanted to be sure.

"Kaprum and Thorne both got death sentences. They're on death row, going through appeals."

Everything else left Ainslie's mind. He could think only of Cynthia, receiving a form letter . . . Cynthia was sharp, she followed cases, would connect the name at once and put everything else in place, including the current interest of the police . . . A form letter—to let her know that her only child, the child she never knew, would soon be executed. He thought despairingly, *Was there no end to the unfair, dreadful hand that life had dealt to Cynthia?* Compassion and the profoundest pity for her overwhelmed him, momentarily eclipsing all else. In the front seat Malcolm leaned forward, putting his head in his hands. His body shook convulsively. He wept.

　　　　　•　　•　　•

"I'm sorry," Ainslie said to Ruby. "There are times when you lose a sense of proportion." He was remembering the protesters outside Raiford Prison, who appeared to have forgotten a murderer's victims. "It all got to me at once."

"I cried last night. This job sometimes . . ." Ruby's voice trailed off.

"When we go in," he told her, "I'd like to go to Cynthia first—alone."

"You can't. It's against—"

"I know, I know! It's against regulations, but Cynthia would never pull sexual harassment stuff; she's too proud for that. Look, you said the letter to her was mailed Friday to the old Bay Point address; she may not have it yet. If she doesn't, I can break the news more gently, and even if she does—"

"Malcolm, I have to remind you of something." Ruby's voice was low and caring. "You're not a priest anymore."

"But I'm a human being. And I'm the one who'll be going against orders, though I need your okay."

She protested, "I have a duty, too." Both of them knew that if something went wrong, Ruby could pay a penalty with her career.

"Look, I'll cover you whatever happens, say I made it an order. *Please.*"

They were at the Dinner Key waterfront and had arrived at City Hall. Ruby stopped their car at the main doorway. The blue-and-white was immediately behind.

She hesitated, still uncertain. "I don't know, Malcolm." Then, "Will you tell Sergeant Braynen?"

"No. The uniforms'll remain outside anyway. You come inside with me, but wait in the auditorium while I go to Cynthia's office. Give me fifteen minutes."

Ruby shook her head. "Ten. Max."

"Agreed."

They entered the main door of Miami's unique and anachronistic City Hall.

•   •   •

In an age when government opulence was the norm and cathedral-style official buildings proclaimed politicians' self-importance, the City Hall of Miami—one of America's major cities—expressed the reverse. Located on a promontory and with Biscayne Bay on two sides, it was a relatively small two-story building painted white, with its name and some minor art deco relief in bright blue. People were often surprised at the overall simplicity, even though the building housed Miami's elected mayor, vice-mayor, three commissioners, and an appointed city manager. Others, usually old-timers, often said the building looked more like a seaplane base—not surprisingly, since it had been a Pan American Airways base from 1934 through 1951, built to serve Clipper flying boats that carried passengers from Miami to thirty-two countries. Then, when flying boats went the way of dinosaurs, Pan Am closed the base and it became Miami City Hall in 1954.

History had been made here. Perhaps more history, Ainslie thought, would be made today.

In the main lobby, Ainslie and Bowe walked to a desk where they showed their police badges to an elderly security guard. The man waved them past. Knowing the location of Cynthia's office on the main floor, Ainslie turned left and gestured to Ruby to take an interior corridor to the right, which led to the auditorium where she would wait. Reluctantly, Ruby left him, pointedly checking her watch.

Before entering the building, Ainslie had instructed Braynen and his partner to hold their present position outside, listen to their radios, and respond immediately if called.

Ainslie continued down the hall until a door confronted him:

OFFICE OF THE
COMMISSIONER
CYNTHIA ERNST

A young male aide sat at a desk in a windowless room immediately inside. In a separate small office a woman secretary was working at a computer. Between the two was a substantial door, dark green, and closed.

Again, Ainslie showed his badge. "I'm here to see the commissioner on police business. Don't announce me."

"Wouldn't anyway." The young man gestured to the green door. "Go right in." Ainslie opened the door and entered, closing it behind him.

Cynthia faced him. She was seated at an ornate desk, her face expressionless. The office was spacious and pleasantly functional, though not luxurious. A window in the rear wall provided a view of the harbor and moored pleasure boats. A plain door to the right probably opened to a cupboard or a small powder room.

A silence hung between them. After several seconds he began, "I wanted to say—"

"Save it!" Cynthia's lips scarcely moved. Her eyes were cold.

She knew. No explanations, he realized, were required on either side. Cynthia would have many contacts; a city commissioner could bestow favors and was owed them in return. Undoubtedly someone in her debt—perhaps in the grand jury office, even, or the Police Department—had quietly picked up a phone and made a call.

"You may not believe this, Cynthia," Ainslie said, "but I wish there were something, *anything*, I could do."

"Well, let's think about that." Her face and voice were icy, devoid of all empathy. "I know you like executions, so maybe you could attend my daughter's—make sure everything goes off the way it should. Mine, too, perhaps. Now, wouldn't you enjoy that."

He pleaded, "I beg of you, don't do this."

"What would you prefer—remorse and tears, some sleazy piety from your old game?"

Ainslie sighed. Unsure of what he had hoped for, he knew whatever it was had failed. He knew, too, that Ruby should be with him. He had made a mistake in persuading her to stay behind.

"There's no easy way to do this," he said, placing the arrest warrant on the desk. "I'm afraid you're under arrest. I have to caution you—"

Cynthia smiled sardonically. "I'll accept Miranda as read."

"I need your gun. Where is it?" Ainslie's right hand had moved and was holding his own Glock 9mm automatic, though he did not produce it. Cynthia, he knew, had a Glock also; like all sworn personnel who retired, she had received her gun on leaving as a gift from the city.

"In the desk." She had risen and pointed to a drawer.

Not taking his eyes from her, he reached down with his left hand, opened the drawer, and felt inside. The gun was under a cloth. Lifting it out, he put it in a pocket.

"Turn around, please." He had handcuffs ready.

"Not yet." Her voice had become near normal. "I have to go to the toilet first. There are certain functions you can't do with your hands fixed behind your back."

"No. Stand where you are."

Unheeding, Cynthia turned and walked toward the interior door he had noted. Over her shoulder she taunted, "If you don't like it, go ahead—shoot me."

Two fleeting thoughts crossed Ainslie's mind, but he banished them.

As the door opened, he saw it was a toilet inside. Equally obvious, there was no other way out. The door closed swiftly. Removing his right hand from his gun, he strode forward, intending to open it—by force if needed. For whatever reason, he suddenly knew he had moved too slowly.

Before he could reach the door, and only seconds after it had closed, it was flung open from inside. Cynthia stood in the doorway, eyes blazing, face tightly set—a mask of hate. Her voice was a snarl as she commanded, *"Freeze!"* In her hand was a tiny gun.

Knowing he had been outwitted, that the gun had probably been stored inside, he began, "Cyn, look . . . we can . . ."

"Shut up." Her face was working. "You knew I had this. *Didn't you?"*

Ainslie nodded slowly. He hadn't known, but barely a minute earlier the possibility had occurred to him; it was one of the thoughts he had dismissed. The gun Cynthia held was the tiny, chrome-plated Smith & Wesson five-shot pistol—the "throw-down"—she had used so effectively during the bank holdup into which she and Ainslie once walked together.

"And you thought maybe I'd use it on myself! To save me and everybody else a lot of trouble. *Answer me!*"

It was a moment for truth. Ainslie admitted, "Yes, I did." That had been his second thought.

"Well, I *will* use it. But I'll take you with me, you bastard!" She was bracing herself, he could tell, for a marksman's shot.

Possibilities, like summer lightning, flashed through his mind. Reaching for his Glock was one; but Cynthia would fire the instant he moved, and he had seen the bank robber with a hole precisely central in his forehead. As for Ruby, barely five minutes had passed. With Cynthia there was no more reasoning. Was there anything he could do? No, *nothing.* And so . . . the end came to everyone in time. Accept it. One final thought: He had sometimes wondered—would he, in the last seconds of his life, return to a belief, even a hope, in God and some future life? He knew the answer now. And it was no.

Cynthia was ready to fire. He closed his eyes and then heard the shot . . . Oddly, he felt nothing . . . He opened them.

Cynthia had fallen to the floor; her eyes closed, the tiny gun clutched in her hand. On the left side of her chest, blood was oozing from an open wound.

Against the outside door, rising from the half-crouched stance from which she had fired her 9mm automatic, was Ruby Bowe.

5

NEWS OF CYNTHIA ERNST'S VIOLENT death swept through Miami like a tidal wave.

And the news media exploded.

So did surviving city commission members, infused with white-hot anger at what they saw as the wanton slaying of one of their own.

Even before the body of Cynthia Ernst could be removed, her death having been certified by paramedics, two mobile television crews were at City Hall, filming and posing questions to which no one had coherent answers. They had been alerted by police radio exchanges, as had other reporters and photographers who quickly joined them.

Sergeant Braynen and his partner, aided by hastily summoned reinforcements, attempted to maintain order.

For Malcolm Ainslie and Ruby Bowe, the post-confrontation events became a mercurial montage. After hasty calls to and from Assistant Chief Serrano's office, they were ordered to remain in place and talk to no one until a "shoot team" from Internal Affairs arrived—standard procedure when death or serious injury was caused by an officer on duty. The team, appearing moments later, comprised a sergeant and detective who questioned Ainslie and Bowe carefully, though without hostility, it becoming quickly evident that Internal Affairs had been informed, before the officers' departure, of the grand jury indictments and arrest warrant for Cynthia Ernst.

The Police Department, itself scrambling for information, declined immediate comment on the shooting death of City Commissioner Ernst, but promised total disclosure at a news conference at 6:00 P.M. that day, which the chief of police would attend.

Meanwhile the chief sent messages to the mayor and city commissioners that he would telephone each of them personally during the hour before the news conference, to report the latest information. It would have been more convenient to have a special briefing in his office, but under Florida's "sunshine law," commission members could not meet together in any place without the media or public being informed and admitted.

From the "shoot team" interrogation, Ainslie and Bowe moved onward to a private accounting in Assistant Chief Serrano's office—behind closed doors, and before Serrano and Majors Figueras and Yanes. During all the questioning, Ainslie and Bowe told no lies, but nor, it seemed, were overly probing questions asked—in particular, how did Ainslie and Ruby become briefly separated at City Hall? Instinct told Ainslie that, justly or otherwise, ranks were closing, with the Police Department maneuvering to protect its own. He wondered, too: Was there, among the five, an uneasy memory of Yanes's covert words concerning Cynthia, spoken in this same room barely an hour before: *She could do the decent thing and swallow a bullet. Save everyone a potful of trouble.* Did they now share a feeling of guilt that no one had protested? And was there an instinct that if probing became too intensive and specific, something they would prefer not to hear would be divulged?

Those were questions, Ainslie knew, that would never be answered.

In the end, what would become the essential police retelling was summarized in a handwritten note by Serrano, to be rewritten and enlarged on as an official statement:

> *Acting with authority derived from three grand jury indictments,*
> *two officers—Sergeant Malcolm Ainslie and Detective Ruby*
> *Bowe—attempted to arrest Commissioner Cynthia Ernst. After the*
> *prisoner was apparently disarmed, with the gun she was known to*
> *own taken from her, and before being handcuffed, she suddenly pro-*
> *duced a small concealed pistol—which she was about to fire at*
> *Sergeant Ainslie when Detective Bowe, using her own police*
> *weapon, shot and killed the prisoner.*

Those facts were upheld, soon after, by the uniformed officers, Braynen and his partner, who, immediately after the shooting, responded to a radio summons from Ainslie and were on the scene in seconds.

Only in a quiet moment later did Ainslie and Ruby talk about what had happened.

"After a few minutes of waiting, I got antsy," Ruby explained. "Just as well, wasn't it?"

Ainslie grasped her shoulders with both hands and met Ruby's eyes. "I owe you my life," he told her. "Whatever you need from me, you only have to ask."

"If I think of something," she said with a half-smile, "I'll tell you. But a lot of it was self-interest. Working in Homicide wouldn't be the same without you. You've taught all of us so much, set great examples. I hope I'm not embarrassing you."

Ainslie shrugged self-consciously. "A little, I guess." Then he added carefully, "Working with you, Ruby, has been a privilege for me." This was not the moment, he decided, to reveal his decision to leave Homicide and perhaps the Police Department. For the time being he would keep that knowledge between Karen and himself.

•   •   •

Preparations for the news conference were made at breakneck speed as lengthy phone calls flew between the Police Department and the state attorney's office. Together they decided that all relevant facts concerning Cynthia Ernst would be disclosed: the three grand jury indictments; Eleanor Ernst's diaries; Cynthia's early abuse at the hands of her father; the pregnancy; Cynthia's plot to have her parents killed; even the fact that crucial evidence concerning another double murder that Cynthia concealed had sat unexamined for a year and a half in the police Property Department. Finally there would be Cynthia's failure to divulge her knowledge of the wheelchair murderer.

As Assistant Chief Serrano expressed it, after consulting with the chief and the Department's public information officer, Evelio Jimenez, "It's one monstrous mess, and no one will come out smelling sweet. There could be problems, though, if anything's held back and then ferreted out by some smart reporter."

Only certain evidence, which might be needed for the trials of Patrick Jensen and Virgilio, would remain temporarily undisclosed. Jensen's arrest, and the charges against him, had now become known.

As for Virgilio, there was doubt about whether he would ever be caught and tried. Metro-Dade Homicide, on learning of his participation in the wheelchair murder, had begun a search for him, as had Miami Homicide, because of his reported slayings of the Ernsts. But Virgilio had fled to his native Colombia, from where extradition was unlikely because of the mutual hostility between that country and the United States.

•   •   •

The news conference was held in the lobby of Police Headquarters, entry being controlled by several police officers near the main doorway, where credentials were examined. A podium and microphones were set up near the main-floor elevators. There, Evelio Jimenez, the public information officer—a former newspaper reporter with a frank, no-nonsense attitude—would be in charge.

Only minutes before the crowded conference began, city commission members, all of whom had already spoken with the chief, filed into the lobby, their expressions ranging from shock to grief. The media closed in on them, but no one responded to questions. When a microphone was thrust in the face of the mayor, he snapped uncharacteristically, "Take that away! Just listen to what they'll tell you."

TV cameras were rolling, microphones lined up like bean sprouts, and pencils and laptop computers were poised as the PIO announced, "Chief Farrell Ketledge."

The chief of police stepped forward. He spoke solemnly, though he wasted no time in coming to the point.

"Without any doubt, this is the saddest day in my entire police career. I considered Cynthia Ernst to be a loyal colleague and good friend, and shall remember her, in part, that way, despite the crimes and horror that are now exposed. For as you will shortly hear in detail, Miss Ernst *was* a criminal, guilty, among other things, of the terrible murders of her parents . . ."

A collective gasp filled the hall. Simultaneously, several reporters rose hastily and left, heading for TV vans outside; others spoke into cellular phones.

The chief continued, mentioning the two murders Cynthia had helped to conceal while a Homicide detective. He then stated, "Earlier today, three grand jury indictments were issued for her arrest. It was during that arrest that Miss Ernst suddenly produced a concealed weapon, which she clearly intended to use on one of the arresting officers. The other officer fired a single shot, instantly killing Miss Ernst.

"We will, if you wish, talk more about that later, but for now I want to deal with today's events, beginning with the grand jury indictments directed at Cynthia Ernst. So I will ask Mr. Curzon Knowles, head of the state attorney's Homicide division, to describe those indictments and the evidence behind them."

Knowles, dressed more formally than usual in a blue pinstriped suit, moved to the podium and spoke authoritatively for ten minutes, relating most of the facts presented to the grand jury. Many in the audience looked up from their notes and listened intently as he described Eleanor Ernst's diaries and the details of child abuse. "I understand," Knowles continued, "that significant pages of those diaries are being copied now and will be available soon." A few questions were asked of Knowles, but none were aggressive. Most of the reporters seemed stunned at what was being revealed; there was a sense that plain words and frankness were the order of the day.

When Knowles concluded, Serrano took over. The assistant chief introduced Leo Newbold, who spoke briefly, then Malcolm Ainslie, who described the murders of Gustav and Eleanor Ernst and the attempt to make them look like earlier serial killings. It quickly became evident that Ainslie had a grasp of the entire complex scene, and for a half hour he responded clearly and confidently to reporters' queries.

He was tiring, though, when a woman TV reporter asked, "We were told earlier . . ." She paused, consulting her notes. " . . . told by Lieutenant Newbold that you were the first one who believed the Ernst murders were *not* part of those earlier serials. Why did you have that first impression?"

He responded impulsively, "Because there's no rabbit in Revelation," then regretted the words the moment they were out.

After a puzzled silence the same woman asked, "Will you explain that?"

Ainslie glanced at Deputy Chief Serrano, who shrugged and told the journalists, "We have talented people here who sometimes solve crimes in unusual ways." Then, to Ainslie: "Go ahead, tell them."

Reluctantly, Ainslie began, "It goes back to symbols—left by a perpetrator at four murder scenes and eventually recognized as religious symbols inspired by the Book of Revelation in the Bible. At the Ernst murders a rabbit was left. It didn't fit the pattern."

While continuing to describe the earlier symbols, Ainslie remembered that all of that information had been held back from the media at the time, and never released later because there had been no need. In the end Elroy Doil was tried, sentenced, and executed for the Tempones' murder only, where no symbol was involved.

Thus, this information was new, and also fascinating, judging by the number of reporters who, with heads down, were scribbling notes or typing on laptops.

As Ainslie concluded, a male voice asked, "Who figured out what those symbols meant?"

"I'll answer that," Serrano said. "It was Sergeant Ainslie who made the connection, and it led to several suspects, one of whom was Elroy Doil."

A veteran print reporter asked, "Is it true, Sergeant Ainslie, that you were once a priest? Is that how you know your way around the Bible?"

It was a subject Ainslie had hoped would not come up. While he had made no great secret of his past, few outside the Department knew of it. Anyway, he answered, "Yes, I was, so in that regard it helped."

Next a woman's voice. "Why did you stop being a priest and become a cop?"

"Leaving the priesthood was my personal choice, freely made. The reasons were private and not relevant here, so I won't discuss them." He smiled. "For the record, I left behind no misbehavior; my acceptance as a police officer should vouch for that." Despite the overlay of seriousness, there was some good-natured laughter.

Soon after, with many reporters eager to get going, the formal news conference broke up, though some reporters and TV crews stayed on, doing one-on-one interviews in both English and Spanish. Ainslie especially was in demand and remained an extra forty minutes. Even then, reporters followed him to his car, still filming and asking questions.

•   •   •

That same evening, and during the days that followed, Malcolm Ainslie was a prominent figure on television as his statements were featured, then repeated, interlaced with new developments. National network news reports carried the Cynthia Ernst story, with most depicting Ainslie as police spokesman. ABC's "Nightline" reported at length the mysterious murder-scene symbols and their biblical interpretation, once more with Ainslie as the star.

The print press covered the Ernst stories, too, showing interest in Ainslie's former priesthood. One probing reporter found a record of his doctoral degree and reputation as a scholar, mentioning Ainslie's joint authorship of *Civilization's Evolving Beliefs*, and that, too, was repeated around the country. His name appeared prominently in *Newsweek* and *Time* reports, and the national Sunday newspaper magazine, *Parade,* ran a cover story with the headline SCHOLARLY EX-PRIEST DETECTIVE LAUDED AS CRIME-SOLVING STAR.

The switchboard at Miami Police Headquarters received many calls from inquiring film and TV producers, all of it defying Assistant Chief Serrano's prediction that no one would emerge from the Ernst debacle smelling sweet. Quite clearly, Ainslie did.

"I really wish all this would stop," Ainslie confided to Leo Newbold.

"The way I hear, the guys up above us have the same feeling," Newbold replied.

Whatever their unease, everyone in authority was clearly relieved that there would be no harrowing trial of Cynthia Ernst.

•   •   •

A few days after the news conference, Ainslie relayed to Leo Newbold his wish to leave Homicide. Newbold was understanding and sympathetic. Many other detectives had traveled the same route, and it was accepted that long-time Homicide duty imposed emotional strains that eventually could be disabling. While Ainslie was awaiting word about new duty, Newbold removed him from current Homicide assignments and placed him in charge of "cold cases"—old homicides being investigated with the aid of new technologies— a productive but "low emotion" area.

After three weeks, Newbold stopped by Ainslie's desk and said, "Figueras wants to see you now."

•   •   •

"Hi, Sergeant Ainslie!" Major Figueras's secretary, Teodora Hernandez, greeted him as he entered the Criminal Investigations chief's outer office. "Before you go in," she asked, "would you do me a favor?"

"If I can, Teo."

"Well, my kids keep seeing you on the tube and reading about you. Then when I said I knew you, they got all excited, asked if I could get your auto-graph." She produced two white cards and held out a pen. "Would you mind?"

Embarrassed, he protested, "I'm not a celebrity."

"Oh yes, you are! Write 'For Petra' on one card and 'For Justo' on the other."

Taking the pen and cards, Ainslie scribbled the names and two signatures. He handed them back.

"I'll be a hero at home tonight," Teodora said as she led him toward the inner-office doorway, which, he noticed, was ajar.

Mark Figueras stood up as Ainslie came in, and he was grinning. "So, our celebrity! How does it feel?"

"Out of place, totally." Ainslie grimaced.

"Well, it won't stop soon. Can you live with it?"

"I suppose. But how about the Department, sir?"

"There might be a problem." Figueras gestured dismissively. "Anyway, forget the formality, Malcolm. This is a talk I've been instructed to have with you—man-to-man stuff. Oh, but first there *is* one piece of formality. You are Lieutenant Ainslie, as of this moment." He extended his hand. "Congratula-tions. A little late, maybe, but in the right direction."

Ainslie wondered what was coming. The promotion pleased him, and he wanted more than anything to phone Karen and share it with her. But he waited for Figueras.

"Career-wise, you're in good shape right now, Malcolm, and there are sev-eral routes you can go—most of your own choosing. The first is to command Homicide." As Ainslie looked surprised, Figueras continued, "Leo Newbold is being made captain, and he'll move to a new assignment. In your case you'd normally move, too, but your record in Homicide is outstanding, and an exception could be made if that's your wish."

"It isn't." Ainslie shook his head. "I already told Leo why I want out."

"I'd heard that unofficially, and I understand it. We simply wanted you to know all the options."

The "we" was significant. Whatever Figueras was relaying had come from the top.

"Okay, let's weigh your future in the Department," the Criminal Investigations chief went on. "You've made lieutenant at age forty-one. In another three years you could be captain, and after that, at the chief's discretion, a major, though nothing's certain, and all of it a little late compared with others, because you were older than most when you started. So maybe at forty-six you'd be a major after fifteen years of service, and above that, as you know, there are fewer jobs and the competition's tough. So you *might* go higher, but major could be your limit before retirement. I'm being frank with you, Malcolm."

"I prefer it that way."

"There's one other thing to be looked at, and I'm really leveling with you here. Recently you've had more public attention than probably anyone in the Department ever had before. One reason is that you've done spectacular work, especially in Homicide. But it was your old background as a priest and scholar that the media jumped on, which brings me to a point."

Ainslie had a notion of what was coming.

"The thing is, Malcolm, because of all that attention, whatever you do in the Police Department now will be noticed by the media and probably magnified. Nothing really wrong in that, but to be truthful, the Department could be uncomfortable. As you know, few people here get consistent public attention, and that even includes the chief—most of Miami's population probably don't know his name. That's how it's always been, and most of us would like to see it stay that way."

"Let's be clear about this," Ainslie said. "Are you telling me that despite all that's happened—my promotion and the rest—you'd really like me out of the force?"

"If it seems that way to you," Figueras said, "then I've done a lousy job, because that's the last thing I wanted to convey. But what most of us here do feel, Malcolm, is that what's left for you in the Department simply doesn't measure up to your abilities. What we'd like to see happen is for you to move on to something more advantageous to *you*, and that would make better use of your special talents."

"Trouble is," Ainslie said, "I haven't done much reading of the want ads lately. Looks as though I should."

Figueras laughed. " 'Want' is an appropriate word. The fact is—and this is mostly what this talk is about—an organization outside the Police Department has been in touch with the chief, the mayor, and maybe others, and *wants* you very much—on highly favorable terms, I understand."

Ainslie was confused. "Is this organization something, or someone, that I know?"

"I don't think so. The person most concerned is the chairman of the board of trustees of South Florida University." Figueras consulted a paper on his desk. "His name is Dr. Hartley Allardyce. Would you be agreeable to a meeting?"

Life was full of unexpected twists and turns, Ainslie reflected. He answered, "What can I say but yes?"

6

THIS MAY SURPRISE YOU, DR. AINSLIE," Hartley Allardyce said, "but we've been talking about you a lot at our university—ever since your talents and background became so widely known."

"Yes, it surprises me," Ainslie said. "Lately, almost everything surprises me."

It was three days after his conversation with Major Mark Figueras. Now Ainslie and Allardyce were at dinner together at Miami's downtown City Club. Ainslie found it strange to be called "Doctor." Though it was valid scholastically, he had not heard it spoken aloud for years, and even as a priest he hadn't used it. In these present circumstances, though . . .

Dr. Allardyce, who seemed to enjoy talking, continued, "The public loves a local hero, always has, and you became one when you solved those hideous crimes. The bonus was that you did it intellectually, using scholarly knowledge, which is why you're so admired by educators, myself included."

Ainslie smiled self-consciously and murmured thanks.

Waving the interruption aside, Allardyce went on, "What has happened to you, in terms of becoming a public figure, could not have occurred at a more opportune time—both for me and for others whom I represent. And, I hope, for you."

Hartley Allardyce was as impressive an individual as his name implied. He was silver-haired, handsome, and deeply tanned, with a confident manner and a buoyant smile. He had been born to wealth, then had enlarged it as the head of an international investment fund, enriching others also. At the same time he was passionately interested in higher education, hence the South Florida University connection.

"I've been chairman of the SFU trustees for six years," he explained, "and in all that time have wanted to develop a lecture program on comparative religions. We have a Department of Religion and Philosophy, of course, but it doesn't deal with comparatives to the extent I'd like."

Allardyce paused as a waiter served their main course, filet mignon with béarnaise sauce. "By the way, I hope you like this wine. It's an Opus One, originated by two of the world's great vintners—Robert Mondavi in the Napa Valley and the late Philippe de Rothschild in Bordeaux. Do try it."

"It's superb," Ainslie reported, and it was. He had heard of the famous wine, though on a detective-sergeant's pay he could never have afforded it.

"Let me get to the point," Allardyce said, "as to why you're here. *Most* university students these days are opting for the hot-action areas of education: business, medicine, law, and engineering. But I'd like to show our young people the value of studying comparative religions.

"Diverse religions say so much—far more than conventional history— about the times in which people live, and their state of mind in every age and society; their fears, hopes, and pleasures; what they dread, consciously and subconsciously, with death always high on the list; and whether there's anything beyond death, or merely oblivion—no doubt the greatest fear of all. *Do* have more wine, Dr. Ainslie."

"Thank you, no. I'm doing fine. But before we go any further, there's something I want to say."

"The last thing I wish is to monopolize. Please go ahead."

"Something you ought to know, Dr. Allardyce, is that while I'm fascinated by comparative religions and always have been, I do not *believe* in any of them. Haven't for a long time."

"I already knew that," Allardyce said, "and it makes no difference. It may even make you more objective. You're sure about no more wine?"

"Quite sure, thank you."

"So the reason I've brought you here is that I have, just recently, raised enough money to build a new Religion and Philosophy Center on campus. A good deal of it comes from a personal friend who is on the point of pledging several million dollars. However, since reading about you and your unique qualifications, my friend has added a condition to the gift. In addition to the building, there'll be an endowment for a professor in comparative religions, to be described as a distinguished scholar. The point is, Dr. Ainslie, my friend wants *you*."

Ainslie's eyes widened. "Are you serious?"

"Totally."

"May I ask who your friend is?"

Allardyce shook his head. "Sorry! Sometimes wealthy donors prefer to stay anonymous; nowadays there are good reasons. Anyway, the commitment on the university's part would initially be for three years, and the annual stipend would be one hundred thousand dollars. Forgive me for bringing up money, but it's necessary sometimes."

There were several seconds of silence before Ainslie said, "I can forgive you for that, Doctor. And perhaps, after all, I *will* have more wine."

"There'll be a few formalities," Allardyce said moments later. "Though nothing you can't handle."

• • •

Karen was thrilled about the pending appointment. "Oh, honey—go for it! It's so right for you. You're an authority on the subject, and you're so good at teaching. I haven't told you this, but after what happened at City Hall, I phoned Ruby Bowe to say thank you—for me, and for Jason. Among other things, she told me how the younger detectives appreciate what you've taught them, and how they all respect you."

He reminded Karen, "There are some more interviews I have to go through before the offer's firm."

"You'll sail through them."

• • •

A succession of interviews took place, the most important with the university's provost, Dr. Gavin Lawrence—quiet spoken and small in stature, but with a firm no-nonsense presence. The provost, with a file open in front of him, looked up from it and commented, "You're certainly academically prepared to go this route."

"There's one thing I have to make sure you know." Ainslie repeated the nonbelief declaration he had made to Allardyce.

"That's in here, too." The provost touched the file. "Hartley wrote a report, saying he appreciated your honesty. So do I, and I agree it's not a barrier." Lawrence leaned back, bringing his fingertips together as he spoke. "Actually, I hear rumors that some of our religion and philosophy professors have discovered their faith waning as they've accumulated more knowledge, of which—in religion—there's been a great deal these past two decades. That happens sometimes, don't you think?"

"It happened to me."

"Well, it makes no difference here, because we simply *don't ask* about the religious leanings of our faculty. What we do care about, of course, is scholarship and honest teaching. I trust that's clear."

Ainslie nodded. "Perfectly."

"There's something else we'd ask of you. From time to time we would like you to give public lectures on your subject. I think, with your name, you'd draw quite a crowd, and since we charge admission . . ." The provost smiled benignly.

As to Ainslie's three-year commitment, "At the end, if everything has worked well, there might be a faculty opening, or some other institution might want you. It's always a help if students like you, and I have a feeling they will. The students really are the key.

"There's one final thing," the provost said. "Tell me a bit about how you would teach comparative religions."

Ainslie was startled. "I've done no preparation . . ."

"Never mind, just off the cuff."

Ainslie thought briefly. "What I would teach is fact—whatever fact is known. As you said earlier, so much fresh knowledge about religions has emerged in the past twenty years and needs examining. What I'd avoid is judgments. Students, if they choose, can make those on their own. Above all, I wouldn't proselytize; that and the study of religions don't go together."

Lawrence nodded thoughtfully. "And in the larger educational scheme— the university's purpose as a whole—how do you see comparative religions?"

"Oh, without question, as important history—human history over roughly five thousand years. And throughout that time, religions have caused countless changes—innovation and destruction, wars and peace, justice and tyranny. Most religions have had their share of saints and scoundrels. Those in high places have *used* religions—emperors, politicians, armies, mercenaries— usually to gain power."

"Religions, of course, abound with positives and negatives. How do you balance those? Which are greater? Isn't that a judgment call?"

"If it is, I'm not up to making it; I doubt that anyone is. What I do know is that no matter how we view the record of religions in history, no other facet of human behavior through the ages has been so all-pervasive or long- lasting." Ainslie chuckled. "I guess that alone shows the importance of com- parative religions in present-day life and education."

There was a silence, then the provost said, "Well done! Thank you, Dr. Ainslie, and you may count on me as an early attendee when your lectures begin."

Their parting was cordial. "I understand that Hartley is planning a recep- tion at his house for you and your wife—a chance to meet others. I look for- ward to seeing you both there."

●   ●   ●

When his post at South Florida University was confirmed, Ainslie submitted his resignation to the Police Department, and during his final few days in Homicide, many who knew him, including senior officers, dropped in to wish him well. For his slightly more than ten years' service he would receive a pension—not large, but, as he put it to Karen, "enough to buy us a bottle of Opus One occasionally."

One thing Ainslie did not do was retain his Glock automatic pistol, as was his privilege as a retiring police officer. Instead he returned it to the armory. He had had enough of firearms to last him the rest of his life, and he did not want a gun in his home, especially with children.

Karen was ecstatic at the final news. She looked forward to having more of Malcolm's time, to be shared with Jason, and their second child, now due in four months. Recently they had learned through ultrasound tests that the baby was a girl. They planned to name her Ruby.

Epilogue

AT LENGTH THE DAY ARRIVED for the reception at Hartley Allardyce's home. More than a hundred guests were expected.

"A little overwhelming, I'm afraid," Allardyce explained to Malcolm and Karen soon after they reached his large and rambling Tudor-style mansion in Gables Estates in Coral Gables. "I started with sixty invitations, then word got around, and so many people wanted to meet you that I had to increase the numbers."

Even as they spoke, early arrivals were coming into an elegant, spacious room with soaring ceilings, opening onto a garden terrace. Outside, off duty campus police had been recruited to organize parking. Inside, waiters began to circulate with gourmet hors d'oeuvres and Dom Pérignon champagne.

"Hartley always does things rather well, don't you think?" Ainslie overheard a tall blond woman say, and he agreed. He and Karen were kept busy with introductions as guests were brought their way by Dr. Allardyce. With bewildering speed they met Southern Florida University's president and several trustees, vice presidents, deans, and senior faculty members. Among those introduced was Dr. Glen Milbury, a university criminology professor. "When my students heard I'd be meeting you," he said, "they begged me to ask—will you take a breather from religions once in a while and come talk to us? I can guarantee a crowded lecture hall." Ainslie promised he would do his best.

Politicians were present; two city commissioners had been introduced, and the mayor was expected. A U.S. congresswoman was in conversation nearby, and the chief of police, in plain clothes, had just arrived when Ainslie felt a touch on his arm and saw Hartley Allardyce once more beside him.

"There's someone special who wants to meet you," he said, and escorted Ainslie to the far side of the room. "It's the donor of our new building and, of course, your comparative religions endowment, who has decided to shed anonymity after all."

They eased through several groups and, near a mullioned window, an attractive, immaculately groomed woman faced them. "Mrs. Davanal, may I introduce Dr. Malcolm Ainslie?"

"Actually, Hartley," Felicia said, smiling, "we've already met. You could even say we're old friends."

At the sight of Felicia—so unexpected—Ainslie found himself startled and breathless. *The same alluring and beautiful Felicia who had lied that her husband was murdered, until Ainslie proved he had committed suicide . . . Felicia, who had offered him a place in the Davanal empire, with a not-so-subtle hint of intimacy to come . . . and of whom the socially wise Beth Embry had predicted, "Felicia eats men . . . If she fancies the taste of you, she'll try again."*

He told her, "I had no idea . . ." Allardyce quietly drifted away.

"I made sure of that," Felicia said. "I thought if you had, you might not have accepted. But don't you remember, Malcolm? I predicted our paths would cross again someday."

She reached out, touching his hand, moving her fingers slightly, and as before her touch was like gossamer. Again Malcolm felt his senses stirring. It had been that way, he recalled, at the beginning with Cynthia.

From across the room he heard Karen's voice and laughter. He glanced over and their eyes met. Did she sense the sudden wave of temptation within him? He doubted it, but wasn't sure.

"We really should meet soon," Felicia said. "I'd like to hear your ideas about the lecture themes you'll follow. Could you have lunch at my house next week, say, Tuesday at noon?"

Ainslie weighed his response. As always with life, doors opened and some closed. This one was still ajar. Quite clearly.

He answered, "May I let you know?"

Felicia smiled again. "Please come."